dreams of
youth

dreams of youth

The Vindicated

***

The first novel in the Dreams Of Youth Series

Christopher Abraham

Oshawa, Ontario

Written & Designed by: Christopher Abraham

Edited by: Megan Berry & Linda Davis

Dedicated to my dearest friend, Corinna

Some faces just can't be forgotten. They leave a mark. A memory. What you choose to do with these permanent clips of life inevitably shapes who you become. It can be a small ripple, a faint spark, and that's all it takes for the next chapter to start. As they compile and form your story, you realize, those memories, those first lines of text, brought you here.

Every thought of you,
Is worth every notion of approach.
When the confines of my dark room wrestle with me,
Your voice beckons for me to walk into the sun.
You were my friend.
You are, my friend, my medicine.
And it's not the kind we take when we get sick.
It's the natural high from grown ups being kids.
The feeling that says, it's okay to be sad and smile.

You gave me a new appreciation for many things, and music is one of them. I hear a song, and I think of you. I think of what was and what could have been. I don't know, how this works, but I know you'd tell me to keep my head up high. You'd share a song with me, and so much would be said in a three-minute span.

In the end, there are no perfect words to explain this feeling.
Our imperfections, after all, explain our goodbye.
It's what brings us together, when words aren't necessarily spoken.
This is my dedication. This is for you.

Sincerely,
These Dreams of Youth.

CONTENTS

CHAPTER ONE
The Sound of Rain

All great stories, journeys and adventures have a beginning and an end. Where the heart and soul of those within it carry extreme weight and heavy burdens. When love is sometimes lost, when friends sometimes fall, when the unexpected comes around the corner and meets the unsuspecting victim head on. This is the case for a young man known as Dusk Hollow, a 21-year-old living with his girlfriend, Sarah Walker, the same age, on the planet known as Eryu.

Within their inexplicable and cold environment, they have one another for warmth. Society on their planet is one of both poverty and modernization, where suburban areas surround a bustling inner city, some of which are full of apartments wedged up close to one another, giving little room for freedom.

Some find themselves in between success and complete despair, an unfortunate way of life that cannot be fixed with the hands of a few, but with the push of mankind itself. Therefore, because mankind has not pushed for a solution, Sarah and Dusk rely on both their inner and physical traits to support themselves on a daily basis, taking up jobs that involve anything from protecting others to fighting in a cage. They are not bounty hunters, or killers. They do whatever they need to in order to survive—constantly changing jobs, routines, and frames of mind.

This lifestyle has its negative consequences—mainly blurring the lines between right and wrong. They begin to struggle with trusting others; random strangers become a threat on the streets that bear down the cold, heavy source of reality.

They know that with each other, they can continue to survive as they always have since their childhood, to live in an unjust world and do questionable things, in order to preserve their own personal world that they share.

Sadly, by ill luck and the misfortune of timing, an argument between them results in the events that unfold hereafter.

Dusk sits by the windowsill in their two-bedroom apartment. Currently in the living room, his eyes lock on the raindrops running down the glass. The sound of thunder gently clears its throat in the sky, while a subtle flash of lightning goes off in the distance.

He looks at his reflection in the window, while not fully visible, he is able to see his face clearly enough past the foggy residue. He gazes at the lack of happiness in his blue eyes, the blankness of his clean shaven face that masks his discontent. With shaggy dirty blond hair , which covers his ears and eyes, he constantly moves his hair out of the way, as naturally as he wakes up and goes to sleep, as a form of comfort.

The living room itself is cast with warm colours and rays of light, the safety net for both Sarah and he. Within the living room, it is fairly empty and open, with only a couch, a bookshelf and a weapons shelf, where their swords rest.

The door to their apartment opens with the click of the lock. Dusk turns to see Sarah walk into the room and close the door behind her. Her brown eyes contain the same look that his show. Her long brown hair hangs loosely and damp. She says nothing and moves towards the couch, sitting down with her arms crossed and a sour expression on her face.

He looks at her and waits, the silence continues. He eventually lets out a large sigh and asks, "What is it this time?"

"You know very well what the problem is Dusk" she says annoyed.

"Enlighten me, I tend to get lost with all the issues you have with yours truly." Signifying himself.

She begins to glare and says, "Don't be a smart ass."

He lets out a small grin and gets off the windowsill, making his way over to her and taking a seat next to her on the couch.

The distance between them seems to remain the same despite his moving in closer. He sighs once more and says, "Alright, what's wrong?"

"The job."

"The job?"

"Yes."

"What job are you referring to Sarah? There's been a few lately."

"It's not one we've done Dusk, it's the one we promised we wouldn't take part in. Why did you sign us up?! You know how I feel about this. There's a line, and if we take part in this then we cross it. There will be nothing left to keep us human."

Dusk lets out a smirk, and his reaction sets her off.

"This is not a game, Dusk! Children should never be harmed!"

His smirk goes away as fast as it let itself show on his face. He removes his eyes from her gaze and he stares at the floor. He then looks at her again, "We need money to live, and it's not like I accepted the job with the intention of harming them."

"You know full well that's exactly what the job is. Threatening families by harming their children is beyond low."

"But I won't harm them, I'm good at lying. I can pretend to do just that, but in reality, the kids will be safe. Nobody loses."

"The families of those children will lose, the amount of stress you put on them is unfathomable."

He lies back on the couch and stares at the ceiling, "Fine, I'll decline it. It's not worth it, you're right. Besides, it's nice seeing you get passionate about something."

For a moment she looks bewildered and blushes slightly, saying with a slight pause, "Were you testing me?"

He shrugs, "Not really, I did accept it. But, I also didn't want to do it. I don't know. Things are just becoming a big blur lately."

She says in return, "Well now you've gone and pissed me off. Making me think you would actually do something like that. It's not us, we're better than that."

He nods his head and continues to stare up at the ceiling. The silence returns as they sit on the couch, the only sound coming from their breathing.

"There's one more thing." She adds.

He raises an eyebrow, this time not sure what to expect. He sits up straight, his arms still resting on the back of the couch.

She opens her mouth, the words slowly come out, his eyes widen as a jolt of lightning slams down near their apartment and the bellowing of thunder covers up the sound of her words, yet his lips mouth the answer to her question, and in turn, results in her screaming.

She leaves the confines of the couch and storms towards the door, this time grabbing her black coat and an umbrella.

Dusk calls out for her, "Sarah please, we can talk about this."

"Go to hell." She slams the door behind her and leaves Dusk in a room that no longer feels warm.

He places his hands to his face and then rubs them through his hair. Dusk then stands up, goes towards the door and grabs his black coat, one similar to hers. He puts it on over his white V-neck shirt with yellow sleeves. As he places his hand to the door handle he stops and turns to look over at his sword.

Debating if he should go and get it, he decides there's no point and leaves their apartment, heading down the stairs from the fourth floor to the main lobby and exiting out onto the porch. He leaps over the railing and lands on the cement, quickly looking to see where she's gone.

The rain patters softly against his coat; he raises his hood and begins to make his way left on a guess.

Meanwhile, Sarah, having made her way quickly away from their apartment, heads towards a small lake not too far from where they are. With mist building up, she treads carefully and silently towards the sound of the raindrops hitting the water. The scent reaches her and she feels a tingle run through her body.

She makes her way closer and sees a clearing, which reveals one of the benches that sit around the small lake. On the bench directly in front of her, with two maple trees on either side, a man sits in a trench coat, his head hanging down with a hat covering his face.

Approaching slowly and cautiously, the man doesn't move. She wonders if he's fallen asleep. Placing her hand to his shoulder, she pulls back immediately. His body, lifeless, falls sideways; revealing a vicious wound across his stomach, blood drenching his clothes.

The look of death on his face shows signs of a painful end. She winces slightly, yet is sadly accustomed to pain and loss. She looks around and sees no one, nothing but the sound of rain welcomes her.

She places the hat back on his head, and lets his body rest. Deciding to call the authorities, she realizes she left the house without her earphone.

"Tragic thing, isn't it?" A voice suddenly greets her.

Sarah turns her head to see a man standing a few feet from where she came from. A man cloaked in black, wearing a hood that hides most of his features, only his glaring red eyes show—a prominent feature—and the subtle white smile that reveals his teeth.

She replies cautiously, "Yes, it's unfortunate for someone to pass away in such a gruesome way as this."

The man nods his head slightly, clearly refraining from showing any further trace of a smile.

Sarah continues to say, "It is also tragic that he met his end, by a coward that hides beneath a cloak."

"Oh…now those are bold words." The man says.

"The truth naturally holds weight."

"What makes you think it was me?"

"Simple" she points at him, "the stench of blood is on you."

He no longer hides his wide smile, and lets out a laugh. "How right you are! But it's not as if I was trying to be anything else. I am clearly a bad, bad man."

Sarah changes her footing and makes sure that nothing around her will cause her to fall.

"Now" the man says, "seeing as how you aren't all that scared, which annoys me, I think I should make you the next example, as planned."

"As planned?" She clenches her fist, "While I may not show fear, I sure as hell know anger."

As he lets out another laugh, she closes the distance and slams her fist into his face. The shock causes him to slip on the wet grass. As he attempts to grab hold of her, she opens her umbrella, blocking his view and sending raindrops into his eyes. She runs past him, as fast as she can, towards safety.

He gets up from the ground and watches as she disappears within the mist. He calls out, "If I were normal, then you would indeed make it through this night." He waves his hand forward and a portal of darkness forms, "But I am anything but." He steps into it and it disappears.

He appears beside her and grabs onto her wrist. Startled, she attempts to break free and holds back a cry. She throws a punch and he dodges it, twisting her wrist, bringing her to her knees. He slams the back of his hand into her neck and causes her to faint.

"Now," he says, "to wait and see what this will sprout into."

He smiles and opens his mouth wide towards the sky, letting out a shrieking cry, "Save me! Please!" He imitates the sound of her voice.

He lifts her up from the ground and holds her beneath his left arm, carrying her as he makes his way towards the street ahead of them.

The cry reaches Dusk's ears. He stops walking and turns, realizing that it's Sarah's voice and that it's come from the direction of the lake. He runs at full force through the marble streets, his feet splashing through the puddles. He makes his way through thin alleyways between the apartment buildings and leaps over a set of railings in order to save time.

With great effort and what he thinks is a matter of luck, Dusk comes across the cloaked figure carrying Sarah down one of the marble streets. They face one another on opposite ends, nothing but the mist and rain around them. With little to no colour, the setting is close to being completely black and white, if it weren't for the glow of red eyes.

"What did you do to her!?" Dusk yells out in a booming voice.

The man drops her body onto the ground. The hairs on Dusk neck rise, the anger in his stomach turns into a knot, he begins to shake.

The man asks, "What is she worth to you?"

Dusk replies, "You seriously have no idea who you are messing with." He grinds his teeth in rage.

With a slight smile the Burden, a title given to those who wear a black cloak to conceal everything distinctive, except for their red eyes, a practically unheard of anomaly, a source of fear and chaos, begins to walk towards Dusk and says, "That answer is music to my ears."

Dusk raises his fists and moves forward, with one fist facing outwards, the other inwards. The man keeps his hands down at his side, slightly raising one forward.

Throwing the first punch, Dusk's outer fist passes by the hood, knocking it sideways, revealing extremely pale skin. Dusk continues to engage in hand-to-hand combat with the man, who guards against the attacks, occasionally swiping with one hand.

The confrontation continues for approximately thirty seconds, until Dusk lands a hit. However, the man—much like what he did to Sarah—grabs a hold of Dusk and twists his wrist. Dusk slams his body into the man and takes him down into the ground. He raises his fist upwards to punch; yet the man places one hand to Dusk's chest, and with a slight push, sends Dusk flying off of him and into a wall.

The strength startles Dusk, causing him to feel vulnerable. His fight or flight instinct begins to kick in, and prompts him to continue to fight. Yet, his efforts are in vain as the man starts to land vicious blows into Dusk's body before he can break away from the bricks pressing against his back.

Trying with all of his might, he pushes past the pain until the man strikes Dusk's upper chest heavily, causing him to cough profusely and lose his footing.

Within the corner of his eye, Dusk can see Sarah get up. He fixes his posture and blinks a few times in order to face the man once more, and in an effort to buy time, he asks, "Who are you?"

The man replies, "My name is Edom, and tonight I am your burden."

Dusk asks viciously, "Why are you doing this?"

"Because creating fear is a beautiful thing."

Both Sarah and Dusk attack at the same time. Edom stops their punches. They continue, but he moves between them, enjoying the sensation of lovers desperately trying to survive.

While fighting, the anger between Sarah and Dusk, the anger that caused the argument in their apartment, is nowhere to be seen, all that is evident is the strength and bond between them, the desire to keep their world intact.

A world, which Edom crushes as Sarah attacks and is caught. She is thrown to a wall and, within seconds, kept there as two daggers that Edom has concealed beneath his wrists, strike her coat.

She cries out, "Dusk!"

"You son of a bitch!" Dusk throws a wide punch filled with rage. Edom knocks the punch away and with one quick step forward, sends a small thin blade into Dusk's heart.

Sarah yells, "No! Stop it!" She screams frantically.

Edom lets his head hang back as he listens to the beautiful cry. "Yes, yes!" he exclaims, "let it sink into your heart!" He pulls out the blade and walks up to her. Grabbing ahold of her face, he whispers, "Let the loss take control."

Dusk heaves and falls as blood pours uncontrollably on the ground. His eyes quickly losing focus as his heart gushes out his life. Tears soak his eyes as the thought of death, the thought of losing Sarah forever, take hold of him.

He moves his arm forward slightly, reaching out towards her. She does the same, screaming out his name. With tearful eyes, Dusk says in pain, "I'm sorry." He watches Edom form a portal, taking Sarah away, leaving behind only the drops from her eyes mixed within the rain filled streets.

One sound is left—but only for a moment—the sound of death. His heart beat stops. His body rests on the ground, permanently, eternally, letting the new sound, the sound of rain, take over as his heart goes silent. The last thing that passes before his eyes is the memory of her smiling face because fear has no hold on his love. Even in death, fear has no hold on him.

CHAPTER TWO
Taste of Metal

Falling through white space, Dusk is enveloped by warm and distant memories. His body descends onto an invisible surface. Colours begin to wash over everything and create scenery—green and vibrant. Without realizing it, he loses control and his mind wanders. Dusk returns to a memory from when he was a child.

His mouth opens and he calls out, "Sarah, wait up!" Sarah giggles and continues to run ahead towards the park. She yells back with a wave and smile, "Catch me if you can slowpoke!" She reaches the swing set and takes a seat, not waiting for him; she digs her feet into the sand. With a heave she pushes off and goes backwards.

With a laugh, she lets her head fall back and looks at the world upside down. As she passes the closest point to the surface, she sees Dusk take a seat next to her. She feels butterflies hit her stomach as the sky becomes closer.

He asks, "How did you run so fast?"

As her swing descends she smiles and passes him "Just luck I guess." She giggles once more. Dusk grins from ear to ear and digs his feet into the sand. Just like Sarah, he gives a heave and puts all of his force into the initial push—the best way to get a good start at swinging. At such a young age, the simple things were all that mattered. The two of them glide through the air and stare at the crystal-clear sky with but a few white, puffy clouds blocking the sun.

Dusk looks over at Sarah. She turns and looks back at him. The two of them pass each other while swinging in opposite directions. Their hands reach out and their fingers touch. Everything flashes white. A warm feeling splashes over Dusk, and his eyes dart open.

He is greeted by a bright light, which seemingly turns out to be more white space. However, after a few seconds, things begin to appear. Dusk sees a gate made of gold in the far distance. He squints and rubs his eyes. Nothing changes.

He asks quietly, "Is this…death…?" Dusk feels a gritty texture on his tongue. "This taste is like… metal?" puzzled, he ponders over why such a strange taste would greet him. He touches his chest and pulls up his shirt. The wound that should be there isn't.

"Your body will be unscathed—a clean slate." A voice answers the question that is lingering in his mind.

Dusk looks to the left and sees a man cloaked in white. The figure pulls down his hood to show the face of an elderly man—one with much knowledge upon his brow.

"My name is Truth. My purpose is to guide those who have reached Heaven's doorstep to the Gate of Acceptance, and to answer any questions that they may have. You are Dusk, I presume?" The man says almost elegantly.

"Yes…that's my name. I guess this means that I'm really…dead?"

"Yes. That is correct."

Dusk goes silent. "Just now I experienced something—an old memory. But I felt like I was really there. I felt like I was little again."

Truth, with his hands concealed within his cloak, walks forward and addresses him. "That which you experienced was a memory in your life that is pure and honest. It wasn't chosen by anyone but your subconscious. It could've been a random selection of many memories or one that serves a purpose to rest your heart."

Dusk places his hand on the ground. He pushes down and feels it move a little. "Cloud texture?" He asks while standing up.

"Yes" Truth replies.

"And what about this?" Dusk points to his tongue.

Truth chuckles "A question I will never grow tired of. That will go away. It's the taste of death. All one must do is drink from the Cup of Afterlife and accept one's fate. The taste will go away, and you will be granted wings to guide you through the heavens and bring you to your eternal rest."

A lot begins to pile up in Dusk's mind. With each answer another question appears. He clears his throat and begins to ask quickly, "The Cup of Afterlife? Where is it?"

Truth moves his concealed hands and points towards the Gate of Acceptance. "Once I direct you, there you will find the cup placed upon a mantle. It will quench your thirst, remove hunger and calm your emotions. You'll no longer need things to be happy. Everything will be all right, despair will never reach you, and tranquility will embrace you. Shall we go now?"

Just then his heart screams out to him. "No," he says. Dusk clenches his fist and looks Truth directly into his eyes. "I cannot be dead, I refuse to accept this. I won't drink from a cup that will erase everything I feel and need. I'm still human and I have someone dear to me that I need to save. I'm here because I failed, damn it! And I sure as hell will do all I can to go back there and correct my mistakes."

A cloud passes above them and removes the glow of sunlight from Truth's expression. His eyes darken. "What you speak of is not territory where one can tread lightly. There is no possible way for you to leave this place. You either rest in Heaven or go to the depths below. You are dead, Dusk. I know that isn't something one wants to accept and, with time, I've forgotten that. So I apologize for being so blunt about all of this. However, we must go now. Any questions you have I can answer on the other side of the Gate of Acceptance."

"I said no." He crosses his arms and stands firm, "No goddamn way."

Truth says nothing. He just looks at Dusk.

Another voice greets them, "It looks like this one has made up his mind."

Dusk looks to the left and sees a tall man with long, jet-black hair, bright blue eyes and a stern expression. He is wearing silver armor that only covers certain parts of his body such as his chest, wrists and lower legs. And, unlike Truth, he has large, white, translucent wings on his back. Dusk is perplexed and mesmerized at the same time. His train of thought leaves him. He works up the composure to ask, "Who are you?"

Truth replies, "This man is Hex, an angel of high regard."

The two beings look at Dusk.

Truth says, "So I guess He sent you to take him by force? I don't approve but I guess he's deserving of the salvation."

Hex replies, "On the contrary, He sent me here because this boy has a destiny set out for him, apparently."

Truth responds in confusion, "What do you mean?"

"It seems this one is caught up in events which are still unfolding. And apparently would serve the Greater Good by returning to Eryu and its aligning planets." Hex looks at Dusk disapprovingly.

Truth's expression darkens.

"And how does He expect to have this one returned? He is no longer alive, he is human in its truest form, and there is no possible way for him to return."

Hex says, "There is but one way."

He turns and looks into the distance. Dusk has to turn around to see what exactly lies in the opposite direction of the Gate of Acceptance.

"That is unacceptable. " Truth blurts out. "There is absolutely no way someone can walk through that gate without a ring—it's blasphemy. He should know better than to suggest such a thing!"

Hex turns his attention to Truth. "Well he's not suggesting it. It's an order that will be followed, despite your personal feelings towards it. He figured the timing is perfect, seeing as how it's my turn to go through the gate." His eyes turn back towards Dusk "And seeing as how now I'm both on a mission and have become a babysitter of a newborn, I think you can cut the tension Truth, I don't have time to argue."

Dusk looks at Truth and then at Hex. He asks, "What's going on exactly?"

Hex replies quickly, "The person who killed you is involved with a lot of troublesome things. But that wouldn't be enough to grant you this second chance. The reason why I have to bring you with me back to your home planet is that, apparently, by some divine reason, you have a light that will pierce through the darkness. A light—I might add—that I do not see nor believe exists." He huffs, "Enough questions. I'm going now. I suggest you follow me. Judging from your reaction earlier, the last place you want to be is here." Hex begins to walk away from the Gate of Acceptance and passes by Dusk.

Truth follows and stops next to Dusk "...I will tell you now, Dusk. If you want true peace, the only way you will find that is if you come with me through the right door. If you decide not to, and tread down a path that no one else ever has, you will be alone, even when the faces of those surrounding you are those you love. So please, think carefully."

Dusk, having done precisely the opposite in his stubbornness for revenge, and from the longing in his heart to rescue Sarah, says abruptly, "I've made up my mind. I'm following Hex."

Truth nods, "Very well, then as it is my job to answer questions for those entering the Gate of Acceptance, I suppose it is also for when a soul leaves through the Gate of Departure. Follow me."

He walks along and Dusk follows suit. The scenery remains the same, with white clouds as far as the eye can see. As he makes his way, noticing the occasional white bird fly overhead and glide through the air, Dusk reflects over Edom's' words. *"Let it sink into your heart...let the loss take control."* This causes him to feel frustration, and he grabs a chunk of his hair and pulls a little to release the strain on his mind.

They reach the Gate of Departure. Dusk stands and gazes, open-mouthed, at the sheer size. Two gigantic, steel gates, that are somewhat rusted, stand tall. It's triple the size of the Gate of Acceptance in comparison.

Dusk asks, "Why is it so big?"

Hex looks at him in annoyance. Truth answers, "To test the strength of the departed. If one isn't able to physically open the gate or move it with their willpower, then it's not meant to be. The ring will be passed to another. And I suppose, in the strangest of circumstances, to keep out people like you."

His final words float through Dusk's ears.

"So what if Hex isn't able to open the gate, what then? Who's going to take the ring?" Dusk asks in return.

Hex sighs and walks towards the gate. He raises one hand, and then closes all of his fingers into his palm, leaving only one pointing toward the gate.

"Open."

The three of them look as the gate opens, creaking loudly, sending vibrations through the clouds. They see what lies beyond the gate, and it is utter darkness. Dusk gets a chilling feeling that runs throughout his body. He rubs his arms.

"So I just walk through that?" he asks.

Truth replies, "It's not that simple, Dusk. What you are about to do has consequences. I cannot tell you what will happen. It's very likely that once you go through that gate without a ring, your body will be torn to shreds and removed from existence. I'll have you know that if that is the case, anyone you love will never see you in the afterlife, though they won't the moment you pass through the door either. However, it is possible that nothing bad will happen, and you will indeed be reincarnated with a second life…however, both are speculation, and speculation is not what I am accustomed to."

"Alright, then I'm going through it. Hex I'll follow you?" Dusk asks.

The angel glances at him and nods his head. "I've never done this either, so keep your head on straight. If you die in the first few moments of this journey then my reputation will be tarnished…though you are already dead, so perhaps it's not an issue I should fret over." Hex replies. He steps forward and disappears as the darkness passes through him.

With one big gulp, Dusk steps forward.

Truth pleads, "Don't be rash…what you are about to do is…"

"Thanks" Dusk replies. He then runs through the darkness, avoiding the logic of Truth, and following the bold nature of Hex.

He hears the steel gates close behind him, screeching as the bars come to a stop. He moves his hand around and feels no resistance. Beginning to feel lost, he steps forward and proceeds in the same direction that Hex went. "Where the hell am I?" he asks himself eagerly, hoping that some sign would appear in front of him.

But nothing shows up.

He continues to walk, endlessly. Fear begins to build up inside the pit of his stomach as his eyes continue to feed darkness into his brain.

"I can't see anything..."

Silence continues.

His voice is swallowed and contained by the depth of the terrain around him. Unable to see anything, Dusk begins to feel weak in the knees. He thinks about what Truth said, about the possibility of becoming nothing but a pile of broken down pieces of who he is.

This thought causes him to breathe heavily. Suddenly he collapses. He heaves and clutches the ground. It feels different but he doesn't take notice to the texture. His eyes begin to blur but, again, he does not notice. He becomes unconscious moments later. A dream of a past event reveals itself and takes his mind for another journey of self-reflection.

A long stretch of road carries on as far as the eye can see. On both sides, trees line up in an orderly fashion—maple trees to be exact. The leaves are yellow, orange and brown. A few begin to fall as the wind shakes through them. Dusk looks around and doesn't see anyone. He panics and turns around desperately. He spins into his older brother's chest.

"What's wrong?" his brother asks.

"Oh...I don't know, I got nervous for a second." Dusk replies.

"Well don't worry, I'm right here. Now let's go home before mom and dad think I took you out to the hover board games instead of getting ice cream." His brother smiles and moves his hand through Dusk's hair.

Dusk giggles "Okay brother, let's go home!"

As they walk down the street, Dusk begins to ponder over something.

"Won't they notice anyways? The ice cream store is only ten minutes away, but we've been gone for a few hours."

"Well when you put it that way, we're pretty much doomed."

Dusk quickly and suddenly changes topics by barking out "Hey, I'm tired. Carry me."

His brother turns and looks at him. "Really, now? You're going to be six years old soon. I can't keep carrying you around."

"Aw, come on big brother!"

"This is the last time, alright?" his brother says with a sigh.

Dusk smiles "Okay!"

The memory fades out, and Dusk finds himself curled up into a ball. With his arms and knees pressed closely to his chest he looks around and his face brushes against something soft. He tugs on it and hears the sound of objects colliding above him. A tint of moonlight pierces through the door in front of him and reveals the contents surrounding his body.

Dusk gets up and moves forward. He places his eye to the opening of light. His mouth opens in horror. The room before him is covered in blood, the window is broken and glass lies splattered across the carpet. He pushes against the closet door but it doesn't budge.

A shadow appears and blocks the moonlight.

"Don't make a sound, Dusk, whatever you do just stay quiet." the woman's voice triggers an alarm in his brain.

"Mom!" he calls out and waits for a reply but receives nothing.

Soon after, his mom says softly, "Know that I love you, all of you. Just don't come out of the closet. Promise me, okay?" she moves back a bit and he sees her face. A soft smile wavers on her lips. He notices the cut on her cheek and the bruise on her forehead.

"Okay...I promise, mom."

A loud boom occurs, and the door leading to the room is kicked down. Dusk moves backwards into the closet to conceal himself. He focuses his eyes on the small gap between the two closet doors. As the stranger makes his way to his mother, Dusk feels his heart clench up. Everything spins and goes blank.

He opens his eyes and sees someone's foot. He moves so that his hands are placed on the ground. Looking up he recognizes Hex looking down at him.

Dusk asks, "What do you want?"

"You've been lying there whimpering for a few minutes. I decided to just watch."

"Well, how thoughtful..." Dusk stands up. "It was a nightmare this time, I think..." he says.

Hex, in the process of moving, stops. "A nightmare?"

Dusk nods his head. "Ye...another random moment I guess. But Truth said it's something related to the heart... or the will... or something."

"Yes, that sounds right...I guess it's only natural you'd have a nightmare. You just left Heaven, the sanctuary. I guess your body thinks it's going to Hell." Hex says coldly. However, his expression shows no malice.

Dusk puts his hands into his pockets.

"Whatever." he mutters.

Walking forward, with his eyes cast down, Dusk begins to notice odd peculiarities in his environment. The grass beneath his feet has golden specs that twinkle on its edges. Wind blows through, and with a cold kiss, presses against his face. He places his hand against his skin and closes his eyes, thinking about an entirely different place. He emerges from his thoughts and looks up to see the vast strange world set out before him.

A pink sky replaces that of what he once knew. Purple clouds are scattered about. Trees stand three times the standard size, rivers flow amongst them with a crystal clear blue shine. It all rests before him, wild in nature, with no set pattern or touch from mankind's desire to shape what they see fit. It is truly free from the clutches of regulation, and breaks through everything he ever thought of as real and true. This paradise of the unknown causes Dusk to simply raise his eyebrows, look around carefully, and ponder on how he will ever escape it.

"This road will take us where we need to go." Hex says, interrupting Dusk's trance of worry. He continues, "There's an elderly lady whom we seek, that has the power to take dreams and put them into reality. She won't be expecting us, but all the same, she won't be surprised either."

Dusk turns his head away from the scenery.

He asks, "What do you mean by a dream? And why didn't the door take us directly to Eryu?"

Hex grins slightly.

"Maybe I'll tell you if you survive this trip…but for now, I'll just say you know nothing."

"No shit."

They walk towards the pathway that Dusk, up until that point, overlooked. It pales in comparison to its wild surroundings. It's dull in retrospect. It seems simple, like something he could gather a couple of friends together and make. The path, boring in nature, leads to the luscious and mesmerizing forest beyond that.

Dusk asks, "So…this place, does it have a name?"

"All beautiful things have a name Dusk," Hex says with a slight pause, "but the truest beauty in life is discovering that name for yourself. So yes, this place has a name, and perhaps you can discover it on your own. If not, someone will reveal it to you eventually I'm sure." He turns to look at Dusk, "So if it helps, you may simply call this place the unknown." His final words ring with a hint of humour, "You can do that much, right?"

CHAPTER THREE
White Crossing

Gazing at an assortment of different flowers resting at the edge of the forest, Dusk feels a hand press against his back. It pushes him forward and into the array of colours. He quickly turns to glare at Hex, but the angel is already walking down the path. Dusk gets back up and follows him. As he catches up, he smells the fragrance of vanilla and lavender that the flowers left on his clothes.

Hex looks back at him and says, "This isn't a field trip."

Dusk says in return, "I'm just trying to remember this place so I can tell Sarah about it when I get back." Hex raises an eyebrow but doesn't pursue the topic. His lack of interest annoys Dusk.

They continue forward, now reaching the entrance to the forest. The river that Dusk thought would stray alongside them for much longer, turns in another direction and soon leaves their sight. The silence between them begins to aggravate Dusk. He starts to focus on the sound that the pebbles beneath their feet make. The chirping of what he believes to be from birds, echoing throughout the forest. The sound of wind moving through the trees and causing them to creek also unsettles him. Everything feels real yet off tune.

He crumbles and caves in to his urge to ask questions. "So I died, and went through a door that could've destroyed everything that I am. Does this mean that I've, well, got a second life?"

"I suppose," Hex mutters in response, his attention elsewhere.

Again, Dusk becomes annoyed and pursues the topic. "What do you mean you suppose? This isn't an every day thing—heck, I'm talking to an angel. I didn't even believe in the afterlife and yet here I am," he says without thinking.

The angel stops and looks around, he leaves the path. Dusk follows and asks, "Look are you going to answer me?"

"I don't know what you expect in reply. You ask question after question. This is the first time I've seen someone walk through the gate who wasn't a classified angel."

Dusk leaves it alone with a grunt.

They reach a bridge made from white wood. It arches across a different river from the one Dusk was gazing at prior. Hex says confidently "Once we cross this we should be about halfway if my memory serves me correct."

"How is it you know where to go? Have you been here before?" Dusk asks, tilting his head in curiosity.

"No I haven't, but before crossing the gate, the angel chosen is given information regarding the journey so he or she doesn't get lost. But they never mentioned being stuck with a chore," he says without blinking. It puts Dusk off a bit but he ignores it.

Hex's attention quickly turns to his surroundings. Dusk however seems oblivious and begins to complain about not having a clue about what is transpiring. "Hex you really need to tell me what's going on, I can't keep walking like this. Hex are you listening to me?" Dusk ask persistently. His voice catches the attention of what Hex has already noticed.

Shadows rush through the bushes on the other side of the bridge that Hex and Dusk stand in the middle of. The water below them remains calm and pleasant, masking the threat. Finally, Dusk begins to notice something is amiss.

One of the shadowy figures leaps from the cover of the forest and into the air towards Dusk. Hex moves in front of him. With an emotionless face he raises his hand. A spear forms from thin air. He wraps his hand around it tightly. The monster roars and raises its claws. With a sudden move of the spear, Hex thrusts it through the monster's throat before it reaches him. He then throws it off to the side. It crashes into the water and floats down the stream.

"What the hell!" Dusk yells out. Another beast emerges. This time he gets a good look at it. It's completely black, its fangs long and sharp with red piercing eyes. "What is that?" he asks.

"One moment." Hex replies.

The monster, wiser then the first, approaches cautiously.

Dusk stands behind Hex. His eyes glued to the approaching menace. The angel remains calm but alert. He stands tall and firm, showing no sign of weakness or fear. The monster glares at him and remains in place. A few seconds pass. Hex says nothing. The monster does nothing, and then when Dusk begins to think he's safe, a dozen of the same threat appear suddenly. They surround the bridge.

Dusk turns around and places his back against Hex's. "Uh, I don't have a weapon Hex," he says worriedly.

"Oh, really?" Hex replies sarcastically.

"Tell me how you made your weapon appear out of thin air, I could use that right now."

"It's not something as simple as teaching someone how to tie shoes, it's essentially impossible."

Dusk huffs flustered and annoyed "Then what should I do?" he waits for a reply.

"Whatever got you here in the first place, don't do that."

The beast closest to the bridge stares at Dusk. "What do you want? You want a piece of me, huh, you little shit!" Dusk yells out in anger "Then come on, try me!" the monster roars. Dusk raises his fists. The sound of water splashing from the left causes him to turn and lose his sense of balance as he's tackled by one of the monsters that was hiding beneath the water.

He's thrown over the bridge and crashes into the river as the monster opens its jaws and attempts to bite him. Hex is only able to watch from the corner of his eye as he faces the others.

The monster slams its mouth shut but misses; Dusk elbows it at the top of the head, which causes him to fall backwards further into the depths of a cold stream. A rush of water enters his mouth and causes him to choke and gag. The monster holds him down underneath the water and his eyes soon see the flickering of light in the depths of blue.

Grabbing a hold of the monster's leg, Dusk twists it and emerges from the water. His hair flicks back. He slams his foot down into the monster's neck in retaliation causing the monster to gasp for air. As the monster struggles to break free, Dusk lets out an unsettling laugh of nerves, runs his hand through his hair and flicks off the drops of water. He takes his foot off the monster. It leaps towards him and receives a punch across the face. It falls, and Dusk begins to unleash a barrage. His fists continue to pummel the monster, but another approaches from behind, but Dusk, still in a fit of fear doesn't notice.

Hex looks over at him. "Imbecile" he mutters. The remaining monsters run at Hex as he returns his attention to them. They leap over the bridge and open their jaws revealing their fangs. He raises his spear and spins it around quickly. It cuts through all of them. Hex then aims his spear and throws it in the direction of Dusk and the monster attempting to flank him. It pierces through the monster's head. As Dusk turns to see, the dead monster falls onto him.

Stunned, Dusk loses control of the monster he was punching and watches as it rises from the water and glares at him. It bares its fangs and charges him, the water rushing into the monster's gaping pit, his head soon accompanying it. Yet the angel throws another spear in the nick of time, and saves him.

Dusk yells, "Damn it, get this thing off of me!" he struggles and then successfully pushes it into the water. He crawls up onto the shoreline and breathes heavily.

One last monster emerges from the forest where it was lying in wait amongst the cold shadows. Hex turns to look at it. It bares its fangs, showing its dominance, its desire to crush and eat the bones of what it deems weak. Hex squints slightly, "I am an angel, a messenger to all that is evil, and you are but a Nightmare meant to be rid from this place. Do you honestly think a child's bad dream can conquer me? I will put you to sleep." The Nightmare runs at him and leaps forward, Hex grabs hold of the Nightmare in mid-air and squeezes tightly, crushing its head and letting it drop.

Still panting heavily, Dusk walks over and crouches to catch his breathe. "What the hell," he gasps, "was that?" he asks.

"Just…pests" Hex begins to cross the bridge.

"No, tell me Hex!" Dusk yells out in anger. "Tell me what's going on, where we are, and what the hell those things were! I need to know if I'm going to make it back home!" The angel ignores him and makes his way into the forest. "Answer me!" Dusk yells in a loud booming voice.

"I just saved your life, you ought to be grateful."

"I have nothing to be grateful to you for!" Dusk yells once more.

Hex stops. His face now showing a clear annoyance towards him, he turns around and faces him. "My tolerance for your ignorance has run out."

"Well maybe I just don't appreciate being viewed as a burden!" Dusk retorts.

"Oh? Since when did how you feel matter? You shouldn't even be here. It's against everything I stand for to let someone such as you go back." Hex says angrily.

"What's that supposed to mean?" Dusk asks.

"It means that, despite your special circumstance, there's absolutely nothing special about you. And now when so many have had to come to peace and accept death, you are desperately trying to go back and see your precious lover. You, for some reason, have been granted another chance and I do not approve."

They glare at one another. Dusk clenches his fist. "Well fuck all of them! I'm going back no matter what and you are going to take me!"

Hex bursts out into a laugh "And you think you can make me? You should rethink what you just said boy," he says with a looming threat. "Because all of the people you just told to 'fuck off' deserve this chance more than you." Dusk's face goes red. He yells in anger and runs at Hex.

"You are seriously...an idiot," Hex says, as the situation deteriorates to the point of an all out brawl between them. The angel raises one finger that strikes a pressure point in Dusk's chest and sends him into a coughing fit. Dusk stops for a moment and then continues to run forward, angrier now.

He raises his fist and throws a punch towards Hex's face. With a sigh, Hex moves out of the way and places his hand against the side of Dusk's ribcage. An incredible force erupts, slamming into him and sending Dusk across the ground.

He gets back up after a few moments of hesitation and pain. With persistence he rushes forward, this time on an angle in an attempt to move in for a quicker strike. Hex doesn't move and waits for him. With a yell, Dusk bends and throws an uppercut towards Hex's chin, however a single finger stops the punch.

Hex looks at Dusk in contempt. "You are turning out to be even less qualified than I imagined." He wraps his hand around Dusk's wrist and pulls on it. He forces him to fall to the ground. He then spins him across the dirt and grass with little effort, throwing him into a tree. Dusk gets up onto his knees and wipes the blood from his mouth.

With sweat trickling down his face, he coughs and starts to think about a way to land a punch. *This is not going my way damn it, I just need answers.* He grins after getting an idea. Hex notices the smirk but remains silent and waits, the extent of his boredom becoming more obvious in his expression with each passing second. Dusk runs at him for the third time. He grabs a handful of dirt as he makes his way upwards from his knees onto his feet. As he approaches Hex, he uses the opposite hand to throw a fake punch. Halfway through it, he changes it to the hand concealing the dirt. With a laugh he throws it into Hex's face. Hex's expression changes. He raises his arm to cover his eyes. Dusk sees the perfect opportunity to strike and aims his arm to uppercut Hex's stomach.

Yet it doesn't go as planned. Hex disappears, causing all of the dirt to rise into the air. Dusk stands there, his arm still raised. Sweat changing from a slight river to an ocean of worry. His smile hangs on, out of place and bizarre. He gulps and slowly turns to look behind him. Before his neck turns completely, Hex grabs him by the shoulder and slams him into the ground. His spear then forms in his hand; he raises it and slams it downwards.

"No wait, stop it!" Dusk yells out in utter fear with tears hanging on the edge of his eyelids. Hex stops, the tip of the spear touching Dusk's nose. It stares Dusk in the face. The sun causes it to glare and shine.

"I'm sorry, alright, I'm sorry," Dusk blurts out hesitantly, not sure if the spear will plunge into his face at any given moment. "I...I just need to know things all right...I don't like this anymore than you do, do you think I want to be here right now? Lying on the ground, dead, or alive, fuck I don't know, okay? I just...I just need to return home...I just need to save Sarah...to save myself."

The angel's eyes lower as he tries to tamp down the fire rising within him. He replies, "You attack me like a stubborn child who doesn't get his way. You want answers yet you blurt out whatever comes to mind. I don't feel like answering them. You have insulted things I hold dear, and are an unknown lying in my bubble of the known." His eyes beginning to heat up slightly as the fire grows, "Prove to me you are worthy and I'll tell you what I know. Show me that your special treatment is not some kind of joke. I may be an angel, Dusk, but I am not perfect, and my selfishness will not accept you." Dusk nods his head, hoping that the spear will soon lower. "Those monsters" Hex says, "... are Nightmare's, the bad...things that linger in your dirty skull."

The spear disappears and Hex raises his hand towards Dusk, "Now get on your feet, and do not show fear in their wake." Dusk taken aback by the gesture, grabs a hold of his hand and is pulled up.

"Thanks..." Dusk says quietly, a tad ashamed of his actions with more questions now looming in the back of his brain, longing for answers.

Hex, having returned to the white bridge, crosses it and heads towards the forest of golden lit leaves. Dusk, in pursuit asks, "So these Nightmares, what are they exactly?" Where do they come from? Where are we? And why do they look like that? Oh and, fear? I wasn't scared Hex!" Dusk spills out all of these words with haste.

Hex places his hand to his face and lets out a groan. "Unbelievable."

"Hex, answer me!"

"No."

The two of them continue to travel through the unknown land in search of the mysterious woman with answers. Yet Dusk's lack of knowledge is causing him to act rashly, resulting in unnecessary arguments. However, with Hex leading him, hope still rests on the horizon.

The angel, now walking with a consistent stride, with his shoulders seeming a little relaxed, asks, "Dusk, what is your last name?"

"It's Hollow, my full name is Dusk Hollow."

"I see."

"And yours?"

The angel smiles, yet Dusk doesn't see it. "Just call me Hex."

CHAPTER FOUR

Amongst the Stars

A girl sighs; she rests her head on her soft, ruby coloured pillow. She stares at the stars through her window overhead. *They're so beautiful,* she thinks. The stars shine brighter than the previous nights with the sky now absent of clouds. To her, the stars are what matter the most. Despite how bad a day might turn out to be, the stars welcome her with warmth when nighttime arrives. And for her, another world is what she needs the most, one with the starry sea of possibilities.

A gentle knock on her bedroom door causes her to turn her head. "Goodnight Essa, I'm off to bed. Sleep well," her mother says with an enchanting voice.

"Night, mom!" Essa replies. She then returns her attention to the stars. "I guess it's just you and me now. It's 11:11 so, that means I can make a wish right? Well…I wish for tomorrow to be a better day… you can grant me that, right?" her eyelids grow heavy and she yawns "Goodnight, stars."

***

The morning arrives swiftly. Warmth soaks into Essa's comforter and eventually causes her to wake up. She rises, stretches and looks up at the sun. "It's just not the same…" she slowly gets out of bed and gets dressed for school. Afterwards she makes her way down to the kitchen. "Mom?" she calls out. She sees a note on the kitchen table.

I won't be home for dinner. I had to go out early today. But it's Friday so we have the weekend together! Just smile darling, and think about the good things in life. I love you.

Essa smiles and folds the note, placing it into her pant pocket.

She grabs her coat and puts it on followed by her scarf and ear-muffs. Everything she wears tends to be purple and black despite her long, red, scarlet hair. She places her mittens on and opens the front door. A gust of cold air rushes into the house. Essa shivers and then takes her first step into the world. The door closes behind her and with it, her sanctuary.

As she makes her way to school, passing children who laugh happily, Essa thinks about how the people who she doesn't know cause her to smile, unlike what awaits for her at her high school. Essa, now in her final year, is surrounded by a generation of monsters, cold hearted as they hide their insecurities behind the lust for others suffering.

Her school comes into view and she begins to walk slower. Yet like a magnet the force pulls her in, each step heavier than the previous one.

The school bell rings. She lets out a groan and sees the younger kids continue to laugh and smile. Being elementary kids, this school wasn't anything but a part of the background for them. Essa enters the prison and feels her face begin to defrost. The students in the lobby look at her. One of them shows no interest, the other two let out a snicker. She walks past them and ignores their looks.

Despite entering the school after the first bell, she manages to be the second student to arrive to class. The teacher, Mr. Linder, greets her with a smile. He is kind and knowledgeable about history and

English, which is odd. Considering his heavy build of pure muscle complimented by his tan skin, one would expect him to fit in a different role. However, perhaps it is why Essa likes him, because he defies the norm.

She takes a seat in the aisle next to the windows. Her eyes immediately glance at the tree in the courtyard. It lies beyond the irregular fountains and perfect gardens. It's not alone, but it stands out. The petals pink in contrast to the maple trees surrounding it.

Her attention then, as a habit, turns and looks at the only other student in the class. She doesn't know his name because she never cares to ask. And even with the roster list that the teacher goes over, not knowing anyone else's name doesn't help her figure out which name is his.

He is always on time and always the first one to arrive in class. But she doesn't understand why. He sleeps half the time, and when he isn't sleeping he's laughing and making jokes with the other students. At this moment however, he's awake. He smiles with a wave. Essa ignores the gesture. Her heart closed off to everyone long ago.

Numbness enters her mind; she begins to wonder what she even learns from this class or any other class. She takes her seat, and then what? What really happens beyond the ticking of time and the desire to escape? She can never remember.

The second bell chimes, and like clockwork all of the remaining students pile in, all of them loud and irritating. Mr. Linder stands against the blackboard and waits for all of them to take a seat. The class settles down. He takes attendance and eventually reaches Essa's name. "Essa Starlight" he calls out. She raises her hand and he smiles, she doesn't need to speak up because her attendance is flawless.

The time goes by relatively quickly with her eyes constantly gazing towards the tree. Essa hears snickering in front of her. She turns to look despite knowing it won't be anything good. She sees a group of the students staring at her. Three of the girls mutter between one another and laugh. Essa looks around and notices that Mr. Linder has left the classroom.

"Just look at her, she's so pathetic it's unbelievable" one of the girls blurts out. The others laugh, everyone except the boy at the other end of the classroom. "To think a girl like her managed to get accepted here. We are supposed to be elites aren't we? Yet they let in a failure like her." The girl doing the talking is the most vocal girl in school, Tabatha Florence, a heartless and life destroying individual with long red curly hair and black eyes.

Tabatha proceeds to turn this into a conflict. "Essa, honestly, can you tell us why you are here?" she asks.

Essa looks at the entire class. All of their eyes staring into her soul. Prying into her essence. "Because my marks show that I'm deserving" she replies.

"Oh is that so? Little-miss-perfect thinks she belongs with us because of her marks?" Tabatha says looking around with a big grin. "What a crock! It takes more than just good grades to make it into this school. You need wealth, an actual meaning to society! But you've been here day in and day out for a year. All because of a special circumstance," Tabatha says with a glare, her voice darker. Essa feels the hair on the back of her neck rise. Her heart begins to pound with the looming threat of anger and sorrow.

Only some of the class is aware of what Tabatha is getting at. She notices this and smiles. "Shall I explain to everyone once and for all?" she says.

"Stop it," Essa blurts out.

Another girl laughs.

"Shut up!" Essa flinches at the harshness of her own words.

Tabatha opens her mouth, "She's here because her father was killed in public, in front of the Principal. And soon after, her brother disappeared. This happened many years ago of course. Apparently the Principal decided that Essa should be granted a chance to experience life here at Westwood. I don't agree. I think trash should stay with the trash. I don't understand how a soap opera about losing a loved one deserves any kind of recognition. So your brother is all alone, probably dead and being eaten to the bone by now. And your father passed away, murdered? So, what!" Tabatha bursts into laughter. Some of the class laughs along with her. A few remain silent.

In a flash Essa stands up and slams her fists into her desk. Everyone goes silent and stares at her. "I don't deserve to be here? I don't want to be here! Why should I have to deal with this kind of torment from the likes of you! My grades speak for themselves. Yet you sit there all high and mighty because your father has money! You're just an idiot who's going to spend the rest of her life oblivious to others pain and suffering. I lost my father and brother!" eyes now watering, "I'm not here on a pity trip. I'm here because money doesn't speak for everything. And I swear to god if you ever mention them again I'll slam my fist into your fucking face!"

The class goes into an uproar. Tabatha sits there, jaw stricken. She doesn't know what to say. However it soon hits her that she was threatened and told off. She stands up to gain face. "I'm going to put you in your place."

Her friend behind Essa grabs hold of her. Everything is now escalating quickly, and even if Tabatha was feeling regret, even if the boy on the other end of the classroom was watching closely, even if Essa felt that something was off, it doesn't matter.

"Let me go!" Essa yells out. Tabatha moves forward, hesitates, and punches her across the face, knocking her to the ground.

Another girl raises her foot, Tabatha's eyes widen in alarm. Essa lies on the ground, looking up, in disbelief of the horror of her situation.

Suddenly a piece of chalk slams into Tabatha's face and then into the forehead of the other girl. The force pinches their skin.

The boy who, up until now, was simply watching, begins to speak. "You're going too far Tabatha, even your underlings are beginning to attempt to jump forward. If you don't watch what you are doing, you'll break your personal goal, and no one will be happy or satisfied."

The looming threat, something vague to everyone else, causes Tabatha to bite her lip. She turns to the other girl and slaps her across the face suddenly. The class gasps. Tabatha then says, "If anyone is going to stomp on someone's face, that's me, got it?"

The girl tries to protest, "But I was only-"

Again, another slap, which causes the girl to give up and begin to tear up. The others, now even further confused, take a step back.

Mr. Linder returns to the classroom and drops his lecture notes on the floor. "What is the meaning of this!" he yells out. The entire classroom jumps in shock. A couple of chairs fall over. Tabatha, about to say something is cut off. He walks over to Essa and helps her up. He then turns and looks at Tabatha. "I'll deal with you and your flock later" he says, eyes showing a lion whose cub has been hurt. Tabatha feels death staring her down.

He brings Essa to the office so she can calm down. After some time he leaves her in order to handle the misbehaving students. Essa sits in one of the chairs, staring through the glass wall overlooking a hallway. A minute later, the boy comes into view. She looks at him, wondering why he is there. Class isn't over for another ten minutes yet there he stands, having avoided Mr. Linder's lecture.

He smiles and opens the door to the office and takes a seat next to her. The woman at the desk glances at him and then returns her eyes to her papers.

Essa turns and looks at him. "What do you want?" she asks.

"I figured you could use someone to talk to," he says in return.

"Well I don't, I'm fine..." she says angrily.

"Oh don't be that way. I'm being nice, and I'm not faking or anything. I promise," he says soothingly.

She lets down her wall. "Fine, then what is it you have to say?" she asks.

"Well," he stretches his arms, "nothing in particular. I was just wondering if you'd like to go for a walk towards your favorite spot."

"My favorite spot?" she says while raising her eyebrows. "Are you spying on me?" she asks.

He chuckles and stands up. "No I'm not spying on you. All you do is look out the window. I figure there's something you like that keeps your attention," he says.

"You know, I could just be staring at something I hate."

"Yes well, that's not like you now is it?" he laughs again. The woman at the desk looks up at him with a glare. He turns to Essa and winks. "Come on, let's go."

The two of them exit the school and head towards the trees on the outskirt of the property. They walk down the pathway leading up to her favorite tree. The pink petals sway in the wind. Essa lets out a smile and the boy takes notice and remains quiet. She reaches it and places her hand against the trunk. Her fingers run along the bark. She places her foot against it and with the other, pushes off from the ground and climbs onto the lowest branch. She lets her legs dangle around for a bit and then musters up the courage to ask a question. "This might sound rude but who are you? I mean, I don't even know your name."

The boy looks up at her with an expression of longing, as if there's a long history beneath his skin. The sun makes it hard for him to see so he takes a step to the side and the leaves protect his face from the sun. "I'm Spike Adams—I know, such a dull name right?" he leans up against the tree and crosses his arms.

"I wouldn't necessarily label that as dull, just, traditional?"

"Kind words."

"So, why did you help me before, in the classroom?" Essa asks, her legs moving around back and forth.

"Help? I don't know what you are talking about. The chalk has a mind of its own. An inanimate object with the sheer drive to cleanse the world of evil."

"Oh really?" she asks with a sarcastic tone.

Spike chuckles. "I'm not like the others. Sure my family has money, but I don't let it decide who I am. As for my marks, well I suppose they could be better. But I spend most of my free time, and the time I should spend doing school work, training."

"I didn't ask." Essa says.

"You wanted to." Spike says in reply.

"I suppose." Essa looks at him closely. She notices that his knowledge of her was far from non-existent. She runs her hand through her scarlet red hair and gazes at his strong jaw line and his tone muscles hidden beneath his clothing, she then asks, "What is it you are training for?"

He closes his eyes and rests against the tree, "To better myself, in whichever way possible, both internally and well," he touches his chest, "the outside."

A gust of wind pushes through the courtyard. Essa feels the tree sway a little. The bell chimes.

"I guess it's time to go back to class." Spike says with a smile as he opens his eyes and says, "Gym is my kind of course. I'll see you there." He leaves with a wave and heads for the school.

Essa watches Spike enter the confines of the school. She then looks up at the sky. "If only the stars came out during the day..." she squints her eyes, as the sun glares down into her vision.

A star suddenly shines bright in the sky, so bright, that it gains attention in the suns ray of power. Then it grows larger, shining brighter. The star puzzles Essa, and then she finds herself watching in amazement as it continues to grow, getting ever closer, bridging the gap between space and life on Eryu. This peculiarity soon begins to worry Essa, as she knows that nothing that falls is safe.

It comes hurtling down towards her, precisely where she is sitting. The speed remains constant. Essa yells and begins to fall off. Just before the star hits the tree it suddenly stops. A brilliant light blinds her temporarily. She blinks quickly as she hangs from the tree branch with both of her hands. She sees a floating object within the bright light.

After a pause, trying to see what is inside, she reaches out with her left hand and places it within the light. An object fits into her grip, melding into her palm, sending warmth throughout her fingertips and towards her heart.

Warm tears form and run down her face, a vision quickly flashes and she sees her family all standing together, smiling, and then that too is replaced by quick glimmers of other faces, of people she doesn't know, of things she has never seen, until it slows down and eventually stops, and all she sees, is a girl that resembles herself, but with short purple hair and strong eyes, looking directly into her soul, *"Fear not this encounter, so much beauty awaits from it."*

She lets go of the tree branch and falls, unaware of her surroundings. She feels everything in slow motion, as she descends, disconnected from reality. The voice—her voice—continues to speak to her, guiding her as her eyelids close, *"From vindicated actions to twisted hearts, the shooting stars form our destiny."* As her body feels like air amongst clouds, a drifting leaf amongst the running river, a pebble skipping across the lake, she opens her eyes as her body lands against the ground and hears one last thing before returning to her senses, *"This is yours to hold, do with it what I could not."*

She finds herself sitting upright before truly understanding what just took place. In her hands rests a book, one strong and sturdy, bound in a unique fashion, so that the brown leather wraps around the contents within acting as if it were more of a shell protecting a heart than simply a wall protecting a story.

Her desire to open it leads her to press her index finger against the cover and tilt it open slightly. A gust of wind shoots out around her, her eyes follow and sees a flock of pink petals leave her favorite tree and float towards her. They dance, and shimmer, and the wind opens the book completely, revealing its white pages.

Completely blank, every single page. Essa, puzzled, closes the book and frowns. She presses it against her chest and then looks towards the school. No title, no story, a book from the sky, where the stars stand together, amongst one another.

She stands up and tucks the book beneath her right arm and rushes to school, a feeling of exhilaration throughout her. Never has she ran so fast towards this place.

A few minutes pass as she makes her way towards her locker, stuffing the unique, leather bound book into it and shutting the miniature door. She looks around, seeing that she is alone, and that up until this point, no one has taken notice of the bizarre circumstances surrounding her break between classes.

Essa then walks towards the gym, ignoring any glares that come her way. As she enters the domain of physical exertion, which strives to achieve perfection and glory, her eyes quickly gaze around for Spike, the only person she seems to deem kind. As she spots him, he also sees her, and he stops what he is doing. For a moment, she wonders if he knows, or if he saw the book fall from the sky in the presence of a star.

Their eyes lock, and then her gym teacher's voice greets her from behind. "So she decides to arrive."

CHAPTER FIVE
Wavering Accusations

A man with his black hair pulled back into a ponytail stands in front of them all. He wears a kimono, which is a traditional garment for those of Japanese descent. It's a long loose robe with wide sleeves that includes a sash that ties it together.

Their teachers name is Mr. Lunar. He looks at Essa first, before turning his eyes to the rest of the class. He yawns and then walks towards the front of the gym so he can address them all with the day's curricular activities.

Once reaching it, he pulls out a wooden sword from the confines of his kimono, to which most of the boys bust out into cheers and grins, excited that they will get to slash at one another. Some of the girls let out a sigh, a few show signs of fire in their eyes, and others grimace, including a few boys who dislike physical trauma.

The gym itself has hardwood flooring and black walls, padded with a contrast of white, so any collisions that may occur do not result in a serious injury. In Mr. Lunar's class, students must participate in any and every activity, even with a high threat of injury unless he deems otherwise.

He looks at all of the students—thirty-three in total. "Today we will be learning how to defend ourselves against an enemy."

Tabatha rolls her eyes and smirks. "With a sword? Really?" she asks. She then sighs and begins to mutter with two of her friends.

"Yes," he replies, "with wooden ones, because even I'd be horrified to give you an actual weapon. The purpose of this is so that you learn some of the basic movements and, in time, refine them." His answer is given with a dull layer of enthusiasm.

Mr. Lunar walks down the middle of the gym. The students form a circle around him.

"Now who would like the opportunity to attack me? Do whatever it is you need to do with whatever your developing bodies have to offer. Real weapons are forbidden. I don't want to have to tell your parents you died during an exercise. So, use your fists, your legs, and even a wooden sword if you want. Any takers?"

Four students step forward. Spike alongside Tabatha, and two other male students. Mr. Lunar looks at all of them closely and then closes his eyes. "Let's begin."

The two boys next to Spike attack first. One of them throws a punch while the other follows up with a kick towards the midsection. Mr. Lunar reacts swiftly. He dodges the punch and raises his knee to intercept the kick. The second boy yelps in pain and falls to the ground. The other students pull him out of the fight. The other boy, frustrated, runs forward and throws a three-punch combo. Mr. Lunar dodges all three punches by back stepping—his eyes still closed. He then moves past the boy swiftly and hits him in the back with the wooden sword. The boy falls to his knees and rolls over in pain.

A large smile appears on Spike's face. Mr. Lunar turns his attention towards him. Spike says in glee, "So you plan to humiliate me as well with your eyes closed? I know you said no weapons but you see I train with a wooden stick. No different from the sword you are using right now. Speaking about defense, I believe my skills will be a prime example for all the students." Everyone gasps and talks to one another. The excitement rises in the gym.

"Alright, that is acceptable. Show me what it is that keeps you from doing well in all of your other courses" Mr. Lunar says.

"Smart ass." Spike goes into his fighting stance and pulls out a stick from a pouch on his back. He flips it out and it forms a medium sized stick, the length roughly double the size of the sword.

Sweat begins to trickle down everyone's face. The atmosphere changes drastically.

Essa feels a strange urge to run away.

Tabatha smirks but then feels something wet on her forehead. She realizes she's also nervous. She looks around and takes a step out of the circle leaving Mr. Lunar and Spike.

Spike trembles with excitement and rushes forward.

"He's insane," one of the students says loud enough to be heard. Everyone watches as the stick moves forward quickly. Mr. Lunar blocks it with his sword and continues to do so against the following attacks. Yet, each one edges closer to his clothing. Spike keeps pressing forward, constantly stabbing and prodding.

Mr. Lunar takes a side step and swings his sword on an uppercut angle. Spike blocks it with his stick, which pushes him backwards. "Let's see how your footwork is," Mr. Lunar says before changing his stance. He waits for Spike to make a move.

"Fine, I'll do all the work." Spike smiles and runs forward. He then tucks his head backwards as the sword swings past his face, making him feel a little nervous. He spins to the side and brings his stick in for an attack at the side of Mr. Lunar's stomach. The teacher simply grabs the stick and stops it with his hand.

Spike quickly becomes puzzled.

"It's just a stick." Mr. Lunar grins. His sword pushes forward and grazes Spike's cheek.

Spike moves backwards and spins the stick all around his body and then slams the end of it into the ground. "Enough of this. Fight me for real. I want to see how long I can last against you."

"You've done nothing to make me want to do so," Mr. Lunar says in return.

"Haven't I?" Spike asks. Just then Mr. Lunar feels the sleeve on his clothing fall off. The class gasps.

"Oh?" he says aloud.

Spike snickers and rubs his nose. "Like I was saying, a lot of practice."

Mr. Lunar smiles and raises his sword forward. "Then let me show you the difference between playing and a battle."

Essa struggles to breathe. It doesn't make any sense to her why she's scared. Perhaps it's because a real fight is about to break out. Maybe it's because someone she'd like to call a friend is doing something so reckless. But the worst feeling is that something is making her think of the book in the star that fell from the sky.

It doesn't take long for the fight to come to an end. In fact, it is over in the blink of an eye. Spike and Mr. Lunar stand focused and ready. Then without taking more than two steps, Mr. Lunar is able to pass Spike and slam the sword at the back of his neck. This causes him to fall to his knees and wave his hands in defeat.

The students gasp. "You still have a long way to go, but this is enough. Any more and I will begin to hurt you. You're fine, right?" he asks.

Spike turns to him and a grin is plastered across his face, "It's like we're already becoming close friends."

Mr. Lunar chuckles at the comment. He then looks at all of the students. "Well now that this is over and done with, let's get to the actual point of the course. I want everyone to pair up. We will begin in five minutes."

Essa runs over to Spike and helps him up. "Are you alright?" she asks.

"Ya, it's okay don't worry about it. I'm far from done. But I know I'm also not ready." His tone of voice changes and he then says, "Just don't judge this as my full potential. This was nothing, alright?" She nods her head in response. Something about the outcome, despite it being simple, was already eating away at him. She didn't plan to bring it up, not now.

The class carries on and seems quite dull in contrast to the initial start. Essa and Spike train together and, throughout the movements, she notices that he is holding back as he keeps up a smile for her. This causes her to put all of her effort into the session. In what feels like minutes, the class comes to an end. She stops moving her arms and begins to feel the exhaustion take over. Spike stretches his arms and then walks over and pats her on the back. "Not bad. You did pretty well for your first session," he says jokingly.

"Don't mock me," she says with a laugh.

"Anyways school's done for the day. Where do you live? I could walk you home if you'd like."

She raises an eyebrow, "Well, I come from Rosendale Street, do you live in that direction? I've never seen you walking that way."

He scratches his chin and asks, "Rosendale…?"

She looks at him for a moment. "You don't know where Rosendale is?"

"Well, I don't know any of the street names. I kind of just go wherever my feet take me." He laughs.

"Most people wouldn't say that and think it's a good thing," she says.

"Well I'll meet you out front alright? I need to go get my stuff together." He replies.

She makes her way to her locker; a strange pulse runs through her hand as she places it against the weakly made steel that confines her secret. She gulps and thinks about what lays beyond it. The form it took as it fell from the sky. "Whatever. It doesn't matter," she says frazzled as she opens her locker and quickly places her hand around it, stuffing it into her backpack.

"Going somewhere?" a familiar voice asks her. Essa turns around and sees Tabatha facing her with arms crossed. "I saw the way you and that lowlife were getting along today in gym class. Don't start thinking anyone here appreciates you. He's just as low as you are in this school's hierarchy. Trash will remain trash." She pokes Essa in the chest and walks away.

Flustered, Essa simply closes her locker and walks in the opposite direction. She doesn't plan to risk the chance of running into her again.

However she still manages to come across someone—someone strange.

A girl sits on one of the benches in the front of the school entranceway. She looks at Essa and remains silent.

As Essa walks past her, she takes a close look. It was clear that her sense of style was different from everyone else attending the school. The girl has long grey hair with white streaks along the bangs. She's very thin and somewhat pale and has a wardrobe consisting of white tights, a pair of black shorts, a black long sleeve shirt and a red-buttoned t-shirt on top with the top button undone.

The girl merely looks directly at Essa without saying so much as a word. Time passes and Essa breaks eye contact, and finds Spike, who walks her home.

***

Hours pass and Essa sits her in bedroom staring through the window in her ceiling. The stars begin to come out. She looks at her backpack that she left sitting on her chair near her desk. "Did you fall from one of the stars I look at every day? Or are you…something else." She closes her eyes soon after and falls asleep.

Morning arrives and Essa makes her way down to the kitchen. "Mom?" she calls out. She receives no response. Essa walks to the phone and calls. But her mom doesn't pick up. This carries on for a while, until she gives up and takes a seat at the kitchen table. She spends the rest of her weekend worrying, endlessly looking for signs of her mother's return.

***

Monday morning arrives and Essa gets ready for school with the little enthusiasm remaining—this time deciding to leave the leather book on her bed. Her mind is clouded with worry. She decides that she will call the police if her mom is not home when she gets back from school.

She makes her way out of the house. As she arrives at school, she sees Tabatha and avoids her glare. Everything continues on as usual.

Except Spike is there to talk to. Eventually third period rolls around and Essa finds herself walking slowly down the hallway towards her classroom. She bumps into someone and takes a step back. "I'm sorry," she blurts out in a daze.

The girl looks at her and tilts her head. It was the one Essa saw that she analyzed and found quite odd. "Are you blind?" the girl asks sarcastically.

"No…just…I'm sorry." Essa says.

"Well it can't be helped I guess." The girl looks Essa up and down, "My name is Cassandra Waver; I figure it's best you at least know whom you walked into with such grace. And you are?"

"I'm Essa Starlight."

Cassandra yawns and places her hands on her hips. "Seeing as how you were rude, I'd say you owe me a favor, how about we skip our classes and go for a talk?" she says.

"Uh, no I can't do that."

Cassandra rolls her eyes and grabs her hand, "Yes you can."

She leads Essa to the terrace on the fifth floor that overlooks a small lake in the distance. They lean their arms against the railing, Essa wondering why Cassandra, so unique, has only caught her attention as of recently.

Cassandra says, "I'll be straight forward Essa, there's something about you that's different from the rest of the students that go here."

"…Well there's nothing special about me, I'm just like everyone else." Essa replies.

"No, that's not true anymore. Not since last Friday."

The image of the fallen star flashes through Essa's mind. "…That's fairly specific, as far as I can recall, that's the first time I have ever seen you."

"I suppose," Cassandra says with her voice trailing off, "that would be…correct."

"Yes, unless you've been spying on me…"

"I'm not into that sort of thing darling, but if I were," Cassandra takes a step closer to Essa, "you aren't my type." She returns her attention to the lake, "Essa…would you care to lend me a hand with something?"

"…What exactly do you need help with?"

Cassandra pauses and takes a deep breath, "When something catches my attention, I learn everything there is to learn about it. I fill in the missing pieces; I fix what is unhinged and hanging loosely in a world full of chaos. Take it as you will, but this means that when something troubling rests on my mind, I seek to find the reason why."

Essa says nothing, letting the silence between them indicate that she is still listening, and truly fixated on how open Cassandra is with someone she doesn't know.

Continuing, Cassandra says, "In this instance, take the new supply teacher."

"Which one?"

Cassandra muses, "The one with the hideous moustache and greedy eyes. He was meant to be a stand-in for the science department but for some reason also had the qualifications to become a guidance counsellor." She turns her body to face Essa completely and leans a little more against the railing, "Those don't normally go hand in hand."

Essa closes her eyes, stands on the tip of her toes and replies, "So, he has a wide range of teaching skills. Is that really reason for alarm and to bring me here?"

"…Something about him is clearly amiss…"

A few students walk into the courtyard and laugh amongst themselves. Cassandra looks down at them with an expression one gives when they see an insect.

Cassandra says, "Essa, what if I were to tell you that you are a waste of space?"

Alarmed, Essa stands firmly on the ground and slams a finger in Cassandra's direction, "I would tell you to piss off."

The expression on Cassandra's face warms up completely, like when close friends make one another laugh. Essa on the other hand, finds it as odd as the entire conversation has been up to this point. She fails to see how beautiful Cassandra is with her contagious smile.

Cassandra continues to say, "That was a good response, your reaction is how I feel whenever someone knows there's something odd but throws a half assed answer at it, so it leaves their mind. Most people dislike thinking, and so they create a wasteland where a wealth of information should be."

"Well, I am sorry if I offended you."

"You didn't, you made me proud." Cassandra continues, "Now, to get to the point. This teacher, whose name is Mr. Fredericton, comically spoken about due to his moustache, has something about him that seems off. I want to investigate what that is, and I want you to accompany me, I want you to use your eyes and see if you can spot what's wrong with him."

Essa crosses her arms, "Fine, I'll come with you but honestly, I suspect it wasn't my fault for walking into you, not in the slightest, not from how you are using this so perfectly."

Cassandra grins, "Let's go."

As they make their way down the stairs towards the second floor, where the guidance room is located, Cassandra places a hand on Essa's shoulder and pulls her into one of the dimly lit hallways and says, "Before we enter the guidance room, there's something I want you to know about me. You can disbelieve what it is I have to say, but keep an open mind." She leans in closer to Essa until their eyes tune out everything around them, "I see the dead."

Essa gulps, "Open mind or not, that's just not something I can believe right away…now just, let's get this over with. I don't normally skip class."

They enter the guidance counsellors' office. The man that looks up at them seems tired and dispirited. As if everything is dull and gray.

He clears his throat and rubs his tired eyes. "Can I help you ladies?" he asks.

Essa takes a step back. His voice makes her feel unsettled.

He notices this and then turns his attention to Cassandra.

She stares at him.

He continues to look at her and remain complacent. Letting her analyze him. "Is there something I can help you with?" he asks her specifically.

"I'm just wondering why you're in this school."

He scratches his face. Rubbing his hand across his exhausted expression. "I'm here to cover for a teacher who is on leave. That's all. Anything else I can help you with?"

"Yes, one more thing," she replies, "explain to me how you're managing to keep that horrid disguise on."

He doesn't reply. He simply grunts. "If all you plan to do is insult me, I suggest you leave. I'm here to assist students but not those who clearly have personal problems associated with make-believe situations."

"I stand by my accusation." Cassandra says while standing her ground, "There is a lust in the air for blood."

"Child, you may actually need my help, there seems to be something broken in your thought process," he replies, his voice snickering slightly.

Essa looks at him in disgust. Cassandra was right—there is something horribly wrong about him, and the only reason she is even able to take witness to it, is because of Cassandra's strong perception.

She grabs ahold of Cassandra's arm, "Let's go…"

The man smiles, "That's a splendid suggestion."

They leave the guidance room and Essa says, "Alright, wasting of time is now complete. I have somewhere, anywhere, else to be."

Cassandra looks at her from the corner of her eye, "Do not offend me."

Essa squints her eyes slightly, "Say what you will, my mind is certainly racing, but my heart is also troubled. I have other things on my plate, it's not empty, I wish it were."

"…Anything I can help with?"

"No."

As they look at one another, Mr. Fredericton exits the guidance room and leaves their sight. Cassandra turns and begins to follow him, leaving Essa without a word, until a loud booming voice startles them, "And where do the two of you think you're going?"

Mr. Linder greets them with a stern expression that quickly turns into a big smile as he addresses Essa, "You're finally skipping classes, that-a-girl!" He pats her on the back three times, laughing with each contact.

Another voice appears, "Are you telling our students that skipping is a healthy lifestyle?" The voice belongs to the school nurse, who is also a new faculty member. She's a slender woman, with long purple hair and strands of glimmering black. She wears a pair of glasses that she continually fixes as they fall down her nose.

Mr. Linder replies, "Oh, Veronica-, I mean Miss. Dixon—what a lovely surprise."

She frowns, "Don't give students the wrong impression." Her eyes turn to Essa and Cassandra, "The two of you should be in class, not wandering the halls."

Replying with a sigh, Cassandra says, "There's nothing wrong with students seeking guidance."

Miss. Dixon raises an eyebrow, "May I ask what may be troubling you?"

"You certainly cannot," Cassandra says, ending the conversation.

"Very well, then where is it the two of you should be?"

Essa clears her throat and says softly, "Gym."

Miss. Dixon looks at Cassandra, "As for you?"

"Gym as well" Cassandra says with a soft smile.

Miss. Dixon replies, "Unlikely. You aren't enrolled in that course."

Growing annoyed, Cassandra asks, "Why would the school nurse know what course I am taking?"

Mr. Linder chuckles, "She has a point, Veronica."

Miss. Dixon glares at him, "Do not address me so casually, Bryce."

He waves his hands and proceeds to cross them, clearly past the point of enjoying the conversation. Miss. Dixon proceeds to say, "It's time for the two of you to return to class. Don't worry about being written up, neither Mr. Linder nor myself are in the mood to fill out paperwork."

Essa smiles, "Thank you." She quickly waves softly at Cassandra and makes her way down the hallway, taking the quickest route towards the gym. The two teachers turn to look at Cassandra. She lets out a sigh and goes the other way, walking casually, her hair dancing behind her as she gazes at the ceiling.

Mr. Linder comments by saying, "They are both unique."

"There's certainly something special about them both, but that's not why we are here."

"I know, it's a waste though."

"That's not for us to decide. We've got our duties set out for us."

"Still, even you seem to be taking a liking to some of them."

"And you haven't? Listen Bryce, if even students are able to feel something is up, that means we're taking our sweet time. We need to act now, not later."

He replies, "Perhaps, but we can't rush things. You are just looking deeply into it, curiosity is not knowledge in the mindset of the young."

She glares at him, "This is the first time that even Mr. Lunar is unable to find the source. This has taken far too long and you know it."

The discussion between them continues, and during this time Essa arrives at her gym class. She changes into her gym attire and manages to enter without anyone taking much notice of her. She soon discovers that on today's agenda, Mr. Lunar has something special set out for them.

The students have the option between continuing their sword practice, or, if they are not up for being whacked by a wooden force, they can partake in the beep test—a punishment in itself—that Essa makes the mistake of choosing.

After running back and forth across the gym at a rising rate, when Essa feels that her heart is going to burst out of her chest, she continues to push forward. Other students begin to fall out and heave on the ground, or quit without putting much effort into the exercise. However, Essa continues to run, her mind focusing completely on everything she's witnessed in a matter of a few days.

With her body screaming at her, begging her to stop, she continues to push forward. She doesn't take notice to the other students watching her as she competes with some of the most athletic. Even Tabatha, who is still running alongside her, begins gasping for breath looking for an end to this nightmare.

It becomes apparent that something is different within Essa. Be it her drive or her physical stamina, she bests her personal score and continues to run, only slightly trailing some of the strongest.

Tabatha, still ahead of Essa, reaches one end of the gymnasium and turns quickly. Her eyes widen as Essa becomes a blur that passes her by a fraction. Not willing to give up, Tabatha chases her, with only seven students still running and her now being in last.

Unknowingly, Essa becomes the focus of everybody's attention. Spike, Mr. Lunar and the other students all watch as she continues to run, surpassing all expectations and continuing to speed up. It becomes baffling to many, some of who point at her and murmur amongst themselves.

One or two students stare with their mouths hanging open slightly, as their swords hang loosely in their hand. Then, the magic comes to an end; Essa stops running and collapses on the ground. Tabatha runs past her and once she reaches the end of the gymnasium, falls to her knees.

Students cheer, some for Tabatha having beaten Essa, others for Essa having put up such a great run. Spike walks over to Essa and helps her up.

He says, "That was amazing Essa, you did a great job."

Not sure of what came over her, Essa wipes the sweat from her forehead, "Thank you. I can stand on my own though."

Spike lets go and she walks towards the changing room, clearly having had enough exercise for the day.

Tabatha, still catching her breath, says loud enough for Spike to hear, "What the hell has come over that girl?"

Spike grins, "She's coming alive," as he waits in admiration for her return.

While in the girls changing room, Essa grabs her towel and wipes the sweat off her face. Sitting on a bench, halfway through changing, she lets her head hang forward and keeps her eyes closed. She grabs a bottle of water, raises her head and squirts the contents on her face, then proceeds to wipe her face once more.

Her eyes open, and within the depths of her pupils, a sign of change. She thinks deeply about everything, but one thing dominates her mind, even more so than the worry of her unreachable mother, she thinks about the book.

She takes a sip of the water, and places her hand on the side of the bench. Her face goes pale. She turns her head, and what she sees frightens her further. Resting on the bench, waiting for her, as if it knew the exact moment to reveal itself, sits her book.

CHAPTER SIX
Painting a Picture

Not letting the book frighten her any further, Essa stands up calmly. She looks at the book, at its leather exterior, and she feels slightly stupid. Of course it's doing the impossible, it came from the sky. She gulps, and with a shaking hand, reaches towards it.

Nothing happens as her hand makes contact. Slightly irritated, she stuffs it into her backpack. She then grinds her teeth, the frustration boiling over.

Tabatha appears at the entrance and rests her hand on the edge of the wall. Essa turns to look at her, and her expression startles Tabatha, who then takes a step back and leaves.

As she exists the change room, once back in her normal attire, this time wearing a red skirt with black leggings, a white button t-shirt tucked in and a red ribbon at the collar, she notices that their teacher, Mr. Lunar, is no longer in the gymnasium.

Spike greets her and she asks, "What's going on?"

"He was just called out suddenly by another faculty member, from their expressions it seemed important."

"Is that so…"

"Is everything alright?" Spike asks compassionately.

"Yes," she nods her head slightly, "...sort of."

With the urge to tell someone, anyone, about her mother and the book, Essa looks at him and feels the need to confess what's troubling her. Spike can tell that she is about to say something, and as her mouth opens to tell the past events, the ground shakes.

Some students notice the vibration in the ground and stop what they are doing. Others continue to laugh and fool around, Tabatha, however, not being one of them. She looks across the gymnasium at Spike, who returns the gaze.

The ground shakes once more, this time stronger, and catches the attention of the entire class. All of the students look at one another in silence, wondering what's transpiring, not used to feeling the sensation beneath them, for tremors are unheard of.

A third tremor occurs, so vicious that it shakes students to their knees. Dust falls from the ceiling and students begin to cry out, some already running towards the exit. Spike grabs a hold of Essa and ensures she remains on her feet, he says to her urgently, "We need to get out of here, something is wrong."

The alarm in his voice matches how she is feeling perfectly, and she exits the gym with him swiftly, other students following them, Tabatha included.

They come across a teacher they don't know the name of, addressing the concern of the students stopped in front of him. The hallway soon fills up. The school, not having a procedure for an earthquake, finds itself in a mess.

"Listen" says the teacher, "everything is going to be alright, the police are already on their way. You are all safe, so please do your best to keep your nerves under control. I know you want to freak out, but you mustn't, it will only increase your overall anxiety. I repeat, everything is going to be alright."

Other faculty members appear, none of which Essa notices are Mr. Linder, Lunar, Dixon, or even Fredericton. The hallway now at a very uncomfortable and crowded level, remains silent as the teacher speaking continues his attempt at calming the students.

Essa turns to Spike, "This is horrible. Do you think the other hallways are just like this?"

"I hope not." He says underneath his breath, "This is incredibly stupid. We should look for another exit. Standing here all bunched together when the ceiling can come crumbling down with the floors above us, is not my idea of safety."

Essa grows pale, "Well that's a thought."

They turn around and Essa quickly spots Cassandra in the crowd a few feet away. Cassandra shrugs, grins half-heartedly and looks very unimpressed with the crowd. Essa walks towards her on instinct and feels a surge of happiness in finding her.

Cassandra's face grows stern and focused; Essa turns to see what's making her look that way, and witnesses the arrival of Mr. Fredericton at the far end of the hallway. Barely able to see him through the amount of students, she stands on her tiptoes.

An eerie smile rests on his face as he asks the teacher who has been talking up until now, "How are the students holding up, is everyone safe?"

The man, oblivious in nature to danger, replies, "Yes, it's good that you are here. This is your forte. You can help me with guiding these students to safety."

Mr. Fredericton smiles and places a hand to his face, trying to conceal how much pleasure he's experiencing, "Oh, yes, we mustn't let anyone fall to harm. We must change the course of events as soon as possible."

The man smiles, "I agree completely, let's make sure they are safe."

"There's just one thing that we need to change in our tactics," Mr. Fredericton says, as the silence amplifies his final words, "...it begins with you."

His hand moves slightly, and with it follows a loud thump. The students look down at the ground and see a round circular object rolling towards them. They stare, puzzled at the fact that in front of them, rests their teachers head.

The first student to open his mouth is cut in half before he can utter a sound. Another student screams, "What the hell is going on!" and the students closest to Mr. Fredericton begin to move in a panic.

Essa and the others, who are on the other end, unable to see everything that is going on, begin to feel a surge of fear coming from the other students like a tidal wave. The pressure slams into Essa, and she feels the urge to vomit.

Mr. Fredericton winks at a set of students who try to run past him, and they are torn to shreds with their blood splattering the walls and students closest. The smirk on his face rising, another faculty member near the front is cut in half down the middle as he moves past the students to assess the situation.

Spike raises his arm in front of Essa protectively.

She places her hands to her face and begins shaking, "What the hell is going on, all I hear are screams and I smell blood…I can even see it from here."

Another student is cut in half. Even with all of the running and screaming, the hallway remains full and clustered. Within all the panic, nobody is able to escape. Above all of the noise, one thing can be heard clearer then everything else, Mr. Fredericton's laugh.

As another teacher is slain, a student trips over the body and bursts into uncontrollable tears. Spike looks at everything that is happening and remains calm and composed to the best of his abilities.

Another student falls prey to the unforeseeable force.

Spike says, "I know it's him…it's definitely him." He looks at Essa, "Stay here, and if you decide to run, go with that girl." He motions towards Cassandra, who in turn looks at him.

Essa struggles to say anything, and Cassandra places a hand on her shoulder. Behind them, Tabatha appears and says, "This is unbelievable…I need to call my father, I can't stay here like this."

Cassandra says, "Calm yourself right now."

Tabatha looks at her, glares, but then breathes deeply, seemingly regaining her composure. Essa, marveling at how that's even possible, watches in horror as a set of students not far away from them are suddenly torn apart. This sets in motion an even stronger fight for survival as every student pushes uncontrollably to escape.

Cassandra does her best to keep Essa safe, and notices that Spike is no longer with them. Off in the crowd, Spike edges closer towards Mr. Fredericton.

She witnesses him slipping on a puddle of blood and falling to the ground. He gets back up swiftly, wiping his hands on his pant legs, his back drenched in red.

Mr. Fredericton looks at him directly, touching the edge of his moustache and twirling it with satisfaction. Spike takes a step forward and a hand grabs a hold of him and pulls him back.

Having reached him, leaving Essa behind, Cassandra yells into Spikes ear, "Don't be rash, you moron! Use your eyes or let me use mine before you run off and get yourself killed!"

Agitated he growls, "The fuck, Cassandra!"

"People are being torn to pieces. I bet you think it's just from thin air, eh? Honestly, don't insult me! Think for once and put your muscles to actual use. That man is using phantasms to do his bidding." She turns to look at the teacher, "Damn it, it's coming!" she pulls on Spike and brings them to their knees, avoiding a close encounter with a blade only she can see.

Huffing, Spike pushes her back, "Look, I can handle this alright!"

Her eyes widen once more and she sends a kick to his head, knocking him to the left, as the blade misses his neck.

He sits up straight once more, "Jesus Cassandra, I said I've got it-"

She slams into him, and the blade misses once more. He looks up at her and stops arguing, if the blade didn't kill him, she was about to.

They both get up and Cassandra pulls him along through the thinning crowd. She says, "We are not playing hero today, we are getting out of here pronto, and we are making sure Essa doesn't witness any more than she has to."

He looks around at the dead bodies and those soon to join as they huddle in fear. He then looks towards Essa, who stands against a locker, with Tabatha close to her, both of them observing their surroundings to avoid the hidden threat.

Spike asks, "Is she safe?"

"We need to hurry, there's one near them."

A gust of wind slams through the students. Cassandra turns and curses as she witnesses a blade pierce through a group of females and aims to take her along with it. Dodging it successfully, she still receives a slight cut along her ankle.

Noticing the trickle of blood amongst the canvas of death, Spike asks if she is all right. She merely nods her head and continues to head towards Essa, avoiding any sudden strikes from the phantasms tearing through bodies.

They reach Essa and Tabatha, and Cassandra steps out in front, keeping them behind her. Spike asks, "So, what's the exit strategy?"

"If we make it past the phantasm that's currently heading towards us, we can reach the exit at the far end."

Tabatha's brow becomes focused, "Wait, you can see what's going on?"

Essa replies, "She can see ghosts."

Cassandra's eyes dart at her, and then towards the phantasm, a large mean looking figure clad in black armor from head to toe, wielding a massive broadsword. She is the only one able to hear its clacking movement, and each step she witnesses echoes throughout her tunneling vision.

Her eyes dart towards three of the exits. One is blocked by a pile of students lying dead against the door, another has a set of lockers toppled over with a student crushed beneath it, although still accessible, the chances of the four of them getting to it safely are incredibly low. The third and final option is the emergency exit at the far end of the hallway, past Mr. Fredericton, who still has yet to take a step from where he initially started.

A gnawing feeling rumbles in Cassandra's stomach.

Spike asks, "Well, what do you see?"

She doesn't reply, but contemplates which route will result in the least amount of casualties.

He asks once more, "Cassandra, what do we do?"

Tabatha, now worrying, "Seriously, Cassandra!"

Essa notices her lips are trembling. Her ears pick up on a noise, a heroic rumbling, and she looks towards the emergency exit behind Mr. Fredericton.

It bursts open and standing in its wake is Mr. Linder, eyes full of fury as he walks through the doorway and past the broken hinges and torn brick. He proclaims in a bellowing voice, "Do not fear this man!" he clenches his fists and flexes his muscles, "I will wring his neck."

Tabatha's eye twitches slightly, "The hell."

Spike grins, "Perfect, right Cassandra?"

"Yes," she grabs a hold of Essa's hand and darts towards Mr. Fredericton, who now snarls and turns his attention towards Mr. Linder.

The four students make their way towards a man of death, relying on Cassandra's eyes to guide them through the thin line on which they tread. Other students, those who remain, take notice. "Let's follow them!" one proclaims, raising their spirits. A dozen run with them, but with no eyes to guide them, become open playthings for the phantasms.

Mr. Fredericton says to Mr. Linder, "So you've come to ruin all my fun. What matter of muscle and bones are you? Thinking you can stop all that I seek." The lust for blood begins to show further within his eyes, "So, there is more to you than your looks suggest, but pawns that shock me," he raises his head, a glimmer of red appearing in his eyes, "are still just pawns."

His hand raises and then falls. With it, Cassandra sees the air around him change, and quickly moves as far to the side as possible while nearing him. Still clutching Essa's hand so tightly that she feels the blood flow.

Spike, who seeks a fight like a child seeks candy, feels Tabatha pushing him forward so he doesn't do something rash. His feeling of jealousy skyrockets as he bears witness to Mr. Linder flexing his muscles further, ripping through the sleeves of his shirt.

Mr. Linder moves towards Mr. Fredericton slowly, and then closes the distance quickly with a mighty punch that collides with Mr. Fredericton's palm. The friction that emits from the collision causes Essa to feel winded and weak in the knees. Spike catches her so she doesn't hit the ground, and the four of them as well as a few lucky souls, reach the exit.

They hear their teacher yelling as they descend down the staircase, "Do not stop running, and do not avert your eyes, live my students, live!"

The plea, the warning, the words of hope strike a chord in Essa's heart and cause her to cry. With her feet landing on each step, sending a slight shock further into her muscles, she thinks about the book in her backpack, as it bounces around, mysteriously, doing nothing to help her.

Spike says, "He's one hell of a man, but he's a goner."

Tabatha nods her head, "If there's invisible blades being flung around, anyone who faces that lunatic would be."

Essa begins to feel everything blur. She looks at Cassandra's back, her strong back hidden by the rich, unique hair. Watching this person she hardly knows protect her, brings courage, and causes her to say, "Mr. Linder will live, he's strong, I know he will make it…I know it."

Cassandra says without looking at them, moving hurriedly down the stairs, "I agree," she turns the corner, her hand sliding across the rail, "with Essa. That man seems to know what he was getting into. Whether he can see the phantasms or not is another story. But those knights of tortured souls are not something I want to run into again, so let's keep moving as far away as possible, while my eyes remain focused."

Spike mumbles, "I want to fight them."

Cassandra says, "Well you can't."

They reach the bottom of the stairs and burst through the doors. The students behind them quickly separate and rush towards the front doors of the school. One of them yells out, "I see the police, we're saved!" Others cry out in relief.

Cassandra stops and raises her hand, not letting Essa, Spike or Tabatha move forward. She then screams, "Stop it! Stop running towards the doors!"

The students closest to the front doors stop and turn, "What?"

then in an instant; their heads are sliced in half in a diagonal fashion. Another student cries, "What the hell, this isn't fair! The cops are right there! Why aren't they helping us!"

Another student falls to the ground and becomes hysterical, the blood from the dead bodies spilling towards her as more fall victim to the freshly appeared phantasm.

Cassandra grinds her teeth, "Appearing this far away from its master…damn it."

The single entity of looming horror faces them, with no other living being in its wake, having slain the other students so quickly that the blood still moves across the ground, trying to find a place in its new home.

It raises its sword, moving it around its body, sending dots of blood across the ground and walls as if it were painting a picture. This gesture unsettles Cassandra further, revealing a trait she does not show often, doubt.

Essa asks, "What do you see?"

"I see death," Cassandra replies, her eyes not averting from the phantasm, the king who paints a picture as she continues to say, "and I seek a way around it."

She formulates a strategy, as the phantasm continues to paint lines with the blood on its blade, seeming to pay no interest in their delay to move forward.

"Alright." Cassandra says, "This is how we are going to play this out. None of you can see this creature. So when I engage it, just remain where you are. Spike," she calls his name without looking at him, "use your eyes, try to see what I see, and maybe, who knows, you might catch a glimpse of what it is you wish to clash with so badly."

Essa looks at Spike, "Why would you want to clash with that?"

His eyes seemingly looking past her, lost in a set of stars of his own, he says, "I will fight anything that spills blood, and I will spill more of it."

She gulps, slightly terrified, and finds herself one step closer to Tabatha.

Without warning, Cassandra runs forward and Essa can see a cut appear across her savior's left arm immediately. She slides across the floor, not losing an ounce of composure, her eyes that of a hawk, seeing all.

The phantasm now finished with his painting of victory moves forward with his heavy sword. He swings it viciously. Cassandra pulls out a blade of her own that she has been concealing. Though small in comparison, with just the right amount of force and luck; she stops the phantasm from taking any of her limbs.

Cassandra runs past the phantasm, slicing his midsection. They try to imagine a blade chasing after her as she then dances seamlessly in front of their eyes.

Spike digs his fingernails into his pant leg, "I can't see anything. It's like she's just dancing around, fighting thin air."

Cassandra grabs hold of a miniature ball from her pouch and throws it forward. It explodes in front of the phantasm and unleashes a cloud of smoke. The others quickly lose sight of her.

Essa asks, "Will she really be alright?"

Spike doesn't reply. He focuses on the odd shape moving through the smoke, the subtle yet precise outline of something not human that causes him to grin. "I see it now," he says aloud.

As the phantasm swings its blade around to disperse the smoke, Cassandra leaps from within it and lands against its chest. She grabs hold of its head and slams her dagger through its face.

She drops back down, creating space between them. Ending the short encounter, the final one the phantasm would ever experience.

Black blood, but blood regardless, drips in a slight trickle down the phantasms helmet, revealing itself completely to the others as portions of its body become soaked in blood. It drops its sword, the impact from it crushing the ground where it rests.

Essa says, "I don't want to remember any of this, none of it..." to which Spike replies, with something out of place in his voice, "Every memory is worth keeping."

Cassandra walks towards the phantasm, as it stands there facing, them. She pulls out a pendant from her pocket and places it against its chest. A light shines, which sends off rays of light that wrap around the phantasms armor, causing the darkness to drift away, leaving behind a faint smile of a man who died long ago. Its body shatters and fades away, black smoke drifting.

She turns and looks at them, letting out a gasp for air. Essa rushes towards her and wraps her arms around her, holding her tightly, she says "Thank you," her voice chokes up, "thank you so much."

Spike places a hand to his side and looks outside, seeing that the police won't be coming to aid them after all, with carcasses lying about. Cassandra speaks for him, "We won't be going that way. It's too dangerous. We will go to the roof and find a way down, we can climb, find something, but we need to leave now."

Tabatha asks, "You can't just fight it?"

Cassandra grins, "Essa is holding me up right now."

Spike walks over and grabs a hold of her, "Alright, we head for the roof."

Essa says, "There's a few things I would like to know on the way."

Cassandra nods her head. They reach a different staircase from before and begin to walk up the steps. A sense of disease, that of silence where silence never existed before greets them. With a majority of their fellow classmates either gone or dead, the path they take seems hard, impractical, and perhaps insane.

So as to not focus on the possibility of them making a mistake, Essa asks, "Cassandra, how were you able to defeat that phantasm? I honestly thought you were making things up, but I also know people don't just get torn to pieces out of the blue."

"Well," Cassandra says, "It has a lot to do with my backstory, which I don't think a thousand flight of steps would give me enough time to talk about. So I'll give you the basics. My eyes are no different from anyone else's, but they are also able to see another plane of existence. You can say it's my nature, or that my teacher opened my mind. I've been able to use my eyes this way as far back as I can remember. As for how I defeated that phantasm. It required two things. The ability to see, though that's not necessarily mandatory, but what is, is a pendant or a weapon that's blessed with the touch of what I and others call, the Tears of Jessica."

Essa asks, "The Tears of Jessica?"

"There is a tale of a woman who could feel and see all, even beyond the curtain of death. One day she felt so much sorrow that she could not stop her tears. And so, as her eyelids let the tears fall, it began to flood the rivers and drench the towns nearest, and then turned fields into swamps, and then oceans, as the water continued to rise. The people were scared, but also sad, that this woman who knew so much, could only cry. That out of all the emotions, sadness became victor, until that is, one day the tears stopped, and the spectre of steel rose into the air. It became apparent that something had changed Jessica, or that she had changed of her own free will. A chord was struck, and from it, a hundred weapons came into existence, weapons with the purpose of releasing wandering souls and giving them peace. Jessica decided that her tears, her one hundred blades, would turn sorrow into peace."

"And you have one of them?"

"Yes."

"What of the pendant then?"

"The pendant was created after, with the purpose of subduing souls that were running rampant. While the Tears of Jessica release the soul, some do not have enough power to utterly vanquish the phantasms, so the pendants speed up the process tenfold. Moreover, if someone doesn't have one of the blessed blades, they can still use a pendant to slow down a soul. Not all can release the fallen, but they can avoid joining their ranks."

Essa thinks deeply for a moment, noticing that they are more than halfway towards the roof of the school. She asks, "Do you know of anyone else that can help us, who has a blessed blade?"

Cassandra shakes her head, "I don't know anyone else who has one besides my master."

Spike asks, "Do you still have the pendant from before?"

"Unfortunately not, a pendant disappears after one usage. It was the only one I had on me."

Tabatha groans, "This is just not what I want to hear."

They reach the roof and Spike kicks open the door with brute force. They exit onto the rooftop and look around, seeing signs of black smoke rising around the school. They can't hear much of anything. The sound of people crying, bullets piercing objects and police sirens screaming, it's all drowned out by adrenaline rushing through them.

Tabatha asks impatiently, "So where's the ladder that gets us off of this roof?"

They look around and come to realize that there is no ladder. Even worse, there's no easy accessible way down from the rooftop. The colour begins to drain from Tabatha's face.

As they stand together, a phantasm emerges from behind. Cassandra spins around and raises her dagger; the force of the blade coming down pushes her knees to the ground. Sweating, she soon finds herself thrown upwards into the air.

Tabatha's lip quivers, "It's…going to kill one of us. I can't see it but…I just know."

Spike remains silent with his eyes staring forward. Cassandra darts past them after getting back up, and throws a smoke bomb at the phantasm. She turns to deliver a blow to its side, but her tactic fails and she is elbowed across the face. She loses her grip on the dagger and slides across the ground.

The phantasm walks towards her and raises its sword. She moves slowly but knows she doesn't have the time to dodge. Then, out of the corner of her eye, she sees an unthinkable sight, Spike running towards her.

He yells, "I can see you!" and slams into the phantasm's midsection. He puts all of his strength into lifting it up and then slams it down. The impact causes a small crater to appear. He leaps backwards as the sword swipes around. The phantasm puts no effort into getting up since its body propels itself up naturally.

Spike grabs a hold of the phantasm's wrist and stops the sword from moving. He then slams his head against the phantasms. Cassandra stares at him in shock and thinks about how recklessly he is acting. The phantasm grabs hold of Spike and pulls on his shirt. However Spike is able to break free and send an array of punches into the phantasm's face.

Spike says in glee, "I can see you, I can see you aha!" he starts to laugh, his eyes filled with the desire for blood.

Tabatha moves far away from them, "You're all crazy…" she says, "You are insane!" she screams out. Suddenly the phantasm begins to glow.

Spike throws a punch and it's stopped. He's then pushed backwards. "Damn it!" he yells and raises his other fist. However the phantasm disappears.

Cassandra screams at the top of her lungs, "Stop it Tabatha, stop giving it something to feed off of!"

Tabatha turns and looks at her, "I didn't do anything!"

Spike looks around "Where is it, Cassandra where is it!"

"I don't know!" she yells in retort "I can't focus my eyes yet… wait…Spike, to your left!" He turns his head and the sound of bone cracking erupts. Blood spurts out. He falls backwards and lies on the ground, struggling to remain conscious.

Essa begins to shake heavily, "Get up…" she whispers "please get up…" she begins to cry uncontrollably, "get up!"

The phantasm looks at her and begins to walk towards her with its sword raised in the air.

Cassandra yells, "Stay away from her! Essa, you need to get away from there right now and run as far as you can towards your right side, you need to jump off the roof!"

Essa wipes her eyes and looks at her "I'll die if I jump!"

Cassandra clenches her fist "And you'll die here in a horrible way if you don't take the chance and jump for it! Aim for one of the bushes or one of the trees!"

Essa shakes her head and places her hands to her ears "Shut up! Shut up!" she cries out frantically with the phantasm only a few feet from her. Cassandra looks at Spike and begins to crawl towards him; she reaches him and feels his pulse. She looks towards Tabatha, "Please, take her and jump."

Tabatha feels her heart clench, "Why…why would I jump with that idiot?" her face begins to twist in fear, "I won't die with scum!"

As fear and disbelief overwhelm everyone and the phantasm raises its blade to strike Essa down, a shimmer of light appears from inside the building. Essa pulls on her hair and kneels on the ground, "Leave me alone!" her voice resonates across the rooftop and is amplified off of the phantasm's armor.

A blade flies out of the building and pierces through the phantasm's chest. It looks down at the tip of the blade and turns around.

Mr. Lunar stands there facing it with another blade already at the phantasm's throat. "You heard the girl, leave her alone." He slices the phantasm's throat with one quick movement of his arm and the phantasm shatters immediately.

Moving in considerable pain, Cassandra utters out, "You possess a blade and the power to see? Who are you?" her eyesight flickers. She leans over Spike and rests her arms on him. Mr. Lunar looks at her but remains silent. She passes out seconds later.

Mr. Lunar places a hand on Essa's shoulder. "It's going to be alright, you're safe now." He looks at Tabatha, she places her hands together and a rush of tears comes down her face. He feels a tug on his shirt. He returns his gaze to Essa who seemingly looks to be on the verge of despair.

Essa asks, "Why is this happening to us, why does everyone have to die?" And for some reason this question bothers him, because what she asks is something he's accustomed to yet can never answer. He places his hand on her head and holds her close.

He finally says, "Bad things happen to good people. People like me hurt the bad things."

She shivers and closes her eyes tightly in hopes everything will go away. But it's short lived. Because as the sense of comfort reaches her heart, so does the looming fear that erupts through the rooftop.

Hovering in the air in a black cloak, Mr. Fredericton smiles. No longer does he have an oddly placed moustache or grey hair. With his eyes now red and his hair short and black, it becomes apparent that he is fairly young, only a few years older than Essa.

Mr. Fredericton muses, "What do we have here, a teacher comforting a student? Now that's against school policy, you know…I thought you'd know better than to lay a hand on a student, one who's clearly showing signs of vulnerability."

He places his feet on the ground, the hole he made in the ceiling now behind him. He places a finger to his mouth and looks over at Tabatha. The meeting of their eyes is enough to cause her to fall down, giving him a laugh. He raises his hands to the air and says, "I love this, all of this!" and then to the side with a swift motion, "this despair is really going to make the boss happy."

The sound of a sheath can be heard. Mr. Fredericton's expression shifts. He says, "So you think you can hurt me? It's fine to have confidence, but your fellow faculty member, ah, what was his name?"

Essa mutters out, "Mr. Linder."

He smiles, "Yes that one. You see, I left him down below covered in horrific wounds. He just couldn't reach me, all of those blades in the way. Ah, a true pity."

Essa asks, "W-who are you…?"

He looks at her and smiles. "I'll answer this one for you darling, since you'll be doing a lot for me in a moment. My name is Nix; my last name is of no importance. I'm here to see to it that you all suffer from tremendous amounts of fear and despair." His eyes turn to Tabatha "Some of who are doing quite a fine job at giving me results." His sinister stare makes her whimper.

Mr. Lunar says in a stern tone, "That's enough. Your confidence is ill placed. That brute doesn't know death. And it certainly won't come from a blade."

"And what makes you say that?" Nix asks.

"Because it wasn't my blade," Mr. Lunar says in response, he then appears behind Nix. A cut runs through the black cloak.

Nix looks down at it and sighs, "I hate fast people. I really do." He yells and turns around with his hand raised forward. The slash of Mr. Lunar's blade is stopped partially. A trickle of blood appears on Nix's hand.

Mr. Lunar says, "Using your hands to block a blade, only a fool or someone who's accustomed to steel would make such a move. I take it you are the latter, with all of those slaves you defend yourself with."

Nix places his other hand to his chest "Now that hurts. I don't have them out now do I? This is a fair battle. So just hush and show me what that blade of yours can do. This is going my way regardless. These two girls are scared beyond compare. Isn't that right darling?" he looks at Essa and winks.

The atmosphere changes and becomes cold. Nix looks oddly at Mr. Lunar. "My, is changing the temperature another unique move you share? I like it a little hot though, this is killing my mood."

The response is simple, the blade in Mr. Lunar's hand shines with a blue tint. He says, "I will cut you with a sharper edge, something slaves would never have the ability to possess since their hearts are no longer involved. You may have their souls, but you've lost sight of the greatest element."

Nix attempts to block the first attack. A deep cut runs down his right arm. He grinds his teeth and goes up close. He throws punches and blocks the sword by grabbing the back of it. He then slams the bottom of his hand underneath Mr. Lunar's chin.

Mr. Lunar responds by slashing through Nix's cloak, grazing his stomach, and then following it up with an attack using his hand, cutting Nix's chin.

The exchange between the two carries on for a minute until a familiar face interrupts it. The ground beneath Nix's feet breaks and a hand grabs his ankle. As he looks down to see Mr. Linder greeting him with a grin, he feels the sharp coolness of a blade pierce through his stomach.

Nix clutches his stomach as the blade leaves him. Blood hangs on the edge of his lip, "I've had enough…of this stupid game." Two blades appear and slam down in front of him, the phantasms arriving to protect their master. A third blade appears, thrusting towards Mr. Lunar's face.

Raising his own blade in time, he blocks the attack. A vein of frustration appears on Nix's forehead. Beneath him Mr. Linder mocks him by saying, "So you've brought out your dogs, huh!"

Glaring downwards, Nix replies, "I should have made you a pile of bones when I had you begging for life."

"I do not beg."

Nix grunts and a swirl of darkness emerge around the tips of his fingers. As he aims it at Mr. Linder, another figure soars through the hole, past Mr. Linder, striking Nix in his wound and causing him to stumble a few steps.

Essa looks and sees Mr. Linder crawl out of the hole and stand beside Mr. Lunar and Miss Dixon. Mr. Linder says, "Nice, I've been wondering where you've been."

"I was helping the students escape, efficiently." Veronica says in a condescending tone.

"Hey now, I took him head on!" he says with a bark.

She sighs, "Clearly, you always end up looking like that when you go in alone without us to guide you. And Lunar, I take it things are a little serious seeing as how your sword has that famous blue tint."

He nods his head, "I can't argue against the truth."

This sets Mr. Linder off "The truth? Come on man, she's talking about me always getting hurt! I'm sure you are just using your sword for show."

Nix stands there quietly, watching the three of them converse. He begins to feel himself twitch. "This is...disgusting," he says in a way that takes the remaining warmth in Essa's heart and crushes it. "All of you are chatting away as if you've won. Honestly, what form of arrogance sunk into your veins? It certainly wasn't one of my blends." Nix places his hand to his stomach and black smoke enters his skin and closes the wound. "I have not come this far...to be mocked." He clenches his hand into a fist and shakes the entire building.

The three teachers give him their full attention and immediately attack together. Nix yells, "I said, I will not be mocked!" his voice shatters all of the windows in the school; glass shards fly about and litter the streets and surrounding cars. The power of his voice causes Essa to trip over her foot and fall backwards.

Tabatha watches her fall, and while she attempts to run forward, the gap is far too great, and Essa disappears from sight.

It's sudden, fast, enough to cause Essa to blink a few times before realizing what's happening. The realization that seconds ago she saw the teachers moving forward and now, falling, cold air, towards the unknown.

She's speechless; her first response is to utter out, "What the hell," as her eyes look ahead at the ground below. She opens her mouth, extends her throat, no sound comes out, her heart races, the thought of death reaching out for her, waiting for her to land in its arms. Her mind succumbs; she says, "Take me far away from here, to a world in my dreams."

"As you wish."

CHAPTER SEVEN
This World and Ours

The sky fills her with bliss with rays of colour unlike what Essa is accustomed to seeing. She falls through a purple cloud and feels a rush of dampness cling to her skin. Her mind lost in thought, she falls without question. As things start to become clear, her eyes widen as she turns her body to see the ground approaching. She falls through another cloud and sees hills filled with trees, an open field with bright rivers running through it and the wide body of water forming a circular lake directly beneath her.

Her first instinct isn't to take in the beautiful scenery or to focus on the two small specks below her. All that comes to mind is her instinct to—as any sane person would do in this situation—scream.

Essa's voice rings out through the sky as loud as she can utter. Her screams are noise without meaning, because so much worry blocks out her reason. She's scared, one moment to be falling from a building and then from the sky itself, towards a place she's never seen before.

Falling, faster now, she closes her eyes and sheds a tear, embracing her fate, until she feels the straps of her backpack give out and tear. Her eyes open immediately. She reaches out to grab hold of her backpack—the only thing left that's familiar.

Out of reach, she watches hopelessly as it moves further away from her taking the book along with it.

Below her, one of the two specs that Essa spotted on her way down, is Dusk with his legs crossed and his hands raised in front of him. His eyes are closed as he focuses on an image of what he desires, a power which he can use to fight with. Hex stands behind him, arms crossed and a look of boredom plastered on his face.

Hex asks, "Are you focusing?"

Dusk cringes, "What do you think? You said I'd get a grasp of having a source of power to use in a fight, but I've been sitting here for what feels like forever, and I can't help but remember you saying this was impossible in the first place. Am I right?"

"Yes. Well you are supposed to be special after all."

"Oh don't you start."

Hex looks at the sky. "Keep focusing, and if you turn to look at me, or anything else, I'll make you regret it."

Dusk nods his head and goes back into his training position, crossing his legs and resting his elbows on them.

Hex reveals his wings, large and white, and spreads them. He kneels slightly and then leaps into the air, soaring upwards, leaving Dusk behind. Who, after feeling a gust of wind, asks, "Hex, are you still there?"

The wind feels refreshing against the angel's face. He moves with great speed and power. Within seconds he comes across the falling girl who's looking around helplessly for her backpack, not taking notice of his approach.

When her eyes move and he enters her vision, she says nothing. Time passes and Hex does not break the silence. He changes his direction so he can descend with her.

She looks at his wings and then at him. Essa says, "I'm dead, aren't I?"

"No."

"Then are you going to save me?"

"Why would I do that?"

Her brow lowers, "Then what are you doing flying! Are you an angel or something! Tell me! At least have the decency to let me know where it is that I'm about to die!" Her eyes full of emotion and a thirst for knowledge, she begins to scream once more.

Hex ponders over helping her, a stranger, as he wonders who she is and where she came from. He pats her on the shoulder and she looks at him with a hint of hope. He says, "I've decided to let you fall into the water below. If you survive I will take that as a—well, one step at a time."

Her mouth hangs open slightly, "You've got to be kidding me… you are the worst!" Her voice rings out loud, "Absolutely the worst!" She cries out and places her arms in front of her face protectively, crashing into the lake.

Waves of water erupt from the impact, crashing into the small bushes and rocks on the outskirts of shore. It catches Dusk's attention. His brow twitches as his desire to turn increases. Once he hears the sound of Essa reaching the surface, gasping for air, he turns to look.

Blocking his view stands Hex, who says, "I believe I told you to focus on one thing, correct?"

Dusk squints, "Maybe, but the conditions have changed. I am fairly sure I just heard a girl gasping for air. I also know you're not one with being gentle and nurturing, so you probably had some part in it."

Moments later, Dusk finds himself swimming.

He opens his eyes and looks around. He sees, through the water, a group of turtles slowly making their way across the bottom of the lake, past a set of rocks and red seaweed.

A few fish swim past his face. He follows them with his gaze, which brings him to a set of legs moving in a circular motion, keeping their top half—Essa—above water. He swims towards her and breaks free from the water's grip, adjusting his eyes to see a confused girl with long, red hair.

Essa looks at him in silence.

Dusk blinks, wipes water from his face and says in a polite greeting, "Hello."

In a slight stutter, she replies by saying hello in return. Her eyes move towards Hex, which causes her forehead to wrinkle, a look Dusk figures matches how he feels on a general basis when in Hex's presence.

Essa says to Hex, "You're an ass, just letting me fall. I'm confused, scared, in a place I have never seen before, and you were going to leave me, my final thoughts, with the image of a rude man with white wings? What if I actually died? Are you that cruel?" Soon, her voice becomes brittle, "I'm just—so damn pissed off! Fuck!"

Her eyes begin to water, and Dusk frowns at Hex. The angel, feeling a tinge of regret, walks towards the body of water and reaches out for her, "I apologize." She looks up at him and takes hold of his hand. He pulls her out of the water and gestures towards the small campfire that has not yet been lit.

Once the three of them take a seat around the fire pit, Hex throws a few logs into it. He then sends off a spark, which produces a green flame. Dusk rubs his hands together for warmth, shivering because of his soaked clothing.

His eyes look up at the angel, "So what did you do exactly, let the girl fall from the sky or some shit?"

Essa glares at Hex, "That is exactly what he did." Her voice regaining composure as her nerves settle, but with the confusion still present as she looks around at her surroundings, trying to grasp where exactly she is.

Essa's face goes red as her thoughts begin to sort themselves out. Her eyes begin to water once more. Nothing is even remotely familiar. "I'm…" she's unable to finish her sentence. She places her hands to her face and covers her eyes. After a moment, she places her hands down and looks directly at Dusk, "I'm lost."

The sense of helplessness makes him feel a sting of pain. He realizes that, for the brief moment he was focusing on obtaining power, he almost forgot what had transpired to him prior. His expression drops, and his eyes turn to the green flames.

A sigh escapes Hex. He says, "This is all unfamiliar to you, yes?"
She nods her head slightly.

"In the sense that you've never seen any of this? That it's all bizarre, out of place, different, even wrong?"

Again, she nods her head, this time wiping away some dampness from her face. Hex pauses and thinks for a moment, letting the flames dance around for them. Eventually he says in a low tone, "How troublesome."

Dusk watches him, sitting on the other side of the flames. Slightly hunched over with his elbows on his kneecaps, the angel's posture saying what Hex would not.

His eyes look up, with the shadows given from the flames reflecting on his face. He says, "I imagine you, more than anyone else, don't understand why even the fire in front of you is green. Or why, the cloud you passed through was purple. How the fall did not break your back, why the water felt the way it did. How it is I have wings, and who that lad next to you is. Can he be trusted? Is he like you? Lost, scared, wandering?"

He takes a breath, blinks and the look of sadness Dusk saw at the white bridge returns to the angel's eyes. Hex asks, "May I know your name?"

"I'm Essa Starlight."

"My name is Hex, and sitting next to you is Dusk Hollow—a twit." Dusk snarls, "Piss off."

Essa feeling frustrated, says, "I am not from here and you're right, all of this is alien to me. The last thing I remember is falling from my school's rooftop."

Dusk's eyebrow raises, "And you're alive?"

She looks at him closely from the corner of her eye, "It seems that is the case."

Hex asks, "Did you do anything on the descent that would save you from death?"

She thinks deeply for a moment and then says unsurely, "I asked to be taken to my dreams. I wanted to be anywhere but where I was."

The angel raises his left arm and moves it around, presenting the world, "And that is where you are, your dreams."

Dusk's eyes widen dramatically as he barks, "Holy shit, so that's it!" As the sudden realization takes over, filling the answer to a burning question.

Essa clears her throat, "What do you mean, my dream? I don't know this place. I can't recall ever thinking about it. Like I said, this is all alien. Right now, I just...want to go home...and see my mom again."

Hex places his hands on his knees and leans forward, "Well that's not going to happen" finishing with a laugh.

Dusk coughs in shock.

Essa gulps in despair.

The angel grins, "I apologize again. Don't let your heart give out on you just yet."

The air around Essa changes, becoming heavy and dangerous. Dusk shifts slightly away from her on the log that they are seated on, and watches as she lifts her head up slightly while looking at Hex. She says coherently, making sure that every word has the same weight and presence, "If you joke around with me one more time. I swear I-"

Hex raises his hand. "This place is not going to look similar to you, because this place is where the dreams of all human things come together as one. But that is where you are. How you got here however, is another matter. One which I cannot answer under these circumstances." He continues on by saying, "I... am an angel. Dusk... Well, you can label him whatever you want, but he's in a very similar situation as you. If you seek help to return to where you came from, perhaps we can help. Though even in one's collective dream, danger can sprout. You will not do well if you are foolish and weak."

"I may be weak," she says and then thinks carefully. Her lips say confidently, "But I'm not foolish. I have faced the most bizarre, hope fulfilling, yet extremely dangerous situations in the past few hours than I have...for as long as I can remember. One random event after another."

Hex asks, "How did it begin?"

"With a book."

"A book?"

"Yes..." she runs her hands through her hair, letting it fall in front of her face. She fixes one side of it, placing it behind her ear, and looks up at the sky. "It fell from the stars, presented itself before me, spoke to me, showed me...something...and that was it."

Dusk, giving off the expression of someone who doesn't believe a word he is hearing, with one eyebrow raised, his mouth slightly open and his eyes looking at her in a peculiar way, continues to listen regardless.

Hex asks, this time softer, "This book. Does it have a leather binding?"

"W-why?"

He motions with his eyes towards a spot between her legs. Essa looks down and sees before her, resting on the earth, the leather book. Her legs shake and, soon enough, the rest of her body catches up. Clearly startled, she says, "I lost it when I was falling from the sky."

"Yet there it resides."

"But-"

"I know. It appeared moments ago, as you began to explain your situation. In particular, when you mentioned it falling from the stars."

Witnessing something incredible, Dusk lets out a sigh of acknowledgment to the girl sitting next to him. Noticing the sound, she looks at him for the first time, taking a moment to let him sink in.

As their eyes meet, he asks her, "What did you go through?"

Her eyes begin to shake from the turmoil. She describes to him the events that occurred which lead her to them. She mentions her worry over her mother, having not seen her before everything went into chaos. She mentions her new friends, the final moments on top of the roof and her descent into what should have been the end.

The green flames cast by the fire begin to dimmer, its luminosity fading away. As Essa finishes recounting what she's been through, the fire goes to sleep, taking along any source of discomfort that may lie between Essa, Hex and Dusk.

The balance of light in the sky shifts, bringing along the change in time. Swirls of smoke loom around the clouds above, while lines that look like dancing snakes, soar through them. Eventually, it becomes apparent that there is no real night, but only a change of colours in the sky.

CHAPTER EIGHT
The Sound of a Falling Tree

Whispering beasts that linger out of sight, accompanied by the hum of heat, hide under the sounds that their footsteps make. Drumming beats of hungers quake, held down by a book that no man could make, or even replicate.

Essa, face red, walks behind the two men who occasionally look back at her, aware that the sounds of hunger roar from her stomach.

She speeds up, reaching Dusk, and asks, "You wouldn't have any food on you, would you?"

He smiles, "Up until a few moments ago, I didn't even know this place was a dream. So, no—no food, sorry."

"How? Aren't you with Hex?"

"The reasons for that are less fortunate than your descent from the sky."

Understanding she would receive no food, Essa holds the book closer to her chest, having nothing to place it in. She looks at a set of bizarrely shaped mushrooms on the trail to their left, the spines both yellow and white, spiraling towards the top.

Dusk comments, "It's a lot to take in. Once you accept that it's all just out of whack, it seems normal."

"So," she looks at him, "how did you get here?"

He thinks carefully about his answer and says, "I woke up, and here I was."

Her face grows pale, "Just like that? From your sleep, you ended up here?"

"Funny isn't it?" he chuckles, placing his hands in his pockets.

She looks ahead, "That's terrifying, having everything taken from you just like that, so suddenly."

His eyelids lower slightly, "Ya...it sure was sudden."

As they collect their thoughts, they look at the change in scenery. On their left rests a forest of red trees. Dusk notices the change in size from the different coloured ones he previously saw, these ones smaller in stature.

On their right, an empty field where the only sight is the wind blowing through the grass. An empty field such as this, one would only see in a dream. Dusk thinks to himself that if he hadn't been told where he was then he would have figured it out by seeing such a sight.

"You know," Essa begins saying, "for someone who looks like you, you have quite the soft voice."

This time Dusk's smile is full of bewilderment, "Is that so? What makes you say that?"

"Well," she says, trying to sound as polite and direct as possible, "you look like you spend most of your time speaking with your eyes. As if you're scared that the words that leave your lips are only meant to be strong, damaging, precise."

He places a hand to his face, and Essa, noticing she caused a shift in his behavior, apologizes swiftly and looks ahead. Dusk thinks about it, and his mind shifts to Sarah—her smile, and then how her expression focuses each time he speaks, as if worried he would crush her world. He then thinks that perhaps he did.

In an attempt to change the topic, Essa says, "I'm from Eryu, by the way. I know that there's a few planets, but, if this dream world is the collection of everyone, I don't think that's world specific."

The thought hadn't occurred to Dusk, he replies, "I'm also from

Eryu."

She asks, "What district?"

"Does it matter?"

Her eyes dart away. He did it—something damaging. Dusk frowns and looks towards the field. Letting the wind take his thoughts along the top of the blades of grass, towards somewhere else, a place that someone, somewhere, dreamt of.

Her voice lower, she asks, "Where…exactly are we going? Does Hex know the way?"

Dusk shrugs, and then turns to look at her, "There's someone we need to meet. But personally, I don't think he knows exactly where to go. If he did, I'd like to think we'd fly there, and save ourselves some time."

"Is that someone going to help us return to Eryu? Even with Hex, being…well, an angel? Because, if he's got wings like that…well maybe he's just a dream?"

"He's an angel."

"Oh…"

Dusk grins, "It's weird eh. The atheist in me still can't take into account that I've been hanging out with an angel for a little while. But yes. This person is supposed to help us out."

"How did you come across him then? If this is a world of dreams, how did he make his way here?"

Dusk shrugs, "He's particular with giving me answers to questions."

Essa, apparently satisfied, then asks, "How come Hex wants to go to Eryu? I can't say I've ever seen an angel before just walking around."

Dusk laughs a little, "I wish I had an actual answer. But before you got here, I was basically pestering him every second I had. And well, I'm not sure we are going to Eryu. Could be any planet really."

"…That's true. How did that work out for you, the pestering I mean?"

He points to his face, "A spear pointed firmly between the eyes sums it up."

They make a turn, Hex directing them towards the path that branches off into the red forest. Dusk, from where he is standing, catches a glimpse of what lays ahead. He sees that the path swirls around in long bends and that it will test their endurance.

With eyes lighting up, Essa says, "Wow, whoever came up with this was something." She remarks on the vast amount of colourful objects of bizarre shapes and sizes hanging from the tree branches. Some melted, others defying gravity.

"Anyway," Hex says, "from here on out, I want the two of you to pay close attention to your surroundings. Essa, stick close to Dusk and I, and Dusk, if you take into account every minor detail, every element, from the height to the texture, you will hopefully improve in finding your inner strength."

Dusk says, "I'm not really pumped on becoming a nature expert, but sure, I'll give it a try."

They enter the forest and walk along the spiraling passage, passing through trees that bend, form archways, twirl, connect and split apart. The leaves, Dusk notices, are all different, none of them having an identical shape. In disbelief, his eyes dart around quickly, trying to see if there's even the slightest similarity, until he starts to notice a very small change within himself—the feeling of noticing the nature, and seeing, rather than assuming what rests around him.

This small change makes him feel incredibly different. He wonders if it's even possible to have felt anything so soon, and decides to keep it to himself. If Hex doubts him, then that's his prerogative.

Concentrating, his eyes dart around at an excessive pace, catching even Essa's attention. Hex grabs hold of a long branch, pulls on it and, with a grin, lets it go. It flies backwards and smacks Dusk square in the nose.

It startles him, causing him to trip and land in the dirt. He looks up to see Essa bending over, lending a hand, "Here, I'll help you up."

He takes her hand and thanks her before brushing off the dirt from his pants. He looks towards Hex with the desire to complain, noticing a smile on the angel's face.

With the trees giving off ample amounts of shade, the lack of light causes Essa to notice, fairly easily, a small, white creature—the first they'd seen in the forest. To her it resembles a bunny rabbit, and this familiarity gives her the confidence to walk towards it, off the beaten path.

Her hand reaches out towards it. As she leans in, she says, "Aren't you just the cutest thing." As her hand inches closer, the way its body jerks makes her slow down the movement of her hand until finally stopping. Her hand now idling in the air in front of the small creature, she begins to wonder if she should have stayed on the path and left this small creature alone.

A red mark rests on the creature's left ear, contrasting against its remarkably white body. Essa notices soon after a small indication of sharp fangs at the edge of its mouth. She moves her hand backwards. The small creature's eyes open. It startles her. She had assumed she could already see its eyes, but it was merely the pattern on the eyelids.

The eyelids open vertically between blinks, showing black pupils—incredibly large and seemingly out of place for a rabbit.

This is no rabbit, she thinks to herself, *not even close.*

Realizing both the animal and Essa's departure from the trail, Dusk says, "Listen Essa, now isn't the time to be looking at the wildlife." With his eyes continuing to look at every inch and manner of detail that the forest has to offer, he stops, turns, and focuses on Essa.

Fallen leaves rise into the air as a blur passes by Dusk—he sees it reach Essa and grab hold of her. He blinks once and the blur raises its arms. He blinks for a second time, and notices the outline of Hex's build, the formation of his spear. He blinks for the third time, and watches as the spear descends into the twitching creature's body.

The silence that was in the forest, which gave Dusk ample time to rummage around in his own thoughts, is torn apart by the shrieking of the creature as its arms extend and try to latch on to Hex. It scratches and digs into the ground, its tongue also extending, slobbering both saliva and black blood.

Hex yells, "Run, now!" He forms another spear and, this time, the edge lights up before he slams it down into the creature, causing it to be silent.

The hair on Dusk's neck rises as he can now hear the rustling of bushes, the sound of tree branches cracking. He turns his head and sees a dozen—which then doubles, and then triples—of the same creature heading towards them. With tongues sticking out of their mouths, arms reaching out and crushing whatever falls in their wake.

His feet don't move for a moment. His intense concentration causes him to analyze every section of the creature — looking at its grotesque body as it stretches, appearing to be on the verge of bursting and becoming something much more terrifying.

Hex yells once more, "Damn it Dusk, I said run!"

He turns away from the sight of death and runs after Hex and Essa, both of whose eyes look at him desperately to come along and catch up. He runs as fast as he can and closes the distance, as the creatures following do the same.

Awkwardly running, Essa begins to resent the book between her arms. In a moment like this, she wishes it would do something helpful, but nothing beyond the unsightly sounds behind her seem to emerge from her silent plea.

A spear is formed and Hex stops—he twists his body and hurls it forward. It passes by Dusk's face and rips through two of the creatures before slamming into a tree and piercing through it, causing it to fall and land on another devilish bunny.

The angel, still slightly ahead of both Essa—who now runs past him—and Dusk, who's close, forms two more spears. He twirls them in his hands and then spins his body, twisting both his arms and legs. He flings both of the spears, which now having a cutting range of one hundred and eighty degrees, cut through another set of five creatures before destroying more of the forest.

Panting, Dusk looks ahead while his arms and legs move of their own accord. His inner self looks backwards, witnessing the change in the creatures eyes as red lines run down the middle, and the creatures heads begins to extend.

This detail, one that Dusk cannot see but feels, makes him wonder if his imagination is running wild. Essa screams at the top of her lungs,

"This is the last time I am friendly to a damn bunny rabbit! There's someone seriously sick in the head for creating that!"

Hex, also running with them, only slightly ahead of Dusk, says, "I have to agree with that notion. Death to the bunny rabbits."

Dusk asks, "Are you enjoying this?"

The angel, holding back a smile, smirks slightly, "Heavens no."

Again, without looking, Dusk begins to feel the change within the creature, as its back rips open, revealing spikes, and its legs and arms continue to grow. The longer they run, Dusk feels, the more dangerous the foes become.

Essa yells, amazingly running at a pace neither of the men can catch up too, "This is a damn nightmare isn't it!"

Hex smiles, this time without holding back and looks at Dusk, "My, she's smart. I like her." He then, raising his voice, says, "Yes, that is exactly what this is, and we are unfortunately playing a part in someone's dream."

Hex then asks Dusk, "Any luck on forging a weapon?"

"That's a negative."

"Pity."

The desire to know what's chasing him grows. Dusk turns his head slightly, and is startled by how close one of the creatures is as he watches it move towards him in mid-flight, arms extended, tongue dancing through the air, eyes wild with frenzy.

Before Hex can form a spear to protect Dusk, an object comes out through the forest and slams into the creature, taking it off the pathway and into a set of trees, which break and fall down.

Hex says, "Keep running, whatever that was, we want no part in it."

A voice rings throughout the forest, "You're a pervert, Kiyo!"

A dazzling beauty emerges from the trees, causing Dusk to slow down, followed by Essa and Hex. The woman standing before them on the edge of the trail, in between both them and the incoming creature, takes a look at the intruders, and then the threat.

She moves her arms upwards facing the sky, and then places her hands behind her head, "Oh my, this is a ghastly sight. At it again are you?"

The creatures stop. They wait on the tree branches and bellow, snarling and drooling. She tilts her head slightly and makes a face of disgust, "You all remind me of someone. I don't like that."

She points at the creatures, "So, I think you all should just go away, okay?" She smiles, winks, and then with the flick of her finger, sends off a green light that causes Dusk and the others to take a step back. The light brightens up the forest and pierces through all of the creatures, causing them to disappear into its depths.

The woman turns around, looking at them once more. She places her hands behind her back, pulling on her wrists to stretch, which move her large chest forward. She has long green hair in a ponytail and wears just a green bra, decorative sleeves with tattoo shaped patterns, and skintight pants. Seemingly fit with her flat stomach and toned biceps, the woman, who seems to be in her early twenties, gives off the presence of someone both mystifying and gentle.

A loud crack rocks through the forest. An extremely tall tree—the tallest to be exact—begins to fall from their right side. The woman, not showing signs of alarm, listens intently as the tree comes crashing down, landing on the pathway behind her.

On the top of the tree—on its side—walks a short boy who, with a sigh, takes a seat, not noticing anyone around him. Appearing to be about eighteen years old, he comes with a set of shaggy, dark green hair styled in a fashionable yet messy manner. He wears a green V-neck shirt with black sleeves that end at the elbow as well as beige shorts.

He begins to speak, still unaware as to the presence of Dusk and the others. "Leaf, honestly, one of these days you are going to throw me, kick me, punch me way too hard and I will break, and be broken, no way of fixing me—just totaled. And I had to kill five of those filthy creatures. The fifth one was stubborn so, as you can see, this tree sort of got in the way." He looks up and notices Leaf facing Dusk, Hex and Essa.

His expression changes. He places his hand to his neck and begins to rub it. He opens his mouth and says, "I guess what they say about a tree that falls making a noise is true after all eh? If uh, people are around to hear it…or was it the other way around?" He begins to laugh uncomfortably before going silent and looking towards Leaf, "So, uh, Leaf, who are these people?"

She muses, "I wonder."

CHAPTER NINE

He Who Stands, Loves

Sitting, legs swinging in a circular motion, the green haired youth plays with his lip as he watches the three who stand out of place. With Leaf's response, he understands that today, this moment, is not something natural.

He points at Dusk, "Who are you?" he asks.

Deciding to remain honest, Dusk replies, "My name is Dusk Hollow."

Kiyo's eyes light up. Leaf's expression changes.

Seeing this, Dusk, once more, knows he said something that will cause a stir. Hex also notices the reaction to the given answer, and takes a step forward.

Legs still swinging around, Kiyo looks at Essa, "Who are you?" His question remaining the same, completely identical, even in his tone of voice.

She hesitates, unsure as to what made them react when Dusk answered. She answers, "I'm Essa" she pauses. Kiyo's eyebrows raise. She squints and says, "Essa Starlight."

Again, a reaction. This time Leaf moves slightly, and Kiyo's legs start to twirl slower. His eyes turn to Hex, and he asks once more,

"Who are you?"

Hex looks at both of them, and then his eyes line up with Kiyo's. He raises his head with pride, forms a spear in his right hand and lets it touch the ground. He says, "I am Hex."

While her eyes gaze at his weapon, Leaf asks, "Just Hex?"

Kiyo's legs stop moving. He says, "Two last names, and one who replies with a weapon. You are certainly not like us."

Unsure how to react to the deteriorating situation, Essa stands closer to Dusk. Hex remaining in front of them, reaffirms his grip on his spear and replies, "What gives you the basis to make such an accusation?"

Leaf snorts and says, "Your lack of knowledge is enough. But if you want to know why we are making such a claim, look no further than at your friends Dusk and Essa. They have last names. Here, last names are only granted to, well, special people."

Slightly hostile, Dusk asks, "We aren't special?"

Leaf smiles, "Don't take it to heart sweetie, but even your scent is different. You are not a dream."

Kiyo comments, "Disgusting angel."

Hex slowly turns to Kiyo, with a look of stone, and says, "I'm itching to remove a dream."

Leaf raises her hands, "Let's not cause a stir." She looks at Kiyo, "Keep your comments to yourself. You know better." Her eyes move towards Hex, "We don't need a fight to happen between us—that sort of conflict will upset our surroundings. There are young thinkers we wish to protect."

Dusk asks, "Are last names really that rare to have here?"

Leaf replies, "At the moment, there are less than five who possess a last name."

"Why don't all dreams have one?"

"The stronger your existence, the more you become aware. It takes a lot of dreamers to even form one of us; eventually a name comes into creation. A last name however, that's another level entirely."

"Why?"

"Because it means you're one step away from being a human. When you form a last name, you no longer need to be dreamt of. You are able to oversee others' dreams—those with and without a name."

Dusk squints slightly, "So then why was it so hard to believe Essa and I were at this level?"

Kiyo jumps off the log and, while walking forward, says, "Two reasons. The first being the fact that the only person in this remote area who has a last name is both wise, strong and full of knowledge. You lot look lost. Someone with a last name who's from here will know the land—every inch of it—from the blades of grass to the falling leaves. Those with a last name also give off a vibe, a scent, a presence." He stops a few feet away from Hex, looking up at him—from his short stature of 5 feet. He continues to say, "Your scent—especially this one—is displeasing and is nothing like what someone with a last name smells like."

Essa says, "This is not something we could have falsified."

Leaf smiles, "Right you are. Now," her eyes looking at Hex's weapon, "may you relinquish that?"

Hex looks down at Kiyo. The spear disappears.

He then says, his eyes still staring down the boy who glares upwards, "I want to know who you are, and then I want you to answer my following questions."

Becoming comfortable, Leaf places her hands on her waist and answers, "I'm Leaf, the one in front of you is Kiyo. We both have a name, but no last name. Otherwise, that's about it."

Hex asks, "Why did Kiyo come flying through the air?"

He notices the pale expression that appears on Kiyo's face.

His face then twitches as he turns to look at Leaf, whose twisted expression greets him.

Kiyo says, "About that…" his voice showing signs of slight discomfort.

Leaf replies, "He has yet to learn the boundaries. He's a pervert."

Essa grabs a hold of Dusk's arm.

Kiyo whines, "It wasn't my fault! Who decides to bath in sun—

nude—suddenly! You knew I was coming back."

"I did not," she huffs.

"You did, but in your arrogance you decided to send me flying through the forest."

"Don't turn this on me," her eyes glare, "you have the wandering eyes."

The banter between them comes as a slight shock to Dusk, Hex and Essa, who up until that point viewed them as both dangerous and cunning. Now, as the two argue over semantics, Hex begins to see that, like a dream, the inconsistencies are present.

Hex yells, "Enough! I am not done asking questions. Do not mess around." A silence falls over them and, for the first time since their encounter, the sound of the trees returns.

With a deep breath, the angel asks, "I would like to know where this person with the last name resides."

Kiyo turns back to look at the tall angel, "What reason do you have to speak to Norma?"

Hex grins, "Is that her name?"

Even Dusk lets out a smile—Kiyo gave them information without noticing.

Hex asks, "What of her last?"

Leaf, arms now crossed, replies sternly, "Only she knows it."

The angel frowns.

Leaf says, "If you seek her, then we can accompany you. That is where we are headed. However, why do you need to talk to her?"

Hex replies, "It's not your concern."

"But it is. She is like a mother to all living dreams. If you pose a threat, we won't let you step anywhere near her."

The angel's eyes go cold. "If she gives me reason to be a threat, nothing can stop me."

Essa clenches Dusk's arm tightly.

He looks at her, gulps and says, "Hex, that's enough. We could use all the help we can get. You say you know the way, but I can tell that's not the case."

Hex closes his eyes and looks upwards, "The information needs updating."

Kiyo lets out a laugh, "It's the dream world, why would anything remain consistent?"

Leaf grins, "You are lucky you found us. Thank the dreamers later, but for now, come with us. It's some distance away."

With the conversation at its end, they venture through the red forest, reaching a pond with stepping-stones lying across it. Kiyo skips across them with long strides. The others follow at a regular pace. As they reach the other side, the path heads up a hill, where the trees part at the top.

There, Dusk notices a pathway as far as the eye can see, with an assortment of puzzling, unique and abstract fountains on either side. With over a hundred, all shooting water in every direction—some connecting into larger waves—the scenery takes on a blue hue.

The fairly dull pathway that was dirt and occasional stepping-stones becomes a beautiful marble path. In the air, lights fly around, catching Essa's attention. The lights are similar to fireflies, shining yellow, white and blue at their tips.

As they make their way through the straight path of waterworks, Dusk finds himself at the end of the group alongside Hex. He takes this opportunity to ask the angel two needed questions. Hex doesn't grumble.

Dusk says, "Hex, we've found ourselves in an odd group. I still don't like you, but seeing as how, of the four people here, I have been with you the longest, I'm going to use that as a reason for us to bond."

The angel grunts and continues to look ahead.

Dusk continues, "How did Essa really get here? We came from above. But she came directly from Eryu. And what sort of book just comes from the stars and speaks?"

Hex looks at Dusk from the corner of his eyes. He then looks forward as he answers, looking at Essa's back. "There are many stories of unique books granting powers such as the power to summon elements, or to animate the dead but I don't know about her. She seems innocent enough, and I did not sense lies when she was telling us about her circumstances and what she's been through. That being said, if she poses as a threat to our mission-"

"I know. You'll kill her."

"Yes, exactly right. It's good you are learning my character."

"It's not easy being around you." Dusk sighs, "I just don't like any of this. And, is this Norma person who you are really looking for?"

"I don't know, but if she has a last name, and if a last name is as important as those two make it out to be, she would be the most fitting to help us out, or at least guide us to where we need to go."

Dusk stretches his arms, "Angels aren't very organized huh?"

Hex does not offer a response.

They come across a spray of water shooting upwards. Dusk stops and looks at his reflection in the fountain. He moves the hair out of his face and looks at his tired eyes. He asks, "This mission that you're on—what danger is waiting for us?" He turns to look at Hex.

The angel gives him a short response, "It is world changing."

***

What feels like hours come to pass and they leave behind the trail of waterworks. They venture past a pair of steel rocks that climb towards the sky, like giants in slumber. Past the steel rocks they come across an open field with a single tree standing in the middle, its branches dancing around organically.

Their journey is not short on amazing sights, both incredibly strange and familiar. They make their way to another forest, one filled with pine trees. They witness each tree having a small circle of water at its base. A pair of tall mountains rests beyond the forest.

Leaf says, "Across the mountain—that one right there," she points, "and just a little further, is Norma's villa."

Hex looks at Dusk and Essa who look tired from the journey. Essa, in particular, who at this point has trembling knees and looks close to vomiting. He says, "Let's catch our rest here, near the trees. Some of us need to regain our strength." His eyes then move to the mountain, resting there, looking at something.

While the others take a seat, Essa dips her hands into the body of water surrounding one of the trees and then brings it to her face.

Leaf ventures and stands next to Hex, who looks on edge as he gazes at the mountain.

Leaf says, "It's quite something, that mountain. It's currently the largest one that's been dreamt up. Probably bigger than what some humans have seen. Though I reckon that's up for debate. Who's really seen it besides us?" She looks at him, "Well then, I'll leave you to it."

After drenching her face in water, Essa plops herself down next to Dusk who's ventured into the forest. He picks at the grass, his eyes taking in his surroundings. Essa watches him, and then places her book between her legs. She asks, "Do you think the dreams here ever sleep? I can't imagine they do…"

He responds quietly, "I don't think so…"

Kiyo, who's not far from them, leans against a tree, his feet in the water as he chews on a piece of grass. His pointy ears listen intently while he lets his body rest, his eyes closed.

Essa pauses, and then, with careful consideration, she asks, "What were you thinking about before you arrived here? You said you were sleeping right? But maybe what you thought about brought you here, a thought that turned into a dream?"

Dusk's eyes move to the left, his mind thinking. He answers, "I was thinking about Sarah."

"Who is she?"

His eyes sadden, "She's someone I hold dear, she is my world…" he smiles faintly, "so, I need to get back to her. To let her know I love her. That I will never leave her side again."

The sorrow in his words makes Essa feel uncomfortable. She decides to say, "I don't see how that would bring you here…"

He tilts his head and looks at her. She straightens up. "I'm not from here, nor am I from where you came from." She becomes confused. Dusk continues, "I'm just…somewhere in between everything."

Essa looks around to try and come to the hidden answer. Her eyes rest on Hex, and then she looks at Dusk. She asks, "How did you and Hex come across one another? If he's an angel, then…how did he get here?"

Dusk lets himself fall into the grass as he rests his hands on his chest. He lets his mind cloud up with thoughts of Sarah from when they were kids. Her smile, the grip of her hand on his. He says, toneless, "The answer to that is simple, Essa. I died."

Her heart skips. She finds her hands digging into the dirt. Her lips tremble slightly. She says, "But I don't understand."

The words that leave his lips are heavy and slow. The reality of his situation causes Essa's temporary shelter from the bewilderment of the unknown to come crumbling down. He says toneless, "I died because I was weak. And then everything—my world—was taken from me…and this flesh of mine that's here right now," he looks at his hands, his voice now flooding with emotion, "I don't know what it is. But whatever it is, it's going to get me back to her. So I can tell her I love her. So I can break the man that broke me."

"Dusk…"

"I should have died a long time ago, but she saved me when I was young. No amount of love could ever repay her for that debt. She needs to be free of the danger she's in." He looks up directly at the light in the sky, the square box replicating the sun, "Hex is bringing me back home. I was given the option between sanctuary and this. So I'm here right now."

She feels lost and out of place. No words come to mind, because any word would be weak and feeble. His circumstances, to her, are more unbelievable than hers. Unable to look at his eyes, afraid she will cry for him. She tears up regardless.

Following his confession, Dusk says to Essa, "So I know for a fact that you will get home." He looks away from the sun, "Do not fear." He sits up and then stands. His stature blocking out the light, casting a shadow across the majority of his body. Essa squints to look at him. "Just follow me."

CHAPTER TEN
Moving Mountains

Having listened to Dusk and Essa's conversation, Kiyo opens his eyes and looks at them, his mind having been made up. He likes them. He steps out of the water and shakes his feet around, getting a pool of water out of his left shoe. Having decided he will go greet them properly in a friendly introduction he takes a step forward.

The ground shakes—a loud and vicious tremor unlike what Essa felt at her school. She grabs hold of her book. In the corner of her eye she sees Kiyo take a stumble and then catch his balance.

The trees rattle, and the sound of their roots ripping from the ground causes everyone to enter their own form of defensive stance. Above the mountain, the sky turns a thunderous and dark gray. Bits of earth begin to soar through the air and crash into the surrounding trees.

Essa falls backwards and sees the ground in front of her crack open. Hex appears and grabs her by the shoulder, lifting her up. Everyone stares up at the mountain, taking in the sudden changes that are occurring as smoke billows up into the air.

Hex says, "That is no normal mountain."

Everything goes quiet. Earth stops falling from the sky. The trees stop flailing about. The ground stops cracking and splitting apart, and water stops cascading through the air.

For a moment Essa feels safe. For a moment she thinks it is just a random phenomenon. But the sound of Leaf screaming, telling them to run away is soon muted by the enormous growl of a monster bursting out from the mountain.

Following it, a large chunk of rock tears through the trees and lands next to Dusk. He makes a run to the right and turns quickly and abruptly as another piece of rock whips past him and snaps a tree in half. He keeps running, faster now. As he turns his head to look back he sees another piece, thinner and moving much quicker towards him. He ducks down and it misses him by a fraction of an inch. Dusk looks around and sees Kiyo and Leaf dashing through the forest at an incredible pace, then to his left he sees Hex rushing along at an equally fast pace, dragging Essa behind him.

Dusk stops momentarily, "Why am I running if I'm dead..." another piece lands next to him, sending shivers up his spine, "...right, just run."

A thunderous shake rocks the ground, causing Dusk's knees to give out. He turns around and sees a horrific black monster fully emerge from the mountain, staring directly at him. Its eyes empty yet full of blood lust. The monster, another form of a Nightmare, slams its fist into the remainder of the mountain and pulls out a chunk.

The mixture of earth and rock is hurtled towards Dusk. His eyes widen and his heart sinks but Hex appears in front of him. The angel, standing sideways, raises his left hand forward. He yells out, causing a bright white light to flash. As the pile of earth and rock makes impact, it shatters and is blown away.

Hex says, "I heard your little speech just now. If you want to save Sarah, you must stand up and fight any and everything that poses as a threat. This is just the beginning. This is but a Nightmare in a young heart. If we can't even destroy this, there is no point in us moving forward."

He forms a spear of light in his right hand and runs forward. At his final step, he thrusts the spear into the air towards the Nightmare. The spear soars through the sky and rips through the Nightmare's shoulder, exploding, removing chunks of rock from its body.

It roars in pure and utter agony, causing it to grab a large chunk of earth from the mountain and hurl it towards them. Hex runs forward and dodges the enormous piece of rock. He leaps up towards the top of a tree with the help of a single flap from his wings. The wings then disappear at his command.

The Nightmare slams its fist down. Hex dodges and moves across the lines of trees on his right. With some time granted, he creates another white spear, however the Nightmare raises its arm. Having little time to properly position himself, he throws the spear in hopes of it landing. It misses the Nightmare's head and explodes behind it. The impact pushes the Nightmare's head forward and its eyes grow fiercer. It opens its mouth and lets out a roar that causes all of the trees to snap, hurtling Hex into the ground.

Dusk yells at the top of his lungs, "Hex!" His fear of the large threat is now gone and replaced by anger. He stands up and clenches his fists tightly. A tree is ripped out of its roots and thrown towards him. It lands in front of him, bounces and goes over his head. He covers his face with his arm but does not budge from where he is standing. The wind brushing through his black jacket, Dusk's eyes grow wild with intolerance for the destruction.

Everything, all sound, begins to fade away as Dusk looks up at the disgusting Nightmare descending from its throne atop the mountain. Sarah's voice begins to speak in his mind, recreating a memory that they once shared.

She appears beside him, arms raised and stretching a bow and arrow. She says, "You're never going to get any good if you just stand there doing nothing." She fires the arrow and it hits the target set out before her, "I know you can do this. It's who we are. Fight."

His eyes begin to glow a faint yellow. Dusk moves his right leg backwards and moves his left hand forward. He pulls it back as if stretching the string to a bow. He raises his arms higher, aiming at the

Nightmare's face. An expression emerges on Dusk's face, containing both pain and passion.

Essa watches from in between a set of trees. Clutching onto her book, she sees the yellow light rising around Dusk. She watches as he holds the string firmly in his right hand, stretching it as far as humanly possible.

The wind begins to wrap around his arrow and catches the attention of the enormous Nightmare. It takes its first step forward and throws a piece of the mountain at Dusk. He continues to hold onto the string, waiting for the right moment to fire. Essa watches in horror as the small portion of the mountain descends towards him. She clutches her book and thinks of everyone she's lost, of the cruel fate Dusk has been given, of the fact she's scared of where she is, of the odd people she's met, from the loss of time in this world.

Essa screams, "I believe in you, Dusk! I will follow you! Please, live!"

The string begins to screech and the pressure causes Dusk to dig his back foot into the earth. A shadow stretches across his body as the chunk of the mountain blocks his vision. He says, "This is but the first step towards being by your side," and lets go of the string.

The arrow shoots forward and pierces through the projectile, shattering it. It continues forward and spins, gaining more friction and power. The yellow light surrounding it, forming it, shines brighter as it nears the Nightmare. Then in a successful strike, it goes through the Nightmare's left eye and the impact ignites into a storm of yellow destruction.

Essa runs towards Dusk and grabs hold of his arm. He turns and looks at her and says in alarm, "Don't startle me like that."

"You did it! But we need to get away. It's still moving."

"What are you talking about? I can finish it right here and now." He says with the belief that nothing can stop him.

"But…you look deathly pale."

Dusk presses his hand to his head and feels sweat pouring down. Suddenly he feels his knees waver and Essa catches him. The ground shakes furiously from the angry Nightmare. This causes Essa to fall to her knees as she holds onto Dusk. He lets go of her and places his hands on the ground. He breathes heavily and places his left hand to his chest, "What...the hell." His eyes widen as he feels his insides contort and pull at his very fiber.

A white light flashes in the sky and Essa looks up. Her heart fills up with hope and she smiles. Standing on the Nightmare's face rests Hex with a spear in his hand. With a mighty hurl, he slams the spear into the centre of the Nightmare's face. He then jumps away, unveiling his wings and soaring through the sky as his spear explodes.

The Nightmare roars in pain and swings both of its hands into the air, trying to smack Hex and cause him to fall. Hex dodges all of the swipes and gets far enough to stop and form two spears, one in each hand. His wings spread wide, keeping his position in the air. The Nightmare makes another thunderous roar, similar to what caused Hex to fall the first time. However he doesn't budge. He throws the spear in his left hand at the Nightmare and then flies behind it. The first spear strikes the Nightmare's right arm as it blocks its face. A chunk of the arm blows away. Hex flies across the other arm and slams his spear into the Nightmare's skin, dragging it through it as he makes his way closer to the Nightmare's upper body.

A stream of white light cracks through the Nightmare's black skin. Essa asks, "Where are Leaf and Kiyo?" She looks around frantically but cannot spot them anywhere.

Hex, now heading towards the Nightmare once more, a spear in hand, hurls it forward. The Nightmare catches it with its sharp teeth that extend across its entire mouth.

It bites down, crushing the spear.

Hex spits in disgust.

The Nightmare begins to speak slowly in a gruff voice, "It will take more than that to hurt me. You white bird."

The fact that the Nightmare can speak unsettles Hex and startles Essa. Dusk continues to wither in pain on the ground, cursing his luck. During this time, the wounds on the Nightmare begin to heal, however one spot remains damaged from the arrow that Dusk shot.

Both the Nightmare and Hex notice this. The Nightmare steps forward, slow and loud, making its way out of the mountain and its remains.

The sky darkens further and the wind picks up, shaking the trees viciously. The Nightmare raises a hand forward, its fingers begin to crack and then the index finger shoots forward, extruding further, stretching and quickly heading towards Hex. The angel curses and flies away from it, seeing that the finger is following him. He soars lower amongst the trees but the finger cuts through them without slowing down.

Dusk coughs out, "This is bad." He clenches his chest, pulling on his shirt. A drip of blood leaves his lips. He sees this and finds his vision beginning to blur.

Essa places a hand on his back and rubs it slowly, whispering, "It's okay Dusk…just hold on, everything will be alright."

A tear builds on his eyelid. He croaks out, "No it's not, this is bullshit. This is a damn joke." He presses his head against the ground and starts to whimper as the pain continues to rise. He screams and forces himself up onto his feet. Essa lets him stand on his own, and watches as he struggles to remain conscious.

In the air, Hex dodges the finger extending from the Nightmare. Another finger twitches and starts to stretch, adding further obstacles for the angel to dodge. Avoiding both of the fingers at once, he spins between them and heads up higher into the sky, wondering where Leaf and Kiyo have run off to.

A set of trees sway. A green dragon made of Leaf's light comes bursting out from the confines of the forest. Standing on its head are Leaf and Kiyo. They head towards the Nightmare. The dragon opens its mouth and breathes a burst of green flame.

Hex flies past the fire and the two fingers following him are ignited. The Nightmare pulls its fingers back, finding someone accompanying them. Kiyo stands on the fingers as they pull back, the fire doing no harm to his body. He stands amongst the green flames and grins. He quickly runs up the Nightmare's arm and heads towards the neck.

Meanwhile the dragon shoots another burst of flame at the Nightmare and it blocks it with its arm. The dragon rises above the arm and moves towards the body. It goes past it and then comes back around, quickly wrapping around the Nightmare. The dragon successfully latches on and confirms its attachment by digging its teeth into the Nightmare's waistline. At this moment Kiyo repeatedly slashes away at the Nightmare's throat, taking chunks with him and sending black blood into the air.

Running up the Nightmare's body, Leaf leaps into the air, her body soaring incredibly fast. She does a flip above the Nightmare's head, landing successfully. She slams her hands together and then places them against the Nightmare's head. A burst of green light wraps around it and descends down its body. Bound by both the dragon and the green light, its head starts to twist and slowly move backwards. Kiyo runs across the top of the chest and slashes the Nightmare's throat. More black blood gushes out.

"You are both vicious little creatures, but you cannot break my neck and bleed me out," the Nightmare says with a cackle.

Leaf says, "Oh silly, no, we wouldn't waste our time doing such a thing." The Nightmare's remaining eye goes wide as it is unable to close its mouth. Leaf continues to say, "Rather, waiting for you to speak again seems more efficient." She begins to put strain on her arms and pulls them back, forcing the Nightmare's head to pull further, quicker.

Kiyo stands on the Nightmare's shoulder and looks off into the distance. "You really did a number on this beautiful scenery," he says and looks up at the sky, "looks like the weather is going to clear up soon though."

The Nightmare looks around frantically, unable to figure out what's going on. Then, suddenly, it recalls the angel. It looks upwards as its head goes on a ninety-degree angle with the sky. Hex, flying above, is waiting to greet the Nightmare, a spear in his hand. He pulls his arm backwards and readies for a powerful throw. As the Nightmare sends out its third powerful roar, Hex yells and launches his spear downwards at the Nightmare's mouth. It cuts through the tremors from the roar and enters the Nightmare's throat, soaring towards its core. As it makes contact, the Nightmare's eye shakes. It goes silent before bursting out in pain.

Leaf lets go and the dragon unravels from the Nightmare, catching Leaf as she falls in the air. She flies around and raises a hand out. Kiyo looks at her and, with one hand casually in his pocket, he raises the other, they grasp hands and she pulls him from the Nightmare's shoulder.

They head towards Dusk and Essa. Kiyo asks, "Do you think the boy is alright?"

Leaf says, "It's strange to see him in that condition, he's different from the other angel."

They descend towards them and leap from the dragon. Leaf flicks her fingers and it disappears in a flash of green light.

"The two of you are something else." Dusk coughs up with a grin, "But good job."

Kiyo smiles and asks, "Are you alright?"

Dusk nods his head and rubs his chest, "Surprisingly I'm feeling better now."

Amused, Leaf says, "It's probably because we took care of the big, bad, scary monster."

Essa says while looking at the sky, "If anyone did that monster in…it's Hex."

The four of them look at him.

He remains in the air with his wings slowly flapping. His arms crossed. He watches the Nightmare erupt from within, the black body dissolving and rising into the sky in white ashes. The sky clears and light shines on the angel's body. He looks at the colourful sky above and closes his eyes, the wind softer now, brushing through his hair. "The weather has indeed cleared up."

CHAPTER ELEVEN
Equivalent Exchange

They stand together looking at the destruction left behind by the Nightmare. With the adrenaline now gone, the feeling differs between the five of them. A look of torment and defeat rests on Leaf and Kiyo's faces as they walk around, looking at the broken trees, torn earth and crushed creatures that were unfortunate enough to venture near the battle.

Dusk stands in the middle of the destruction. Pieces of ground uprooted and resting upon each other, forming obstacles that weren't originally there. Extruding and broken. His eyes slowly look around as he thinks about the arrow he successfully formed and the consequence his body felt after the release.

Not far from him, Essa watches as Leaf and Kiyo tread carefully around the collective environment dreamt of by humans. A place equally important to them as a family member would be to a human. Leaf looks away from the others to wipe her eyes. Kiyo lets out a sigh and watches her, his hands resting in his pockets. Essa keeps the book close to her chest.

In a taut voice, Leaf says, "Let's go. There's nothing that can be done here."

Dusk takes a step forward and stumbles. As he lands on his knees he clenches the dirt. The others look at him. Hex walks towards him and looks down at him. The others wait.

"Get up" Hex says harshly.

Dusk looks up at him in teary eyes, "You think I don't want to? I can barely move my body Hex!" his voice now strangled with emotion, "I wish I could."

Kiyo steps forward but Leaf holds him back, "Let them work it out."

Hex says firmly, "I said get up."

"Listen I-" Dusk tries to reply but Hex interrupts him.

"I said get up."

Dusk glares at him, "I said I can't do it! What don't you fucking get!?"

"I SAID GET UP!" Hex's voice roars and causes Essa and Leaf to flinch. His chest having rose from his yell, he shakes as he calms down.

Teary eyed and frustrated, Dusk cries out, "You son of a bitch, you want me up? I'll get up and I'll kill you!" He grinds his teeth. He digs his hands into the dirt. He breathes heavily like a raging bull and lifts his body up. One knee followed by the other, one-foot accompanied by the next. He wavers as he stands. He takes a step forward towards Hex.

The angel waits. Dusk swings a punch, one that anyone could easily dodge. Hex does not move. It lands across his cheek, cutting it open. Dusk falls forward. The angel catches him and holds him up.

Dusk's voice quavering, "Why can't I move my body properly Hex? Why am I so weak!" he buries his head against the angel's chest. "Why am I so weak!"

The angel replies, "But Dusk, what's weak about striking an angel? To me, that's what strong is. You overcame the pain. There's nothing weak about you. But I can tell you need to rest. So I will help you walk."

The compassion leads Dusk to burst out in tears. Hex holds onto him and looks towards Essa, he blinks before slinging Dusks arm over his shoulder, "It's time to go."

With Dusk in an emotionally unstable state, his body still stricken by the after effects of his usage of the bow and arrow that he created, Hex walks with him towards the clearing in the mountain, through the destruction and towards the other side.

There in the horizon they see a house—Norma's villa. In its beauty Dusk forgets about the pain for a moment and looks at the elegance that humans create when dreams unite.

Norma's home has a lake that rests behind it and stretches around, forming a beach on both fronts. Pastures of lime green grass connect from where they stand and where Norma's house resides. Only a handful of trees are present, but all of them are incredibly large and create ample amounts of shade. The colours of the leaves are red, green and gold.

Beneath the trees rest little cottages, large in their own right; some having decks attached, others leading out to the water's edge. Yet they pale in comparison to Norma's villa. The villa is made up of different kinds of wood dreamt of by many. The wood in some sections has a golden tint, while in others its ruby red with a dark layer of brown throughout.

Closer to the villa are two totem poles that stand erect, evenly spaced apart with the villa resting in the centre further back. The figures on the totem poles are birds—a kind never seen before in Essa's or Dusk's memory. They are red with a spiral of white going around the centre half.

Essa looks at the porch that wraps around the entire villa with vines hanging off of it. As the light from the sky warms up the wood, it also catches a shine throughout the windows, particularly the one at the highest portion of the roof. Essa realizes that it's a clock.

They walk through the field towards Norma's villa. Large sunflowers sway in the wind, blue petals from smaller flowers fly off and dance in the air. Leaf leads the way and turns to look at Dusk, "I think before we visit Norma you should bring him to the water."

Hex asks, "Why the water?"

"It has healing properties. I'm not sure it will work on him, but it's worth a try."

Kiyo frowns, "Does the water not do that in the real world?"

Essa replies, "Not even close. The water is either polluted or full of dangerous monsters. Humans avoid oceans and large lakes. Man-made beaches are generally the only water people swim in."

Kiyo scoffs, "How disgusting."

"Tell me about it" she lets out a sigh. She winces and touches her forehead, noticing a trickle of blood. "I must have gotten hurt before."

Leaf says, "Well you can go to the water with Hex and Dusk. Kiyo and I will go to Norma's villa."

Hex replies, "No. I'll go with you to Norma's villa. Kiyo can go with Dusk and Essa."

Leaf squints, "Kiyo will end up dragging Dusk. There's a height difference."

"A height difference?" Kiyo raises his arms, "the hell you starting that for now!"

Dusk coughs, "I can walk there myself. I'm starting to feel better. But if the water can help, then that's where I am headed."

Kiyo puckers up his lips, "Fine, fine, I don't have to carry you. I'll come with, so you don't drown or something."

Dusk replies, "How kind."

Kiyo then points to Hex, "I'd let him drown though."

Leaf yells, "Kiyo!"

Hex looks down at him, "What good would your height do if I were in need?"

The boy's eyes lighten up "Smart ass! I-"

Dusk places a hand on his shoulder, "You can help me walk after all, let's go."

With that, the group splits apart momentarily. Hex and Leaf head towards Norma's villa while the others head towards the beach.

On their way towards Norma's home, Hex looks around, noticing that near the huts, those he sees shimmer slightly. The faces of the people seem light, the eyes holding little emotion. Their movements are slow and what they appear to do is trivial. He asks, "What's wrong with them?"

Leaf looks over at the people he is referring to, "Them? There's nothing wrong with them. But what you are witnessing is both the birth and creation of a name. That shimmering is the battle of dreams colliding. Sometimes people come and go before receiving a name, others succeed."

He grunts, "I see. Then if you have a name, are you still in danger of disappearing?"

"Yes, but" her eyes move forward, "only if those who dream of us die."

The door to the villa opens before they arrive. They stand at the bottom of the stairs leading up to the porch. Hex sees an elderly lady step out from the villa. She greets him with a smile.

Hex says, "Hello Norma," in a pleasant tone, his eyes fierce as a smile spreads across his face. Leaf looks at him in alarm.

The elderly lady returns his slightly sinister smile, "Hello angel."

He raises his chin, "I'm looking for someone that can help me out. A special service if you will."

A twinkle emerges in her eyes as she says flirtingly, "I'm quite old, I'm afraid I don't have much left in me. But perhaps I can do that sort of playful thing one more time."

Leaf's expression darkens.

Hex replies, "I've been lead to believe that since you have a last name, you are the one that I should seek. So we can get to where we belong."

"We? Is this a group affair?" she chuckles, "Are you sure you belong?"

He does not answer her question.

Norma, enjoying the talk, takes a step to the side, "Well don't just stand there, come on in. We can discuss your journey."

Hex turns his head to Leaf and asks, "I suppose a playfull atmosphere is to be expected? You are all formed of dreams after all."

Leaf grimaces, "Yes, but for Norma, it came after she got her last name. And let's be honest, she's perverted."

Hex smirks from a rare moment of surprise. They enter the villa.

Meanwhile, Dusk stands with Essa and Kiyo on a deck that shoots out into the lake. Looking down at the water and his reflection, Dusk asks, "So, I just jump in for a swim and I'll start to heal?"

Kiyo nods his head.

"It's really that simple?"

Kiyo nods his head again.

Essa rolls her eyes slightly and places her book on the deck, followed by her shoes and socks. She dips her legs into the water. "It's not that bad, perfect for swimming."

Kiyo replies, "Of course it is, it's a dream world."

She turns to look at him, "Dream world or not, you're a pain in the ass."

He blinks and crosses his arms, mumbling something underneath his breath.

Essa pushes herself off and into the water. As she moves around, Dusk leaps in.

The two of them lie in the water and begin to feel their bodies heal and feel lighter. Their blood drifts off and evaporates in the water; water particles then rise into the air and disappear.

Dusk takes the time to turn around and look off into the distance. The clear, blue water makes him feel at ease, yet the pulsing sensation in his body troubles him. As minutes pass the sensation begins to subside, putting him at ease. His eyes close. He listens to the water splashing against the wooden poles that support the deck.

Essa ducks her head under water and then pulls it out, flipping her long, elegant red hair backwards. The water streams down her body. She squeezes her hair into a ponytail to remove some water and then raises a puddle in her hands and looks at herself for a brief moment. She notices a hint of sorrow in her eyes. She spreads her hands apart, letting the water return home. She falls backwards into the water and floats, looking up at the sky to clear her thoughts.

"Dusk…" she says softly.

"Ya?"

"Do you think we can really get back home? Back to where we

came from…to be with the ones that we love and hold closest? Even if the ones we cherish might be few…even if they don't cherish us in return?"

He lets his mind wander before replying, "Just follow me."

She smiles slightly, her eyes also closed as they drift in the water together. "Alright" she says, "I trust you."

As time passes Dusk exits the water and raises his hand to pull Essa out. She grabs hold of it and is brought onto the grass. Kiyo produces and throws them a set of towels. After a few minutes of drying their bodies and Essa having retrieved her book, the three of them go to the villa and knock on the front door.

As they wait, Essa turns to Dusk, "I was worried before. Back when you were crying."

He looks back at her, his eyes hopeful, "Thank you."

Kiyo, standing in between them lets out a great big huff—being so short that they are able to converse above his head. He knocks on the door heavily and crosses his arms. The door opens and Leaf lets them in.

Inside the villa rests a long table in the middle that looks as though it can seat twelve. On the left side of the room is a large window with a chair. It overlooks a garden and three trees. On the right is a fireplace with two long, thin windows on each side. A few feet away from the fireplace is a staircase leading up to the second floor.

Norma, who is already sitting at the end of the table, located in the centre of the room, beckons for the others to take a seat. Hex who has been standing up until this point, takes the seat closest to her.

They all find a chair to their liking. Dusk sits next to Essa in the middle, two seats away from Hex. Leaf and Kiyo sit directly across from them. Norma clears her throat. Dusk looks at her closely, wondering if this woman can get him back home.

Norma says, "It has been brought to my attention that three of you desire a trip to Eryu. I believe the home planet for both you and the girl?" her eyes resting on Dusk.

Essa says, "My name is Essa Starlight."

Norma smiles, "To speak your name so freely… I envy you."

Her eyes move towards Dusk. "And you my dearest, are Dusk Hollow."

Dusk looks at her eyes closely and sees a galaxy of stars and light swirling together—a world of possibilities, of life and nurture. He hears her ask, "Do you want to go home?"

He replies, "There's nothing I want more than that."

Norma smiles, her eyes drift to Essa who says, "I will do everything I can to make it back home."

Norma clasps her hands together and sits in silence, looking at both of them analytically. She observes their posture and the way they present themselves. How hope, fear, anger and loss riddles throughout their core. She lets out a soft smile, "My loves, you can indeed return."

They move with excitement and lock eyes as they finally have a sign of hope. Light shines through Essa's demeanor. With a large smile she says, "What do we need to do?"

Norma smiles slightly, the galaxies in her eyes swirling around. She says, "It is what I must do that will get you home. I'm afraid."

Kiyo asks sternly, "What do you mean?"

She replies, "I will die."

Leaf says tightly, "Don't kid around Norma."

The elderly woman lets her universe look towards the strong woman before her. "What is required costs a hefty toll on the one granting it. It has only been done once before." Her eyes move towards a set of picture frames on the wall. They contain images of a man and a woman smiling together.

"This world," Norma says, "my sweets, has three categories. One is imagery, simple and magical. It presents the landscape that humans' dream of which merges together. Their subconscious agreement is what shapes our home with time." She smiles, "The second category, is you and Kiyo and all others who have a name. You are gifts, my children. And I am thankful for every passing moment that all of you venture throughout this world and rid the Nightmares that plague the dreams of the young and old." She places a finger to her lip, "But that is where your power ends. Hunting and slaying Nightmares, you are restricted here."

Kiyo barks, "What of it? So that's all we can do, so what? I don't see why that means you have to die so they can return to reality."

"The Nightmares are growing." Her eyes move towards the door, indicating where they came from. "And we are not. If the Nightmares continue, then…I will continue to lose you, my children."

Leaf says, "W-what do you…what are you implying?"

"Seven have fallen in a short period of time."

Kiyo and Leaf are taken aback. Kiyo digs his sharp nails into the wooden table. Leaf shakes her head, "How is that…possible?"

Norma's brow lowers, "These things transpire my love…perhaps they were outnumbered, taken by surprise, worn out. The Nightmares are getting worse and are increasing. I have the power to change things and move them in a better direction."

Kiyo says with a painful expression, "By dying? Don't pull that kind of shit. Norma, you are not dying, you can't."

"I must."

"No, you don't need to! Let the humans' sort out their own damn dreams! Let them grow up and figure it out and make sacrifices! They are the ones that made that bloody monster out of a mountain! They are the ones who can't control themselves…"

Norma looks at Kiyo and says brittle and low, "Humans are good and bad Kiyo. They experience both ends of the spectrum and feel every single emotion. Emotions not even you or Leaf are aware of. Sometimes humans succumb to a certain one and it shapes them, it makes them do things that…are cruel and terrible. It induces fear into others and sometimes those who stand up against it are killed."

Kiyo's eyes begin to water.

"Kiyo, if too many fall, I will lose you. I will lose you even if you win against every Nightmare here. I will lose a child. So I need both you and Leaf to listen to what I am about to say."

He looks down at his knees and clenches his eyes closed. Leaf feels her throat constrict and struggles to breathe. Norma says, "The third and final category is someone with a first and last name, namely me. I am no longer a dream. I am not a human. I'm something more, something less, and something different. I have the power to open up a gateway between our world and theirs. This power requires something of equal value, an equivalent exchange. For the door to open and remain open long enough for the journey to the other side, then the value of that is I. So, I must speak my last name aloud, and that will open the door."

Dusk and Essa remain silent. The hope they felt has been replaced with grief for what must be lost. Hex looks at Norma and she nods her head. She says, "This must be done now. There is no time...for us to say our goodbyes."

Leaf cries out, "Wait Norma!"

"I'm sorry." Norma smiles faintly, "now listen to an old woman's last wish."

Kiyo begins to cry and Leaf feels her eyelids grow heavy from the water trying to spill out. Norma says, "I would like the two of you, to venture to reality. Make the Nightmares go away, so that all dreams can continue to exist."

Suddenly Norma stands up. Essa looks at her with her mouth slightly hanging open. She doesn't want this to happen, she wants to find another way.

Dusk looks at the angel, "Hex..."

The angel says nothing. His lifeless expression indicating he has nothing to say. That the events unfolding are how they must be. Dusk looks towards Norma, he asks himself if he is willing to go through with it, and the answer hits him quickly causing his stomach to feel unsettled. A voice whispers inside of him, *"Yes."*

Frustrated with himself, Dusk asks, "Hex, are you okay with this?"

"That is a stupid question" Hex replies, "Of course I am."

Kiyo bursts out of his chair, "How dare you!" He yells and Essa watches his fingers become more like claws.

The angel looks at him, "I have a task. An order. It is to save humans, in turn saving you. If one must make a sacrifice for the greater good of many, so be it."

"You have no right to decide!"

"I did not decide, Norma gave her answer before I asked the question."

Kiyo's lips quiver and he looks over at Norma helpless. Hex continues, "I will be going through that door with or without you. I don't care if I am alone on this journey."

Dusk speaks up, "I would never waste away someone's sacrifice. I will go through the door if Norma opens it for us."

Kiyo looks around at all of them, clearly distraught, he says, "Norma don't do this, please..." begging her to rethink her decision.

Leaf says quietly, "I will go through the door."

Kiyo's eyes slowly move and he looks at her in disbelief. She averts his gaze. Norma smiles, happy to see one of her children swallowing their own emotions for her sacrifice.

She says, "My last name is-"

Kiyo leaps onto the table and darts towards her, "No! Don't do it! I won't let you! Stop!"

Her smile, so large and pure, causes her galaxies to close, with love filling her being, "Youth."

The room around them breaks apart. The chairs rise with those still sitting on them. Wind begins to push heavily, causing Kiyo to fight against it as he reaches out towards Norma.

"No! Damn it!"

He loses his footing and grabs ahold of the table, using his other hand to try and grab her, "Take my hand! Please don't leave me!"

Everything becomes loud, chaotic, out of control. Essa watches as a dream unfolds and removes itself, becoming something else—a gateway home. They are all pulled into a swirling vortex of white, gray, black and blue. Essa lets her mind wander as she sees what to her looks like her own special galaxy of stars. She sees a floating mirage of Norma pass her, the elderly lady smiles and says, "Hold that book close my dear."

Kiyo, still struggling, fighting against the vortex, looks helplessly as Norma fades into the outer walls of the gateway, becoming the pathway that will lead him away from home. She looks at him and closes her eyes, disappearing for good.

They all fall downwards, making their descent to reality. As they fall, Kiyo, now having given up, stares helplessly upwards and says in a croak with tears streaming down his face, "I didn't want to lose you either, you were l-like…a mother…to me…Norma. Norma!!!!"

CHAPTER TWELVE

The Descent

They descend through a sea of nothingness, a prospect of everything and nothing. White empty space to some, stars to others, even gray clippings of past memories emerge for them. Blurs flash by, showing imagery that's slightly noticeable yet unrecognizable.

Dusk, his body feeling light, asks, "What is this?"

The vortex holds obscure markings. Dusk focuses his eyes to try and make it out. Yet the shapes disappear if he stares for too long. So he decides he will close his eyes, and feel them. See them in his mind rather than with his sight.

He sees images, only recognizing some of them. He spots one of his family, his father and mother laughing while his younger sister, older brother and he run towards a table with food on it. He grimaces. Another image is that of his father and uncle. He sees other images that don't relate to him at all and wonders if it belongs to one of the others or someone else entirely.

A warm light begins to emerge. Dusk feels his body suspend in the air. The others continue to fall. He looks to them in alarm, but the light brightens and then casts away everything. He opens his eyes and finds himself standing in a field of white grass.

No sky, no trees, nothing. Silence welcomes him. Neither sound nor the movement of wind can be felt. Dusk looks around and sees no one else. Everything around him is white empty space; the only form of texture is the grass beneath his feet.

A girl appears in front of him facing the opposite direction, her body contrasting the environment. As he gets closer he recognizes the length of the hair, the colour and style. "Sarah?" he asks and slowly places his hand on her shoulder. She turns around and what he sees startles him.

Thin lines of blood stream down her face from her eyes and mouth. "You let me die," she says. "Look at me, this is all your fault." She places her hand to his cheek, "look at what you've done to me." A cackle of laughter rings through Dusks ears. Sarah then begins to twitch and her body slowly turns to ash.

Soon nothing is left of her. Feeling anxiety overwhelm his body, Dusk cries out, "Where am I? This shouldn't be happening, do not torment me! Where is she!?"

He turns to see the white grass turn black, it spreads towards him and begins to wrap around his legs and up his body. As it reaches his face he gasps and tries to claw it off.

A voice replies, "She is nowhere, she is everywhere."

Dusk claws and digs his fingers into the darkness, he screams, "Don't fuck with me!"

The voice begins to laugh, cackling as it consumes Dusk. Bringing forth a shaking realization that the voice that's speaking is coming from his head.

"You know better than to scream" it continues, belittling him, "she's as good as dead, you just like to fill your mind up with her, your heart."

He now finds himself in a dark room. The floor a harsh wood, rich in a red tint while the walls are gray brick, shadows echoing off of it.

Dusk yells, "Where am I!"

The voice replies, "Such a stupid question."

Dusk grinds his teeth, "Who are you!"

The voice laughs, "Again, a stupid question. Don't make me feel a fool Dusk! I am you. The darkness within your soul that you claim does not exist. I am the monopoly, the chance of change. I am the pitch-black concrete of smeared blood that exists in your conscious, your bones; your very fiber. I am the you that kills, that lives, that has fun. So do not ask me who I am. Ask yourself, why aren't you me already."

"Cut the bullshit!"

A set of torches emerges, ten on each wall all lit up. The flames burning high, casting orange hues that flicker shadows. The light reveals a chair opposite of him at the end of the room. A figure sits upon it, with red eyes piercing through the darkness accompanied by a white smile. The voice beckons, "Come closer, if you want to see for yourself."

Dusk steps forward, he sees that the chair is made of red leather, and that the man is wearing a black suit. A silver watch rests on his wrist. His white hair is parted slightly so it does not cover his face. His face, Dusk sees, is identical to his in every single detail despite being very pale. The man looks at him, his lips blue, and his eyes red with a white stripe down the middle.

The person moves his hand from his face and smiles; sitting slightly slouched with his left leg sitting on his right knee. "As you can see, the only differences are miniscule. I am you. No. You are I." The man places a finger to his chest and smiles.

Dusk says toneless, "You are nothing. I'm falling through a gateway. This is just a side effect."

The darkness's smile turns into a grin. It shakes its head, "A natural reaction…but dull. I expect more from you." It sits up straight in the chair, its voice becoming modulated, pleasant, "This is no dream. This is your mind. You're here because your focus brought it upon yourself. And now you are bearing witness to me, the greatest gift you could hope for."

Dusk grunts, "I can simply pass this off as a dream. If you are in my mind, then I'll forget about you in time."

"I won't let you," the man—the replica—says as a threat.

Dusk replies, "What do you expect to gain from this encounter?"

It begins to smile, "I've gained so much already. You acknowledge my existence."

Dusk eyes waver, the man laughs and says, "We are going to have a lot of fun together, just don't get yourself killed again."

Dusk raises his chin, "Is that how this started?"

His darker self nods its head, "What made you, well you, is now open for grabs. All of your emotions are realigning, you are changing, and I am going to make sure I become the largest portion. I will be-come-"

Dusk closes the distance between them and grabs a hold of his darker self by its black tie and pulls it upwards, lifting the figure slightly out of the chair. Dusk says, "You aren't going to do shit. You will remain here in this dark room where you belong."

The darkness lights up and says, "I love your eyes, so much anger."

Dusk lets go of the tie and says, "I will kick your ass if you try anything."

The figure frowns and rests its head on its left hand, "Please, I have a name. Call me Hollow." He yawns, having established his presence, he waves a finger around in a circle and says, "You may go back to whatever that old woman is having you fall through."

The darkness, the black room disappears and the white grass returns. Dusk turns to see if his darker half is still with him but he can't see him. Noticing a strong return of the taste of metal, he spits numerous times. Dusk then lets out a yell, "Damn it!"

Hex calls out, "Dusk?"

He turns and sees the angel standing in the field, his white armor blending in, but his jet-black hair standing out. Dusk asks, "How... how long have you been standing there?"

The angels eyes look around, he says, "That doesn't matter. Does this place mean something to you?"

"No."

Hex's eyes lower slightly, "I see."

Dusk asks, "Where are the others? If you are here then that must mean-"

"Unfortunately I'm only here because I flew towards the white light that appeared before you. The others are still falling. We might be as well, who knows" Hex pauses, "Was that girl…"

Dusk, his voice elevating says, "So you saw…yes" his eyes waver, "that was her…sort of. Did you see anything else?"

The angel stares at him. Moments pass. He replies, "No. Oddly enough I felt an inclination to look into the abyss of white, and then felt my body stiffen, and I was unable to move. I could not hear, nor feel."

"Oh" Dusk says, "Is that really all that different from your usual self?"

The angel tilts his head slightly, looking directly at him. The white grass begins to disappear. The flickering gray blur returns and pulls them down further towards the other side.

Dusk lets his thoughts drift away. He says lightly, "I'm tired of focusing…of thinking." He closes his eyes and the angel watches him drift in silence. Before him, the angel watches the most complex being he's come across in all of his life. Someone, he thinks to himself, who could also be the least significant.

While they fall, Hex looks out to see if he can spot one of the other three but has no luck. The descent increases in time, until time itself loses all meaning. The seconds feel more like hours, causing drowsiness followed by the carrier of sleep to arrive.

A shimmer occurs in the vortex. Hex watches it dart across the faint images, curling them as it makes its way around in circles. A hand made of the clippings bursts from the wall and reaches out, grabbing a hold of Dusk and Hex. It pulls them towards the rest of the blur, causing them to merge into it.

Dusk stares in horror as he finds that both Hex and he are standing back in Norma's villa. Across from them, Norma stands at the fireplace with Leaf, the two of them discussing something he cannot yet hear.

He calls out, "Hey! Why are we back here!?"

They do not turn or respond.

"Hey!"

"They cannot hear you" Hex says as he moves up, standing beside him.

Dusk points forward, "What the hell is this?"

"A memory I presume. And we are bearing witness."

Leaf slams her hand into the fireplace, she yells, "Watching over him is insane! Norma, you know what he is."

"You cannot judge him on that. He's different but he still has a name. I gave him that name."

"You shouldn't have. Myself or one of the others could have easily dispatched of him."

Norma says, "We don't harm dreams Leaf. You know that."

"Yes well, he's a special circumstance. Now we've got a ticking time bomb walking around with us."

"I want you to watch over him."

"What!"

"Yes. If you watch over him, you can shape him and keep him away from turning into what he was supposed to be."

"I didn't sign up for that. I have enough to handle with these constant Nightmares emerging all over the land."

"Leaf, just do me this favor. Keep him close and you'll see what I saw. You'll see the love within his eyes."

She lets out a sigh and steps away from the fireplace, covering her face with her hands, "Fine" she lets her shoulders slide down, "whatever."

Norma smiles, "Thank you."

Hex feels the inclination to turn around. What he sees causes him to place his hand on Dusks shoulder. His attention caught, Dusk turns and steps forward. He says quietly, "Jesus…Hex, what the hell…"

The angel looks at a room before them, this one much different from where they watched Norma and Leaf talk. At the far end of it, leaning against the wall with her legs pressed together, her knees close to her chest and her arms wrapped around them, sits Essa.

Clearly younger, her hair a mess, she stares angrily at them. Dusk looks at her and moves his hand up and waves. Her expression does not change. They look around at her bedroom and see the chaos, books torn apart, her bed hanging off its frame. Holes in her walls, picture frames scattered across the floor with broken shards of glass.

Essa mutters, "I hate this, I hate all of this." She begins to rock herself back and forth, tears streaming down her face. She screams, "Why did you leave me! Why did you leave me all alone! Where are you!"

Moonlight comes through the window in her ceiling. Dusk sees Essa bury her head behind her knees, clenching her legs. His eyes move toward where the moonlight rests. He sees a picture frame but is unable to make out its contents before everything changes.

As new scenery emerges, Dusk asks, "What is the point of all of this?"

"To observe," Hex says calmly, "and maybe learn."

The third memory forms itself and they see Kiyo sitting on a log covered in moss amongst a forest of gold. His legs dangle around, his eyes looking at seemingly nothing.

A woman appears who looks to be a younger—much younger—version of Norma. Her gray hair is replaced by the evident colour of blonde. She wears an elegant purple dress with gold bracelets around her wrists. She asks, "I thought I'd find you here. Do you have a name, child?"

Kiyo looks at her irritated, "No."

She smiles softly and walks towards him.

Kiyo hesitates.

She reaches him before he moves and she places her right hand against his cheek. She says, "Child, we all face ourselves. We wonder if we are good or bad. An answer always finds its way to us, and for those who cannot find it, others help them do so."

She takes a seat next to him on the log. Norma asks, "What would you do if you were to find out your name?"

He frowns, "I don't need to know it. I'm fine without it."

"Are you?" she asks politely, "or are you frightened?"

"I'm not scared of anything!"

She smiles, "We are all scared of something. We're the dreams of humans. Few of us can openly admit to being strong enough to have no anxiety. But, I will tell you this. Knowing your name will give you a better understanding of the differences of what you are feeling right now. Of the good and the bad."

Her hand presses against his chin and lifts it up, "Would you like to face this fear and journey with me?"

His lips press together tightly. He asks, "Why should I listen to you?"

She replies, "I never said you have to. But, with a last name, I feel like I should do what I can to help you. I know you have a name somewhere in you. I am willing to find it for you. It has a cost though, and with that cost, I would like you to do something for me."

He frowns and asks, "What would I have to do?"

She smiles, "Listen to my final wish."

The scenery begins to morph and the colours rearrange themselves until all pigments and shades become one, become nothing, become whole. Hex pulls on Dusk's shirt and brings him out of the trance that associates itself with the showcase of memories. The others still haven't joined them, and the two continue to fall, lightly, effortlessly, without control of their own bodies beyond the simple movements of their arms.

"Hex…I'm tired…of this place."

"…So am I." Hex replies.

"Do you think the others will make it out?"

"I wonder…if it's us who should fear the inability of escape."

Dusk chuckles softly, "I suppose we should." He then closes his eyes and decides that if he is going to continue falling, he might as well let the darkness beneath his eyelids comfort him and let the white and gray blurs beyond remain alone. The angel looks over at him and watches his companion drift off into sleep. He then looks ahead into the abyss of emptiness; for an angel never sleeps, he simply waits.

CHAPTER THIRTEEN
Capturing the Flower

As a story unfolds, so do others in parallel, carrying similar fates. When one falls victim, another rises. When one perishes, a new life is born. There is also the circumstance of those who have yet to meet but share the same path and strive for the same goal. While Essa, Dusk, Hex, Kiyo and Leaf fall through the door in hopes of returning to Eryu, the city itself, the main hub of the planet, continues to carry on with its daily routine. And within this hub a similar story is taking place, where a group of individuals are about to experience something far greater than what they had anticipated.

In the southern region of Eryu a few blocks are known as the convict district. This name has been given due to the lack of cameras throughout the streets to protect its citizens, the lack of drones, which roam the streets, or the presence of police officers. This is due to the fact that when any of said three controls shows themselves, the people riot in protest. The people themselves are not convicts, yet their nature of rallying against the control has placed this nickname upon them. Because of this, a huge influx of casinos, bars, strip clubs and other archaic past time enjoyments exist amongst the streets.

One bar in particular is known for hosting shady individuals as well as wild brutes, yet it doesn't stop the business from flowing. Inside this bar, known as the Devils Den, two men sit at the counter.

The bartender walks up towards them and asks, "Care for a drink?" to which the man on the left waves his hand signifying he doesn't as he turns in his chair and glances over at a booth.

The man on the right simply nods his head and his glass is refilled. He takes a long sip and then looks at his friend and says, "You know, staring isn't polite. Nor is it in any shape or form an efficient way of concealing yourself, let alone your intentions."

The man on the left smiles, "At this point, Tail, I'm less concerned about blowing our cover than I am about her sneaking off on us again while we enjoy our beverages. Remember last time? Sapphire almost killed us both."

Tail shrugs and takes another long sip. If one were to describe him in one word, the word would be 'cold'. This applies to him perfectly due to the fact that his emotional response to anything is limited and uncaring. Moreover, his apparel perfects this impression as he wears black jeans, black boots and a black sweater with no sleeves, although his right arm is covered up completely in a white bandage. His hood is always up and along with his long black hair; a portion of his face always remains hidden, which includes his right eye.

This choice of dark clothing is the opposite of his friend, who wears red jeans, black shoes, a gray shirt with a red leather jacket, and short styled red hair accompanied with a scruffy face. Moreover, he has a sword sheathed on his right side with a gun on the left, whereas Tail has no visible weapons.

The man places a cigarette in his mouth and lights it. He breathes in and then exhales a cloud of smoke, which forms a circle. He says, "Besides, she knows we are here. I can't remember the last time Fleur wasn't aware of us being close. You could say she's bored now and just wants to have another round with us."

Tail replies before taking another sip, "Then go ahead and play with her Gunther, I have a drink that has yet to be finished and I'd very much like to do so in peace."

"But I don't want to…not alone" Gunther whines slightly, he then looks at Tail, "Come on, we always face her together."

Tail grumbles, "And yet due to your stupidity she continuously escapes, but not before making a snide comment about my apparel."

"Well you do wear alot of dark clothing. Anything you want to share?" He says sarcastically as he takes another hit from his cigarette and lets the ashes fall in front of him.

"And you are dressed like a red beacon, honestly…who wouldn't notice you are after them. You're like a raccoon making a mess of things, dying to be noticed."

"What can I say? It's fashion."

Tail looks around and then his black emotionless eyes rest on Gunther, "Fashion is when a few wear clothes that distinguish them from the rest, in turn leading a new wave. You however have been wearing the same damn style of red clothing forever and not a single person has yet to say to themselves, 'hey that looks good'."

"Well, we haven't looked back at the places we've visited. For all you know there's countless people wearing red clothing. Even one person would be a testament to my good taste."

"Your testament has a count of zero and no sight of rising." Tail finishes his drink and places the empty mug on the counter. As he ponders over having another refill, Gunther taps his shoulder and nods his head in the direction of one of the booths. Sure enough, a figure cloaked in black rises up from the table, masked in the darkness of the dimly lit room, and heads towards the exit.

A smile spreads across Gunther's face. He says, "Everything is ready, and this time will be the last. Are you good to go or has all that alcohol gotten to your head, Tail?" He doesn't receive a response. He turns to see his friend is no longer sitting at the bar. "There's no fooling around with you, is there?" Gunther says to himself quietly.

The cloaked figure—known as Fleur—reaches the exit door and places her hand against the handle. When it doesn't open, she lets go and quickly moves towards the staircase that leads to the rooftop. As Gunther starts to move toward her, a group of four large, bulky men step in his way with their arms crossed. They average in height between 6'2 to 6'5, which makes Gunther's height of 5'11 seem puny in comparison. He looks up at them and asks, "Can I help you gentlemen?"

One of the men replies with a smug look, "You can start by getting the hell out and leaving that girl alone. She told us all about you and your friend. Disgusting. You are perverts unlike any other."

Gunther blinks, "Perverts…I swear, this is all a misunderstanding." He raises his hands in the air, "I swear, she's an old friend of ours up to no good. Though I do have a picture." He proclaims, "Can you lot look at it to confirm if it's her?"

"The hell, a picture?"

"Yes, let me show it to you." He reaches out and grabs the closest man by the throat. Gunther says, "In the foreground, a man is crushing the throat of another…" He looks at the other three, "…with the rest to follow." He squeezes tightly and the man gurgles up blood.

A man yells, "You're a dead man!" and throws a punch at Gunther, to which Gunther slides his hand past it and sends his own into the face of the man with ease. Then, twisting the shoulder, Gunther slams his hand into the face once more.

He then moves forward. The other two circle him. He patiently waits for them to strike, taking the time to inhale and exhale more smoke. He places one hand to his ear and presses the button to his miniature headset. He says, "Initiate plan b, she's heading to the rooftop."

One of the men yells out, "Who the hell are you talking to?"

Gunther looks at him with amusement and says, "The legion of perverts you daft prime ape." This angers the man and he runs at Gunther. With a spin kick, Gunther hits the man across the face and sends him into a nearby table, causing the ones sitting there to grow angry and stand up.

Gunther coughs slightly, "Oh…great."

The fourth man backs away until he finds himself unable to move. He looks down to see shadows wrapping around his feet. The shadow covers his mouth and then, with a slight tug, snaps his neck.

The sound causes Gunther to wince. "Tail…we don't have to kill everyone we come across that causes mischief. Oh, and I see you've managed to keep the entire room under control." He looks at every customer in the bar who's being held down by the shadows and unable to move. He smiles and says, "Ten out of ten for effort."

Tail replies, "Shut up." He walks out of the shadows. The bartender gulps as he looks at them. Gunther raises an eyebrow and the man ducks behind the bar. Tail taps on the counter. The bartender peers up to look at him. Tail says, "A refill, if you would be so kind."

The man nods his head hurriedly and pours Tail a large glass of whiskey. Tail raises his glass in appreciation and looks at Gunther and says, "She's off to a good start. Will they be up for it?"

Gunther heads towards the staircase and says, "I doubt it." with a smile. He removes the cigarette from his mouth and tosses it backwards, letting the remaining ashes float off into the air.

On the rooftop, Fleur makes her way towards the edge. She looks down at the street and across at the closest building. She contemplates whether or not she wants to make the jump or find another route.

Hiding above the clouds, a spaceship known as the Trinity hovers. Small in size, capable of holding up to twenty people comfortably, it serves well as a carrier for its crew of eight members lead by Gunther.

Three of the members walk towards the hanger that will let them jump from the ship and towards the ground. They strap themselves with air-gear, which is a set of leather straps that have gears attached to them. The straps wrap around like a vest, with shoulder and leg guards. The get up is complete with a skintight black suit, the key—to give as much maneuverability as possible.

Of the three members, two are females, sisters with black hair, one long and the other short. The third member is a man with shaggy blond hair and blue eyes.

The hanger doors open and the three of them jump out into the night sky, embraced by the darkness, heading downwards towards Fleur. The man falls faster than the other two and takes the lead.

They pierce through the clouds and the city lights reveal themselves. The wind rushes through the gears. They direct their arms and legs to determine the speed and positioning of their descent. In a matter of thirty seconds they reach their target and change their body movements.

The gears start to spin and use the air to slow their descent. The wind wraps around their bodies, providing cushioning for any sudden impact. They land on the rooftop silently without alerting Fleur.

The girl with long black hair—known as Abigail—raises her arm and reveals a miniature barrel beneath her wrist. In turn the other female known as Baylee does the same.

They aim at Fleur's arm. The man then raises his hand up and presents three fingers, signaling the time limit before they make their move. He brings down one finger, then another. As the last one comes down, the sound of air quickly being cut can be heard as darts go through it.

Fleur turns around to see the darts and the ropes connecting them to the barrels on Abigail and Baylee's arms. She raises her arm to protect herself, resulting in one of the darts successfully wrapping around her wrist, the other dart also successfully reaching its target. Both of her arms are pulled forward.

Abigail says, "Alright that should do, what's next Dexter?"

The man walks forward towards Fleur. He pulls down the facemask that's concealing his mouth. Dexter says, "This is the first time you've met us, but we know all about you. We know that your hands are a fundamental resource when using your illusions. With those held up, you're useless."

Dexter pulls down her hood and sees an elegant and pretty boyish face. She has short pink hair and a similar shade of pink within her eyes. A small scar rests on her forehead. Dexter looks at her closely. He moves the cloak and sees no signs of cleavage. He frowns and Fleur asks, "Would you like to check in between my thighs? I thought you knew all about me." She smiles and continues in a silvery tone, "You've never seen a woman trapped in a man's body before?" she winks, "and what's this nonsense about me needing my hands to create an illusion? I mean that's not wrong. But, there's more to it than that."

Her body disappears. Dexter steps backwards and he says, "Abigail,

Baylee, move back!" They all look around desperately for signs of Fleur.

She emerges behind them and claps her hands and says, "Time to fall asleep." A petal falls in front of Baylee, she reaches out and touches it. As she makes contact, a stream of flowers erupt from it and cover both sisters in vines. They lose their ability to move.

Dexter yells out, "It's an illusion, just focus on freeing yourself. Those flowers aren't real, you can escape!" He takes a step towards them and hears a slight crunch. He looks down. A small flower, crushed, rests beneath his foot, and a scent floats up towards his nostrils. He feels his knees weaken and he falls down, unable to move. "This isn't good…" he focuses all of his mental strength into moving his right hand to his ear to contact the others. "Sapphire…we couldn't catch her."

Standing on the roof of a building not too far away, a woman receives the call. Parts of her body, including her lower abdomen, left arm, both legs and right eye, are cybernetic. She has long light blue hair, blue eyes and wears a tight aerodynamic suit. "I will handle it," she responds.

Fleur runs below her on the street. Sapphire raises her left arm. "L-Cannon, initiate protocol—BOOM SHOT, fifty percent." Her hand forms into a barrel and a beam of blue light shoots out from it. As Fleur continues to run, the ground in front of her erupts from the impact of the projectile that Sapphire shot.

Fleur leaps over the broken cement that litters the street and continues to run. She takes a sharp corner and goes down an alleyway. Sapphire chases her, leaping across rooftops. Her right eye analyses Fleur and looks ahead to see which route she will try to take. "L-Cannon, initiate protocol—FLARE AMMUNITION, fourty percent."

She leaps into the air and twists her body as she fires the flare. It lights up the sky above Fleur, causing her to run into a wall from distraction. Fleur falls backwards and gets up quickly. She mutters, "You're a real pain in the ass."

She goes into another alleyway and continues to run. Yet the alleyway is long and narrow. "Shit." Fleur mutters as she realizes this and runs as fast as she can.

Sapphire walks confidently towards the beginning of the alleyway while on the rooftop and sees Fleur halfway towards the other end. Raising her arm once more Sapphire says, "L-Cannon, initiate protocol—STUN GUN."

Sapphire fires a stun bullet. Fleur decides to block it with her right hand. The shock electrifies her. She clenches her teeth and fights through the pain. She stumbles and hits the wall, but pushes herself off and escapes the alleyway. Sapphire places her hand to her ear and says, "Gunther, she's been stunned. The use of illusions should theoretically not be possible anymore. How's Tail?" Her analytical voice shows sign of warmth as she asks about her companion.

A moment passes and Gunther replies, "Tail says to stop worrying about him, he's not a child. As for Fleur, nice shot! We just came across Dexter and the others; the idiots got caught in an illusion. They won't be moving for a few minutes. Do you know where she's headed?"

Sapphire looks ahead and analyzes the most plausible areas that Fleur will strive to reach. Three areas of note come to her attention. The first is the sector of large towers that are the borderline between the south and central district; this carries off into a small river with a bridge leading to a national park that carries on for a few miles. However it eventually leads to central district that is always under high surveillance amongst its bustling streets and skyscrapers.

The second option is the south districts steam crate; a huge hole in the ground where steam rises, a natural resource that Eryu uses to dispose of its garbage.

The third and most likely destination is the open field right before the train that connects the south district with the east, north, and west and then, as a last stop before returning to the south, central. This would give Fleur the opportunity to increase her possibilities of escape tremendously.

Sapphire says, "She's heading towards the train station."

"The station? Isn't that a bit of a relic? It takes hours to get to the

East with it."

"Yes, although Fleur isn't on a sightseeing trip, she simply needs a good spot to jump off. Common sense Gunther, you should know that much."

"Oh hush…this district makes me so darn nostalgic I lose my ability to think."

"That doesn't make much sense."

"I suppose so, but when I find myself surrounded by dimly lit streets made of marble and rock, it takes me back, you know?"

Sapphire closes her eyes momentarily. "I'll meet you two at the station, and if you can, try to wake those three out of that illusion. " She cuts off the communication and jumps down into the street and heads towards the train station at the eastern side of the southern district, beyond the cramped streets filled with cool, damp air.

Puddles splash beneath her feet, the windows reflect her blurred movement as her legs pick up the pace to close the gap between her and Fleur. All the while, thoughts of when she was a child start to cloud her brain.

On her way towards the train station she passes few people since many stick to the darkness and the confines of the buildings. It's not quite nighttime yet; the sun is still within the sky's boundary casting its light upon the tops of buildings and streets. When night does approach, the streets fill with the convicts and delinquents. They go out and enjoy the wildness that the other districts look down upon. Those districts don't protest however since it's away from them. Sapphire thinks about this in the back of her mind. Each step she takes awakens a small echo of the past from when she and the others were a part of this life. She leaves the confines and reaches the open area leading towards the train station.

It's a wide open space, quite large. Stones form the majority of the plaza, where dirt pathways connect it and lead outwards to small shops and little resting areas that have benches beneath trees that overlook ponds. In the centre, away from the distractions, Sapphire notices Fleur amongst a crowd of people heading towards the building made of wood, polished and slick, one of the few historical buildings left in Eryu, the station itself.

The crowd is made up of about a hundred, Sapphire estimates, as her eye observes all of them. Yet she doesn't lose sight of Fleur and raises her arm into the sky. She shoots a signal flare from the tip of her index finger. Since it's not an attack of high impact weaponry, she isn't required to state the prerequisites to unlock it.

The flare lights up the sky with green smoke, causing the crowd to become startled. It disperses slightly. Fleur continues to hide amongst them. She sees that she won't be able to get to the station while the slow pace and mixture of confusion carries on amongst the citizens.

Sapphire sees this as her chance to move in and capture Fleur once and for all. No more running around or hiding, the years of chase can rest. Or at least that's what she thinks until Fleur activates an illusion unlike the previous ones.

A sea of pink petals engulfs the crowd and fills up the entire plaza. Sapphire is unable to see one step in front of her. Her eyes lose track of Fleur. She says in protest, "This isn't possible, your right arm shouldn't be able to move."

Fleur reveals herself momentarily within the confines of the pink petals. She says mockingly, "I'm not restricted to using my hands. I hope you enjoy this beautiful sight, a beautiful lie."

The petals start to spin and slash at Sapphire's skin. She knows the pain isn't real or even the blood, but faltering for one moment can put her in a fit of panic. Closing her eyes, she focuses on her sense of hearing, but that too isn't effective against the loud gushing sound of petals flying past her ear. So she focuses on her scent, but this also fails.

Sapphire realizes that this illusion is able to control all of her senses, except touch. The moment she figures this out, she runs forward in hopes of coming across Fleur.

She reaches out and grabs ahold of Fleur by the collar and raises her arm forward, her hand turning into the cannon. "L-Cannon, initiate protocol—STUN GUN." Fleur's eyes widen, the pink glare of fear shines throughout the fury of petals. But nothing happens. Sapphire looks at her arm with worry. Fleur smiles.

Sapphire asks, "Why isn't it working?"

Fleur says, "Now…this is precious. It seems I have a guardian angel! You won't be catching me today, pretty!"

A sword appears behind Fleur. The blade presses against her throat—Gunther at the other end of it. She laughs and says nervously, "My, that was fast. You're getting good at tracking me down, love."

He moves in and wraps his arms around her. "Don't call me that, Paige will gut us both."

She smiles, "How troublesome."

Gunther moves back, his blade still at her throat. He looks over at Sapphire, her expression full of anger. She clenches her fist. Her arm comes down, as her hand returns to normal. Sapphire asks, "Why did you disengage my ability of attack? You put me in harm's way Gunther."

He looks at her with the guilt of being caught in the act and says, "Look, I knew you'd go overboard and I didn't plan to leave you out too dry. We need her conscious; her being put into a state of drool isn't going to do us any good. The bounty lowers when the prize is broken."

"That's inexcusable. I have the right to make the moves as much as anyone else on the Trinity."

"Yes, but the limit to your power is within our hands for a reason, don't let it get to you."

"You pulled a selfish act."

Fleur looks at both of them and rolls her eyes. "A petty quarrel between friends…oh how cute." Sapphire turns around and backhands her, leaving a solid red mark across her face. Fleur spits out some blood, glares at her and says, "How tasteless. Thankfully this body of mine isn't easy to harm, you bitchy pest."

As Sapphire takes a step forward to deliver another blow, Tail appears behind her and grabs her arm. "That's enough Sapphire." His voice catches her attention and quickly soothes her.

Fleur grins.

Gunther shakes her and says, "That's enough trouble out of you. You won't be able to activate another illusion for a few minutes."

She rolls her eyes.

He continues, "It's nice to see your eyes still have their charm though. I was beginning to think you lost that art." He puts his sword away and twists her arm.

She says mockingly, "Oh please, you chumps are a pastime of enjoyment for me. I can do whatever the hell I want and that includes-"

The impact of a body suddenly falling on top of Fleur renders her unconscious. Sapphire takes a step back. Tail simply blinks and Gunther looks upwards to see a gray portal in the sky.

What they were all unaware of during their conversation was an opening from above. A gateway with gray images swirling about, bringing Essa to Eryu and causing her to fall downwards, landing on Fleur.

The gateway closes and they all look at Essa as she sits on Fleur's back. She says, with her voice shaking, "I can-n't believe I fell-ll from the fucking-g sky again…"

CHAPTER FOURTEEN
Trading Secrets

Gunther asks Essa, "Who are you?"

She simply looks at him and remains silent. Her eyes drift, looking for the others, wondering if they've come through the portal as well. She asks in return, "Where am I?"

Gunther looks at her carefully before he replies, "You are in the southern district of Eryu." His hand rests on the handle of his gun.

She lets out a sigh of relief, "I'm back."

"You came from that rift in the sky?"

"...Yes."

He looks upwards, toward where the portal had been. He then returns his gaze and asks, "Where did you come from?"

Her eyes avert, "You wouldn't believe me."

His grip relaxes slightly on the gun handle and he says, "Give it a shot."

She looks at him straight in the eyes, "I came from a world of dreams, but my home is here in Eryu."

He scratches his chin, "You're right...sort of out there."

Essa looks behind her at Sapphire and Tail. She then looks down at Fleur who still rests beneath her. Essa stands up and crosses her arms, taking a step back, "Sorry about that."

Gunther looks at Fleur and then his eyes light up, "Oh no need to worry about that. She's a prize, just slightly damaged now."

"A prize?"

"Yes."

"What do you mean?"

His expression darkens. Essa hears a rush of wind and then a sudden shock. She collapses onto Fleur. Tail says sardonically, "That was sudden."

Sapphire stretches her arm, "It had to be done."

Tail places a hand to his face, "I thought I was the cold one."

Gunther sighs, "We will detain her for now. We're bounty hunters after all. People aren't fond of us, so when our business is discovered it's kill or—well we will see. After all, she might mean a lot to someone out there…once we learn who she is."

Tail raises a finger, "There's a fine line between us and slavers. She looks to be 18—still a child."

Gunther lets out a laugh and says, "Oh come on Tail, don't start. Now let's take these two back to the Trinity and be on our way. There are some familiar faces I would like to see."

Sure enough, the sound of a ship cutting through wind appears overhead and hovers over them. A ship that Gunther takes utter pride in, with its red splash of paint over the white exterior that forms the body. The ship is his signal of rebirth and escape from poverty and oppression, from fear of death to a world of endless possibilities. The ship holds his family of companions, his life and his dreams.

After picking them up the Trinity flies through the clouds above Eryu, making its way from the Southern district to the west. Within the ship, Fleur is placed in a cell located in the bottom portion of the Trinity. Her hands bound and eyes covered. Essa is also placed in the cell, but she isn't given the same treatment as Fleur.

Isolated from anyone or anything, Essa wakes up in a daze. She notices the comfort of the cell. The furnishings seem normal, with a small window looking out into the distance.

While Fleur remains unconscious on the bed at the other side of the cell, Essa looks around, and then a panic kicks in. She doesn't have her book. She realizes that when she fell it was not with her, despite her holding onto it so dearly.

As she shifts her bodyweight on the bed, she looks down at her waist and sees a red pouch that was not there before. Her hand touches it and she looks inside. Her heart bounces uncontrollably in her chest. Resting in the pouch is the book, somehow within its confines of space and size.

She closes the pouch and looks away, her eyes shaking. She looks around at the cell and wonders who has taken hold of her. Her fingers dart around one another, and she looks at the ground.

She sits back down and clenches the bed sheets. She looks within her pouch once more, a warm sensation runs across her fingers as she touches the binding of the book. Unable to explain the sense of relief, she gulps. No logic or form of reasoning can explain what she sees, how she feels, and why it's happening. But she refrains from speaking or thinking and merely embraces the fact that, for whatever reason, the book will remain with her.

She decides to lie down on the bed facing the window, embracing the sight of the cloudy night sky, the book resting at her side, out of sight. As she lets her mind drift, a question rises up within her and she says aloud, "The air did not seem as cold…how long have I been gone?"

Meanwhile in the Trinity, above the floor where the cell rests, is the main hallway that holds the rooms where the ship-members sleep. At one end is the kitchen with its own bar as well as booths to accommodate more than the existing crew members. The other end of the hall leads to a joint path, one way leading toward the next floor, where engineering, health and repair centres are set up, the other leading to the bridge where all of the crew members are currently.

They stand together in a circle while the ship is set to autopilot. Joining them is Paige, the pilot of the Trinity, and Rudy, the navigator as well as additional fire support. Paige has short brown hair and piercing blue eyes. She wears a white tank top with a black, unzipped jacket, along with blue jeans. Rudy has black hair tied back in a ponytail and wears glasses, as well as brown cargo pants and a white shirt. The two of them are not much for fashion.

Paige says, "So, we've caught Fleur finally, for good this time—I hope."

Gunther smiles, "With some extra baggage. It's nothing we can really explain right now. When we reach the rock we can settle everything."

"Well, as long as it doesn't pose an additional risk to my ship, Gunther." Paige says while poking him in the chest, "Because if it does, you'll be the first to hear about it."

"How about we change the topic of discussion to how Dexter, Baylee and Abigail managed to get taken out by a single person, shall we?" Gunther quickly directs the conversation to them.

Dexter mutters, "…That's so unfair"

Baylee sighs, "It's not our fault…"

Abigail says, "Happens to the best of us."

Tail remarks, "I can't remember it ever happening to me."

"Likewise." Sapphire says while crossing her arms.

Paige raises a hand to silence the others. She looks at Gunther firmly and says, "This is the last time we go on a goose hunt for Fleur. We have her and it's going to stay that way, otherwise just let her go. I'm fine with whatever you decide, but this is the last time we make that decision. I won't let my ship come into harm's way over foolish behavior."

Gunther grins with his childish expression.

She pokes him in the chest again and says, "No trouble, got it?"

"I promise, on my life, nothing weird will happen."

A loud thud rocks the Trinity and turns everyone's attention to the hood. They see, through the windows, a boy who's landed on their ship. He quickly slips downwards and his shirt is caught on a small piece of metal extruding from the ship. A piece that has, over time, begun to peel off and thus serves as a chance of luck.

A moment of silence ensues. They blink, stare, blink once more, and then take into context what's happening before their eyes. A boy is hanging from a piece of metal sticking out of the ship's body, a piece that hasn't been fixed due to the lack of time. Something weird is happening. Something which, moments ago, Gunther said would not take place. And it has—in a very odd way.

After another set of blinks, and thoughts about how unlikely it is for someone to remain on the hood of a moving spaceship, Paige rubs her forehead and then gives Gunther a quick look. She says, "I guess that's the extra baggage?"

He mutters, "Honestly…I have no idea what that's called…"

Sapphire says, "Maybe another one of those rifts in the air?"

Tail says, "We didn't see anything this time."

Sapphire replies, "We weren't looking."

With a shrug, Gunther starts to head towards the exit, "I'm going to go take a nap. Let me know when we've arrived at the rock. If the kid hasn't fallen off, he has a cell waiting for him." He gives a slight wave and leaves them all standing there, bewildered by the boy hanging onto the ship—a short boy with green messy hair.

***

Fifteen minutes pass and Kiyo still remains hanging on the hood of the Trinity, his expression far from happy. The ship begins to descend as it heads towards their destination, a small island that they call 'the rock.' Its size is quite small, with a sandy beach and palm trees. The rest of the island is taken by a large rock formation that has been tunneled into to form a base.

The Trinity lands on the beach of the small island and a set of doors open up to let the crewmembers out. Gunther, after being woken up from his nap, leaves the ship first, accompanied by the others. They head towards the front of the ship and see Kiyo fall down and into a tree. He falls through the branches and lands headfirst into a pile of sand.

He sits up and spits out the sand from his mouth. When he sees Gunther and the others walk towards him, he remains silent and on guard.

Gunther asks, "Who are you?"

He hesitates momentarily and then says, "I'm Kiyo, and you are?"

Gunther smirks, "I have no need to give you my name just yet. Why were you hanging from our ship these past fifteen minutes?"

"I fell from the sky…did you expect me to just let go of what was keeping me alive?"

Gunther grumbles, "The sky?" and turns and looks at Tail, "What's with all of these people falling from the damn sky?"

Tail shrugs.

Gunther thinks for a moment before asking Kiyo, "Do you have a friend with long red hair?"

Kiyo waits for a moment and then says slowly, "Depends."

Gunther muses, "Oh, on what?"

Kiyo points at him, "On who you are." His voice clearly agitated.

Tail grunts at the wise move of the short boy.

Gunther scratches his chin and then lets out a large sigh. He looks at Sapphire and says, "Care to handle this? I need another nap."

She frowns and says, "You just woke up."

He waves his hands upwards and says, "Well clearly it didn't do its job." He leaves them and heads towards their base located within the confines of a rock structure. Making his way there he says, "Might as well bring the two sleeping beauties along."

They venture into the base. The inside is chiseled down, creating smooth surfaces on the floor. Light fixtures hang from the ceiling, casting warmth over the cool rock surface. A main foyer serves as the focal point of the base. Tables and chairs are set up near a bar.

A staircase leads to a balcony overlooking the foyer; it has three rooms that anyone can use to gather some rest. Additionally, beneath the staircase, is the cell.

Kiyo enters the cell first and takes a seat on a bed. He stares intently to see Essa enter shortly after, a slight wobble in her step. He asks, "Are you alright?"

She nods her head and looks as Tail places Fleur on a bed and then leaves, closing the cell door behind him. For a moment, Kiyo and Essa simply look at each other. Words rush into her, a desire to apologize, hold him, anything to let him know how much it means to her that she's back.

She says, "Kiyo…I"

"Stop…I don't want to talk about it."

"O-okay…"

He digs his nails into his knees, "Where the hell are we?"

She shakes her head, "I don't know. When I came across them they were quick to subdue me. I think they are bounty hunters…or slavers."

Kiyo's ears perk, "Slavers?"

She runs her hand through her hair and says, "Ah, don't worry about that. Listen, things are…probably going to be very weird for you, as they were for me when I was in your world. So, feel free to ask me anything."

Kiyo looks at her intently before saying, "I'll probably just figure it out on my own."

"Whatever works."

His eyes wander over to Fleur as he asks, "Did you come across Leaf yet?"

Essa, now pacing in circles, says, "No, you are the first one I've come across."

He doesn't respond. He leans his back against the cool surface of the wall and stares upwards.

Essa takes a seat on the bed.

A voice beckons to them, "Well what in all matter of luck do we have here?"

Sitting up, Fleur looks in their direction, her eyes still covered and her hands clasped together. A smile faintly shows itself on her face. She licks her lips, those of a boy, and causes Kiyo to lower his brow as he tries to determine if she's a male or female.

Fleur says elegantly, "Would one of you care to remove this annoying blindfold?"

Essa says, "I don't think that's such a good idea."

Fleur grins, "What makes you say that dearest?"

"It's just a feeling…"

Fleur, her head now bobbling up and down as if she understands the feeling of the confused girl, says, "I have no ill intent toward fellow cellmates. I just want to see who I'm sharing this familiar place with."

Essa gulps, "So you've been here before?"

"Oh, countless times."

Kiyo says, "You aren't very good at staying away then, are you?"

Her head turns to look at him, a grin still plastered on her face, "Well, it's not every day I have something from the sky fall on me." Her head turns to Essa, "I think the least you can do is let me look at you."

Essa hesitates. She looks at Kiyo and he nods his head, motioning not to be afraid. She walks towards Fleur and leans in to take off the blindfold.

Fleur moves quickly, coming close to her neck. She takes a sniff and smiles, asking, "Who are you, girl?" as she looks up at her.

Essa removes the blindfold. "You can take a look for yourself."

Fleur's pink eyes blink. She frowns, "I see." She then looks at her surroundings, "This place—still as cheap as ever."

Essa takes a few steps back and Fleur watches intently. She stands up and looks down at her bound hands. She smiles, and they disappear.

Essa cries out, "What the hell!"

Fleur raises a finger to her lips, "Shhh, it's okay. I'm a woman with a lot of tricks up her—okay, his—sleeve." She lets out a laugh and hurries towards them, quickly grabbing a chair and spinning it around so she can sit on it, her arms resting on its back as she faces them. "So," she says, "do tell. Why on earth did you land on me?"

Essa's lips pucker up, "It's not like it was intentional."

Kiyo interrupts and asks, "Who are you? How are you able to make things just disappear?"

She looks at him and then lets out a long, loud sigh, "Fine…fine, listen. I'm a unique figure, and my lovely quality is illusions. I don't get tied up ever, I just make it seem that way. I have a soft spot for that man Gunther." She presses her head to her arms, "So from time to time I pay him and the rest a visit."

Essa asks, "So you deliberately get caught?"

Fleur smiles, "But never have I been knocked unconscious in the process."

Essa asks, "Why do they want to capture you so badly?"

"Well, naturally, it's because I am Fleur Godwin. A lovely lady who's got a bounty on her head for ten million. Why, you might ask? Well of course I'll tell you! It's because I've caused over five billion in damages to the Federation and stolen over twenty billion from banks. One might say I'm a hell of an entrepreneur!" She lets out a laugh.

"So the price on your head is very large…and Gunther is going to cash it in?"

"Oh," Fleur waves her hand, "he won't do that. He and the others know that they won't put me in harm's way. I sure as hell piss off their pilot, but I know better than to get on her bad side. So this is the last time I plan to fall into their hands."

"Why…would you…?"

"It's complicated history love."

Kiyo bluntly asks, "Are you a boy or a girl?"

Fleur winks at him and says, "Wouldn't you like to know. I'm a girl in a man's body. But, I am actually a woman. But that's also another story. And I really want to know about the two of you. So! Tell me— who do I have the pleasure of speaking to on this dreary night?"

Essa, having taken a seat on the bed says quietly, "Well…"

Fleur interrupts, "Are you suicidal? Because that's not the prettiest way out-"

"No!" Essa yells, "It's complicated."

Fleur frowns and says, "Complicated, huh? Well how about this. We make a trade? One question each—a special deal between cellmates. Then we can let one another speak and reveal themselves on their own terms, afterwards. What do you say?"

Listening to her voice full of elegant praise and silvery danger, Essa finds her hand slightly shaking. She holds it down with her opposing hand and looks at Fleur directly. She gulps and says, "Fine."

Fleur smiles and says, "Well, you first. Go on, ask away."

Essa thinks calmly. Her mind decides between crucial interests. She can either ask Fleur about the meaning behind being a woman in a man's body or she can figure out the relationship between her and Gunther, in hopes of maybe finding a way out of this cell. The decision comes quickly. "Your history with Gunther. I don't expect you to tell me everything. I certainly don't trust you. But I know you are the kind of person who will keep his—her—word about it. So, tell me one thing between the two of you."

Fleur genuinely smiles, admiring how Essa approached the situation and question. She says, "If it were not for me, he, as well as his friends, would be dead—or worse, slaves to a very cruel man. A man that also experimented on others and myself. People I care about. So, because I saved him, there's a bond that won't break." She points at Essa, "Now it's your turn to answer my question. Where did the two of you come from? And don't tell me the sky. There's more to it than that."

Essa says, "I…I don't think I can openly talk about it without sounding insane."

This catches Fleur's intrigue. She leans forward. "Darling, I've been called many things in my life, insane being one of them. I also know that it means…little. You'll realize a convict such as I will be more understanding than a person who's kept up in themselves so they can have a comfortable, normal, average life. So, I implore, tell me your secret."

Kiyo decides to answer on Essa's behalf. "We've come from a world of dreams. This place is where everything that exists is due to the collection of what humans dream about. I am from there, and my name is Kiyo. Essa, originally, is from here but, for unforeseen reasons, ended up in the dream world. Through the sacrifice of someone very…very close to me, we were able, along with three others, to enter a gateway that brought us back here to reality. So, now we are here… and I am unimpressed with what humans claim to be. Locking us up in a cell. Disgusting."

There's a moment of silence between the three of them. Fleur moves her right ankle around in circles. Essa waits to hear words of laughter and contempt—or even an accusation of lunacy. But no such thing occurs. Fleur merely raises her hand to her chin and tilts her head slightly. She says, "That's quite something…I'll believe you though. Since you spoke to me as an equal, a tone most cannot hold true when it's towards me, but most of all, your opinion on humanity…now that's…spot on. I have other questions, but I will keep my word. You both interest me greatly, don't be alarmed if I follow you to find your other secrets. To see what you mean by being a dream, and how one goes to and from such a place."

Essa says uncomfortably, "They aren't secrets. Just hard conversational topics."

Fleur laughs and says, "That's what a secret is."

CHAPTER FIFTEEN
Honesty or Death

A faint knock is heard on the wooden door that separates them from freedom. Fleur gets off of the chair, repositions it and then makes her way to her bed. She takes a seat and with a wink she creates an illusion of her being bound and blindfolded.

The door opens. Gunther looks over at Fleur who tilts her head and says, "Are you letting me free from this miserable place?"

"Not today." He looks over at Essa and Kiyo, "The two of you, come with me."

Fleur asks, "And of me?"

He scoffs, "Unlikely." As he directs Essa and Kiyo out of the cell and makes his way to the door, he turns and looks at Fleur, and says quietly, "Don't go running off just yet." He closes the door behind him.

They walk up a few steps and head towards a wooden table that's set up for them. Gunther takes a seat on the other side, and they sit down in the only two chairs on their end. Gunther leans in his chair and rubs his hand through his hair before placing it on the table gently.

Standing behind him are Sapphire and Tail, who both seem to look as threatening as Gunther does as he places his gun on the table. Kiyo's ears perk up.

Gunther says, "As you can see neither of you are bound. You can take that as a sign that we trust you. But we don't. What that actually says is that you can try whatever you want. You will fail and we will kill you. From this moment forward, the two of you will answer my questions. The quicker we finish, the better."

He closes his eyes and lets out a yawn.

Sapphire sighs.

Gunther continues, "Now, this is your chance to explain to us why we should let the two of you live. Don't waste it." His eyes rest on Essa, "Let's begin with you." She tenses up as he asks, "Did you come through that gateway in the sky?"

"Yes."

"Where did it connect to? Another planet?"

"It wasn't another planet...it was another, well, place. Look, nothing that we tell you is going to make much sense."

He pulls out a cigarette and lights it, inhaling and then exhaling. He says, "That's not for you to decide. Just answer my questions." He pauses and then says, "So you both know one another?"

Essa gulps and looks with anxiety at her predicament, "Yes."

Gunther nods his head. He asks, "How?"

Again, another question that Essa finds difficult to answer. She looks at the table, her head beginning to heat up as her heart races. She begins to feel her blood pulsate throughout her body. She feels the eyes staring at her.

"I asked how."

Essa looks at Kiyo from the corner of her eye. He remains firm, bloodlust beginning to show in his eyes. She sees the situation deteriorating. She either risks telling the truth and sounding like she's insane, telling a lie and risking death, or not saying a word and hoping that the gun stays on the table and not pointed at her head.

Her eyes tear up; Kiyo looks at her and his expression changes.

She decides she will risk telling the truth.

She closes her eyes and recounts the events that have led her to where she is. She thinks about the note her mom left, of her friends at school who went through hell to protect her. She thinks about falling through the sky and meeting Dusk and Hex. She thinks of the Nightmares, the mountain, and the woman who gave up her existence so she could return home.

Essa opens her eyes, and Gunther sees a fire in them. As the warm liquid runs down her face, her expression is that of a rock holding back a demon. She says, "I am from Eryu, the northern district. I was at my school when a massacre began to unfold. As I found myself trapped, I fell to what should have been my death. I ended up in another place. I ended up in a world of dreams. This place exists because of all of us, and that's where I met Kiyo. Now we are here."

Gunther frowns. He places one hand on the table closest to the gun.

Essa looks at it and then back at him. She says, "I am telling the truth."

Silence.

He replies, "Is that all? Is there no crucial element that played a role in you supposedly going to a world of dreams?"

Now Essa finds herself at yet another crossroad. She can either confess the information about the book she has in her possession or she can lie. The gun on the table causes her to think long and hard. She opens her mouth hesitantly. "There's…a book that…brought me there."

"Do you have this book on you?"

"…Yes."

"May I look at it?"

She opens her small red pouch.

Sapphire leans over to see, and is surprised by the book that Essa pulls out from it.

She places it on the table and slides it towards him. Gunther looks at it, places his hand on it and then opens it up carefully. She watches to see his expression, but it remains neutral.

He flips through the blank pages and then closes the book. He hands it back to her and says, "There are some interesting drawings you have in there."

Her face pales, "W-what?"

He says, "In your book, there's some interesting imagery on the first few pages. The rest are blank however."

Essa, her heart beginning to hurt from the strain, opens the book and sees on the first page, a drawing, so precise, that she feels like she is there. The scene is of Cassandra fighting a phantasm which, in this case, is also drawn. She turns the page, and sees a drawing of herself falling from the school's rooftop. On the third page is yet another drawing—this one of her sitting at the fire with Hex and Dusk. The fourth is of her running in the forest away from the Nightmares. The fifth, of the mountain. The sixth and final page shows Norma opening up the gateway.

Gunther says, breaking her from her trance, "If I were to believe you. I would be required to act upon the information given, and detain you." Her eyes widen. He continues, "But, even though a part of me believes what you're telling me, there's a lot that I know has yet to be said." He stands up and picks up his gun. He walks towards her and places the barrel against her head. Kiyo snarls but finds that he is being held down by shadows.

Shaking, Essa looks at Gunther. He says to her, "In my line of work, I put a bullet between the eyes of those I do not trust. I cut down those who pose a threat, and if there's sign of profit, I go for it. There's only one thing that stops me from acting on this impulse that has taught me to survive. It's more than a gut feeling, and it's a feeling I have only felt with one other person."

Essa quickly thinks about Fleur. Her eyes widen in worry. Gunther continues, "The feeling tells me that for whatever reason, I should ignore the logic and rules that I follow and instead, protect the clear sign of trouble sitting before me. It's telling me that even though by trading you in a lot of good can be done, that the possibility that something bad will happen is unacceptable. And so, by saying," he removes the gun from her head and waves it around, "that I do not believe you, I can then ask other questions, and move from being a captor to a kind and caring man, who may or may not choose to help you. So I have one simple question, and answer truthfully because I may change my mind. I want you to tell me your full name."

She looks at him carefully, bewildered and perplexed by the situation. She doesn't hesitate to answer and give him her full name. She says, "I am Essa Starlight, and don't you dare point that gun at me again."

The look on Gunther's face changes dramatically and swiftly. It shows that of a man in pain, of a man who's happy, of a man who's impressed, interested, and content. Gunther opens his gun and reveals that there are no bullets inside. He places it into his holster and says, "Well miss Starlight, you are the second anomaly in my life that will make me break my own rules. How may I be of service?"

"You can take me home."

He lets out a laugh and walks towards a railing separating them from the bar a few feet below. He looks off at the moonlight coming in through the holes in the rock, "I still need to ask a few questions before that, but this time so I can help you. Tail, you can let him go now."

The shadows that were binding Kiyo disappear. He cracks his knuckles and lets out an annoyed huff while Essa notices that neither Sapphire nor Tail have a heavy presence about them, and seem to be easing up incredibly fast.

Gunther says, "About three months ago, a school in the northern district had a massacre take place. More than fifty per cent of the students were found in pieces amongst the school grounds. No faculty members are reported to have lived, and four were reported missing. Rumor has it that a man in a black cloak was responsible. Is this the school you attended?"

Essa's eyes shake. She says, "It sounds...like it, but three months, that just can't be right. I have only been gone for a few hours...or a few days...but not three months."

"Hm, well, the north district near the school is a ghost town now. Many parents moved away or have locked themselves up. The security has also risen, though, it's not like the security is all that impressive around here anyways."

Essa, still fixated on the time, says, "Three months ago. I...I...it was…. how long was it…" Essa looks at her fingers and tries to count the days, "Five…no four…wait…maybe five…it couldn't have been any longer than five days…where did…no…that's impossible. There's no way three months have passed since then! I need to go home now. My mother…I need to find her. Maybe she's home and has been wondering where I've been…"

Sapphire says, "Listen, we understand that three months can come as a shock. But if you need to return home, then you will."

Gunther hums, "Yes, don't fret. When the morning arrives I will accompany you home and you can answer the other questions I have for you. For now, you are both free to do as you wish."

Kiyo grumbles, "What is there to do here?"

Gunther, the cigarette in his mouth practically gone, takes it and drops it. He points to the bar, "Drinks, night sky, sleep."

Kiyo replies, "Sounds dull."

Gunther says, "When members of the Trinity spend time on the rock, we tend to drink and dance. Of course, we do that everywhere. There are rooms above the stairs if you wish to sleep. We will be here if you need us."

With the conversation now over, Kiyo and Essa leave Gunther and the others. They head up the stairs. As they reach the top, they look down to see Dexter dancing with Abigail and Baylee, while Gunther wraps his arms around Paige, looking at her lovingly, while her hands are pressed against his chest. Over at the bar, both Rudy and Tail sip on some beverages that Sapphire serves them.

They head into one of the available rooms and close the wooden door behind them. The hinges screech, needing to be oiled.

An opening in the rock forms a window that lets fresh salty air enter the room. It looks out toward the sea, with only a set of palm trees blocking out the view on the farthest sides.

Essa places a hand on the ledge. She asks, "Do you hate me Kiyo?"

He looks at her. After a moment he says, "No, I understand why Norma did what she set out to do… I just wish she didn't. She was like a mother to me. Giving that up is hard, to the point that just thinking about it angers me. I can't hate you for that though—it was her decision. Once I find some Nightmares, or some bad people that I can tear apart, I should be a little better."

Essa thinks about what it would be like to give her own mother up and wonders how she would feel. She says, "I hope we find the others soon."

"I just want to find Leaf." He looks up at the moon and asks, "What do you plan to do once you return home?"

Essa leans forward, "I haven't thought about it…right now you are all that's been consistent for me in what's been apparently three months. So I just want us to stick together until we find the others."

"Alright." Kiyo shuffles a little, "Essa, I have a question."

"Yes?"

"…Humans…this place… To me it feels like there's a lot of hostility. Like the world isn't meant to be safe. It feels like it's only natural for so many Nightmares to sprout. Is it like this everywhere?"

She looks at her hands and says, "Kiyo, in this world…there's honesty, and there's death." She looks at him, "And often times, honesty is death in itself. I'm sure there are good people and good places, but… I'm still looking for a perfect place."

Essa listens to the music coming from the foyer—a mixture of techno and old-fashioned tunes compiled together. "I think I'm going to try and catch some sleep…I can't remember the last time I slept…" She goes and lies down on a bed and looks over at Kiyo. He sits down and stares at the floor. She asks, "Are you able to?"

He looks up at her, "I can't. I've never even seen a person slumber. I'm neither accustomed to the night or the day. It's just shades of light and dark in my eyes that pass by while I share the company with others. I don't know why…and I don't know how…but the darkness here is cold and depressing…I sort of understand how you humans fear." He pauses, flexing his hands and looking down at his fingertips. Connecting his eyes with hers, he says, "Just sleep. I'll be here when you wake up." He pulls his legs up and lies against the wall, his eyes now looking out at the sea.

The night takes Essa and leaves Kiyo alone with the sound of music and laughter. But that too dies out as the hours pass. Left in a world where few remain awake, he sits alone, for the first time without Leaf.

CHAPTER SIXTEEN
Mother

The night passes and morning comes. Essa wakes up fidgeting and a little restless after having slept for the first time in months—three months. She rubs her eyes and looks around only to see that Kiyo isn't in the room. Becoming a little uneasy, she leaves the room and quickly rushes down the stairs. She looks to see if anyone is in the foyer but it's empty. So she leaves the confines of the base and walks out onto the beach. There she sees everyone set up in chairs overlooking the water while they casually drink alcoholic beverages.

"Hey, Essa!" Gunther calls out, "Why don't you come on over and have a drink?" he asks in an outgoing manner.

She holds back a frown; the thought of the gun barrel against her head crosses her mind. "Uh no thank you." she says earnestly as her eyes desperately search for Kiyo. She breathes a sigh of relief when she sees him lying in a canopy that's set up between two palm trees.

Sapphire says warmly, "It's going to be a long day. There's water here."

"Oh, alright then…" Essa walks over and takes a seat next to Sapphire, who hands her a glass with water to the brim and ice cubes dancing around in circles. Essa looks at the water and hesitates before taking a sip.

Dexter says, "It's not poisoned." He walks over and pours himself a glass and gulps it down. She looks at him and then takes a sip of her drink. The cool water splashes against her dry throat and chips away at her frustration and exhaustion that's built up over her journey thus far.

She watches Dexter run off into the water to go swimming with Abigail and Baylee. Despite being in their mid-twenties, they enter a splash battle with giggles. Essa then turns her attention towards Gunther and Tail. Her interest is caught by the fact Tail's hood is up, covering his face. So she asks, "Aren't you hot wearing that?"

Tail looks over at her and then back at the water, "It blocks the sun." He says in an protective manner.

"But, the sun is good for you, gives a tan."

"On the contrary, it gives skin cancer. I can bear with a little heat, child."

"I'm not a child."

"How old are you?"

"18."

"Then you are a child." He states impassively.

Gunther laughs, and Essa gives up with the impression that Tail is one for having an answer to shut down any conversation. She moves her gaze to the water and lets her mind float away for a few moments before asking Gunther, "I want to go home, is there a way of getting there from here?"

He nods his head, "There is a way, yes. Are you a strong swimmer?"

"No, not really."

"I guess sharks wouldn't help that much either."

Essa taps her finger on her chair and grumbles. "Then what are my options?" She asks.

Gunther places his hands behind his head and leans back in his chair. "Simple, I take you and your friend on my little baby."

"…Little baby?"

Tail takes a sip of his drink and looks at his empty glass, "He's talking about the miniature ship aboard the Trinity. We use it to fetch supplies when landing the Trinity becomes a risk not worth taking.

Naturally, he calls it his baby."

Essa asks, "How is that natural?"

Tail explains, "It's natural for an idiot I suppose, I can't explain it myself."

"Alright, that's enough" Gunther waves his hands and turns in his chair to face Essa. "We can head off in an hour once everything is prepared. I'll take you home and drop you off with your friend and then we will go our seperate ways. Before that however, I may have a few questions, so I would like for you to answer them. Oh, and don't tell anyone about our business; bounty hunters aren't all that adored by the crowd, let alone the Federation."

Essa says, "You get me home and you'll be the farthest thing from my mind," indifferent to his circumstance.

"That's a tad cold. Tail must be rubbing off on you already." Gunther grins and looks up at the clear blue sky, "I say, it doesn't look like we have any worries, a clear sky, a destination that's only a few hours away by ship. It's going to be a good day."

The hour passes relatively fast. The miniature ship known as the Ember is set up and ready to launch. Essa and Kiyo take a seat within the Ember and look out the window to see Gunther talking with his crewmembers. They see Dexter laugh and pat Gunther on the shoulder. Abigail and Baylee give him a hug. Paige kisses him on the lips. Sapphire nods. All the while, Tail remains in his chair, impassive and silent.

"They are like a family in an odd sort of way, don't you think?" Essa asks Kiyo while she gently admires what's unfolding in front of her.

Kiyo says, "I guess so, though now that I think about it I only know a few of their names."

"…That's true, isn't it…I think I'll ask him when he comes back."

Essa continues to look outside the window and see Gunther chat with his companions. A minute passes and he gives a final wave and turns towards the Ember. He walks into the ship and takes a seat in the cockpit. He stretches and then starts hitting away at the buttons. Gunther turns to look at Essa and Kiyo, and asks, "We will be going now, are you both all set?"

Kiyo says with a yawn, "Yup."

Essa says, "As ready as I'm going to be."

Gunther nods his head and the Ember starts to rise from the beach. He looks down as the ship drifts around in the sky. He sees his companions all standing together, talking and laughing. Essa notices a sincere smile on his face.

The Ember rises high into the clouds and heads towards the main capital of Eryu. But the quiet and relaxing journey soon becomes riddled with dark clouds. They become dense and thick, forcing Gunther to lower the Ember. He fidgets a little in his seat. A rumble of thunder can be heard overhead.

He grumbles, "This is strange, this weather came out of nowhere…"

Essa pays close attention and silently agrees. The change in weather is abrupt and bothers her. Soon the water below disappears and the top of trees can be seen. As the sky darkens further and removes the direct rays of sunshine, they start to go over the Southern district's convict area.

Essa asks, "So Gunther, what's your last name?"

His eyebrows raise, "Oh? What does it matter?"

"It matters a great deal." She replies, "I find that people who don't give their full name are hiding something. It's indirect and I don't like it."

"Alright, alright, fair point. My last name is Blaze."

"What about the other two?"

"Sapphire and Tail? Sapphire's last name is Freestone; Tail's would be, let's see, oh yes, now I remember, his last name is Ryker. And if you are wondering about the rest I can go into detail."

Essa looks out at the gloomy clouds, "You might as well. It'll kill time."

Gunther laughs, "It will kill time eh, fine. Dexter's last name is Keating, as for the sisters Abigail and Baylee, their last name is Fletcher. As for Paige, hers is…" he pauses for a moment, thinking deeply, "Shit, good thing she isn't here. Okay, I think it's Hudson. Oh, and Rudy's is easy, it's Black. Does that satisfy your curiosity?"

"Yes, thank you."

The Ember slows down and lowers itself even closer to the Southern district. More thunder rings throughout the sky, causing the ship to shake. A flicker of lightning goes off in the distance and strikes a building.

Another one echoes off in the distance, its light branching off through the clouds like branches on a tree, moving freely and organically. Gunther says with slight alarm in his voice, "This weather is becoming fickle."

He takes a drastic turn that catches Essa and Kiyo by surprise. Another bolt of lightning erupts.

Essa asks, "That would have hit us, wouldn't it? How did you know it was going to strike there?"

"I didn't. I just realized I don't particularly want to go through the Central district when we are this close to the ground."

"Wait, so then if you hadn't decided at that moment we would have been struck?"

"Yup!"

Kiyo asks, "How much time will this add to the journey?"

"Hm, I'd say another hour or two at most. This ship is fairly fast, but this weather is going to impede the progress we can make. At least we aren't going by foot or ground transportation. It would take days if we were doing that. And now I have time to ask questions."

Lightning begins to go off steadily, lighting up the clouds with yellow and orange glares. The Ember shakes once more when a loud bang of thunder rocks above them. Rain starts to poor down and the windows start to fog up from the difference in temperature.

Essa asks, "What is it you want to know?"

Gunther replies, "I have just one thing lingering on my mind. Don't you find it odd that a gateway can be opened up from the dream world to here? Don't you think that's dangerous? What if Nightmares come spilling out of some pervert's imagination? If a thing such as that is even possible. It's really, a big…interesting topic."

Kiyo says, "You don't need to worry about that. The gateway has a heavy toll, and no one on the other end is going to be taking that expense upon themselves anytime soon."

"And one last thing, sorry. Where are the friends you came with? If you came through the same gateway, why did the two of you drop at different times?"

Kiyo remains silent. Essa says, "We don't know…"

Gunther looks at the rearview mirror and sees their expressions. As another loud bang of thunder goes off, louder this time, he groans and then freaks out.

A male body falls through the air, clothes drenched from the rain. It moves past the Ember and descends quickly into a set of mist.

Essa recognizes that it's Dusk and yells at Gunther to descend.

Gunther says, "Bloody hell, you kids fall from the sky often or what!" he pushes forward with all of his might and the Ember drops on a ninety-degree angle. "Paige will kill me if she finds out how I am piloting this!"

Essa yells louder than he, "Stop worrying about Paige, I'll kill you if we don't save him!"

Falling through the mist at a dangerous rate, unable to see through the darkness and losing the reliability of the limited navigation systems, Gunther relies solely on his eyesight to which he is straining. He curses underneath his breath, "Damn it, where is this brat?"

"Come on, hurry! We need to catch him!"

"Look I'm trying my best here but I don't see him. We are going to die at this rate, and we have no damn way of getting him inside the Ember while in midflight!"

Essa screams, "Does it look like I care!?

"You should you crazy girl!"

Kiyo looks at the ceiling of the ship and inspects the corners. He asks, "Is there a way to detach the ceiling?"

Gunther bites on his lip, "No, it's not much of a convertible. Why? What are you suggesting?"

Kiyo says with a hint of skepticism, "If we remove the ceiling and are able to pass Dusk, we can then change the angle of the pod and he can land inside."

Essa remarks, "That's a good idea."

Gunther says, "No, absolutely not, that's a horrible idea. First, that will mean damaging the Ember, a priceless pod I might add, and that will only anger Paige. Second, not only will she be angry but my life will be forfeit. Third, you just have to think logically, that boy will simply splatter on impact. All that blood, just thinking about it. You know who's going to have to clean it up? I will! Hey, are you listening to me?" He turns his head and his jaw drops.

"Sorry." Kiyo says, as the ceiling flies off of the ship and a gust of wind sends waves of rainwater into the Ember. Essa raises an arm to cover her eyes from the rain as her clothes become drenched from the piercing drops. Kiyo slams his fingers through a wall and balances himself as the Ember continues to descend.

The mist clears briefly and they are able to spot Dusk. His body continues to fall, but slows down as it spins. Essa asks, "Why isn't he conscious?"

Gunther points out, "Neither of you seemed to be all that aware of your surroundings from what I recall."

Suddenly, a second body flies past the Ember with white wings on its back.

Kiyo remarks, "Oh…I recall just fine…stupid piece of shit ship."

Gunther asks, "What was that?"

Essa screams, "Hex!"

He falls forward with his wings tucked in for maximum speed. His eyes set on Dusk as he reaches out to grab him. The angel swoops past him and wraps his arms around him, immediately opening his wings and changing their direction. Dusk slowly opens his eyes and feels warmth spread through him while the cold rain slams against his body. Hex looks at him and asks, "Are you alright?"

"You saved me just now, didn't you?" His eyes close and open as he tries to gain his bearings.

Hex says attentively, "Why of course, that is what angels do."

Dusk coughs, "Essa…might be a tad jealous on the free fall save."

They land on the ground and Hex gently places Dusk on his feet.

He watches as he pulls himself together, and then Dusk places a hand on Hex's shoulder and says, "I guess I owe you one." Dusk looks around and then up at the sky to see the intense thunderstorm. The rain hits his face and causes him to squint. "I'm finally back home."

He wipes the rain from his face and looks over at Hex. "I never really noticed but you stand out with that white get-up you have going on, especially with the wings."

"I suppose that's an issue worth noting. For now I will simply keep my wings out of sight." Hex has his wings disappear. "So, Dusk, now that we are back to your world-" he is interrupted as the Ember appears above them and makes an abrupt landing. Dusk turns to look at the worn out miniature ship.

The doors open and Essa comes running out. "Essa!" Dusk remarks, and then smiles at the sight of her, "It's good to see you are alright."

She jumps and wraps her arms around him. He's slightly embarassed by her enthusiastic embrace, yet he doesn't stray from it. He returns the warmth. The rain continues to fall and bounce off of their shoulders. Kiyo walks out of the ship and leans against the door. Gunther stands behind him and asks, "That one had wings, did he not?"

Kiyo turns and looks at him, "Starting to believe our story now?"

Gunther huffs and looks over at the three of them now heading towards the Ember.

Essa looks at Hex, "So you let me fall but Dusk you'll catch?"

The angel grins, "It's nice to see you as well." His eyes move over to the small ship in front of them. "What happened here?"

Gunther raises an eyebrow, "Eh? You mean the Ember," he points at Kiyo, "you can thank this one. He thought we'd be able to catch Dusk in the air."

Hex says, "That would have surely crushed him on impact."

Kiyo grumbles, "Stupid angel."

Hex replies, "I see you also made it. Where is the other one?"

Essa replies, "We still haven't come across Leaf yet. We were hoping you would have."

"No, sorry."

Gunther says, "Well, I assume the two of you are with Kiyo and Essa so you might as well come inside the Ember. Not that that will do much in preventing the rain from soaking our clothes."

He lets them all pass through the door and closes it behind him. He stands tall and looks at the newcomers in his ship. Dusk takes a seat along the wall where a small portion of the ceiling remains, limiting the amount of rain from hitting him. Essa sits beside him. Kiyo stands against the wall with one leg raised behind him, foot pressed against it. Hex stands in the middle with little care about the lack of roof overhead.

The Ember rises into the air, Gunther says, "So, still taking you home Essa?"

"Yes please."

"Friends included?"

Hex asks, "Is there a problem?"

Gunther says, "Well, are your wings dreamt of or are you an angel? Because otherwise I'm simply perplexed by how everything is turning out. I'm only bringing Essa home and then I will be on my way. I don't care where it is you have in mind, you will be going with her or not going at all."

"You talk a lot."

"You don't talk enough."

Dusk asks, "What am I missing?"

Kiyo replies, "Gunther here is an ass, and now he feels guilty so he's doing us a favor."

"Look," Gunther says defensively, "I'm not an ass. Now, while I still get used to the fact that not one, not two, not even three, but four people have fallen from the sky, I just can't help but sense that something off-putting is going on. And I want nothing to do with it, alright? That's my decision—I want no part in this. It's not worth it."

Hex lets out a slight sigh and looks over at Essa and Kiyo. Essa fidgets in her seat and Kiyo looks the other way. Hex says, "I care little about what's gotten you to ramble on. Indeed we have come from the sky. Now if you don't mind, we will keep our business to ourselves. But if it's of no trouble we will travel with Essa to her home, alright?"

"Alright." Gunther takes a seat in the cockpit and raises a thumb up, "Then with no more delay, let's get going." With that he refrains from talking, and focuses on the flight.

The ship makes its way out of the Southern district and through the Western district. Dusk and Essa look at their homeland and remain quiet. Hex stands beside Kiyo and the two of them look up at the sky. The clouds continue to block out the sun. The pounding of the rain becomes less noticeable and in time they all tune it out.

As time and distance pass, the five wander off into their own thoughts respectively. The bond that has started to connect the dots continues to grow as new faces join. Dusk feels a void in his heart grow slightly in the absence of his one and only. Essa in turn feels her heart grow with the notion that she's actually on a journey instead of hiding in obscurity and fear. Hex wonders what is required of him and where he must go, and if the things he saw in the gateway matter in some way, shape or form. Kiyo wonders where Leaf is, and Gunther ponders over the cost of the ceiling.

As their minds all wander and reflect, they enter the Northern district; the home of both Dusk and Essa. Where everything began. It's nostalgic for them in different ways. So much so that, through thinking over it, Essa turns to Dusk and asks, "Is this where you were born and lived as well?" to which he replies with a nod and a slight smile. She can see a light in his eyes masking the pain further beneath it. She doesn't ask about it, or about Sarah. Essa chooses to focus on her own goal for now, in hopes that when she arrives home she can finally wrap her arms around her mom and cry so that everything can go back to normal. And that's where another fear waits for her—does she want things to go back to the way they were, before she met the others? The thought troubles her.

Her eyes widen as the surroundings become familiar and she recognizes the set-up of the trees, the angle of the roads, and the height of the buildings. She says, "My house, it's right over there!" The excitement takes hold of her and she points wildly at her neighborhood.

They all look and eventually spot her house. A large oak tree rests on her front lawn and its height surpasses that of the two-story building. The Ember lands on the street. Everyone exits and steps onto Essa's property. She quickly rushes towards the front door. Hex and Kiyo follow her relatively fast. Gunther looks at the exterior of the house for a moment while Dusk looks around to see if he recognizes the neighborhood.

Essa reaches the door and, as her hand reaches out, she stops momentarily. The thought of being gone for three months rushes through her mind. She shakes her head and then quickly opens the front door without pondering over why it isn't locked. She walks into her house and yells out, "Mom!" she runs into the foyer and turns to look in the kitchen. She sees a kettle brewing on the stove. Her eyes lighten up. "Mom, I'm home! Where are you!" she yells anxiously. The others walk into the house silently and wait for Essa to reunite with her mother.

Her heartbeat starts to rise. She runs into the foyer once more and then heads down the hallway, "Mom!" she starts to panic. A set of footsteps can be heard from above. Essa stops and turns to look at the others, "She's here!" she runs upstairs and as she reaches the second floor, she stops.

What she sees doesn't relax her. It doesn't bring her joy or happiness. The person standing in front of her is someone she knows, but isn't her mother. Essa, her voice wavering, asks, "What are you doing here…Cassandra?" She takes a step backwards, "Where's my mom…" she moves down the stairs, distancing herself.

The dimly lit hallway casts a shadow over Cassandra's presence. She takes a step towards Essa. Essa screams, "Where is she?!" as a flash of lightning goes off outside, piercing the hallway with light.

Cassandra looks straight into Essa's eyes, and says softly "Essa…"

Essa runs down the stairs and into the living room. The emptiness brings her to her knees. She places her hand against the living room table and takes a seat on the couch. Cassandra walks down the stairs and tightens her grip on the railing. She sees Hex looking up at her from the bottom. She asks, "You are?"

"I should be asking you that. Essa never mentioned anyone else living with her, and you are certainly not old enough to be her mother."

Another crack of lightning goes off, followed by a loud roar of thunder. The tension begins to build between Cassandra and Hex. The others stand behind him, filling up the hallway.

"There is a lot that needs to be said. My name is Cassandra, and the last time I saw Essa she was falling off a rooftop."

Dusk asks, "Wait, you were there?"

"Yes, along with a few others. I assume she's talked about it… Well, it's been three months since then. And I was beginning to think I would never see her again. So if anyone is a little startled right now, it's me."

Gunther, deciding to take part in the conversation, asks, "Yet, you are in her house?"

Dusk frowns, "Three months…what's going on?" He looks at Hex. The angel merely shakes his head.

Cassandra says, "I'll explain. Let's go into the living room." She walks down the steps, past Hex and into the room, temporarily defusing the hostile encounter. They all look at one another briefly before agreeing to follow her and take seats around Essa, whose eyes seem lost in thought.

"Where is my mother?" Essa looks up angrily at Cassandra, "and why are you in my house?" The mixture of emotions is evident in Essa's voice. Gunther feels a little uneasy and tries to find a more comfortable position on the couch opposite Essa. He rests one leg upon the other and places his right arm on the back of the couch.

Cassandra places her hands together, "There's one more person who ought to be here shortly, and then I will explain everything, I promise."

The frustration can be seen boiling up on Essa's brow, but she doesn't protest. Moments later, the front door opens and can be heard from the living room. Kiyo turns his head to see a male walk in wearing black jeans and a black long sleeve shirt with the buttons open revealing his chest.

Essa looks at him and then back at Cassandra. "Tell me, before I lose it, why are you and Spike in my house, boiling a kettle like its normal and looking at me with pity!"

Spike places himself against the wall. Neither Kiyo nor Hex are able to take their eyes off him—looking at him closely to determine if he's a threat. Dusk elbows Hex, catching his attention. The angel looks away from Spike and then towards Essa. Kiyo turns his curiosity towards Cassandra.

Cassandra says, "Essa, about your mother." Another flash of lightning goes off followed by silence.

After all of the hardship and struggles, the pain and loss, the mishap and interesting play of events, Essa finally gets to find out what matters most.

Cassandra pauses briefly, her eyes look around the room, at the brown rug on the hardwood floor, at the drapes and curtains covering the large windows, at the chandelier hanging from the ceiling, until nothing else can hold her attention, she says with no sign of emotion, with words that are heavy and cold, "She's dead."

CHAPTER SEVENTEEN
It Goes Back

Those two words leave Essa in silence. The others feel the hair on their necks rise. Spike crosses his arms, feeling uncomfortable. Gunther clenches his fist.

Essa asks very quietly, "H-how…did she die?" Already fighting the urge to burst into frantic tears and say it's a lie.

Cassandra, searching for the the right words, says, "Your mother's been dead for seventeen years Essa."

Essa asks in disbelief, "What the hell are you talking about…?"

"Essa, there's a lot I'm about to tell you, but before I do… I need you to tell me a few things so that I can truly give you the proper answers. I need to know where you've been these last three months and how you found your way back here."

The sound of concern in Cassandra's voice throws Essa further into confusion and despair. "Where I've been? Who the fuck cares where I've been!" She yells hysterically, "Tell me what happened to my mother!"

Hex and Dusk both recall the scene they witnessed when Essa was full of rage and pain in her room. With an apparent disconnect from the person they know, a new side of her personality is revealing itself right in front of their eyes.

Cassandra, finding it hard to continue, looks at Spike. He nods his head, letting her know that it's alright to continue her approach. She looks back at Essa and says, "I will tell you everything you need to know Essa, I promise. But I need to know where you have been, up until now."

Essa digs her nails into her legs and glares at her, "I've been stuck in the sky for all I god damn know. I was there for a day! Not three months! I.I…What is going on…How could she be dead for seventeen fucking years!" she places her hands to her head and rocks herself back and forth.

Cassandra says, "Essa…"

Essa screams, "Fuck you and your questions!"

Seeing the situation deteriorate, Gunther clears his throat and says, "I uh…might have worn out the question card. So, for Essa's sake, stop darting around and tell her what she needs to hear."

Dusk says, "I can vouch for her, I was also there."

Hex says, "Indeed, so was I, as well as Kiyo over there."

Cassandra looks at them knowing she needs to hurry and tell Essa everything, she says, "In the sky? Explain."

Hex isn't fond of how she asks, so he ignores her.

Dusk sighs and says, "There's a world that's… well… It exists because of humans. The way Essa arrived is different from how we did, but I was there when she fell from the sky. It was sudden and random, but she certainly was there. And I think it has something to do with the book she has in her possession. But…I don't see how this has anything to do with her mother…"

"The book?" Cassandra looks at Essa.

Spike says, "I think you ought to explain about the loss of her mother more carefully. Don't stray from the topic…not now."

Cassandra, feeling a little ashamed, redirects her full attention to Essa, "I'm sorry…Essa, the reason I ask is because… and this will come as a shock…" she pauses, "you suffer from a disorder that has kept you from reality. So much so that you believed your mother was alive to this day. We thought your disappearance was due to an intense episode from the shock of what happened at school…all of those deaths… we were sure that it put you into an episode. But your disappearance…after we failed to protect you, and you vanishing like that… we didn't know what to think."

Essa looks at her in disgust and begins shouting frantically, "I have a disorder? WHERE IS MY MOTHER! TELL ME WHAT HAPPENED TO HER OR I SWEAR TO GOD I WILL RIP YOUR THROAT OUT."

Cassandra stands up and shouts, "ESSA!" startling even herself with the volume of her voice, she lowers it before continuing, "do not threaten me. Let me explain. I will tell you about you and your mother." She sits back down, "Essa, when you were only one year old, your father was found dead in his office in the central district. Your brother went missing the same day—he was supposed to be visiting him there. Soon after, your mother, stricken by grief, fell ill and passed away. All of this shock, of the only faces you know disappearing, put you into…a rare phenomenon. Children can forget events, but certain ones stick, and this was enough to cause you, from the age of one, to block out the truth."

Hex asks, "How are you aware of this? If she was but a child, then so were you, how would you know, or even care about Essa?"

She replies, "My mother was close with Essa's mother, and so she took her in. When I became old enough to understand, and having grown up with Essa, I took it upon myself to help out—look over her. Do what I could in any way possible—as time went on and as we grew older, I realized that no matter what I did…Essa would forget key things the following day, such as who I was, or where she spent her time."

Essa, unable to find words in her disbelief, looks hopelessly at Cassandra as she continues.

"Eventually, with the help of a few others, we saw fit to place Essa back in her home, here, where she grew up. It never sold, because…a man with a lot of power saw to it that it remained hers and hers alone. So Essa lived on her own from the age of 12 onwards. From then on

I, along with the help of Spike and even Tabatha, as well as a few other students who grew to care for Essa, took turns in ensuring she was safe. We would make her food like a mother would, leave notes, and ensure the house was clean and so forth."

Essa says quietly, "This is a fucking joke…there's no way any of this is true. I've seen my mother with my own two eyes on countless occasions!"

"That was you projecting her…it's a part of the trauma."

"A part of the trauma! I can distinctly remember Tabatha being a cruel bitch!"

"She took that role upon herself…because the only thing that would help you remember anything is minor trauma…but all of this changed a few days before you disappeared. You began to keep your memory Essa."

Essa, beginning to rock herself back and forth, places her hands to the side of her head and clenches her hair, "I just can't accept this lunacy…I can't."

Cassandra looks down at her hands and says, "Because you put so much mental capacity in conjuring up your mother…you would forget everything that wasn't essential to survival. Your friends from one day became strangers the next. But we always looked after you, in hopes that one day you would be able to keep your memories, and you finally have…we just don't know how."

You could feel the tension in the air, a discomfort for everyone, and an utter hell for Essa, sitting there facing a truth that seems so far-fetched. Essa begins to wonder if there are any memories she has, and when nothing comes to mind, she shakes further.

Gunther decides to ask, "How did you make all of this possible for her? If she was just a child I can understand your mother taking her in, but I don't see how you kept her house, and even had her attend a school with a bunch of students. I also disaprove with you having put her in smaller traumatic situations."

Spike, speaking for the first time says, "Tabatha…hated what she had to do, but it was the only thing that worked. For every moment she was cruel, a slight improvement was shown in Essa. She was able to remember small, positive exchanges from previous days that she would normally forget all together."

Cassandra says, "As for how we made it possible. I guess Essa can thank the president of Eryu, the man her father worked for, Alex Inker."

Essa grinds her teeth, "I won't thank a soul for this, and for this curse you are deciding to reveal to me. I...need my mom...I need her...to come back." Tears begin to stream down from her eyes, her voice quivering with sorrow, "how am I supposed to believe in anything you say to me? How am I supposed to believe in anything?"

Cassandra speaks softly, "Look into my eyes. What you will see is the love and adoration of a friend and a guardian." Essa looks up at her. Cassandra continues, "We would never lie or make you cry unnecessarily. We've tried to tell you the truth multiple times...but it wouldn't work. Whenever we tried to tell you, you would revert and lock yourself up in your room. In those moments you were aware, but the grief, so strong, would cause you to forget...but you were never like this, you never argued in disbelief, this time is different."

Spike says, "We introduced ourselves to you each day, hundreds—thousands—of times. And then, one day, the day of the massacre, you seemed different. Your mom was missing, she wasn't there, and your mindset was changing. You were retaining information. You were starting to remember us."

Essa's eyes shake, "The day the book fell. A few days before the massacre...I can remember..."

Cassandra says, "Whatever it is, however you got it, either by fate or random chance, or even by direct influence, your mind isn't sick anymore. You remember us."

Essa says, "This...doesn't make any sense." Her eyes wide, stretching the skin. The fear and disgust overwhelming her as her body shakes furiously. "To tell me my mom's dead, that I forgot who you two were everyday, that people like Tabatha were what, my friends? You label all that treatment as friendship!" She screams hysterically. "And this book is the reason for my memory returning?" She opens up her pouch and pulls it out, "This stupid book!" she hurls it across the room.

Cassandra winces. She then replies, "One of the most effective ways for your memories to carry over to the following day is mistreatment…for your sake…it's not a lie, Tabatha and others took on that roll. Some of them enjoyed it…that's true, but Tabatha hated it, hated herself, but did it so you might remember her, someone else or something the next day. There's been many of us who have been with you, in that school and the one before it."

Essa bursts into tears. Cassandra jumps from her chair and wraps her arms around her. Kiyo stands up along with Dusk and Hex. They all refrain from moving closer, not sure if she needs the space or not.

Dusk says to Hex, "This is messed up."

Kiyo remarks, "A Nightmare if you ask me."

Cassandra says, "We have, and always will, be here for you…and even if you forget us tomorrow, we will be with you. Because that's our duty as a friend, because we love and cherish you."

Essa pushes away from her, a tear rolling down her face. Spike looks, clenching his jaw. The others look at the apparent truth that came out of nowhere—the change in events. They can't help but feel sad for her.

Essa says, "I won't deny that in my heart you both mean something to me…but I cannot…I won't accept this." She stands up, turns around and leaves the room.

Gunther decides to ask, "Seeing as how you two nitwits just hit her with a load of world breaking shit, do you think she will retain her memory? Perhaps, she retained her memory because the people at the school where you all went were massacred. But oh, it must be the book right?"

Spike replies loudly, "What's it to you, huh? It doesn't explain the regaining of her memory prior. Her noticing her mother's absence was a sign she was getting better before that took place."

Gunther looks at him in annoyance, gets off from the couch and picks up the book. He says, "Have any of you actually looked inside of this book? Because I have and I don't see how it could be the source of her memory returning. So the way I see it, you just fucking risked a whole lot on a theory. Say she was getting better—maybe this will throw her back over the edge."

Spike walks towards him angrily and grabs him by the collar, "Again, who do you think you are?"

"Simple, I'm the man with my gun pointed directly at the one spot you care deeply about, and here's a hint, it's not your friendship."

Spike looks confused and then looks down to see the barrel pointed at a particular spot.

Kiyo lets out a slight laugh that causes everyone to look at him. He leans forward on the couch and says, "The way I see it is the risk has already been taken. You humans sure are thick in the head."

"Just let her rest." Dusk pleads.

The others all take their seats once more and remain silent. A room full of strangers accompanied by the sound of rain pattering against the windows as the only distraction.

Finally Spike asks, "So what are you, if you're not human?"

Kiyo replies, "Me? When did I ever state I'm not human?"

"Another world, sort of creates that label."

Kiyo smiles, "Fine. I'm your dream."

Dusk lets out a sigh, "Kiyo here is from the dream world. Where Essa, Hex and I were. He's formed from human dreams coming together."

Spike replies, "I find that hard to believe."

Kiyo grunts, "Yet you had confidence in stating I'm not human."

Hex says, "You expect Essa to believe in what you have to say about her and her past? Start by believing in the words coming from those she's travelled with since her disappearance."

Spike grumbles, "For all I know, you took her from us."

Cassandra interrupts the argument. She looks at the book in Gunther's hand. "May I look at that?" He throws it over to her and she catches it. Opening it up, she looks at the image on the first page. Her eyes quickly look towards Spike. "Come over here, you need to take a look at this."

As Spike makes his way over, and the two look at the images in the book, Gunther begins to wonder if he missed something crucial. As he ponders, Cassandra says to them, "The first image is of me fighting a phantasm, and this image here is Essa falling from the school…but who could have drawn these…"

Gunther replies in a scoff, "Maybe she did."

"No, not the Essa I know. She can't draw beyond smiley faces and stick figures." She looks at the book, "Whatever this means, it's an unknown element and perhaps the answer to Essa's cure."

Dusk says, "So perhaps we should return it to her. None of us know what that book means or what its purpose is. But it seems to have chosen her and, with no signs of danger coming from it thus far, I think it's safe to say we don't have to worry about it right now."

Hex smiles softly and says, "A good decision."

Spike grunts and says, "If it is indeed the book."

Gunther looks at Spike from the corner of his eye and says, "My thought exactly."

Cassandra says, "Alright then, I'll bring it to her shortly. Enough arguing. I would like to know who the two of you are." Her eyes rest on Dusk and Hex. "This would be the time for us to sort everything out, since we are all in this room together. I want to know who's been with her for these past three months."

Gunther pulls on the collar of his shirt and cracks his neck. "Well, I for one am merely here out of courtesy, I hold no relation or companionship with the others. I've spent little time with any of them and I was simply dropping them off. However, this dream world business has caught my attention on more than one occasion so I'd like to listen. They did fall from the sky after all."

Spike asks, "Can we trust you?"

"Is there any reason for me to not be trusted? Is the information valuable? Are people at risk? I only know one thing, that girl is going through one hell of a time. Before I leave I want to know the story, that's all. Then I will leave knowing she's in good hands. Even if her safety is in the hands of literature itself."

Cassandra looks to Hex and asks, "What about you, care to elaborate on who you are?"

Hex replies, "Not really."

Dusk says shortly after, "How about we hear more about the two of you, before you ask us who we are. That's only fair, seeing as how you claim to be her guardian."

She bites her lip, "Very well. I will let Spike talk about who he is if he desires to but I can certainly talk about myself. As I said before, my mother was close with hers. My mother was also someone very unique. Everything I know is because of her. Such as the ability to see souls from the afterlife."

Hex twitches slightly and looks at her in alarm. Sitting before him is a threat that could undermine him completely and he wasn't even aware of it. He budges in his seat and decides to take control of the conversation for his benefit and the safety of his mission. He asks, "What else can your eyes see? I would like to know."

She pauses, and then says looking at him, "If you want complete honesty, I am aware that the three of you are different. But that's all I can tell. If I also take into account what Kiyo is, a dream, I know that the two of you are not."

Spike asks, "So then what are they?"

"I'd like for them to answer that."

Dusk twitches. He redirects the conversation and says, "So, Spike was it? What about you?"

Spike replies with a scoff, "If it's a matter of specifics, then all I am willing to tell you right now is that I am a man that will always strive to better myself. If there's a challenge, I will take it. I will also die before I let harm make its way further into Essa's heart."

Hex says, "Noble, but stupid."

Gunther muses, "Talk about putting a rope around your neck."

Kiyo feels his eyes begin to roll around in his skull as the conversation drags on. He slouches and turns his head to Hex, "This one I know at least is an angel."

Dusk feels a flash of anger at the undermining of their companion. He knows Hex doesn't like being put on the spot. He slouches in his seat.

Cassandra and Spike look at him with surprise, "An angel?" They ask simultaneously.

Hex closes his eyes and takes a deep breath, similar to that of an angered bull or a hawk sharpening its gaze when its about to strike. His eyes open, his shoulders become broad, his back straightens, his aura rises and the air in the room shifts. He says, "And what if I were to say that me being an angel is something I disagree with? That the information is dangerous to bring to light, and that it's better if the subject is dropped completely. Is that acceptable, do you understand?"

Gunther, now sitting on the arm of the opposing couch, says, "So, you want me to claim that I saw someone with white wings flying, but that it wasn't an angel?"

Hex gives off a dangerous smile. "I'm advising you never mention the white wings at all."

Gunther winks and says, "But information is business."

Cassandra's eyes lower, and she focuses on him, "But you are, aren't you?" She finishes her sentence to the appearance of a spear hanging in front of her face. Dusk places a hand to his forehead and lets out a sigh.

Hex says, still smiling, "Heavens no."

She doesn't flinch. Her eyes battle Hex's and, after a noticeable gulp, she says, "I can clearly see you want all of us to keep the notion of you being an angel under tight lips. So I will. But nevertheless, you are an angel. So do me a favor, put that away—act appropriately. There are many strange things this is true, but if secrecy is your plan of action, you're not doing well."

He scoffs but the weapon disappears.

"Act appropriately," he says. "It's easy for you to say that, but what knowledge do you have of angels and how they are supposed to act? Half of you think we aren't real, the other half blindly asks for our help. Neither of you understand."

Spike asks, "But you are here for a reason, are you not?"

"Yes." Hex says, "But the reasons don't involve you."

Cassandra asks indirectly, while looking at Dusk, "Do they involve him?"

Dusk snaps out of his discomfort and his reaction is clear. He is now paying full attention to Cassandra. The danger that Hex felt, he can now see. His focus shows itself to a woman who is both young and analytical, someone who will find the answer to a question without fault. No secrets will exist around her. She is a gift and a curse.

Hex remains silent. Dusk says, "My name is Dusk Hollow." He pauses, blinks and thinks for a moment before continuing, "I suppose if we follow the time frame with Essa's disappearance and how that somehow adds up to three months, then I was killed around that time. I'm not an angel however, I gave up that right." Hex's eyes dart to him—something he said causing the angel to feel a tinge of regret. Dusk continues and says, "So we are here to stop... well," he looks at Hex, "what we are stopping I don't know. But I have a personal goal and it's to save Sarah—someone who was taken from me when I was killed." His eyes return to Cassandra and Spike, "Us coming across Essa was merely by chance, and now she's back home. So where we go from here is our choice. If Hex knows what to do, I am going to follow him, but again, my main goal is to save someone I love. Nothing will stop me from doing that."

A moment passes and Cassandra's eyes pierce into Dusk, "So, a dream world, an angel, someone who gave up the right to be one. How is it you two entered the dream world?"

Dusk replies, "Through a door that connects the dream world and Heaven."

"What about the dream world to Eryu?"

Kiyo says, "With the sacrifice of Norma."

Cassandra asks, "Who's Norma?"

Kiyo replies with anger in his voice, "My mother."

Her eyes avert, "I am sorry to hear that." She regains her composure and says, "I imagine then, if there was a sacrifice, that the door between the dream world and here is not something that happens often." She pauses, thinks and then says, "Dusk, I know who you are or, at least, I recognize you."

The angel raises an eyebrow. Gunther wonders what other puzzling information could be given.

Dusk frowns and asks, "How do you know me?"

Cassandra says, "I know who you are, because I read about your death in the paper."

"…I guess that would make sense, location wise. So you know about me. This just proves the point I did die, that I did go through the dream world, that I am here right now, and that Essa was with us for those three months." Dusk says with a sense of completion. Yet Cassandra continues to look at him, he notices a look of pity in her eyes.

She says it abruptly, "The issue is that you could have faked your death, making all of this moot and a hoax. However, if you are telling the truth, then explain to me how you've confused your death from a year ago with Essa's disappearance of three months."

He feels the conversation slip from his mind, "A…year…ago?" The words leave his lips while everything else closes in. For a moment he hears the laughter within him coming from the dark corners of his heart. All he can do is turn and look at Hex for an answer, an answer he needs to hear, an answer he hopes the angel can explain.

CHAPTER EIGHTEEN
Time

The crucial factor of life and death when simplified has one true answer—time. It is this variable that separates everything and also joins it. This truth also applies to what happens after death, yet time seems to lose all meaning for those who experience it. Because of this, few question time and take it for granted while it, in turn, takes that opportunity to continue expanding further. This knowledge is one of many principles that angels keep in mind and refrain from telling those who perish and awaken before them, since time has no more meaning to the dead. But if it were to hold meaning, it would crush the one seeking the answer.

The angel sees the fear within the depths of Dusk's eyes. Yet he knows that the answer will not extinguish that fear, but only ignite the spark and cause a fire to spread throughout his body.

Dusk asks impatiently, "Hex, answer me, what is she talking about? Is there something I need to know about when I died?"

Hex continues to look at him with a hint of concern. He replies, "When you died and woke up, nine months of your time had passed. It's not the same for everyone, it's related to acceptance of death. For some, they awaken in minutes, others years."

Dusk feels a slight hesitation in believing every word Hex says before he asks, "So then…that means Sarah has been in the hands of that bastard for a year…?" His eyes dampen and he continues to say, "And because I couldn't accept my death…the fact that when I was dying she was being taken right in front of my eyes, I had to lose nine months of that time, nine months in which anything could have happened to her?" he places his hand to his throat and feels the dry constriction of his muscles tightening, making it hard to swallow. Dusk realizes that he inadvertently put Sarah through an additional nine months of hell. He looks in anger at Hex and says, "And you didn't tell me, so that I wouldn't argue and I would accompany you?"

Hex replies, "No…I would not do that to you."

Gunther reaches for a cigarette and places it in his mouth, quickly lighting it. "I hope you all don't mind," he says as he puts the lighter in his jacket pocket. "So, are we at the point where Dusk has to prove that he's actually dead? This is truly a night of fairytales all in one room isn't it?"

Cassandra crosses her arms and says; "Dusk, if you are from around here then it's possible you were buried in Mithras graveyard."

He nods his head and says, "My parents are buried there."

"Well, it's only a few blocks away from here. This is going to sound cruel, but if we can confirm your body is buried in the ground, then I will believe everything that's been said and I will put my faith in Essa actually getting better."

Hex looks at her, enraged, and asks, "You wish to desecrate his grave?"

"I see no other way to find the needed evidence"

"Evidence? I've had enough of this ridiculous gathering." Hex stands up and unveils his brilliant white wings that fill up the space around him, "How is this for your evidence?"

Both Spike and Cassandra stare at the wings with a loss for words. Even Gunther who's caught a glimpse before is struck by the purity before his eyes, causing his cigarette to hang loosely in his mouth.

The small light that's given off causes Dusk to look up and briefly forget his troubles. While Kiyo, with a smirk, says below his breath, "Well there you have it."

Cassandra takes a moment to regain her composure before apologizing to Dusk. "I think this conversation has reached its end," she says as she stands up. She then leaves the room and heads upstairs.

Hex says, "Kiyo, go with her." Kiyo huffs but doesn't protest. He follows Cassandra, making their way to Essa's room, where they stand outside.

Meanwhile Hex tries to console Dusk, yet fails. Dusk rises up from the couch and leaves the room. He heads into the hallway and towards the front door. Hex follows him and watches him leave the house. Dusk makes his way towards the street and stops. He looks left and then right, trying to figure out which way he should go. With his mind clouded, the frustration lets the darkness in his heart chuckle within him. He clenches his fist.

The front door opens once more and Hex presents himself. Dusk ignores him and decides to walk left. His feet leave the confines of Essa's property and meet the pavement. As he makes his way down the street, he soon finds Hex beside him. Annoyed, he glares at Hex and asks, "Why are you following me? Stay at the house."

"I'll pretend you didn't just order me to do something. Besides, that girl asks far too many questions. I have no desire to remain in that house."

"I'm like this because of you."

"Dusk…"

He remains silent with no desire to argue, his mind screaming at him. The last thing he wants to do is have a scuffle with no weapon. He wants to save Sarah, not feel pity and remorse. The two of them make their way down the street and continue to move from block to block, edging closer to where Mithra's graveyard is.

As they make their way towards the graveyard, Gunther, who still remains in the house, decides to walk around and see what Essa's home is all about. He looks at the clean furnishing and at the warm colours amongst the furniture. Then he looks for valuables—in particular, imagery. He notices Spike watching him, but he pays no worry. His eyes come across a set of pictures sitting on a desk at the far end of the living room.

He looks at the five frames and recognizes that they are only of Essa. He smiles slightly, seeing her at different ages, from a small toddler to a more recent one with her long red hair and vibrant smile. He wonders who took the photos and then shakes his head, figuring that Cassandra or someone else did when they were watching over her.

His own smile wavers slightly when he sees a picture of Essa's family. It's the only one he sees that shows more than just herself. In the picture, the father and mother look at Essa lovingly, while the mother holds her between her arms and the father has his arms wrapped around the mother. A boy stands at the father's side, holding onto his father's fingertips. Gunther looks at the picture for a while. He gazes at each person, and focuses on the boy. He looks at the innocence within the boy's expression and the trust that's between him and the family.

Gunther notices Spike walking towards him, so he diverts his eyes and looks around at the house while pretending to be interested in what he sees. Spike looks at him warily before making his way towards the kitchen and says, "Seeing as how everyone's split up, I'm going to grab something to eat. You can eat some food as well, if you'd like. Fairly sure Cassandra was in the process of making tea."

He follows Spike. As he reaches the hallway, he turns around once more to glance at the photograph and then exits the room.

While he and Spike get settled in the kitchen, Kiyo and Cassandra stand across from one another upstairs outside of Essa's room.

Cassandra begins the conversation by saying, "So, a dream huh?"

Kiyo says in return, "For someone who has the patience to be forgotten every day, you have a hard time keeping an open mind about things that are out of the ordinary."

This aggravates her but she recognizes the truth of that. She doesn't retaliate, but instead decides to be friendly. She says, "Look, I'm not normally that cold and direct when I speak, but you have to understand that I haven't seen her in months and I was worried. You could have all been playing along, trying to harm her. But I know now that's not the case. I can see that you care about her as much as I do."

"I do care about her, yes, I think that's true…I can't really say why, and I haven't known her all that long, well, in my time." He pauses, "Do you think she's alright in there?" Kiyo motions towards the door.

"I'll check on her, just stay here." Cassandra knocks on Essa's door but receives no response. "Essa, I'm coming in." She opens the door and sees Essa sitting against her wall, knees close to her chest, identical to how she was when Dusk and Hex saw one of her memories.

She looks up at Cassandra with wet eyes and says, "Do you remember when you talked about the Tears of Jessica? How she was so overcome with remorse for her loved ones that her tears eventually turned into something useful?"

Cassandra closes the door behind her and walks towards the bed. She takes a seat and replies, "Yes, I remember."

"How do you think she would feel if she were in my position? Would she be-e able…to even fee-l if she found out that someone she loved was actually gone for 17 years? How would she even react? She would have broken, Cassandra, and her tears would have done more than flood small towns." She places her head down and says, "And what of my tears? When will they do anything but make me feel weak and alone?" She clenches her knees and looks at Cassandra, "Please, leave me be."

While Essa remains in her room hunched up against the wall, with her eyes cast towards the clouds, she thinks about nothing, she thinks about everything.

Meanwhile Dusk makes his way with Hex towards the graveyard that he believes his body resides in. The rain isn't as fierce as it was earlier, and softly becomes a faint mist surrounding them. The walk is accompanied only by the sound of a heartbeat—the one residing in Dusk's chest.

The graveyard appears before them, and Hex notices Dusk slows down. Very tall birch trees surround the exterior of the graveyard, with a few throughout it. The grass hasn't been trimmed in weeks. The lack of care to the place of the dead slightly disturbs Hex. He accepts it, however, since not a single person crossed their path the entire time they spent walking to Mithra's graveyard. This place is abandoned.

Dried out flowers rest in front of the older fashioned graves, while further into the graveyard, past the birch trees and into a small patch of freshly planted saplings, a large wall made of marble displays a list of names. Each name coincides with a fallen person who's chosen to have their body turned to ash instead of being planted into the ground.

Dusk sees a man standing in front of the wall, his eyes scanning through the list of names. The man appears to be in his early twenties. Dusk walks close to him and glances at the wall, looking for his own name.

As Dusk looks at the names, he locates those of his father, mother and brother. He reaches out and places his hand to their names. The man to his left looks over at him and to where his hand is placed. Dusk continues to think back to the faces of his family, and he lets go of the wall. He notices the man looking at him.

The man has short shaggy blue hair. His eyes are also blue. He wears a white and silver outfit that gives off a somewhat militaristic presence.

Dusk asks the stranger "Is…there something I can help you with?"

The man's eyes slowly return to the monument. He replies, "No, I was just looking at your feeling of remorse."

Dusk says, "I see…" His eyes return to the wall, looking through the syllables and letters that feel so strange, yet have meaning when put together. "You're here to mourn someone you've lost I imagine."

"I suppose I am." The young man looks at the names in front of his eyes. Each name sounds somewhat familiar to him, yet also unknown and alien.

The rain begins to fall heavily once more and he looks up at the sky, letting the rain drip down his face. He places his hands in his pockets and turns around, "Enjoy your time of mourning, I'm sure those you have lost are happy knowing you have come to visit them." The man says as he walks away.

Dusk turns and looks at him strangely. If only the man knew that Dusk was visiting his own body. What would he have to say about that?

The angel's eyes rest on the strange man momentarily before he returns his gaze to Dusk. "I notice names on the wall that share your last name."

Dusk nods his head, "My mother, Samantha Hollow; my father, Joshua Hollow and Seth Hollow, my brother."

"May I ask what happened?"

A flash of pain pinches Dusk's heart as he thinks back to the blood staining the floors in his old home, the desperation in his mother's voice, the final time he saw his brother. "I don't want to talk about it."

The angel looks at him slightly, "Very well, what is it you wish to do here?"

"I think you know the answer to that already Hex. I want to know if my body is buried here. If they knew about the murder then someone would have found my body. It was out in the open. I also don't see my name on this monument."

Hex gets a bad taste in his mouth, "Digging up your own body. This is absurd."

Dusk snaps, "It might be to you Hex, but I need to know!" He places a hand to his face, "I'm sorry, my emotions are out of whack... with Sarah and just, me being here. I need answers to the questions drilling away in my skull. Okay?"

The angel looks at Dusk, at the unique and complicated companion in front of him. "Alright, but you might not like what you find once you dig up your grave."

"That may be, but first let's find it."

Dusk and Hex look around the graveyard to find what will give proof to Dusk's situation. The proof is clear, Dusk finds his grave a few minutes later and feels sick to his stomach. He bends over and places his hands on his knees. He stares at his name written on the plaque, 'Dusk Hollow resides here, a loving son and nephew.' He then feels the urge to hurl, and turns his head and vomits. "I don't know what I'm doing." He coughs after wiping his mouth.

Hex remains silent.

"My uncle…he must have been the one to take care of…this. It tears me up knowing my death is this real…I know, with all of the things we've gone through, that this shouldn't come as a surprise. But it still makes my stomach churn." Dusk stands up and focuses on his drenched clothes. The rain continues to fall. His expression changes. "You know, it's been raining since we arrived. Maybe that's a sign."

"A sign? There's a lot that you humans like to believe is done for a reason, but the weather is something of chance…I'm sorry Dusk, that this is making you realize what you are."

Dusk glares at him, "And what am I? I'm surely not normal. I felt like I was about to die when I formed that arrow…it felt worse than death. Like my fiber was being torn…"

"…Dusk."

Dusk laughs through his pain, "And here we stand, without a shovel. I honestly don't know what to do anymore." He runs his hand through his hair and begins to cry, "I don't know what I expected coming here, but if my body is really in the dirt, then what am I? How can I feel and have this physical presence, this… me… What did I do to deserve coming here?" He says this, turning to Hex and walking through the long wet grass. "Why am I here!"

Hex keeps his composure, unfazed by Dusk's sudden breakdown. He decides to shed some light, to ease the pain Dusk is being over-whelmed with. "Individuals think about themselves, not the concept of everything as a whole. We place ourselves as the centre of attention and, because of this, we break when things tear at our foundations. Dusk, you're here because, believe it or not, I need your help. This world and the many that accompany it are changing, and darkness will spread towards the light. Love will perish, families will crumble, and hope and happiness will no longer be a consistent thing. I don't know where this darkness is or who is bringing it. I don't know any more than you do right now, but you are here because someone has put that faith in you. They saw something others may overlook. Now, I also know that the time of saints is over, it was never here. I know that

Sarah is your world, your foundation, and you're wondering how you'll ever be with her, or save her. How your body is possibly in the ground. But you are still walking forward. Your tears are proof of that. You have been dealt this pain—now overcome it and conquer it so that no one else has to see their own grave."

Speechless, Dusk looks at the grass and then asks, "Can you... help me?"

Hex walks past him and stands above the grave. He raises his hand into the air, and a swirl of white light flickers in his hand.

"Stand with conviction," he tells Dusk as he places the white light into the ground.

The dirt begins to part. Both Hex and Dusk step back and watch as the ground gives way and the coffin is revealed.

Dusk says quietly, "So you can do more than use spears..."

As the dirt stops moving he takes a step closer, the white light now entering the coffin. The cover opens up and rises into the air.

It takes thirty seconds for the dirt to move, a minute, for the light to enter the coffin—eventually time loses all meaning, Dusk looks at the confines of the coffin, at the piercing truth to who he is as a living being. He looks at the truth—at what's become and what is. His lip quivers slightly, his eyes grow heavy.

Dusk asks as he looks at the coffin, "This is the truth?"

"That appears to be the case. Are you alright with the outcome?"

Dusk watches the coffin close and the dirt shift back together, reforming the grass so that it appears as though nothing has disturbed it.

"Only we know. That's how I want to keep it..." He looks at Hex, "Let's save Sarah, let's save everyone."

The angel nods at Dusk's response, and the sky begins to clear up as the dark clouds part. A stream of light shines through and lands on their shoulders. The heavy aroma of loss begins to clear up and hope begins to prosper. Hex muses, "The weather is truly...a fickle thing."

As they make their way out of Mithra's graveyard, Dusk stops for a moment and says, "Before we continue, there's another place I'd like to stop by. It's where I lived with Sarah. If I'm going to save anyone,

I'll need my sword."

"Sounds reasonable to me. It's about time you aren't useless in a fight." Hex returns to being cold and abrupt. Dusk sighs and, as they begin walking once more, he turns onto another street. They make their way to where Dusk spent his final moments before his death, before everything became a question.

***

Hours pass.

Back in Essa's home, she lingers in her own thoughts. She faces her own truth. All of this time, her love and adoration were towards the wrong person. But her mother—she still loves her, she loves her family.

She says, "This is all so messed up" and rubs her forehead. She stands up, picking herself up from the ground. She walks towards her window and looks out at the street, noticing the clearing in the sky.

Her hands clench the windowsill. She places her forehead against the glass and looks down to see Dusk and Hex returning to her house. Unaware that they had left, she sighs but smiles at the sight of them. With the sun setting, she watches them. She notices the sword hanging on Dusk's waist, and the expression on his face—that of determination. She isn't able to put her finger on it, but the bond between both Dusk and Hex seems to be stronger. She feels it just by the way they walk beside one another.

They enter the house and she turns around, pressing her back against the windowsill. Essa questions what to do next, having spent hours kept up in her room alone, knowing everyone else is waiting to see what happens to her—if she will forget them. But she knows she won't. She knows something is different, and she knows it has something to do with the book.

Essa closes her eyes and visualizes the book. In her mind she grabs ahold of it from her bed and runs her hand down the spine. She opens the book and looks at the blank pages. She flips through the pages and closes the book in disappointment. Despite knowing in the back of her mind that the book is the cause for her adventure, she has no evidence to prove that's the case. Yet the pages aren't blank anymore. Opening her eyes she thinks that, even if it brought her to the dream world, she has no idea how or why. The time she's spent with the book has been a gift and a curse.

She places her hand on the door handle, stops, and thinks. Undoubtedly someone will be on the other side, and she will have to face them. To look into their eyes and know that she has so much missing from her memories while they know all about her—a time gap, a loss in stature and footing.

She opens the door. She sees Cassandra and Kiyo standing across from one another. They both smile gently at her. She returns the smile. It feels wrong but she tries with sincerity.

Turning, she looks at Cassandra and says, "While I might not remember everything you have done for me, and while my heart is heavy with what might be the truth, you did save me that day. Thank you."

Cassandra replies, "Your acknowledgement is enough for me...I've missed you."

Essa turns towards Kiyo, "And Kiyo, for what it's worth, thank you."

This takes him by surprise but he nods his head and feels a little more comfortable within all the strangeness that surrounds him. The three of them make their way down the stairs and onto the main floor where the others wait for them in the hallway.

They spot Dusk and Hex standing near the door. Cassandra looks at his sword and asks, "Where did you go?"

Dusk replies calmly, "I went to go visit my grave."

Cassandra's face goes pale. The others look at him wondering if he's alright and what he found. Essa asks, "Why did you feel the need to do that?"

Cassandra says, "It's my fault, I was pushing for information."

Gunther comments, "Yes, you really did."

Spike defends her. "But it was necessary."

Dusk says, "It's alright. That's over with now." He looks up at Essa, who is still a few steps up on the staircase. He asks, "Are you alright?"

She answers, gaining the strength to do so, "I'm fine."

Gunther moves slightly at the statement, but enjoys hearing it nonetheless. He looks at her and admires her determination despite the hurtful truth she faced hours prior.

Essa asks again, this time giving no room to avoid answering, "Dusk, why did you visit your grave?"

His eyes twinkle slightly as he looks up at her, a little smile on his face, "Because one must face the truth even when time loses all meaning."

"Time…" the words leave her lips.

"A year's worth. Not as much as you but…nevertheless, I sort of understand what it feels like to, well, be surprised."

She feels the need to cry again, but doesn't. She stays strong and says, "We have something in common then."

"Of course we do." He says, "We fall from the sky."

The others take a moment to look at one another.

Kiyo asks, "What is it we are going to do now?"

Cassandra and Spike look at him as if they are unaware of the reason behind the question.

Then Essa makes her statement, "From now on, whatever it is that's going to happen, I know that my life is different and there's no reason for me to feel rooted down here. Everything is expanding, I need to grow with it, and I know that being with Dusk, Hex and Kiyo is where I'm supposed to be."

Spike asks in alarm, "But what is it they even plan to do now that they're here?"

Dusk smiles, "Save everything from destruction."

Cassandra lets out a laugh and Spike says, "You must be joking. Save everything? Save it from what?"

Essa says, "From the man who destroyed our school."

Dusk says, "From the man who took the one I love."

Hex says, "From darkness."

Kiyo says, "And to find Leaf."

Cassandra looks at all of them slightly bewildered and says,

"Look…that's… understandable, but let's be realistic here. The planets are not in danger. What proof do you have? There have been… traumatic events but that's still…just events. There's no way for any of that to happen easily when you're talking global. I don't know about this Leaf situation, but in regards to the rest, it's just…"

Essa says, "Listen, you don't have to believe us. But I'm going with them."

Cassandra replies, "Wait, let's think this through."

"I've done enough thinking Cassandra. I just want to start moving forward. I can't stay in this house any longer."

Before the conversation can continue, Gunther moves past everyone in the hallway and heads for the door. He turns and says towards them all, "I think I've spent enough time here and I can be on my way. I wish all of you the best of luck."

Essa looks at Gunther, "So, you're going to leave?" She isn't sure why, but there's something about Gunther that troubles her, and him leaving their group so abruptly could be a problem.

"Yes. You are here with friends and you're safe. I have my own family to be with." He gives a slight wave and turns around to leave. His sudden desire to exit gives no time for the others to thank him for his help in bringing them together.

As his hand touches the door, a loud explosion is heard coming from outside. He yanks the door open to see the Ember in ruins—flames bursting through the debris.

"What the hell!" he gasps, "my baby!"

He runs outside and then stops as a figure rises from the debris. He pulls out his gun and yells in anger, "Give me a reason not to blow your head off you miserable scumbag! You just destroyed something I love—I'll kill you!"

The others exit the house and stand together, wondering if what's standing in front of them is a threat. A figure emerges from the smoke and flames. A beautiful woman with long silver hair appears. She looks at all of them until her eyes rest on Hex. The angel notices her gaze.

Hex walks forward and the others watch as he closes in on the stranger. Gunther looks at him and keeps his gun pointed forwards. The stranger takes a step forward and waits for Hex to get close to her. As he stands in front of her, he raises his hand forward and she does the same. They place their right hands together.

Hex asks, "Do I know you?"

Her silver and blue eyes sparkle slightly, "I am Andromeda." The pale beauty says elegantly. She slides her fingers down Hex's palm and then places her hand to his chin. "You don't know me, but I know all about you."

He asks, "Why are you here, and why did you make such an entrance?"

Gunther barks out, "Ya, I'd like to know as well. What kind of fucked up way of introducing oneself is this? That's a few million, below your feet, lying in ruins."

Andromeda looks at the debris and flames. "That is regrettable. Unfortunately, my method of travel is a tad destructive. I aim for open spaces but it's not easy to do so when in certain environments. As for who I am, I'm a guide for your kind." She directs the statement to Hex.

Dusk asks, "A guide for what?"

She looks at him, "To lead you to your task—where the evil rests. But to also ensure answers are given. The fog that clouds your minds will soon be lifted."

Essa says, "This is what we need—a direction."

Cassandra comments "Essa this is strange, I don't like this. Don't be rash."

Essa replies, "I'm not being rash…I'm being open."

Andromeda walks past Hex and towards Dusk. She looks at him closely and places her hand to his cheek. "Both of you are why I am here. However, if these are your friends and they wish to help then I can bring them as well."

Dusk asks, "Bring us where?"

"To the one with the answers of course."

"How can we trust you?"

"Trust is instinctive. Do I seem threatening to your senses?"

Dusk thinks for a moment. He looks deeply into her eyes and senses nothing that provokes him. "No, you don't seem threatening."

Gunther rolls his eyes, "Oh come on! She's got trouble written all over her. Look, I don't know what this nonsense is all about but if there's some," he makes quotation marks with his fingers, "adventure going to happen," he crosses his arms, "I want nothing to do with it. I want the payment for what you just destroyed and I want to carry on my way."

Hex turns to look at him, "I'm sure we won't need your assistance any further."

The comment makes Gunther scoff. He places his gun in its holster and walks towards Hex, standing face to face with him. "Listen, angel, I just want what's rightfully mine and then I will carry on my way."

The newcomer walks towards them. "I apologize for the destruction of your vessel, I will transfer the funds into your account. I can also offer you transportation to where it is you wish to go. However, this will have to happen after I bring the others to their destination."

He looks at Andromeda and lets out a sigh, "Today is just a damn mess. Fine, but don't try to screw with me. My patience is running low."

Spike places a hand to his hip and says to Cassandra, "Let's just stick with Essa. We can discuss what we do next once we go where this woman is going to bring us."

Cassandra scowls but doesn't protest.

The others slowly come to an agreement, and turn their attention to Andromeda.

She smiles for the first time and raises her hands. "Please step closer, we have to stay within the limit I'm afraid."

The stranger's eyes glow softly and a gust of wind wraps around the perimeter of where they are standing. Essa turns to look at her home and watches as it disappears from sight.

CHAPTER NINETEEN
A Man Who Knows

The scenery changes and Essa's neighborhood is replaced with the sound of water splashing against rock. She finds herself in the confines of a cove. Butterflies rush through her stomach as she notices the ground approaching at an alarming rate. As she and the others make contact, a loud burst of energy is given off. The environment around them shifts, sending sand, rock, grass and water to move against the flow of nature.

Water gently flows across their feet as the shoreline is under the water slightly. Essa takes notice that where they are looks similar to Gunther's hideout, seeing the palm trees and large bodies of rock. She figures it is another small island outside of Eryu's main city.

As everyone observes their surroundings, Andromeda seals the power that's disturbing the nature around them. She walks forward without a word. They watch as she reaches a wall of rock and places her hand against it. A symbol appears and emits a flash of yellow light. A doorway reveals itself in the rock. Andromeda enters the hideout.

Spike raises the question, "Has the thought occurred to any of you that this is a trap?"

Cassandra mutters, "It hasn't left my mind."

Everyone enters through the doorway. It closes behind them. A long hallway leads them to a wide-open space, where a glass wall overlooks the water. On the left side, a modern staircase leads up to a balcony with tables resting on a steel floor. Windows large enough to fill the entire room with light rest on each wall. On the right side, a smaller hallway leads to a set of rooms, also cast in cool steel that reflects the sunlight and the surrounding colours.

Essa says, "This is quite extravagant." She admires the chandelier hanging from the ceiling and the red carpet beneath their feet that covers the centre of the floor, one of natural stone casting a hue of orange.

A man appears at the top of the staircase to the left of them. He wears very modest clothing which consists of gray and white. They fit loosely on his upper body and the collar shows his skin. He walks down the stairs elegantly. His white and silver shaggy hair swings freely with each step. As he reaches the bottom, his silver eyes—similar to Andromeda's—become visible and sparkle as they make contact with everyone.

Hex looks at him and says with both hesitation and excitement, "You've changed in these past years, haven't you Wish?"

Wish smiles and gives a slight bow, replying in a carefree manner, "Only to keep my spirit lifted in dire times friend, and I see you've brought others with you."

Dusk asks, "How do you know one another?"

Wish smiles and responds, "Care to answer that for him Hex?"

Hex crosses his arms, "Wish is an angel like me, but his circumstances are similar to yours Dusk."

"Similar to mine?"

"Yes, he's gone through the door just like you, without a ring."

The others don't quite understand what's going on since this pertains to information that Dusk and Hex kept from the others up until now. Essa tries to make sense of it, while everyone else just tries to digest their beautiful surroundings and the appearance of the strange man.

Wish says, "How right you are Hex… and this must be Dusk. I've been looking forward to meeting you. But I'm sure you have no idea what's going on, so don't fret!" Wish taps Dusk on the shoulder and then takes a few steps back and spins around, "Let's go sit down, shall we? Andromeda, some refreshments if you will."

She nods and carries on her way. The others follow Wish as he leads them up the stairs and towards a set of glass tables in front of the windows that overlook the island. He gestures for them to take a seat. He then slides across the table on his rear and falls into a seat. His light mood—somewhat childish—causes the others to look at him oddly. Kiyo, however, enjoys the sight of someone different.

Before Wish can make a statement, Gunther states, "Just to clarify, I'm here to receive payment for my ship. I'm not here for anything else."

Essa looks at him with ill amusement. His characteristics of being a bounty hunter show more over time.

Wish leans back in his chair and places his hands on the table, balancing his posture. "Gunther Blaze, a licensed bounty hunter for the past seven years. With a crew of eight on the ship known as the Trinity, one of the companions of the Dawson. You specialize with a sword and gun, with signs of having the skill of producing fire. I assure you, you are meant to be here, and you will receive adequate funds."

A slight silence takes place before Essa asks, "Wait, fire?"

Gunther stares at Wish. "Listen, I don't care what you think you know about me. I just want what's rightfully owed."

Enjoying the protest, Wish says, "Don't be alarmed Gunther, information is my game. Your other secrets are safe with me. I believe some things should not be said aloud. I can assure you, however, that what I have to say is worth more than money owed…which you will receive, so rest easy."

Gunther's expression as his face begins to go red.

Wish then looks at Spike, "Now for you. Spike Adams, recently a student and witness to a school massacre. You specialize in a long stick technique, also proficient in hand-to-hand combat. You show an inner trait of adapting to the situation and learning quickly. You have no family, your closest relative having past away. Now your friends are your closest bond, and your strength comes from your master. But that's a dark tale, isn't it?"

Before Spike can make a comment, Wish looks at Cassandra and continues.

"Cassandra Waver, you also attended the same school until recently. You are one with the afterlife. You see ghosts and have the task set out for you to put them to rest, taught by your master—your mother. But that too is a sad tale." He pauses, "I'm sure you and I will get along."

Wish looks at Essa, "Essa Starlight, up until recently you were unaware of the truth of your mother, but now that you know of it you feel a need to continue moving forward, shown in your quick decision in coming here. It may be rash and yet, naturally, the right move. With you there is…a book…" his calm look changes slightly, his composure then returns.

As the others begin to stare hopelessly at the man who is able to look into their souls and deepest secrets, Wish looks at Kiyo and says. "Kiyo, you have no last name for last names are given in time. You're close to two people, Norma, who gave away her life so you could be here, and Leaf, who you are looking for. You hate that the decision to bring you here was not of your own accord and you have a thirst to destroy what created the circumstances that have unfolded… you are, to put it bluntly, a vengeful dream."

Wish's piercing eyes then turn to Dusk. At this point, everyone can only look and see what will be revealed about him. The angel slides his right hand across the glass table and says, "Dusk Hollow, your life is that of tragedy and love. You seek Sarah out for she is your world and only form of consistency. Everything else prior to her has turned to ash. She is not only your hope, but she is your heart. Death took you as well, but you've been sent here to face a fate unknown and rare to anyone else. It is unheard of, cruel, but this is your destiny, and you are not one to roll over and do nothing. You exist to fight."

Finally Wish looks at Hex, Dusk loses his focus and thinks about Sarah.

Oddly, Hex has a large grin on his face and says, "Wish, you're as efficient as ever in making others uncomfortable with your innate ability to learn about who they are. Must we cover me as well?"

"But of course friend, that's only fair." Wish smiles. "Hex, the name given to you upon birth. You are here to seek out the darkness that threatens the planets and humanity as a whole. And I am the one who has all of the answers for your task."

Wish looks at everyone, "I assure you all that when I say you are meant to be here, I mean it. You all possess particular traits and skills that will help save humanity. I'm sure such a statement as saving humanity seems comical and childish. What's the threat to humanity? Why us? Is this man serious? Well, despite those and the other questions plaguing your mind, unfortunately this is not a game. A force known as the Burdens is about to unleash the likes of hell into your everyday lives. The death toll will be incomprehensible, and few are even aware of this threat."

Gunther places a hand to his face and slightly shifts his body weight forward. "If you know of this threat, why tell only us and why have you kept it to yourself until now? Why play this game where you guess who we are? Gathering information isn't impossible so don't expect me to be dazzled by your—quote, unquote—skill."

Wish replies, "I see. Then perhaps if I confess one of your darkest secrets, you will believe me? Listen, all of you. The reason I have not come forward, or anyone has for that matter, is because the Burdens have the power to quash anyone who opposes them. My life, the power I possess, it would not be wise for me to risk all that I am, the answers I know, so humanity can deny the truth, as it does when facing danger yet to come. But right now, telling all of you, this is what I am meant to do, even if it seems selfish."

Cassandra places her arm around the top of her chair and says, "This still seems farfetched, but at this point I know that doesn't matter. Look, these Burdens or whatever, what exactly are they setting out to do? And what is it you want us to do about it? Specifically Hex and Dusk." She points towards them and continues to say, "Because Spike and I, we are no heroes. We care about two things; ourselves, and Essa."

Wish rubs his face slightly and says, "I want all of you to stop the threat naturally, if it is possible. As for what they wish to do—it's to bring forth fear and use it to devour everything. You may only care about little, but even the little things will be gone if the Burdens succeed."

Hex asks, "Do you know who the members of the Burdens are specifically? Why are they called the Burdens?"

"I do not. And the name comes from a source."

"Do you know where they reside?"

"I do not."

"…Do you know the powers they possess? How they plan to use fear? When they plan to attack?"

"I do not."

Dusk throws his hands into the air, "Well what the hell, I thought you had the answers to everything. But you don't know anything regarding our supposed purpose. And this crap about them being the Burdens, how vague can you get? The man who killed me mentioned something about being a Burden. Is he related now?"

Wish, after a moment of silence, replies, "Perhaps."

Hex says, "Wish, this is strange. I believe you, as I always have, but for you to not know. Either you are losing your ability, or this threat is something that neither of us can contain by ourselves, a power that chokes yours out."

Wish's content smile finally goes away, "I'm afraid it's the latter. Taking into account I also do not know the number of enemies that humanity will face, along with the fact that humanity itself still does not know anything—very little is in our favor. But I did not lie, I have all the answers, and those answers do not exist. Merely letting you know there is a threat is all I can do, so that the preposterous claim that humanity is in danger, sounds less so."

Spike says, "The answer is that there is no answer? Well what the fuck. You are the one who decides humanity won't listen to you and then you tell us, there's no answer? How about doing some reconnaissance."

"I did, and I found all of you."

Spike scoffs.

Wish says, "It's not so simple."

"Nothing is simple. But you could have told us more if you tried harder than to just sit here in this elegant hideout you have. Honestly, who just tells someone to save humanity while they themselves do nothing? You preach pretty words but show nothing. I call that weakness."

At this moment Andromeda walks up the stairs with refreshments and places one for each of them on the table. Chiseling into the tension between Wish and Spike.

She stands behind Wish slightly to the left. They all look at her. The similarity between her eyes and Wish's becomes evident.

Wish replies, "Nothing is fair. True weakness is thinking life is."

Spike scoffs once more.

Hex asks, "Who is she?" Motioning towards Andromeda.

Wish raises his hand and she wraps hers around it, "She is a part of me, but she is also her own being. An android with the knowledge of what I possess but with her own freewill to act."

Gunther takes a large gulp of water and then another until the glass is empty. He places it on the table and stands up. "Well, I've had enough of this bull shit. I can tell that there's nothing more to discuss. I don't care about some big bad guys called the Burdens. I've seen true hell. So despite how bad some things may be, don't expect me to be fazed and feel the need to help. I don't care about your supposed knowledge, or this guide you sent who destroyed my transport ship. I care about my money."

Wish looks at him from the corner of his eyes, "Perhaps you would change your opinion if you knew that the man that took Dusk's life and the man who put Essa in life threatening circumstances are part of the same organization."

Dusk feels his face heat up.

"Unfortunately," Gunther looks at him, shifting forward, "I don't care."

Essa barks, "Well I do!"

He looks at her for a moment and then returns his gaze to Wish.

"Very well." Wish says, "You will find rooms to rest in downstairs."

Gunther turns around and places a hand gently on Essa's shoulder. Without looking at her, or saying anything, he lets go and makes his way down the stairs.

Kiyo watches Gunther enter one of the rooms and decides he's heard enough as well. "I'll see all of you in the morning," he states impassively, and leaves the table.

The others remain seated. Essa plays with the rim of her glass as she remains in thought. She asks, "Who else is aware of the threat?" trying to remove her frustration from Gunther's cold stance.

"Besides everyone in this hideout," Wish says, "the High Council is aware, consisting of its twelve respective members. There is also a group that keeps to themselves known as LINK."

Spike asks, "LINK?"

"It's a group that resides amongst the stars. Their leader has similar qualities and resources in relation to me. So it's natural they are aware."

Hex asks, "Can we rely on them for help?"

"Doubtful. They, as well as the High Council, have their own motives to look out for. While everyone wants the Burdens to falter, they won't make a hasty move."

Cassandra finishes her glass and pushes it across the table. "So that means we take all the risk. A risk that might be more than any of us can bear, because apparently those who know are chicken shits." She looks at Essa and says, "This is not our battle. Let's go home. If the High Council isn't doing anything, what can we possibly do?"

Essa says softly, "Cassandra…my home is with them, with you, but it's not back there. I don't care if the High Council is avoiding the problem. If I can do something, I'll do it."

Spike listens closely. He looks at Essa and says, "Well then it might as well be us. Those with power who are afraid to act are of no use." His eyes rest on Wish, "I've heard enough. I don't care where we go or what happens. I will succeed."

He leaves the table abruptly. Cassandra decides to follow. Placing a hand on Essa's shoulder, she says, "Just think carefully," and then departs.

Wish says, "It seems they are all agitated."

Andromeda rubs his shoulder and says, "That's to be expected with sudden but sparce information. Not to mention you claiming to know all the answers but having little to say. As well as claiming the existence of humanity is in danger yet, no danger being visible. "

Wish's expression scrunches up a little, "True, I was a tad unforthcoming." His eyes cast towards the night sky, "May I ask the three of you to let Dusk and I have a little word?" Wish looks at Dusk and places his hands together. He continues, "There are things we need to discuss."

Dusk replies, "And they can't hear it?"

"They can if you wish, however I deem it somewhat personal."

Dusk takes a moment to think. "Let Hex stay here…" he looks at Essa and says softly, "I'll tell you later, okay?"

She feels slightly taken aback, but with her own world of problems she nods her head and stands up. Perhaps part of her is hurt—a gap clearly evident between their young bond—however, she knows that he too has a world of his own. A world she doesn't know.

As she leaves them, Andromeda follows. Both Hex and Dusk remain seated. Wish stands up and walks towards the window. He leans against it and crosses his arms, his eyes cast out at the sea, barely visible in the darkness. He says, "Dusk, what I am about to tell you will be alarming. And before I tell you, you need to understand that no one knew about this except for me, alright?" He looks at him. "Not a soul."

Dusk replies, "…What is it?"

"If I know Hex well enough, I'm sure he's attempted to teach you the power that angels possess, the ability to focus and then conjure up a weapon. Am I right?"

Dusk looks at Hex before answering, "Yes, that's true, well, sort of…he's a bit of a…poor teacher."

Hex's eyes squint a little.

"Well, it's dangerous for you to do that, so I advise you not to. In fact, any strenuous activity, any form of intense emotion will be dangerous for you."

Dusk lets out a laugh, "What the heck are you going on about?"

"The moment you went through that doorway, you traded away your right to rest. You're in a halfway state. To use that power means to use your own life force, ending your presence here at a faster rate."

"So what are you saying?"

Wish's face grows firm, "What I'm saying is, you're neither alive nor dead, and time is running against you. The same applies to me. We do not possess the rings that keep our bodies whole. We are anomalies."

Hex and Dusk both look at him strangely. Hex says, "Wish you need to explain this further. I understand that going through the door without a ring is against the rules, but he is no different than he was upon death."

Dusk asks, "What ring?"

"I'm sorry to say that you are wrong Hex." Wish says, "Dusk and I, when we use our power, it shines a hue of yellow. It's the hue of life. While white is what normally shines from the power of an angel. I lost my classification as such when I left through the door without a ring. In Dusk's case, he left without a ring…but he wasn't even an angel. By being unstable, our physical presence relies on our existence and our existence is used up with each glow of yellow. So I ask, have you ever felt weak, have you done what I speak of?"

Dusk says, "Yes…once, when I formed an arrow."

"And what happened?"

"It didn't kill the monster—well, Nightmare, I guess is what we called it."

"Do you want to know why you felt weak?"

"…Yes and how about you explain to me about this bloody ring?"

Hex answers swiftly, "Dusk, all you need to know is that when an angel is granted the task of going through the back gate and into the dream world, they are required to wear a ring. It keeps them in check so that they don't do something, like go insane. It also limits our power so we are not overwhelemed by our own strength. There is no quick rejuvenation here, what breaks does not heal."

Dusk states, "And no one ever thought about telling me, or giving me one of these rings?"

"You are neither an angel, nor worthy."

"Yet I was worthy enough to come with you."

"…Not to me, not at that time."

Dusk looks away, feeling hurt.

Wish decides to tell Dusk more about his circumstance. "Dusk, I want you to listen. You felt weak when you shot that arrow because a part of your existence latched onto the Nightmare, and since it did not die, it didn't return to you. By using your inner power, you are flipping a coin where the odds are that the power you expense will not return. Each time you make a move, you need to ensure that it returns to you, but that cannot always be the case. If you use that power on an inanimate object that has no life, it will disperse once it's been used. If you use it on a dead body, it will not return depending on the circumstance. If you use that on anything that is alive yet lives through its use, it will not return until the being is dead. So know this Dusk, you do not have the luxury of using it at your freewill, and I advise that you cease to do so."

Dusk feels the sense of despair linger over him—more horrible news. He says, "This is just…" He stands up and clenches his fist, "I'll use my power as I see fit. I chose to come back. I will fight." He turns to walk away.

Hex glances at him and listens as his footsteps grow farther and dimmer. "This is troubling to hear. Now he's even more useless in combat."

"Don't be harsh Hex, he has a sword at his side. If anything he has what he needs."

"But against a threat that you know nothing about? I think he needs that inner power."

"But that power will result in his demise."

"All living things die."

"But his fate is uncertain, as is mine, where we go once we perish…"

Hex looks at Wish in alarm and then thinks about it deeply. "Wish…why did you go through that door?" As he asks this, he wonders what will become of both his friend and Dusk. He is unable to think about it analytically and relies on an answer.

"Friend, my actions are always simple. I went through it to find Wing, that's all. Now I suggest you take that cold side of yours and let it remain hidden when you are dealing with Dusk. He's going to need you. He will have many questions, I can assure you, and while I could give him answers, it's better if you do."

"Need me? I don't think that boy will ever need my help."

"Hex, he's needed you since the moment this journey of his began."

The words sink in and Hex thinks about the way Dusk always stays close to his side, the way he adapts to the situations around them and his reluctance to back down. It's been ages since he has had a companion. Perhaps he has become blind to certain things that humans show.

Hex says, "How much progress have you made on Wing? Since that time." Trying to change the conversation into another matter.

Wish grimaces slightly, "I have an idea, but I'm keeping that to myself. I feel it is my right after taking on this toll."

The mysterious topic continues to develop between them.

Meanwhile, Dusk makes his way to one of the empty rooms and slams the door behind him. Essa sees the door close. She crosses her arms around her legs on the bed she sits on in the room across the hall. Cassandra sits beside her and Spike stands in front of them. The three return to their conversation.

Essa asks them, "What happened after I disappeared?"

They both answer, "A mass of confusion mixed with hell."

Cassandra then says, "We were out of the fight when you disappeared, but I was lingering in and out of consciousness. What I saw was the conclusion of the battle. That man, Nix, he broke off a chunk of the roof and disappeared in the debris. The teachers then looked for you while taking care of us. But it became clear that you were just... gone. When the police were finally able to make their way into the school, they found whatever survivors were left and helped them out. Half of the school's population died on that day. The school closed after that and then, as a result, many of the neighboring streets became a ghost town. The mourning families either kept in their corners or left, trying to find salvation for the hell that took place. You could say they were running from the fear of facing it. If Spike and I were lucky with anything on that day, it was knowing we don't have family members to worry over."

Essa says, "Not having family members…I guess we all share that similar trait. I…never mind." She pushes past the thought and asks, "What about the teachers that helped us? Mr. Linder… Lunar… Dixon?"

Spike scratches his chin, "About them… Well, besides them being the only faculty to survive while also having incredible strength, it became clear that they weren't your average teachers. We clued in immediately and asked them time and time again. They didn't tell us much, but we know that they work together, and that they take on jobs. I guess they knew something troubling might happen in the school, but didn't know what. Before we could get anything else out of them, they flat out disappeared."

Essa says, "Disappeared… there's a lot of that going on huh?"

Cassandra says slowly, "I suppose."

"Do you think Gunther knows them? Perhaps they are bounty hunters as well?"

Spike and Cassandra both shrug. Essa bites on her lip. "Well, thank you for filling me in. I want to sit down with the two of you again, and just chat about everything, alright?" She looks at them with clear eyes. They both smile and agree.

She then makes her way out of the room and crosses the hall to Dusk's door. She hesitates for a moment and then knocks softly on the steel panels. There's no response. She places her hand on the doorknob and twists it, slowly opening the door and looking inside to see sheer darkness. The light from the hall creates a small path towards Dusk.

She asks, "Dusk, can I come in?" He gives no response, so she takes it upon herself to enter the room. She closes the door behind her and flicks on the light. Essa walks towards him and he looks up at her with little interest. "Are you alright?"

His eyes slowly become level with hers as he sits up straight. "I've had better days."

"What did he tell you?" Her curiosity kicks in.

"It's nothing."

"Dusk…it's never nothing." She points out.

"Well then, apparently the only thing I can do that has potential, like that arrow I used back in the dream world, is killing me."

"…What?"

"I know. How is it possible when I'm already dead? Well from what I got, it can get worse. So I don't know. Wish left out what it means in the long run but I put two and two together. I'm essentially going to meet a horrific end."

"I'm sorry… but what will you do?"

"I'm not going to stop. I'm going to get stronger. He knows I'm a fighter. I'll find a way around this."

"Well you have me, okay?" She says comfortingly.

He looks at her with a slight smile, "Thank you, I'm here for you as well. We will both get through our struggles together. That's what it means to be friends."

She smiles hearing those words and pats her legs. "After all, I just need to follow you." She pauses and says, "Well, I'll leave you to it then. I'm going to get some sleep. I'll see you in the morning." She waves softly and leaves the room.

Dusk stands, the slight smile removed from his face. He walks to the door and turns off the light. He finds his way back to the chair he was sitting in and sits back down. He places his hands to his face and bends over slightly. He says to himself, "Were you aware of this?"

The darkness within his heart replies, *"Naturally. The question is; what do you plan on doing? I'd say you need me more now."*

"I don't need you. Asking you was a mistake."

"Oh you need me. You already find solace in the darkness. I'm winning." The voice starts to laugh and Dusk slams his fist into his knee, "Shut up." He silences the voice and rises abruptly, slamming the lights on.

***

Night soon passes into an early morning, where both Hex and Wish sit casually across from one another. Wish takes a sip of the tea he is fond of and lets the warm aroma settle over his weary mind. Hex looks at his friend and at the obvious changes.

Hex asks, "Are you still able to go without sleep?"

"I can go a few nights, but sleep does greet me. It's just darkness, but it refreshes me all the same. And while I can also go a long while without the need for sustenance, I enjoy it."

"Is that so." Hex looks out at the sun, wondering what it feels like to take in the world for all its worth rather than to look at it as an object— to feel the wind, the rays of the sun, the emotions that plague humans.

Sets of eyes cause the hairs on his neck to rise in alarm and he turns around to see Dusk staring at them. His alarm goes away, the lack of sleep can be seen from the bags underneath Dusks eyes. "Trouble in paradise?" Hex asks.

"Something of the sort." Dusk says as he takes a seat at the round table. He looks at it and then at Wish, "Was this here yesterday?"

With a chuckle, Wish replies, "No, I like to sit at this table in the morning, so it's something I set up each day. Brings me closer to the beds."

"Oh, right." Dusk says as his eyes drift off.

Hex and Wish look at one another with the same thought; Dusk is having trouble facing the news of the day prior. As the three of them sit at the table in silence, the others wake up and greet them. Soon everyone sits at the table and Andromeda fetches them toast and orange juice, a balanced breakfast.

Neither Hex nor Kiyo take much interest in the food, but Kiyo decides to try it out anyway and finds enjoyment within the texture and taste. As they all dig into the meal, a few eyes of suspicion look at Wish. He continues to enjoy his cup of tea, the tenth one since they arrived in his home.

As he places the cup to his lips, ready to finish its contents, to then ask for the eleventh, his eyes widen slightly. He looks over at Andromeda. Her eyes also showing concern.

Hex sees the reaction between them and he asks, "Is there something wrong?"

Wish places his cup down and the noise of it clashing with the plate causes everyone to look up. "It's begun," he says. A large screen appears across the glass windows and everyone turns to see the Eryu News being broadcast.

A female reporter stands before them, clearly frightened. She says, "Just now, five individuals have started wreaking havoc in the capital of Eryu. Sources say that they are destroying everything in their path. Both local officials, as well as nearby Federation starships, advise everyone to stay indoors while they handle the situation. I repeat; five individuals are wreaking havoc in the city." At the end of her sentence, a building behind the reporter ignites in flames, the windows burst and the foundations crumble. The reporter screams and the camera is cut as the building falls towards them. The footage switches to an aerial view, where a drone overlooks the devastation.

Gunther grumbles, "I'll be damned."

Hex asks, "Are they the Burdens you mentioned Wish?"

Wish replies, "No, they are just tools of fear."

CHAPTER TWENTY
Just a Tool

Every tool has a sense of purpose, a source of reasoning behind each action and placement for its use. If a tool is known as a threat, it is only a threat because of those who wield it. Yet to think such a term is clear, like the contrast between black and white, is foolish. So foolish that Wish questions his own choice of words in the face of the beginning of what's to come.

The group looks at the destruction that is taking place in the city. As flames quickly spread and the chaos ensues, those responsible are slightly visible within the smoke and ash. Yet the small glimpses of five individuals walking forward is lost amongst the thousands of citizens who run in fear as those who are trying to fight back are slaughtered.

With all the causalities, Essa begins to see what took place at her school happen all over again. The massacre, the displacement of power, the loss of innocence and the feeling of fear in the hearts and minds of those who, up until that point, were barely aware of its existence.

An explosion goes off at the base of a building and causes the foundation to cave in, sending the tower crashing down into its neighbor. Glass shatters and falls onto the crowd below it. Soon after, the first signs of police force can be seen as they rush forward, passing through the crowd of fearful people. The force of two dozen men and women march forward with their guns raised, they stop and place themselves accordingly, with ten kneeling, while the others stand behind them. The twenty assault rifles wait patiently for the tools of fear.

That patience is quickly met by one individual. A man walks forward, his face calm and showing no signs of stress. As one of the officers orders for him to stop, a piece of metal shoots up from the ground and pierces the officer's heart.

The police officer looks down and falls over. All composure is soon lost and the remaining nineteen officers let loose a barrage of fire at the man.

The bullets head towards him and yet he does not fidget or budge. The drone in the sky focuses on the man and everyone in Wish's hideout get their first solid glimpse of the individual. He has short black hair, styled upwards. His clothing consists of a white and silver skintight suit. The style reminds Dusk of the man he met in the graveyard.

The mysterious individual, with his jet-black demeanor, raises his hand forward in a fist and opens it to reveal a piece of metal in his palm. It morphs into a wall in front of him, stopping all of the bullets. As the police officers continue to fire, the man places his hand against the metal wall. A sword shape appears in the metal and then extrudes towards the police officers at a considerable speed. The bullets bounce off of the metal sword and, as it reaches them, rises into the air and points down towards them, spreading apart into ten miniature swords. The blades soar forward and pierce through the unfortunate ones. The remaining officers begin to stare helplessly as their comrade's bodies are pulled into the air and whipped around.

The bodies begin to fall and the remaining force begins to disperse. As a few succumb to shock, a small group rushes forward towards the mysterious man in a last ditch effort to close the gap. However, it's pointless. The man pulls a piece of metal from the wall and shapes it into a sword. He then slams his fist into the wall and chunks of metal soar forward. One of the officers is hit and his head is crushed. Three others make it past the debris and come face to face with the man, who quickly cuts through one of their throats, decapitates the second officer and cuts through the waist of the third.

One of the remaining officers panics and unloads the remainder of his bullets at the man. Yet agility surpasses the skill and accuracy of the officer's aim. The man reaches the officer and slashes his sword downwards, splitting the officer's body in two. As the man turns to finish off the last officer, the sound of a gunshot goes off, and the man looks at the officer who chose suicide over facing a gruesome death.

Essa and the others are unable to believe their eyes.

The police force stood no chance in the presence of one man.

Gunther starts to feel a chill run down his arms, a mixture of excitement and fear all at once. He says, "So there's something worth killing after all."

Cassandra places her hand to her lip, "The way he was using metal like that… If he's with the group that's causing all of the destruction, then he's either the leader with this unique trait or… all of them have a power like his…this is bad."

As they digest what they are seeing, they do their best not to turn away in disgust and imagine that none of this is happening.

The man looks up at the drone and pulls a small piece of metal from his pocket. Gunther leans forward and says, "What's he planning to do?"

The man throws the piece of metal into the air and it finds itself crashing through the centre of the drone, causing it to explode. The image on the screen cuts off. Gunther lets out a subtle sigh, "He's not my problem, that's for sure."

Essa glares at him. "He's all of our problem at this rate!"

Hex says, "Tools of fear, that's what you just said earlier Wish. This man is just a tool?"

Wish replies, "More or less."

Spike asks, "What makes you think they are just tools?"

Wish says quietly, "Because nature is ever-changing. Sometimes we see things that are morphed cruelly. I don't know many who would willingly put themselves in a situation where they must face off against everything at once. That's usually what a tool is used for, to create damage but protect the user."

Spike replies, "But he could simply be a man with enough courage to make his own move."

"Yes, but that's not what I see. I see a man weighed down by…a burden."

Hex clears his throat and says, "Alright then, as of this moment, Eryu is under a new management. I don't see a man of that caliber being taken out by average people. They won't hold out and the Federation isn't here yet."

Kiyo's nose feels itchy so he rubs it. He comments, "New management Hex? I doubt it. After all, we're going to go there and stop him. Right?"

Hex looks over at Kiyo, "Naturally, we're the new management."

Wish and Andromeda think to themselves for a moment. Wish then says, "Alright, Andromeda can take those of you who wish to stop this destruction from happening."

Gunther turns and looks at him, "No thanks. I have my own ride and its destination is much different. It's been fun, but as of now I am getting as far away from this mess as possible and collecting my much desired profit." His eyes then look over at Hex, "By the way angel, as magical as it is to be in the presence of someone like you, others do not think the same. Most believe that you defy logic, while others believe it's possible and want you for greed alone. I'd bring you in but I know the result."

"The result?" Hex looks at him carefully. "Are you threatening me?"

"Just passing a warning. You are like livestock, as we all are. There's a price on everything, even in times of destruction. While you plan to go do heroic things, people like me will only think about themselves and how to get a step ahead."

"You are quite forthcoming for such a person."

"I play by my own rules." Gunther grins and turns to look at the glass window. "I hope you don't mind some renovations, do you Wish? You can subtract it from what is owed."

Andromeda looks at Wish in alarm and Wish tilts his head and says, "I was tired of those windows anyway." A moment later, the windows shatter, glass shards scattering across the floor. Everyone covers their faces to stop the debris from harming them. Gunther smiles proudly as the Trinity sores in the air outside of the hideout.

In disgust, both Cassandra and Essa look at him. Cassandra says, "You're just going to cause a mess and then leave thousands—hundreds of thousands—to die?"

He replies, "Listen missy. I did my job. In fact, it wasn't my job but a favor. I'm not risking my life for a noble cause. Nothing in this universe deserves my life. I will only protect my family. Wish here decided his own path, so am I."

Wish replies, "What makes you think this danger won't involve your family sooner or later?"

"When it does, I will burn it to ashes." He looks at Essa and continues, "Essa, you have no physical abilities or skills that will aid you in fighting the enemy. If you come with me, you can get away from all of this. You'll be safe."

She stares at him baffled and says, "Come with you? Absolutely not! I'd rather help than run away."

"Essa, there's nothing you can do."

Her eyes widen. Her upper lip quivers slightly. She points her finger forward and proclaims, "Don't you dare lecture me. You're right to leave. No one needs the help from someone like you. Your selfishness won't help anyone. Protect your family if that's all you will do…I don't know what Fleur sees in you."

For a brief moment, Essa can see a flood of sadness show in Gunther's expression but he masks it so quickly that she wonders if it was her imagination.

He says with a slight smile to cover up the pain the words held, "Is that so." He places a cigarette in his mouth and lights it. Inhaling, exhaling, and then with a large inhale, finishes the cigarette in one swoop. The ash falls to the floor and blows away as the wind from outside moves inwards. His eyes drift towards the Trinity and he feels confident seeing his ship. Gunther says, "Listen Essa. It's commendable you want to go help out, but you are weak. Weakness will result in a needless death. I'm selfish, but I'm smart. Come with me. I will keep you safe." He looks at Wish, "You agree, right Wish?"

Essa feels the choice slipping from her hands, "Don't ask him. It's my decision."

Wish looks at her and, for a moment, he hums to himself. He says, "I agree with Gunther. You should go with him."

She turns to him with a gasp, "But what about all that talk about being the ones to help save everyone!"

"That does apply, but not to everyone. He's right to claim his own path. I did, you all can."

"This is ridiculous! You don't know what I can do!"

"What can you do?"

"…That doesn't matter."

"It does. It matters greatly. Because talk will only result in your demise, and that is why I think you accompanying Gunther is a good idea. He's not a bad person, despite his tendency to be rash."

Essa says, "Hex…" as she looks at her companion, "…please tell me you disagree."

He replies passively, "I agree with them."

Her face goes red once more and she looks at Dusk. With his hands in his pockets he fakes a smile and shrugs slowly, his expression showing that of nervousness and yet no reluctance to agree with the others.

Essa looks downwards, "Fine…" she turns towards Gunther, "just so you know, I won't forgive you for this."

Gunther replies, "I'm not looking for your forgiveness. Forgiveness means nothing to me."

Wish places his hands together and leans on his toes. "Well, with that sorted out, are the rest of you ready to depart with Andromeda?"

Spike and Cassandra look at one another and whisper between themselves. Cassandra looks at him and nods her head. She turns to Wish and says, "I'll be accompanying Essa."

Gunther says, "The more the merrier."

Essa walks away from them in disgust and leans against a wall. She digs her nails into her skin. Biting on her lip, she struggles to hold back her tears of frustration. This is not what she wants. This goes against what she feels she must do.

As the others converse amongst themselves, Spike walks towards her. He stops in front of her. He places his hand through her hair and moves it away from her face. She glances up at him and looks into his eyes. She sees flashes of his younger self and it startles her. She then realizes it's just memories returning.

She places her hand to her pouch and says, "I'm pathetic aren't I? I can't do anything but cry and scream."

He lets out a laugh and then raises her chin before saying, "The Essa I know is the opposite of weak. You might not be able to break someone with a punch or withstand one, but your willpower is unlike anyone else. So don't be alarmed but I'm going to go with them."

Her eyes water as she says, "I know you are. You always face a challenge."

"It's to keep you safe."

"Oh shut up. You're my guardian angel I know." She looks away and wipes her eyes with her hand and then against her clothing. She takes a deep breath and looks at the others. "Please be careful. I don't know what I'd do if you got hurt." She looks back at Spike and says, "I'm trying really hard to figure myself out…to figure out why I have this damn book with me." She lets out a little laugh, "And it would help if familiar faces remained, so I can show my appreciation."

He shows a genuine smile and says, "Everyday was like meeting you for the first time. It was like finding the feeling of a true bond over and over again. It saved me more than you know."

"Oh." she rubs her eyes, "Don't go making me cry okay?" she smiles weakly, "Make sure you whack the bad guys really hard with your stick."

He grins, "I've got it."

Cassandra walks over to them and says, "Are you ready to go?"

Essa replies, "Like I have a choice." As she shrugs her shoulders, she looks over and sees Dusk, Hex, Kiyo and Andromeda stand together. They motion for Spike to join them. He gives her one last look before heading towards their company.

Wish says, "I must thank the four of you who are going, for doing something that I myself am avoiding. It feels wrong but it must be done."

Spike grunts, "Feel free to join us champ."

A twinkle goes off in Wish's eye, "In time I suppose." He looks at Hex and says, "Please be safe. They've sent you to do the work of a hundred men."

Hex says wryly, "But I'm an angel, friend. I'm enough."

Wish looks at him closely, making sure to remember what could be the last time they cross paths. He says, "Alright, the four of you and Andromeda can depart from here. I need to start refurbishing this place as it stands."

Spike says, "Ya, play house keeper while we fight."

Wish doesn't reply and merely focuses his attention towards Hex.

They gather around Andromeda and move away from the others until enough space separates them. Dusk looks over and directly into Essa's eyes. Her annoyance lifts as she sees him. They stare in silence. A hand gently rests on his shoulder. He looks and sees Hex.

The angel says, "Stick close to me, and we will succeed. You will be able to see her again."

Spike crosses his arms and asks, "See who again?"

Kiyo grins slightly at the alarm in Spike's tone of voice. Andromeda's eyes glow a faint silver. Wind moves around them.

They disappear, leaving the others behind.

Essa, now taken from the company of those who brought her back home, feels a tinge of pain in her heart.

Gunther, avoiding the chance of looking at her, says, "It's time for us to go."

CHAPTER TWENTY-ONE
Greetings, Threat

The landscape changes and with it they find themselves in the confines of Eryu's city centre. They are met with utter devastation. The buildings surrounding them are on the verge of collapsing into themselves. A few bodies lay within the rubble with pools of blood scattered about.

Kiyo looks around in temporary shock. The feeling of disbelief rattles in his stomach. He can't fathom how people can do this to one another, destroying everything that has been built. The only monsters in his existence have been Nightmares. He's now witnessing where those Nightmares come from, and the sense of ease disappears with the understanding that humans are trouble.

As they all look off into different directions, Dusk asks Hex, "What do we do here? Where do we go next? Hex…"

The angel replies, "We need to find those responsible for this and then ask them why they've done it. If they protest, we make them talk. If they confess, we ensure that the information is accurate."

"This is a lot to take in. I feel like we are getting side tracked."

"We aren't. You just feel that way because this may not directly relate to Sarah's disappearance. Now that you're back in Eryu, your urgency has risen."

"Of course it has. It's been a year Hex."

The angel looks at him and says confidently, "Then we have no more time to waste." He walks forward and into the sunlight cascading between two buildings. It shines on his armor. The light flows around Hex, providing the others with a path to follow. As he continues to walk they see the first true signs of someone worth following. An angel who does not fear what lies ahead.

They venture into the city, moving past broken vehicles and fragmented images of what once compiled a living street. A building on the left starts to crumble and a chunk of the wall falls down, the debris below absorbing its impact.

Making their way forward, each of them looks around for signs of life while staying alert to danger. The stench of death begins to make its way into the air and clings on desperately to its surroundings as if hoping it can return to its former body.

Andromeda's eyes scan the road ahead. She moves forward, watching carefully the moment a sound is made. To guide others is her duty, but to return home is her desire. The two feelings coexist within her and she doesn't mind. She thinks of Wish and the gift he gave her by putting a part of his being into her makeshift empty shell. Now she breathes like a human and feels like one too. She feels the disgust and sadness around her. She feels the fear itching towards her heart.

Walking close behind her, Spike keeps his eyes closed. He avoids tripping by using his instinct, using any opportunity to challenge himself. He doesn't want to see the children lying dead on his left side. Or the elderly lady on his right cut in half with her arm crushed to pieces. He knows they're there but with his eyes closed, it doesn't bother him. He has been through worse, yet he still doesn't have a desire to witness it. Gore is not his thing. He questions his rash decision to venture towards this battleground. Wondering when he stopped acting like the rest of society and like a sadomasochist seeking the opportunity to quench his thirst for blood. It's not the blood that's spilt by others that invigorates him; it's the wounds he causes and receives that speak to him—letting him know he is alive.

His eyes slowly open to look at the death. The realization that crosses his mind causes him to take it all in. His desire to spill blood, to test his strength, exceeds that of protecting Essa. If she were what mattered the most, he would be with her right now. He knows it, and so must she.

Still ahead of everyone, Hex follows his instincts. Walking down streets where their feet are the only sound the echo copies. His mind wanders and he begins to think of the past, breaking his own rule of concentration. He thinks about the words his maker—his leader—told him in confidence.

The voice resonates in his mind and says, *"The boy will be the deciding factor but his fate is not certain. He will be led by his own emotions and desires, and eventually they will boil to a point he cannot contain. He will clash against you if he sees no signs of saving that girl. Do what you can to keep him contained and bring him with you as you move forward. It's time we fix the factor that makes humans destructive to one another."*

He looks behind and sees Dusk gazing off into the distance. If the angel has a fear, it's seeing someone he's spent time with go insane with emotion. Emotion leads to death. His eyes return forward to see what they've been after, the group responsible for this temporary hell.

Across the plaza that separates them from one another, the one who was on the broadcast looks at them closely. Hex and the others stand in place, seeing that the man is with four others.

The man raises a hand and says, "There's something about you that's different. You aren't aiming your guns at us or screaming and begging for mercy. I'll be honest. I don't like it. You're making our lives so much harder." His expression darkens, "Stop prolonging our happiness."

Dusk says, "Happiness? You sick fuck, what right do you have to speak about happiness? Look at what you've done to those around you."

Hex asks, "Who are you?"

The young man replies, "My name is Slate and I am fully aware of what I am doing."

Hex frowns, "And?"

One of the other four, a young man appearing to be in his late teens with long green hair and green eyes, says with a laugh, "You're quite the entitled one aren't you? I'm Vince and oh how I would just love to tear you to bits."

Another one, a young man standing at about 5'2 with short shaggy brown hair and black eyes, says, "That's enough Vince. Let Slate handle it."

Hex raises a hand to his ear and says, "What was that, short one? I didn't hear your name."

The short young man replies, emotionless, "My name is Tern."

Hex, now clearly antagonizing them, looks at the remaining two. One, a young girl with long blond hair and piercing yellow eyes, and the other, a man familiar to Hex and Dusk, someone they met in the graveyard only a day ago.

The girl, known as Lucil, puts her hair into a ponytail and says, "Listen, can we go now Tern? Let Slate handle them. The quicker we finish things, the better it is for all of us."

Tern nods his head and looks up at Slate. "You can handle this, right?"

"Of course, just go."

The remaining young man, the one Dusk met in the graveyard, looks curiously towards them. Something in his eyes shows a longing to connect, to destroy. "I'm going to remain here as well," he says, "I want to see how this plays out."

Tern looks up at him and says, "Do as you will but remember the gift I gave the two of you. Use it if you must. Be safe."

Vince yawns and says, "Have fun with the rabble then. Alright Tern and Lucil, let's go. I'll lead the way."

The three of them leave, removing the illusion that there was a prior balance. Dusk stares at the familiar man and says, "I don't under-stand, why are you here?"

The man ignores the question and replies, "What was it that that arrogant man wanted to know. Was it my name? Then, let this sink into your mind. I am Echo, and all of this, is just the repetition of what you as a society have done time and time again."

With a wild look in his eyes, Spike walks past Dusk and towards Slate and Echo. He pulls out his weapon from behind his back belt, and the small weapon extends into a full long stick made of steel. He licks his lips and picks up his pace, striding towards them.

Echo says, "It appears this one has a death wish. I like that. He's interesting."

Slate replies, "In the end, we will destroy everything, even them. Don't get too attached. It won't do you any good."

"I know…things like that simply break."

Spike, having gotten close, picks up his pace and yells at them, screaming out at the top of his lungs like a soldier in the field of battle.

Dusk says, "We should help him. We can't let him go in alone."

Kiyo replies, "It's best we wait just a little. We have the numbers, let's use that wisely."

"So we just let him act as bait?"

"No. He wouldn't run towards them if he didn't have confidence. The brave are motivated to do great things. Facing up against the lack of purity in their own hearts."

Hex watches as Spike closes the gap, now halfway towards them. He says, "A man like him is rare to find. He doesn't scream in fear, but with the shrill of laughter. While the Federation, the organization meant to protect you humans, watches from afar, even farther than we. A man like that doesn't care about the consequences. He just wants to fight, maim and kill."

Slate raises his left hand into the air, forming a fist. His fingers extend and a sphere of metal emerges, resting on his palm. He hurls it towards Spike, along with a second piece shortly after. Spike dodges both pieces that tear chunks out of the ground from the velocity and weight they hold.

Another piece forms in Slate's palm, Spike's speed not giving any cause for alarm. This time he brings the sphere close to his chest. He wraps both hands around it and squeezes tightly. He then moves his hands away and the piece of metal hovers in front of him. He says, "There's…something special in moments like these."

The piece of cold steel shoots forward, making its way through the air towards Spike. This new type of attack causes Spike to react differently. He slashes the ground in front of him with his weapon, sending pieces of dirt into the air that collide with the metal sphere.

An explosion occurs, sending shrapnel in every direction but his. As the dust settles, Slate is able to see that not a single scratch rests on Spikes skin. He says to him, "I admire your courage, but you will die here. Luck eventually runs out for everyone."

He forms another sphere in the same fashion as before. It shoots towards Spike. Again Spike slashes the ground to protect his body. Another explosion occurs and smoke filled with dust blocks his vision. Slate bursts through the smoke and slams forward. Spike blocks the attack with his long stick, barely managing to stay on his feet from the sheer force of the impact.

Slate flips over his body and sends his foot backwards. It connects with Spike's waist. Slate then follows this attack with a spinning punch that makes impact with Spike's jawline. Slate finishes the barrage with a punch to Spike's chest.

Spike retaliates by swinging his long stick from his right side. Slate ducks underneath it. The long stick then moves at an admirably fast rate with complex movements, quickly making its mark on Slate's forehead.

As Slate falls to a knee, he moves out of the way as the long stick comes slamming downwards into the ground. Spike presses forward, throwing more combinations at Slate, yet the attacks fail to hit as Slate dodges them by moving from side to side.

Slate slams his hand into the ground. He makes contact with a piece of shrapnel in the dirt. Slate grins and Spike notices. He slams his foot into the ground, preparing to use a heavy attack on Slate. The piece of shrapnel that Slate touches morphs and connects with all of the surrounding pieces in the ground. It then bursts outwards into the air, like a snake coiling around its pray, and aims itself at Spike.

With a quick reaction, the long stick is used to stop the impact. Sparks are sent off as the two pieces of metal clash. Slate's eyes flash as he recognizes a perfect opportunity. He rushes forward and leaps into the air, slamming his knees into Spikes face. He spins around him and grabs Spike by the collar. He flips his body over his own and slams him head first into the hard surface below.

The blood begins to form a puddle beneath Spike's head. With his legs still raised into the air, he looks as Slate walks towards him.

Andromeda says to the others, "We need to help him, now."

Spike spins himself quickly, catching everyone off guard. His left leg swings far enough to make impact with Slate's face, knocking him off his feet. As Slate regains his footing, Spike slams his long stick forward into Slate's stomach.

Slate wraps his hands around the long stick and looks forward. A trickle of blood drips down from his lip and onto the long stick. Spike tries to pull it from his grasp but fails. His eyes drift upwards to see the satisfaction on Slate's expression.

The young man says to him, "Bad move."

The weapon morphs and leaves Spike's grip. It rises upward and reforms in Slate's hand, taking on a slightly different appearance. It then smashes across Spike's face and knocks him down.

He gets up, only to receive another blow to the face. He gets back up again, his arms hanging loosely. Slate sends another slash forward. Spike raises his arm and blocks the impact. The blow doesn't affect him. The long stick is sent towards him a few more times and he blocks each blow. As he begins to feel the adrenaline kick in, his eyes grow wilder. He stops blocking the impact of the long stick and runs at Slate. He slams his palms into Slate's chest.

The impact pushes Slate backwards and causes little drops of blood to escape through his mouth. He grows angry and says, "It's still not good enough. You're weak." He swings the long stick forward. It changes direction and makes contact between Spike's eyes.

The impact brings Spike's movement to a stop. His thoughts leave his head and his body is riddled with pain, shooting through his nerves like a river on fire. He bites on his tongue to draw away the pain, and regains focus.

Spike moves his hands forward, trying to catch the next attack, yet it passes through his guard. Once it reaches his chest, he slams his hands onto the stick, holding it tightly. It extends, morphs and slashes his chest. It then wraps around his ankle and yanks, bringing him to the ground.

His body is pulled across the ground and whipped back and forth. He is then slammed into the dirt numerous times before being thrown up into the sky. The metal extends as the distance grows. Spike, as sturdy as he is, cannot hide the look of pain on his face.

He turns to see the long metal stick that was once his, pulling him back towards Slate. However, with swift action Kiyo appears and, with one swipe of his long nails, he cuts through the metal, freeing Spike from Slate's grasp.

Kiyo says, "I thought you could use some help."

Spike laughs in mid air, "Just don't kill my buzz."

He lands on the ground and together Kiyo and Spike dash towards Slate in hopes that Echo will continue to watch, rather than act. If they are given the chance because they are being misjudged, then it's the perfect opportunity for them to finish Slate off.

They reach him and make their moves of attack—Spike now throwing punches and Kiyo slashing. Slate defends himself perfectly by blocking each punch, pushing the fist out of the way. Then, with a push of his palm, he slams it into Spike's chest.

The blow staggers Spike, and for the second time he questions the pain that has enough strength to make his body collapse from ecstasy. He catches himself to ensure he doesn't let his enjoyment of the thrill result in his death. There's so much more to experience and obtain from this encounter.

Kiyo uses Spike's loss of thought to push him forward towards Slate, catching him off guard. He runs around them and, while sticking close to the ground, he avoids any counter attacks of the morphing stick and slashes Slate across the leg.

Blood trickles down Slate's leg. His eyes look at the stream of red soaking through his pant leg, the blood that he cherishes, the bond between him and his friends. He begins to see a change in the tide.

Slate clenches both of his fists and says loudly, "I will not let humans shed the scarce blood that keeps us alive!" All of the muscles in his body flex and he lets out a loud roar. His suit changes into a pitch-black shade with a glowing white and gold prism in the centre of his chest. He clenches his teeth and raises his arms to his side, his muscles bulging. He yells, "I will eradicate those who endanger us!"

Kiyo comments, "It looks like we hit a nerve."

Spike says in turn, "Perhaps you struck one in his leg?"

They look at each other and smile.

Slate pushes his legs forward and slams his hand into Spike's face before Kiyo can react. With a strong grip, Slate moves forward, pushing Spike along with him until he lifts him into the air. With a mighty slam to the ground and push, he drags him head first along the dirt.

Slate then turns around to look at Kiyo with ferocious eyes, his breathing heavy and fast. He pushes forward and meets Kiyo head on. He grabs both of Kiyo's wrists and pushes them out of the way, grabbing ahold of his waist and lifting him up into the air. He slams Kiyo into the ground and then grabs his ankles. He whips Kiyo through the air into a building to the right of where they are fighting, causing a portion of the cement to crumble and windows to shatter.

Turning his head, Slate watches Spike rise from the ground. He sees him crack his neck, removing the strain in his muscles. Spike wipes the blood from his mouth and looks at it on the back of his hand.

He steps forward and meets Slate in direct combat. He throws a left punch, followed by a right and then an uppercut, which strikes Slate underneath the chin. The blow doesn't do much and Spike quickly dodges a punch and then throws another of his own. He continues to engage in the fistfight until Slate makes contact with a punch to the side of Spikes chin, which has enough force to spin him around entirely. As he spins around to face Slate, he sends a kick of his own at Slate's face, yet Slate ducks down and returns a kick, striking Spike in the chest.

His body wobbles backwards. He places both of his hands to his chest and coughs up blood. Spike then turns with just enough time to see Slate already standing at his side. With one backhand strike, Slate sends Spike flying into a building close to where Kiyo was sent tumbling, now causing even more portions of the frail structure to crash into the ground and destroy the silence.

Slate looks over at Dusk, Andromeda and Hex. He then returns his attention to where Kiyo and Spike were sent. He says, "I'll leave these three to you Echo." He walks towards the crumbling buildings. Causing a shift, turning five against two into three against one.

Dusk says, "This is not going well. We can't let him kill them."

Hex replies, "You won't fare much better trying to help. A sword is effective, but useless to a man who can warp all forms of metal."

"They won't survive."

"Have faith, they will live. And so will we."

Andromeda steps between them. She wraps her arms around their necks and says, "Look over there, he's been eyeing us down the entire time. Something tells me that we are in for our own share of fun."

Dusk looks at Echo, who still remains standing far away, watching them closely. Echo's watchful eyes bask in the sunlight of despair, warmth coming from the fires that spread amongst the city. The standoff continues, and the time begins to have a toll on Dusk's patience, as the fear of what lies ahead creeps up on him. He places his faith in Hex who stands with him. Two versus one has proven to be ineffective, yet Dusk knows Hex is stronger than all of them combined. And with the help of Andromeda, Dusk feels confident in their chances.

Yet the calm collectiveness, the cool nature of gratification and anger in Echo's posture, in his existence, rattles Dusk further. He finally gets up the courage required and steps forward with his hand ready to pull out his sword that rests on his waist. As soon as he steps forward, his world takes a sudden turn. Hex pulls him backwards and throws him to the ground. Before Dusk can yell out in shock, a black cloak appears and wraps around Hex, darkness identical to the one that took Sarah months prior. Dusk's eyes struggle for a moment but he sees that Hex is holding off another figure, pushing back and failing to break free.

The man in the black cloak lets out a shrill laugh as his hands get a hold on the angel's throat. Dusk catches a glimpse of the face and the intense contrast between his and Hex's long hair, black against white.

The man says, "Play with me birdy!" and flies off into the air with Hex through the sheer power of pushing off from the ground.

Dusk watches Hex disappear from sight.

In one instant, in a swift moment, Hex took the Burden head on, while Dusk was only able to stare. A cloak of darkness, an entity not even Wish could analyze. This is fear.

He places a hand to his chest and says, "I've already made a mistake…"

His eyes look towards Echo and he sees a young man whose eyes reflect his own despair. He looks up into the sky, only hoping that Hex can handle himself against the sudden threat. Dusk then, with great difficulty, pushes everyone out of his mind and returns his attention to Echo who still stands across from him patiently.

Dusk says, "I can't let everyone fight while I stand here. I'll cut my way through this, I'll kill him." He begins to run forward, keeping his hand on the hilt of his sword, leaving Andromeda behind him, forgetting he still has someone to help him while in his fit of rage.

Echo tilts his head forward a little and continues to wait.

Dusk runs at him, closing the distance, and Echo doesn't move an inch. The footsteps grow farther apart, the speed increases, and Dusk feels his power growing within him. His confidence spirals higher and higher. He reaches Echo and starts to pull out his sword to deliver a quick upper strike. Echo stops this from happening, grabbing ahold of Dusk by the wrist and throat simultaneously. He throws Dusk onto the ground. Echo opens his mouth and utters his first direct words to Dusk since the graveyard, in a slow and definitive manner.

"Greetings, threat. You have lost."

CHAPTER TWENTY-TWO
The Birth of Flames

Amongst the dimly lit clouds between dusk and dawn, is the Trinity. It rides upon the wind that has no demand of its own, its contents both cool and warm. It flows with a natural purpose, to bring the Trinity and its inhabitants along its weightless and guiding path.

The rhythmic pattering of Essa's tapping foot rings clear throughout the Trinity's bridge. It catches everyone's attention, yet no one wishes to ask for silence—the sound keeps them alert. Aware of the circumstance between Gunther and Essa, the crew keeps the joy of Gunther's return amongst themselves. They understand that while a battle wages on below them, they are slowly but surely decreasing the distance to safety—or at least the mirage of safety.

Her foot creates the silence amongst her peers as her eyes stare off into the sky, imagining that the clouds are the towers, and that the vast ocean of blue is the road. Essa thinks deeply about the weight of everything that's being left on the shoulders of Dusk, Hex, Kiyo and Spike. Friends that she's known for a short amount of time yet who have been in her life longer than that. These names mean more to her than she can explain, and with a clear mind, she wonders if she felt this way before and just isn't able to remember, like with her family.

She looks over at Gunther and sees him talking quietly with Tail and Sapphire. The three of them together look completely natural, almost as if they are the definition of what it means to be perfect. But nothing is perfect. Essa knows that everyone has their inner demons, and that those inner demons are why she's stuck with them, fleeing while her friends risk their lives against a threat that might only be the tip of the iceberg.

Essa grinds her teeth and says loud enough for everyone to hear, "I rather die than be someone that flees in the face of adversity. Life isn't about having more strength than the opponent, it's about having the guts to show up in the first place. I want to fight even if I have no strength behind it. I want to show that my love for my friends is equal to their determination to protect human lives."

Her words cause everyone to look at her, even Paige, who rarely removes her eyes from the controls.

Essa continues, "So if you think I'm going to be quiet and accepting while you keep me on this ship, you're wrong. I will find a way there, and if any of you try and stop me I'll make your life an utter hell. A hell that will make the danger you are fleeing from look pathetic."

A small grin appears on Cassandra's face, while Rudy places his hands behind his head and twists in his chair to see Gunther's reaction. The others show a glimmer of anger by being labelled as cowards.

But the most noticeable reaction is from Tail, who coolly responds, "I guess this means Essa here has the real flame, doesn't it Gunther? As reckless as that is."

Sapphire says, "I remember when you were like that."

With his arms crossed, Gunther doesn't laugh or grin. He states, "No flame, however large it may be, will cause damage if it decides to ignite itself below the sea. Essa, what you want to do is sheer suicide. Someone will always have to protect you while you run off into danger to show support. I get it—I know why you want to help. But if we do, there will be casualties amongst us. And to make things perfectly clear, we are bounty hunters, we work for the highest pay, but even then, we can turn it down. Our job is to bring Fleur back to our main ship—the

Dawson—and collect our pay. Whatever happens down there is not of our concern."

The flame within Essa's eyes grows fiercer, and she yells back, "What use is a bounty hunter if the people that hire him are all dead!"

A flash of a dark memory appears in Gunther's head. He winces at the pain and turns his head to look away. A memory of when he was young lingers in his thoughts—the scars on his body, the blood dripping down his wrists. The loss and fear in the eyes of all the children around him. A cold white room with padded walls with only an observation window to break the isolation. Lost children with no escape, only the fate of what lies beyond the only door that faces all of them.

He says, "Essa, a lot of people die. People die every day. But right here, this is my family. I don't plan on putting them in harm's way."

Essa rubs the palm of her left hand and her tone becomes softer, "But, Gunther, my family is down there right now...why can't I be with them?"

His eyes widen, the words strike him and he looks away completely. Sapphire sees the lack of conviction in his eyes as his opinion sways. Tail remains silent but sees the same change within Gunther.

Cassandra walks towards Dexter who's standing in the middle of the bridge, and says, "So, is it natural for the Trinity to take its time flying through the clouds when all it has to do is enter space?"

A twinkle sparks in his eye, and she smiles having caught what's going on. She turns to look over at Abigail and Baylee. The two girls remain silent yet seem to be ready for a mission.

Rudy places his hand to his ear as he begins to listen to a broadcast. His eyes squint for a moment and then widen. He says loudly and quickly, "Paige turn on the broadcast. Guys, you are going to want to see this."

A moment later a screen appears above Paige. Everyone turns to see Vince, one of the five attacking Eryu, send wind ripping through buildings.

The destruction and chaos pushes Essa to become loud again. She yells, "This! We can stop this! I know we can. Gunther please, do what you want but let me go back there! And if you really care about more than just money, then come with me and help me stop this from happening. We're the only ones who can! I know what Wish said is true. I just know."

He asks, "You know?"

"Within my heart, I know. I just do."

He places his hand to his forehead and rubs it, his mind continuing to linger back to the room full of children, where he stood in the middle of it alongside Tail and Sapphire. The three of them innocent, yet aware of how cruel the world can be at such a young age.

And, as if by sheer coincidence, everyone's eyes rise up to look at the destruction being carried out by Vince. They see the symbol on Vince's chest change and begin to glow as his clothes turn green.

The blood drains from everyone's faces. All but Essa and Cassandra.

Sapphire places her hand to her chest, Tail's jaw opens slightly, and Gunther clenches his teeth and squeezes his fists.

"That son of a bitch!" Gunther yells.

Essa isn't sure why this sudden anger bursts out from him. Her eyes stare at the symbol on Vince's chest then back towards Gunther's blazing eyes.

"I will show you a real flame girl." He exclaims, "I will burn everything those bastards cherish into ash. Then look at me and tell me your flame is greater than mine, just try it." His teeth continue to grind, his nostrils flare and he yells out, "Change of plans! We're going to fucking destroy those pests one at a time."

Paige, without hesitation, without putting up an argument about the success of their mission, changes the course of the Trinity and heads towards the capital of Eryu at full force. Every one of the members aboard the Trinity begins to prepare themselves.

Cassandra and Essa watch in awe at the shift in atmosphere. The signs of concern and worry over leaving have been replaced with sheer anger and the will to face any danger. Essa wonders what wound has just opened within their chests.

A trickle of sweat drips down her forehead and Essa pushes her finger against it, feeling the moistness spread across her skin. She turns and looks over at Gunther. With his back pressed against the wall, his lips remain pressed together tightly. Essa wonders if the rise in temperature is coming from him. She asks herself quietly, "Can he really use fire?"

She moves her feet forward and walks towards Paige. She stops and stands behind her. Essa's eyes take in the view and she sees how close they are in such a short amount of time. She realizes that up until that point, the others were stalling, contemplating, worrying, and because of this they hadn't gotten very far. She turns and looks over at Gunther, her opinion of him beginning to change, and she knows she has been too quick to judge him. Yet she fears it's too late to apologize because the man standing in front of her now cannot see her or anyone else. It seems as if to her, he is lost in his own thoughts, where everything is burning. For a moment, Essa wonders if the Trinity still feels like home to Gunther, or if it's become a cell he wishes to break out of.

Turning her eyes back towards the view, she sees the shoreline of Eryu, the waves splashing against the rocks, the birds flying in flocks across the sky, as they avoid what lies below. Further beyond that, clouds of smoke rise in the air. She squeezes Paige's seat. Her heart begins to pound. As the others come close to being ready, she looks down at herself and sees only weakness. She refuses to become a nuisance, and from that strong desire, something begins to grow within her.

Paige says, "We're arriving in five minutes guys, get ready and head towards the hangar doors. We're going to be dropping you off from the air."

Essa asks, "The air?"

A hand presses on her shoulder and she turns to sees Dexter, "Follow me" he says. She does so without question and leaves the bridge where Paige and Rudy remain, ensuring the Trinity arrives as swiftly as possible.

Her feet tap against the floor, one after the other. She begins to walk faster, following Dexter's pace. She soon finds herself running, running as fast as she can, as he makes his way towards the hangar.

Once they arrive, she sees both Baylee and Abigail wearing their air gear already. The hangar doors open and the wind comes swooping in, causing everyone's hair to thrash around widely.

Abigail says, "We're about ready to head in. You haven't done this before have you Essa?"

Essa says in response, "No, I certainly haven't."

"Well it's not too bad once you strap yourself into this—which doesn't take long. Most of the work is maneuvering yourself accurately as to avoid any collisions." Abigail raises her hands, "Just follow my actions."

Alarmed, Essa raises her arms and the air gear straps onto her. She looks at Baylee who simply nods her head as if to say it's normal.

"Now," Abigail says, "the three of us are going to be descending with you while Gunther, Tail, Sapphire and Cassandra will form the other group. We'll be heading off in about two minutes. Don't worry, once you are in the air just guide yourself and keep your legs together. Once you come close to the ground, spread your arms apart. You will feel the change in the drop and you'll slow down."

"Wait, wait, this is a lot to take in. Isn't this rash?"

"Well, yes, it is, but there's no time to train you."

"…I'm going to fall to my death at this rate."

Dexter chimes in, "The three of us use the gear the most out of everyone on the Trinity, and we'll make sure you don't splatter on the ground." He slaps the back of her shoulder with a smile and steps towards the open hangar doors. "Alright." He says, "It's just about time to do this."

Cassandra walks into the room with Gunther and the others, already wearing the air gear. Essa turns to see her, and Cassandra gives her a slight nod and says, "You'll be fine, I'll be right behind you."

Dexter says, "Alright, it's time." He waves Essa over and she walks to him, taking a place between him and Baylee. The wind rings loudly in Essa's ears and she starts to have trouble hearing anyone talk. She notices the others using hand signs and then, without notice, she finds herself falling through the air. Again, the sky greets her, and, again, her first instinct is to scream.

As she descends, and the city of Eryu is still quite far away in the distance, she feels her body fill with adrenaline rather than fear. Her eyes watch the others and she mimics their movements. Despite having never used air gear before, she finds herself somewhat comfortable. Her eyes look to her side to make sure her pouch—her book—is still with her.

The fall continues. Baylee and Abigail begin to turn so Essa follows, Dexter slows his speed and Essa gets closer to him. He starts to turn and ends up next to her shortly after. He gives her a handsome smile and she tries to hide her blush. It feels crazy to blush while falling towards a potential demise. It's even crazier how fast the tides have taken a turn.

***

Not far behind them, Gunther leads the others. They head through the sky fairly quickly to ensure the gap between both their group and Essa's is as small as possible. Gunther's eyes remain on Essa for the time being, hoping that she will come out of this entire ordeal alive.

Meanwhile, as the two groups fall through the sky towards Eryu, on the ground a threat awaits them. Vince looks up at the sky. With a grin he stretches both of his arms before crunching his hands. Air begins to gather in his palms. The golden prism on his chest casts a glow on his green clothing.

Lucil asks, "Do you see something you like?"

Vince's smile widens as he says, "I get to tear up the sky now."

Tern looks up and, while squinting, can see eight small figures in the air starting to increase in size.

Baylee and Abigail, the closest to arriving in Eryu, begin to feel a change in the air. Baylee looks at Abigail and shows concern.

Abigail turns to look at Dexter, who shows the same sense of concern. It becomes apparent that the reason their groups are so close together, and why there's so many of them, is because they won't all be making it towards the ground unscathed. There's strength in numbers.

Squinting, Dexter sees a shift in the wind ahead of them. He yells out for the others, yet the speed of the wind reaches them first. It brushes past Abigail and misses the others. Essa notices the intense air pressure and the spontaneous movements of Abigail. She begins to feel the fear creep back into her heart.

Dexter yells once more, and another gust of air moves past them, followed by another and then another. Abigail and Baylee move out of the way of the air attacks and continue to press forward. Another air attack, faster and smaller in size rushes towards them. It strikes Baylee in the leg, causing her to spin around. Abigail yells out and reaches out for her. Baylee regains her composure with little time to celebrate before another small air attack strikes the side of her arm. This time it sends her off course completely.

Unable to reach her, Abigail watches in horror as Baylee descends at a rapid speed. Dexter presses his arms close to his sides and speeds off towards her.

Essa watches as her group begins to split apart.

Seeing the chaos in front of them, Gunther and the others cut through the air at the fastest rate possible and soon merge with Essa and Abigail. Then, moments later, Gunther, Tail and Sapphire push forward, forming the front while keeping the rest behind them to ensure them some needed protection.

Looking down, Gunther sees that Dexter has successfully grabbed ahold of Baylee and is now preparing for a heavy landing.

The gusts of air continue to head towards them and occasionally strike them. The closer they get, the stronger the attacks feel, until one of them cuts through Sapphire's arm. Gunther takes note of this and they split off from one another. Essa and the others do the same, all realizing that the farther apart they are, the less likely they'll all be hit.

Halfway now towards their desired landing, the adrenaline rises even further in Essa's body. Everything starts to move past her at a faster rate. Her mind is racing, trying to keep everything under check as she sees the mistakes being made and the misfortune of the wind.

Her eyes rest upon Tail as she follows his movements. Occasionally taking a quick turn, she manages to avoid the slicing wind that passes them. She hates how weak and feeble she feels, having no choice but to continue falling towards the predator waiting below. Yet, as she and the others close the gap and start to make out the green haired killer who's attacking them, everything takes a turn for the worst.

His bellowing voice rocks through the sky and pierces their ears, "Come, let me rip you apart!" followed by a shrieking laughter. A long slicing gust of wind is sent from both of his hands. It tears through the sky and is the first attack that can be easily seen. But seeing it does them no good, for its size and speed is impossible to avoid for anyone who isn't used to air gear.

It strikes both Essa and Cassandra. It tears through Essa's side and pierces a rib. She winces in pain and loses her control and sense of direction. She starts to scream as her body takes a sharp turn to the right and heads towards a set of towers.

Gunther turns his head to see this and feels the light drain from his eyes. Her body crashes through a set of windows and leaves his sight. Soon after, he turns his head and looks away. There's no time for remorse.

Memories begin to flood into his head and he tunes out Sapphire's calling for him. He simply descends into both his own mind and towards the evil below.

A ticking sound—that of a clock moving its hand around vibrates in his skull. Gunther sits strapped in a cold steel chair with ragged clothes on, torn and dirty, his face full of cuts and bruises, with the floor below containing a mixture of blood and tears.

A voice, cruel in its nature, asks Gunther, "Do it, use the fire, or bleed out like the rest."

Wounds on his wrist let out Gunther's blood. With all of his might, he continues to restrain himself from crying out in pain. To show tears would be to show weakness, and he refuses to let his opponent get that satisfaction.

As he battles the stress and tries to remain conscious, the blood continues to pour out. His eyelids begin to grow heavy. Another voice starts to play within his mind, that of Sapphire saying, "It's okay you know? One day, you, Tail, Cecilia and I, even Max, we can all get away from here. We just need to be patient, because I know there's good within us, and the world can't be that evil, evil enough to let children be tortured."

A slight tear forms in his right eye. His head begins to fall forward as his neck takes on invisible weight. Tail's voice now begins to ring in his ear, "Gunther, it's alright to be angry. It's an emotion like the rest. Sometimes, it's the right thing to feel."

Their smiling faces, young and happy, flash past his eyes, and then he sees Cecilia, her short silver hair, her sparkling blue eyes, her thin build and soft smile. Gunther slowly turns his head and looks over to see Cecilia sitting in a chair beside him. Her head hanging forward with a lifeless expression, her wrists having been cut just like his own.

He slowly calls out, "Cecilia…" his voice both dry and sore. "Cecilia, please…wake up." His eyes begin to water and tears drip down his face, washing away both blood and dirt. He stares at her rigid body—her skin paler than it was when she was alive. As he stares, her smiling face, her short shiny hair, disappears from his mind.

He grinds his teeth and turns his head, facing the camera in front of him. He clenches his muscles and the blood begins to pour out faster. "Cecilia! You murdered her! You fucking murdered her!" he slams around in his seat, flailing his body around.

A man stands on the opposite side of an observation screen that separates his presence from them. He grins with his arms crossed. He says through the microphone, "You will join her, or you can control the gift I've given to you."

Gunther flails around even more and then stretches forward, his eyes bulging in their sockets as he says, "I'll fucking burn you, I'll turn you into a pile of ash!"

Steam begins to rise from his skin. The wounds on his wrist begin to close as sparks of flame scorch them. "I WILL BURN YOU, MELT YOU, AND MAKE YOU NOTHING!" His body bursts into flames and he is soon engulfed. Unable to control it, it begins to harm portions of his skin as he screams out, "Cecilia!"

The memory fades, the smile of the innocent girl he met in that dark place along with it. Her soft smile, her faint resemblance to a long lost sister, all of it gone.

He opens his eyes and sees that the target is closer. His eyes show a small flame within the pupils. The wind that whips around his body ignites the flames within his heart, given to him by a man of hell, blossomed and controlled for those he loves.

The flames that flicker around Gunther's body do no harm to his skin or clothing. As he fears for Essa, as he hates the sense of loss, he pulls out his sword and wings of flame begin to spread around him. They dance with the wind.

His flames stay close to him as he leads the way. Sapphire and Tail descend on his left and right. Abigail remains behind them staying close to Cassandra.

Tern and Lucil approach Vince and look up at Gunther and the others. Tern says, "It seems your barrage hit a few, but you've angered one to the point that he's burst into flames."

Lucil says, "It almost makes me feel less unique."

Vince cracks his knuckles and laughs. "Let them get as close as they want. I'll rip through them all."

Despite Vince's confidence and Lucil's slight admiration, Tern feels an unsettling presence coming from Tail, Sapphire and especially Gunther. A feeling that suggests his inferiority but more importantly, a similarity.

He looks at the man who's one with fire and wonders how that came to be. He wonders what burning passion resides within him to allow him to control such a thing. His eyes begin to reflect the warmth of the fire in the sky above. He sees the passion, the flame. He sees the birth of something profound.

Tern says quietly, trying to hide his confusion, "Their names will be worth remembering. I wonder if ours will be after that heat that scorches everything it touches, reaches us."

CHAPTER TWENTY-THREE
Nicknames

In times of anger, decisions are made at a different pace. The mind tunes out anything unrelated to the cause. The heart pumps through the veins a boiling liquid that gives life to the one experiencing it. For Gunther, reaching this point of anger means casting away any sense of security and wielding his curse as a weapon. His fire, the one everyone has within his or her heart, shows itself.

Gunther lands on the ground and flames surround him, scorching the earth. Hot wind presses against Vince, Tern and Lucil. Two raise their arms in defense yet Vince simply moves his arms to the side and beckons for a fight, his eyes asking for it, his thirst for it multiplying with each level of danger.

Tail and Sapphire land moments later with Abigail and Cassandra. The five of them face off against the three villains.

Gunther barks out, "Who are you! Tell me, who thinks it's clever to destroy and smile doing so? I want to know before I burn those who wear that disgusting emblem on their chest."

Vince looks at the mark and places his hand against it, rubbing the edges of the prism. He raises an eyebrow and says, "This little thing? It's just a mark. But you, your eyes are filled with bloodlust all because of what, this?" Vince laughs, "because of this mark? So what if it's on my chest!"

The anger spreads throughout Tail and Sapphire. Tern begins to feel an increase in danger from the three of them. He starts to look around for an escape route.

Vince continues, "If you must know. We here, we are the vindicated. Every action we do is out of love for each other, and despite what you see we are actually fighting agaisnt a bigger evil." He places his hand to his chest, "but that being said, removing humans from the world doesn't really weigh me down. For, I am the Push."

Lucil says, "I am the Current."

Tern moves his eyes to Gunther and the others, "I am the Bond."

Sapphire raises her arm forward and prepares an attack, her hand forming into a cannon. "Childish nicknames."

Vince retaliates, "Nothing childish about being true to one's self, you'll see exactly who we are…starting now!" He slams his hands together and a loud bang erupts, followed by a surge of air that wraps around his hands, moves up his arms then back towards his hands. He sends it forward with a spin of his wrists.

Sapphire raises her left arm, the cannon, forward. Within its tunnel, a red beam begins to glow. "L-Cannon, initiate protocol—ANNI-HILATE, seventy-five percent." It shines brighter and fires. It makes impact with the wind from Vince and erupts, destroying the ground within the vicinity. The red beam presses forward and Vince slams his hands together. He raises one hand forward and does a ripping motion with his finger, sending a wind slicing through the beam, dispersing it.

The fight blows up from there. Gunther charges forward and uses his air gear for an increase in acceleration. He uses it to attack Vince from an unusual angle. His sword slices forward and cuts Vince's arm. He lands behind him and slashes forward then upwards and then side to side. He continues to push forward. Vince doubles back and throws waves of air to push Gunther away and disperse the flames. Yet the fire refuses to die and only increases in presence.

Lucil flicks her fingers and a spark of lightning erupts from it.

It heads towards Gunther. Abigail yells out to warn him. He turns and slashes his sword down into the lightning. It explodes and, for a brief moment, the flames rise up and cover everything around Gunther, hiding his presence. As the flames return to their normal state, not a scratch can be seen on him. Lucil frowns and sends off another spark of lightning. This time he dodges it and ignores her, continuing to press after Vince.

Vince yells out, "So one on one with me, is that it?!" As he says this, he finds himself stopping suddenly. He looks down to see a set of shadows wrapped around his ankles, quickly spreading up his body.

Tail does this with the use of one hand as he says to Abigail and Cassandra, "The two of you need to go look for Essa, Dexter and Baylee. When you find them I want you to stay with them. We will come find you once we are done here."

Cassandra asks, "Are you sure? I can help."

He looks at her from the corner of his only visible eye, "I know you can, that's why I'm putting my trust in you to go find them. Don't betray that trust. Especially the faith Essa has in you."

She gulps. Abigail grabs her hand and says, "Let's go."

They exit the battlefield and disappear in the direction the others fell, heading into the streets and crumbling buildings.

Vince struggles to break free of the shadows. He sends a wave of wind into the ground but it does little. He looks at Tail in disgust until a voice catches him unawares.

Gunther says into his ear, "You should never look away from me." He then appears in front of him and the heat of the fire slams into Vince. He cringes and feels the flames start to scorch his skin. He sends a wave of wind towards Gunther but it's far too weak to do anything. As the sword rises to cut into Vince, Tern makes his move.

Tern strengthens the gravity field around Vince, forcing Gunther to his knees. His sword almost leaves his hands completely. The shadows from Tail are torn apart. With Vince now free, he leaps backwards and slams his hands together. Rubbing them as he spins them, he lets out a wind that spirals and slams into Gunther, knocking him further backwards.

Gunther uses the air gear to hover over the ground and as he prepares to push forward, another one of Lucil's lightning bolts strikes him, causing an explosion.

Vince grins, "So, like I was saying, shall we do this one on one?"

Gunther wipes a smidgen of blood from his cheek and watches it evaporate. He says calmly, "Sapphire, you have my permission to use full force for the next minute. Make that girl repent."

"With pleasure." Sapphire takes her first step forward since she landed on the ground. Tail can't withhold his smile as he watches in glee.

Lucil looks at Sapphire in disgust and says, "What the hell? You think I'm scared of you?"

Tern looks towards Sapphire and then at Gunther. His mind begins to race and his eyes start to look around again for an escape. He sees Tail attempt to send shadows towards Vince once more. Tern presses and slams his hand forward. The shadows are forced down by the gravity. Without knowing it, he's stepped into Tails trap.

Shadows approach Tern from beneath the dirt and burst out behind him. He spins around and emits a much weaker field of gravity to push away the shadows. As he attempts to spin back towards Tail, a punch is sent into his face. He falls onto the ground. He gets back up only to receive a knee to his waist. He coughs and raises a hand forward. A force of gravity slams into Tail and makes him stumble. Tern then manipulates the gravity further and knocks Tail's chin upwards but that isn't enough to create a distance between them.

Tail says, "It looks like I had an appropriate hunch. Your attacks grow weaker if used in succession. How about you show me the emblem on your chest so I can remove it?"

Tern snarls slightly, "You're getting ahead of yourself."

As they face off, Vince laughs hysterically as he gets into the feel of the fight and starts to push Gunther back. His attacks grow in strength through his excitement and adrenaline rush.

He cuts chunks out of the ground and sends debris and earth into the air. As Gunther runs sideways and wraps around the battlefield, he passes a group of buildings by using the air gear at its maximum capacity. Vince takes complete glee in tearing through it, killing anyone unfortunate enough to be hiding within. The building comes crashing down and sends off a cloud of smoke. Vince cuts through the smoke and attacks widely, now uncertain as to where Gunther is.

A flash of flame erupts through the smoke and Gunther rushes forward, putting an immense amount of strain on his air gear. The metal begins to melt from the already unbelievable heat. He heads straight for Vince with the intention of a head-on collision.

Vince pulls back his left hand and then slams it forward with a yell. The attack connects with Gunther and tears away some of the flames. New ones form in its place and the distance between them becomes miniscule. Vince pulls back both of his arms and the smile of satisfaction is replaced with a tinge of worry. He yells out and slams both of his hands forward. The ground in front of him is blown to pieces and destroys everything on its way to Gunther.

Pushing the air gear to its upmost degree, it breaks and sends Gunther through the wind. Most of the flame around him is blown off. With a yell, he slashes his sword through Vince from the right shoulder down towards his left midsection. The cut is deep enough to cause Vince to drop both of his arms, take a few steps back and begin to fall.

He catches himself before falling to the ground and holds himself up. His eyes look around to see Tern dashing around and holding off Tail. He thinks about the gift around his finger that Tern gave him, and then decides he won't use it. He sees Lucil being beaten to a pulp by Sapphire with intense punches and kicks followed by a cannon attack that sends her through a wall and tumbling on the ground.

Blood gushes from Vince's mouth. Tern and Lucil both notice the change in his behavior and the large wound on his body. Vince raises one hand forward and gives the thumbs up. With a slight smile he raises both of his arms and spins himself around, causing a tornado to form around him.

Lucil screams for him. Tern sets off power he's been withholding and it puts Tail off his feet, causing Sapphire to become distracted.

Tern runs and grabs ahold of Lucil and says, "We need to go, now!"

"We can't leave him!"

"He'll make it okay! He's letting us get away first. Don't worry! He's going to make it." He pulls on her arm and she looks back until she can no longer see Vince at all.

Tail gets up onto his feet and wipes the dirt from his pants. He fixes his hood and turns to look at the wild tornado. The wind pressure is enough for him to feel his feet slide across the ground. He uses his shadows to keep himself in place. He looks to see Gunther standing at the edge of the tornado, staring into its depths with a face riddled with intense anger.

Sapphire says, "Gunther, they are getting away."

He replies sternly, "It does not matter, this one will do for now."

Tail asks, "What is it you plan to do?"

"Get some answers, and leave nothing." A new set of flames burst around him. He steps forward into the tornado. The flames cast off into the wind, and in a matter of seconds it becomes a fire of its own.

He walks within the eye of the tornado and approaches Vince who is on his knees breathing heavily. The gash on his body is mortal, the blood already forming a pool around him.

Looking up, Vince says in pain, "Can't say I'm happy with the way this turned out." He coughs and smiles, "But I can't deny that this is the most alive I've felt…since I was born."

Gunther looks down at him with a sense of disgust as well as some form of pity toward the dying young man. The sound of the wind ripping around them echoes in his ears while the heat from his flames press against the tunnel surrounding them. He asks, "Why do you wear that emblem?"

"What does it matter?"

"It matters a great deal. That emblem—I know who it represents. A bastard I can never forgive. A person who took away more than my sense of freedom, but also the lives of those I care about. He warped everyone close to me."

Vince looks up at him, letting his hand drop from the wound, giving up on stopping the blood from pouring out. "Is that so…then, I understand your anger. It's almost a pity I was on the opposite end of it."

"I see no pity in that."

"Why? Because I destroyed this city?"

"No, I could give two fucks about this place. What you did is worse, you spilt the blood of someone I hold dear."

"So that's it…that's why you're able to stand here right now without a sense of fear. These flames, your flames, you're not normal either. What did he do to you? This man?"

Gunther pauses at the question and decides not to answer. Instead he asks a question of his own. "Before I cut through you, who are you, really?"

Vince's smile wavers slightly as his breath becomes heavy and his vision begins to blur. His voice lowers as he says, "I'm just another familiar face…a clone that the man you hate has made…but I don't regret what I've done." He looks up, with a larger smile, "Because what I did, I did for the ones I love. What would you do for the ones you love?" He closes his mouth abruptly and his lips press together tightly as he feels the approach of death.

Hearing the truth, Gunther's anger leaves his heart for the time being. He looks at Vince, stricken by the words that have been spoken. He answers, "I would do as you have done, because I am the fire, I am the birth of flames."

"I like that…birth of flames…its…kind of…coo-l…" Vince's head drops forward and he falls onto the ground. The wind around them disperses. Gunther turns to look over at Tail and Sapphire, who await to hear what he has to say, but words are not needed, for the tears in his eyes say all they need to know—the tears of a flame.

CHAPTER TWENTY-FOUR

Friend of the Family

Broken glass, cool wind, ringing ears; Essa slowly turns her head. The piercing sensation in her ribcage causes her eyes to roll around in the back of her head. Ticking, itching, aching sensations dance around together. She moves her eyes forward.

As they blur, shutter and try to make out what rests before her, she sees a figure that soon morphs into someone she knows. Mr. Lunar. Standing at the windows, looking out into the distance. She notices his slick clothing consisting of a black suit and tie, his hair still in a ponytail with a black band and his sword sheathed on his side. She asks with a wince of pain, struggling to stop herself from screaming, "Mr. Lunar, what are you doing here?"

He does not look at her or give an answer. Another voice responds, "It's nice to see you've woken up, but that wound doesn't look to good. Let me take a look at it."

Essa looks up to see Miss Dixon, the nurse from her high school, one of the three teachers who fought Nix alongside Mr. Lunar and Mr. Linder when they were being attacked.

Essa sits up slowly. Some shards of glass fall. A few cuts rest on her elbows. She brushes off the few remaining pieces of glass stuck to her clothing. She winces in pain once more, noticing the stream of blood coming from her midsection. Looking at Miss Dixon she asks, "What's going on here?" She clutches herself in pain.

Miss Dixon runs over and places her hand against the wound and the pain begins to fade momentarily. Essa looks in awe.

Dixon sees the sense of curiosity and says, "I've formed a small barrier within your ribcage. It will stop the bleeding, and stop the wound from getting worse. However it's only a temporary fix. As long as I concentrate, you'll be fine."

"I didn't know you could do something like that."

Miss Dixon smiles and says, "How could you?"

Essa blinks, still unsure how to respond to the familiar faces.

Mr. Lunar says, "Take a look outside at all of this destruction. That is why we are here Essa."

She turns and sees a tornado brewing in intensity. "I don't remember seeing that on my way down."

Miss Dixon replies, "You were out for a while."

"So you just watched me?"

"We had other concerns before yours."

"Such as?"

The tornado catches fire and ignites the sky. Essa returns her attention to it and says nothing, wondering if the flame is coming from Gunther. Wondering if he can truly use fire.

Miss Dixon hums slightly and says, "Well…"

Mr. Lunar comments on the tornado, "It appears Gunther has decided to let loose. It's been quite some time. I wonder how hot his blade has become."

Essa raises an eyebrow and asks, "Miss Dixon, I'm aware the city is under attack. What I want to know is why the two of you are here… and how do you know Gunther?"

Miss Dixon replies, "Please, just call me Veronica."

"Okay, Veronica, can you tell me?"

"Well…" her voice fades and her expression shows that she's looking for the correct thing to say.

The doors behind them open and Essa sees Mr. Linder walk in with his huge smile. He's also wearing a black suit and tie, but his muscle mass makes him look a tad odd. The uniform suits Mr. Lunar and Veronica much better.

Essa twitches slightly while looking at Mr. Linder, wondering how he ever successfully pulled off being an English teacher since seeing him now made that seem ridiculous.

He opens up his arms and says, "Essa, how are you!?" He walks past Veronica and picks Essa up, spinning her around. His happy behavior throws her off further. His smile seems out of place when so much destruction is going on—that and the pain still speaking softly in her side.

Mr. Linder places her down and pats her on the head. He asks, "How've you been? I thought you were dead for sure. It's nice to see you made it out of there alive!"

"Uh, ya…I'm doing good I guess." She starts to look for a way out of the room, the reunion being more than unwelcome.

Veronica walks forward and places a hand between Essa and Mr. Linder. "Alright, that's enough. You are only scaring the poor girl. I haven't even told her who we really are yet or why we are here. And if you haven't noticed, she just fell through a window from up above."

He replies, "What the hell! You haven't told her yet?" Mr. Linder looks at Essa, "I'm sorry, you probably think I'm being irrational." He looks at the broken window and then comments, "Tough skin."

Mr. Lunar says, "You are always irrational Bryce." His eyes still look at the tornado, its fire starting to disperse.

Veronica says, "So, it's time we tell you who we are, but first, we must know-"

Essa replies, cutting her off, "Ya, there's always a 'but first.' I'm here because I was using air gear, but that got torn off and I ended up here. I should be down there where the tornado is, however that clearly isn't the case."

Mr. Lunar asks, "With Gunther?"

Essa raises an eyebrow, "Yes, and again, how do you three know him? Are you all bounty hunters as well?"

Bryce smiles, "In simplistic terms, yes."

"Are you friends?"

"We tolerate him. He's a hot head at times."

She scoffs, "I don't deny that."

"Where have you been since the last time we saw you?" Veronica says, returning the attention to Essa's whereabouts up until then.

"Ugh, that's a long story."

Veronica laughs, "Then we don't have time to hear it. Though I'm sure we will find out about it as information gathering is second nature for us."

"Why is that?"

Mr. Lunar looks away from the window, "Because we are just like your friend Gunther. However we're a step above being simple bounty hunters."

"And being a step above lets you figure me out?"

Veronica says, "Correct. For example, we know that where you went was not on Eryu."

Bryce continues, "We also know that you have only known Gunther for a short while."

Getting slightly annoyed, Essa asks, "Well, how is it you know that those flames are Gunther's? After all, isn't all fire the same?"

Mr. Lunar asks with a flicker in his eyes, "Are all swords the same to you? Do all footprints share the same imprint? No, there is always a characteristic—a detail—that separates it."

"…Then what exactly is his?"

Veronica answers for him, "Emotion, love."

Essa turns and sees that the tornado is now gone. She bites her lip and asks, "Why were you at my school for such a long period of time? What was the mission?"

Bryce answers, "We received information about a member of the organization known as the Burdens and we believed that your school was one of their targets. However, the information was minimal, and for months we felt that we were wasting our time. We finally figured out their plan the day before but it wasn't enough time to stop the massacre."

Essa frowns and replies, "So you three knew about the Burdens, yet all of those people died?"

The three look at each other before Veronica says, "You know about them Essa?"

Her face flushes. She clearly gave herself away. "I've just heard things is all."

Bryce says, "Well not many people speak openly about the Burdens."

Mr. Lunar says, "Regardless. You're here now and you are alive. We failed at your school but at least some survived."

Essa asks, "So...why are the three of you here? I still don't know that."

Veronica grins and says, "It's not every day someone who crashes through a window asks all the questions."

Essa raises her chin and retorts, "It's not every day my teachers turn out to be imposters."

Bryce responds quickly and gruffly, "Behave, you're in the president's office."

Essa looks around at the walls and sees artwork of the stars, planets and famous spaceships. She sees a large banner that hangs from the top of the ceiling to the floor, with a background of deep red. She sees a desk toppled over with all of its contents spread across the floor.

She hears the doors open once more. Four soldiers walk inside; followed by the man that Essa can only assume is the president. She looks at him and feels a knot in her chest form.

Instinctively she reaches for her pouch and notices it's no longer with her. Before panicking, she looks around and sees that it's close to the table and chair. Taking note of her focus, Bryce goes and picks it up. As he lifts it into the air, the book falls out of the pouch and hits the floor. Everyone in the room turns and looks at it.

Their expressions put her off, as they are all frightening. They glare at the book. Unknowing as to why, she wonders if, up until that point, everyone else has had the same opinion towards it. She watches Bryce pick it up. He opens the pouch and continues to frown. He places it back into the clearly miniscule pouch with its vast compartment within. He approaches her and hands it over in silence.

Essa asks, "Is there something wrong?"

"No." he says sternly, "Just, I haven't seen a book like that before." He then turns and stands next to Essa as the president makes his way further into the room.

She wonders why the book is unsettling, and not the pouch. Before her mind can wander further, the soldiers move out of the way and the president comes into view.

He looks familiar, to the point that it causes her head to ache. She winces from the pain and stares at him. It begins to dawn on her that she's met him once before. A friendly smile is on his clean-shaven face with piercing green eyes and brown hair. His wrists crossed and resting behind his back.

He greets her politely, "Hello Essa, how are you faring?"

Her eyes widen. An image passes through her mind and she puts the pieces together and says, "You're…the man who…kept my home for me."

The others look at him, curious as to what Essa is implying. He says, "I'm glad you can recognize me. It appears you're getting better. I've waited for this day for a long time…" A hint of sadness attaches itself. He asks, "Have your memories returned? Or is this coming as a shock more than a nostalgic reunion?"

She says, "I…I only know of you because Cassandra mentioned something about someone powerful who looked over me. And when I just saw you now, I felt like it was you."

He replies, soft spoken, "You're right, it was me."

Her eyes water slightly, unknowing as to why she feels that way. She asks tremulously, "Why did you go through the trouble of looking after me? I was so…young. I wouldn't have been able to blame anyone, especially in my condition, if I was just left to die."

His face grows firm and he says, "I would never leave you to die.

You were, and still are, the youth of this generation. Your family and I were close. Losing them was like losing my own family. If I were to abandon you…it would have been like abandoning a child—my child."

One of the soldiers begins to grow wary of the length of the ongoing discussion, considering the circumstances taking place outside. He leans in and whispers to the president. He nods his head in understanding of the soldiers concern.

Essa asks, "How did you know my family?"

"I knew your father primarily. He then introduced me to the rest of your loving family. He and I worked together. Back then I wasn't the president of Eryu, I was simply a common official. But your father…" His eyes begin to light up with warmth, "… He was an incredible man. He could have been anything…"

Essa clears her throat and asks, "May I know your name?"

He looks at her in bafflement and says apologetically, "I'm sorry, I forgot to do something so simple. Essa, My name is Alexander Ixar and it is my pleasure to finally see you again. I know the circumstances are dire, but I, will always be here for you."

Her body shakes but she knows deep within her heart that this man is good. She nods her head and begins to feel a rush of emotions collide. An explosion outside of the tower catches all of their attention and pulls her back into the reality of what's transpiring. Now is not the time or place to ask personal questions.

Veronica says, "We should be safe in here. My barrier can handle an explosion. Even a falling building won't destroy it."

Essa asks again, "Why are the three of you here?"

Mr. Lunar replies, "Isn't that obvious? We've been hired to protect Alex."

Bryce nods his head in agreement.

Alexander says, "Essa, there are fifty men stationed within this building. We will be safe for the time being."

She says rashly, "It's not about us being safe…why are you all in here when so many people need your help outside? That's where we should be. Not here hiding."

Mr. Lunar says, "Essa… The president's life is of a higher value."

Alex raises a hand and says, "It's not that. Unfortunately I have tasks required of me to ensure the balance of Eryu and its aligning planets. The High Council and the Federation are also…helping. If I die, it will put everything into a free-for-all. I wish I could be out there helping, believe me, but a man who's better suited to politics, does not throw strong punches."

Mr. Lunar continues, "Not to mention, if the Burdens show up, not even this barrier will hold."

Veronica huffs but doesn't argue.

Essa takes a slight step back, "…So, you're all stuck in this cage… scared of what's coming." She begins to reflect on what Wish had said before everyone left his hideout. How there are those who know of the danger yet have not taken action.

A flash of anger sparks within the three bounty hunters. Mr. Lunar clenches the hilt of his sword and says, "I will never be put in a cage, only an illusion of one can be made and that is when I strike. The ones being slaughtered are the unfortunate, but a lot goes on that you do not see."

"…Alright." Essa clutches her pouch. "Whatever, I'll be going now. I have to help the unfortunate." She looks at Alex, "It was nice seeing you again."

This catches them by surprise.

Alexander says, "Surely you don't mean to go back out into that. You're safe here."

"It's not about being safe. Gunther and the others are fighting. I'm ashamed that I'm here while they put their lives on the line."

Mr. Lunar looks at her with a tinge of respect, "That is admirable. I will not stop you."

Bryce bursts in protest, "You can't go out there Essa, a girl like you will-"

"Will what!" she bursts out, "I'll what, say it!"

"…You'll die."

Her scarlet red hair reminds them of someone else that they know.

Her eyes burn and she clenches her fist, pointing a finger forward. "I will not die. I will do what I set out to do. So protect Alex, make sure he accomplishes his duties. But do not impede my progress. I do not fear those Burdens. They will fear me when they see the wrath of someone who's lost everything more than once."

CHAPTER TWENTY-FIVE
Carnage, the Star

Outside of the tower protected by Veronica's barrier, a blur of darkness and light moves through the sky. Translucent feathers fall with trickles of blood staining the tips. The blur moves closer towards the tower, turning and spinning frantically. Within the mixture of chaos, Hex fights the madman who refuses to let go.

Having continued to battle him through the sky since being with Dusk, Hex grows angrier at each passing second. The Burden, the first he's encountered, is strong enough to hold him and keep him from getting an opening. What's worse, the insane smile of satisfaction, the eyes that roll around in his head, the dark piercing glare, white skin and long black hair. It all screams lunacy, yet Hex knows it's more than that. The Burden, he's simply playing around.

They slam into an invisible wall and it stops both of them. The Burden, who is closest to it, turns his head and sees that they haven't struck a wall, but something protecting it. He looks upwards and downwards, then directly forward.

Hex breaks free of the grip and throws a punch. The Burden raises one hand forward and sends Hex into the ground fifty floors below.

The man reaches out and touches the barrier, feeling a slight wavering on his fingertip. His smile grows.

Veronica feels the pulsation on the barrier and walks towards the windows. She looks down and sees a man is hovering in the air at the barrier. Her face grows pale as she notices his black cloak, torn at the edges, flying loosely around him. She sees him looking up with a smile still on his face.

She backs away from the window and turns to the others, "We need to get out of here right now."

Mr. Lunar and Bryce rush towards Essa and Alexander without a second to waste. They grab them gently and bring them towards the doors leading out of the room. Two soldiers follow from behind while the remaining raise their guns forward towards the windows. Veronica runs past them to join the others.

The Burden moves through the air towards their floor. He arrives and stops, placing one hand against the barrier. He pushes, watching it waver slightly. He backs away. He raises both arms forward and, with a fierce yell, pulls his arms backwards. His chest rises and his jaw stretches. The force of his yell sends off a power that shatters through the barrier. The windows burst into shards of glass, cutting through some of the soldiers.

In retaliation, the soldiers begin to fire at the Burden.

Veronica forms a small barrier around those nearest her at the exit leading towards an elevator. She looks at them and says, "You need to leave now."

Her eyes return to see the Burden float his way towards the windows. He takes his first step on the tile flooring and scoffs at what's before him. The soldiers continue to shoot at him but the bullets that pierce through his body just fall back out through his skin. He cracks his neck and then slams his foot into the ground. It sends off a quake that knocks the soldiers into the air. He runs forward and snaps all of their necks before a single one of them returns to the ground. He holds onto the last soldier and throws him out the window, like a god removing a rat.

Essa's group watch and see the wounds start to heal. He looks at them and stands, waiting patiently to see what their move will be. The look in his eyes causes Essa to feel sick and afraid, longing for an escape. She feels foolish for thinking she could face him.

Alexander takes a step forward in the face of danger but Bryce places a hand on his shoulder and says, "Don't, you must go with Veronica."

She turns and looks at him, "You're not coming?"

"That's right." He says, "Me and Lunar here will remain, show that bastard he's picking a fight with the wrong people. Isn't that right Lunar?"

"I couldn't agree more." Mr. Lunar pulls out his sword and readies himself to attack the moment Veronica steps away.

She looks at both of them and says, "I plan to see the two of you alive. Don't you fail me."

The Burden takes a step forward, and Mr. Lunar rushes at him.

Bryce yells, "Go, now!" as he runs, following Mr. Lunar.

Veronica grabs ahold of Essa's hand while Alexander runs ahead of them with the two soldiers at his side. They enter his private elevator. The glass doors close behind them. They see the Burden throw Mr. Lunar across the room and against the elevator. The glass cracks and he slides down onto one knee. Veronica places her hand to the glass and watches him stand back up. They see Bryce throw a punch and connect with the Burden's fist. The elevator descends.

The elevator continues to move silently, passing each floor. The five of them stand quietly. Thinking and reflecting on how quickly the situation went from safe to horribly dangerous.

Alexander opens his mouth to speak but suddenly the elevator shakes and stops. A red light begins to flash.

Essa asks, "What's going on? Is he already after us?"

Alexander says, "No, this alarm is only activated when a severe event is happening on the main floor."

The two soldiers look at one another through their helmets and make sure their guns are locked and loaded. Essa wraps her arms around herself and rubs to get warm, feeling cramped in the small space.

Veronica continues to focus and ensure that the barrier around them remains strong. She says, "What exactly is our next course of action Alexander?"

"Don't fret," he says, "I'm a little untrusting of people, or perhaps paranoid, so this elevator has its perks."

She raises an eyebrow, "Do any of these perks involve moving?"

"Indeed they do. Like this." He places his hand against the wall and a panel reveals itself. It scans his hand and a blue light takes the place of the red one above. The elevator jolts and then slowly rises for a moment. It stops and then, with another jolt, begins to move sideways.

They look through the glass walls surrounding them on three sides, and see only darkness with the occasional dim light on the outside, serving as a reminder that they are not lost.

Eventually the elevator stops and changes direction. It proceeds forward and an exit is revealed, their escape to the outdoors. Essa's face goes pale when she realizes that the elevator is going to proceed out the exit. As it does so, she clenches her pouch.

The elevator leaves the building yet remains attached to its side. A view of fire and torn streets rests in front of their eyes as they hang within the sky. Alexander feels a clutch in his chest of dissatisfaction at what has become of his city.

They begin to descend. In the distance, they can see a bright yellow light rise into the air. It circulates and then expands, enveloping everything around and below it. Essa and the others watch the yellow light, wondering where it's coming from and if it's dangerous. It shoots downwards towards the ground. They do not see it make impact, but they assume it does. A wave of energy moves throughout the city and reaches them shortly. It slams into the building and causes the elevator to rock heavily and then drop. One of the hinges comes off, worsening the acceleration.

Veronica focuses on the barrier now surrounding them, yet the speed of the drop causes it to move and let a portion of the elevator exit its protection. The remaining rope tugs tightly on the hinge and causes them to fly forward against the glass window in the elevator.

They feel themselves fall towards the windows on the third floor. The elevator crashes through, and pieces of metal and glass tear off and imbed themselves into the walls.

The elevator slides across the concrete floor, tearing it apart. The glass within the elevator cracks with the pressure of everyone's weight upon it. Essa feels a strain within her neck and places her hand to it. She winces slightly and turns to look at the others. A few scratches and bruises can be seen but no one appears to be severely injured.

As the elevator comes to a stop, the soldiers stand up and proceed to help Alexander onto his feet. One of them moves towards the elevator door and pushes against it. It doesn't open. He decides to place his fingers into the slight opening and pull sideways, causing it to open with a screech. He looks through the opening and sees a group of soldiers from a different regiment, one that reveals their faces to the public, aiming at him. One of soldiers gives a signal to withdraw their guns.

The door is opened up from the outside and Essa and the others are able to escape from the broken shell of what was once their escape. They quickly merge with the group of soldiers and Essa's distress rises. She's aware that the number of bodies means little towards the man many floors above.

The soldier who began opening up the elevator door, one of the two from Essa's group, asks the soldier on this floor who is in charge, "What's the situation?"

The man replies, "Grim, I'm afraid we're mostly what's left. There are a few of us below but it won't do much to aid our situation. There are two individuals who are ripping through all of our defenses with what appears to be a mixture of lightning and what others have said looks like gravity itself. We're here right now as a second barricade. Now, why the hell are you here with the president?"

"The top floors have been compromised. We're all that's left."

Veronica comments, "There are still two up there."

The man looks at her, "True, there are two."

A slight light appears at the end of the room at the staircase. Essa, as well as another soldier, catch sight of this.

"They are coming. Quick! Form a perimeter." The solider cries out.

The soldiers run ahead and set up a line with all of their weapons aimed forward. The man in charge of his group says, "Burst shots people, and keep on your toes. We cannot be easy targets."

Essa looks around and gets a sense of their new surroundings. The entire floor is open concept, with only pillars supporting the roof. A few desks linger at the far ends of the room but it's obvious that the floor has been cleaned out. With nothing in their way, it's first strike wins—or at least it would be in a normal circumstance.

The ground shakes and dust falls from the ceiling above. Essa looks up and a small piece of the ceiling breaks off and falls, bouncing off of her face beneath her right eye. She rubs her face.

Veronica says, "Stay close to me. Things are going to get bad before they get better."

Their small group of five merges together and they find a spot near a set of pillars. The two soldiers keep their guns aimed forward, however Essa starts to notice the difference in their stance. A sense of calmness emits from the two of them and she wonders if they are either very capable or just downright unaware of the danger coming from below and above.

Essa looks over and sees that a soldier stands behind each of the pillars. There is also a line of men that has set itself up in front of the stairs. She feels a slight surge of confidence.

Another spark goes off followed by an explosion at the staircase. Smoke rises. A soldier runs up the stairs, his face burnt. He screams, and everyone watches as he is struck by lightning and scorched to death. Ashes fall.

Sweat begins to appear on the soldier's faces as well as their palms. They move slightly—uncomfortable and nervous. The man in charge gulps and wipes his hand on his pant leg. Seconds pass. A shadow appears on the wall. The soldiers wait, their fingers on the trigger. The shadow moves, and the top of someone's head can be seen. They see brown shaggy hair.

The boy known as Tern presents himself. Before he reaches the top of the stairs, the bullets begin to soar. He looks over and watches as they stop in front of him and fall to the ground.

Tern reaches the top of the steps. He walks forward slowly and keeps his one hand forward, a set of rings on each of his fingers. The soldier in charge yells out for everyone to hold their fire. The bullets stop. Tern's expression changes into annoyance. He runs to the right and the soldiers then see Lucil, the girl with blond hair, as she reaches the top of the steps. She flicks her fingers and forms a spark. It soars into a group of three men, killing them instantly.

They break off, Tern continuing to run towards the pillars, unaware of the ambush waiting for him. Lucil sends off another spark of lightning, this time only striking one soldier. The men split off as directed prior to the fight. They continue to shoot when the opportunity presents itself, and unlike Tern, Lucil must dodge the bullets. One grazes her side and tears through her suit.

As Tern approaches the pillars and runs past the first set, he realizes his mistake. The soldiers he passes turn and open fire. He throws his arms forward and sends off a huge surge of gravity that tears through the pillars and crushes the soldiers. Yet many more open fire and he begins to cringe and clench his teeth to hold up the field of gravity protecting him. He waits for their guns to run out of ammo and dashes forward. He drops his shield of gravity and slashes through the throat of the solider closest to him.

Essa unknowingly grabs onto Veronica as she stares at the chaos ensuing in front of her eyes. Veronica glances at her and says softly, "It will be alright."

The two soldiers with them begin to converse between themselves. Essa looks at them and then at Alexander. His face remains rigid yet he keeps his composure. Her eyes return to the soldiers, she realizes that one of them is a female by the sound of her voice.

The man says, "You've noticed the delay right?"

The other replies, "Thirty seconds."

"Should I take the shot?"

"No, you always do. I'll take this one."

"I'm a better shot though."

"Doesn't matter."

"It does if you miss."

"Damn it just let me take the shot. I've got this."

The soldier aims carefully. She watches Tern spin around and send another soldier into a pillar and then continue to fight. He crushes the bones of those around him, tearing through the occasional soldier's neck. The female continues to watch, slowly mouthing the seconds on her lips; waiting for the moment Tern uses his next big shot of gravity.

Her lips move, "Twenty seven, twenty eight, twenty nine, thirty." She presses down on the trigger and watches as Tern uses his gravity, throwing two soldiers into the ceiling. As his hold on gravity lessens, Tern catches sight of the spinning bullet. Unable to use his gravity fully, he is able to make a very small barrier on his face. The bullet slams into it and sends him off his feet, cutting his cheek open.

The man says, "You messed up."

The one who took the shot replies with, "Well in retrospect, I hit the target."

A shriek of anger comes from Lucil. They turn and see that she's spotted them. She sends off a massive wave of lightning towards them. Veronica watches the bolts of lightning crash into the barrier and split off, destroying a set of pillars and striking a few soldiers. Lucil continues to send off the bolts of lightning, aware of the effect of striking the barrier.

The soldier in charge yells in anger and aims his gun at her, cocking the grenade barrel attached to his gun. He fires, and it explodes in front of her, scorching her face and severely damaging her right shoulder. She sends off the largest bolt of lightning yet, and barely misses him, killing the soldier to his left.

He runs forward and swings his empty gun at her. She ducks and slams her fist into his stomach. Taking a step back, he swings the gun once more. She knocks it from his hands. He throws a punch forward and she moves her head out of the way. He throws another and she ducks underneath it, slamming her hand between his two arms and into his face. With one quick squeeze, his face turns into a pile of gushing blood. The leader of the soldiers falls to the ground, his efforts in vain.

Lucil's white suit turns yellow, and the prism forms on her chest. Her anger then guides its way to the mass of soldiers approaching Tern from behind. She raises her only functioning arm and sends off a large bolt. It tears through the pillars and turns the men into flaming flesh.

Tern rushes into a crowd of soldiers and picks up a knife. He slashes through them and dodges their attacks, fighting against seven using only a knife. His weapon makes contact with another soldier, tearing through their guts. Tern continues to cut away at them, his movements quick and agile.

Unable to send off another precise shot, the two soldiers with Essa, Veronica and Alexander watch hopelessly as the others are butchered one by one.

Essa stares, her heart slowly becoming numb. She asks, "Why are they here? Why are they doing this?"

Alexander replies, trying to calm her, "Sometimes people have the same beliefs but come at it from opposite ends. Strong beliefs and the inability to see the other side can lead to misunderstandings, the desire to protect ones own and ultimately war. However there are those who simply have the thirst to destroy. I'm afraid the moment you fell through the window you landed yourself in a tough predicament. One where we have to learn if what we are witnessing is a huge misunderstanding, or a wickedness unlike any other. I won't say everything will be all right. But I will tell you that we won't let anyone's death be in vain."

Tern yells out and the ground beneath his feet cracks. The gravity throws the soldiers around him into the pillars, snapping their bones like brittle cookie crumbs. He breathes heavily and walks forward. With no one standing between him and them, he reaches out as if to pull them in his direction.

Veronica says, "This is bad."

A smile appears on Tern's face as the sweat causes his hair to stick slightly to his forehead. He opens his mouth to speak but the windows surrounding the west and north of the room shatter. More soldiers spill in. His voice falters and he quickly sends off a force of gravity as the bullets soar towards him. He looks over to see the same look of despair and anger on Lucil's face.

The soldiers run towards Tern. Essa notices the air gear attached to their bodies. She sees them soar through the sky and dodge around the pillars. Tern is forced to spin around and turn his head back and forth. A soldier comes at him from between two pillars. Tern sends his hand forward and crushes the man. Another soldier comes from behind Tern and raises his knife. He grabs ahold of the soldier's wrist and sends him into the ground, breaking him with a push of gravity.

Meanwhile, Lucil walks forward and continuously snaps her fingers together causing sparks to form around her. It shocks a few of the soldiers closest to her. She then snaps them harder and a bolt soars forward, tearing through a crowd of them, scorching them to their graves.

The second round of fighting commences and Essa begins to tremble in anger. She realizes that everything she said to Gunther was pointless—that he was right and she was in the way. She looks at Veronica and sees her expression of complete focus as she continues to hold the barrier around their small group, keeping them from harm's way while all those outside of the barrier fight for their lives and that of their president.

Lucil's sparks begin to grow larger. She finally runs forward and Veronica turns to watch as one of the two threats makes their move. Lucil makes her way past a group of soldiers and dashes up a pillar, flipping over into the air and sending off a dozen bolts of lightning that strike the men in the face. She lands on the ground and sends a spin kick, snapping another's neck.

A soldier pulls out his knife and stabs forward. She sends a jolt into the knife and electrocutes his body. She runs past him and sees a wave of bullets being shot at her. She dashes forward and slides her hand across the ground. Lightning moves across the cement floor and then scatters through the air, causing the bullets to explode.

She gets close to another set of soldiers and spins around them, slamming her hand, arm and elbow into any that get close, instantly breaking bones and causing them to fall to the ground motionless. She does a backflip when a soldier swings a low kick, and as she lands on her only functioning hand, her legs wrap around his head. She swings him around and snaps his neck as he lands on the ground. She looks around and sees that she's made progress towards her goal.

She stands up and feels her mangled arm hang loosely at her side, the blood drenching what remains of her skin, with pieces of her suit still attached. She looks at the remaining soldiers around her, at their guns and their fearful eyes.

Her eyes slowly turn to see one soldier holding a rocket propelled grenade launcher on his shoulder. With little time to react, and the fact he's standing on her blindside, she counts down the seconds before the incoming pain. He presses down on the trigger. She moves her remaining hand forward and the missile explodes a few feet in front of her. Pieces of shrapnel cut into her sides. Blood leaves her lips and she screams, sending off a bloody wave of lightning, tearing through everyone around her.

Tern sees this and cries out, he watches her stumble forward. She catches herself and takes a step. The two soldiers with Essa aim their guns. The one who took the shot at Tern fires once more. The bullet spins towards Lucil. She raises her hand forward to light up a spark, but the bullet tears through her palm. The spark is unable to ignite. Soon after a set of bullets pierce right through her stomach and out her other side.

She stumbles and falls to her knees. The prism on her chest begins to dim along with the yellow on her suit, returning to its original white shade, now mixed with blood. Lucil looks down at her palm and presses it into the ground. She looks forwards, staring into Alexander's eyes and says, "I just need to kill you...then everything will be okay."

A bolt of lightning tears through the ground and slams into Veronica's barrier, the pressure causes her to raise her second hand. She concentrates as the lightning continues to strike against the barrier.

Alexander looks at the young woman trying to kill him, unsure of what he feels. As Veronica focuses more on the barrier, Essa feels some pain.

As this takes place, Tern runs forward and pushes past those in his way, only to get cut off by more. He stops and slams his hands together, tearing apart the men in front of him.

The lightning doesn't ease up. Lucil focuses on her breathing and watches as the lightning envelops the barrier, revealing its width and height.

The ceiling above breaks and a black cloak lowers itself. Lucil turns her head to see the Burden set himself on the ground. He looks around with satisfaction; all of the carnage getting him excited.

His eyes turn to her and his smile turns into disgust. He sees the lighting being cast from her hand. He says nothing, simply acts.

Tern's eyes widen and he screams, "Lucil, use it! Use it!"

She stares at the incoming and overwhelming threat. Her hand raises, the lightning stops. The ring on her finger activates and sends off a force of gravity as the Burden reaches towards her. It cuts through his arm but doesn't push him back. He slams his hand through her chest.

For a moment, Lucil regrets having ever been born.

She falls towards the ground as his hand leaves her body. She looks towards Tern. His eyes showing that of utter horror as he fights back tears. He cries out and forgets about his surroundings. A blade soon stabs into his back.

The soldier who successfully struck him says, "I...I did it...I got him!"

Those become his final words as Tern sends off a high-pressure wave, turning the man into a pile of mush as his body is torn into a million pieces. Tern removes the blade from his back and drops it on the floor. He cringes. He stares at the Burden who looks bored after fatally wounding Lucil.

One of the fingers on Tern's hand begins to dissolve. Lucil watches and a tear rolls down her face as she sees his finger decay into a pile of ash. Yet Tern shows no sign of pain. His eyes stare wickedly at the Burden. The others watch in confusion at the events unfolding in front of them. As the tools themselves are broken by their wielder.

Tern says angrily, "You were supposed to let us handle this, we are so close! And you strike her down? Can you not control your sick, sadistic desire to kill!?"

The Burden simply blinks.

"Answer me!" Tern screams.

A smile spreads across the Burden's face. Tern's eyes change and the prism ignites on his chest. His suit goes brown and the ground around him breaks apart and rises into the air. He grinds his teeth together and screams, screams so much that even the Burden winces slightly before being stunned at the fact that Tern, in a second, closes the distance between them.

Two hands slam into the Burden's chest, and he is pushed with such a forceful amount of gravity that it sends him through the wall and out of view. Tern turns and looks at the others. He decides their worth pales in comparison and rushes towards Lucil. He wraps his arms around her. She looks up into his eyes and places a hand to his face gently. She sees his look of despair. She opens her mouth but he shakes his head and says, "Save your strength, everything is going to be alright."

She whimpers slightly, "But he's right there…he's so close."

"I know, but for now let us rest." He shows a sad smile, "Let's just pretend everything will be alright."

"Tern…"

"Can we let go of this pointless mission and go?"

Her eyes grow watery, "I think that's what we should have done from the start."

He lifts her up and looks at Essa and the others. He then stares at Alexander and says, "All we needed to do, was kill you."

A burst of gravity, so forceful it reveals itself as a circular sphere, appears around Tern and Lucil. They then rise from the ground and burst through the ceiling, leaving them alone.

Veronica's hands lower and the barrier disperses. Essa looks at her and sees that her face has gone pale. Veronica says quietly, "Are they… okay?" wondering if Bryce and Mr. Lunar are still alive.

Essa places a hand to her lip and says, "What…just happened? For a while I thought those two were working for the Burdens. But that man struck one of them down without hesitation."

One of the soldiers takes off his helmet. He runs his hand across his stubbly face. He says, "There's hierarchy in everything."

Alexander says, "No. That was pure carnage. That man has no heart."

The female soldier takes off her helmet and reveals long brown curly hair and tan skin. She says, "Pity, that's one less spot to strike with a bullet."

Standing together, the five of them gaze at the fallen. Essa questions the difference between them and the Burdens, if those around them are used and discarded. She thinks that even if they don't treat them cruelly, the system is faulty. Every dead soul has someone precious. The thought of giving up life when it's not for loved ones puzzles her.

While deep in thought, she doesn't notice the intense glare Veronica gives to the soldier who spoke moment's prior. She hears her say, "What are you doing here Michael?"

Essa glances at the male soldier.

Michael says, "I was hired. You can bitch another time."

A voice interrupts their badly timed argument, "Where do you think you are going?"

They see the Burden walk through the opening in the wall. His smile out of place—large, gruesome. He places a hand to his chest and says, "If you want to do good, then try and kill me." He tilts his head, "Because, what can be worse than I?"

Essa's heart sinks.

The Burden speaks to them in an orotund fashion, reciting his poem, "So this is the enemy? Nice. I've been wondering where the friend of friendly was hiding." He raises his arms into the air and begins to move them around as if leading an orchestra, the only sound coming from his dead tone and the movement of his cloak. "Call me Grim, and this here is Reaper." He points to the empty space around him,

"Born as brothers, hand in hand, they say I've got the ability to clutch. So what's your purpose?"

He tilts his head, and then shakes his hands. "Don't tell me—it must be dying. Can't be anything else. See, my cloak is darker than any colour, so say goodbye to light. I take the warmth and turn it into ash. Just try to laugh. I'm the calmer half. And if you think you can win, understand winter is my blessing." He gives a slight bow, "You should envy me, friend, I control your destiny and I decided you can meet me. Don't cry for it will be quick."

He takes a step forward. "I'm not into torture, that's the obsession of another man. Want to meet him?" he cracks his neck. "I can arrange the meeting. The pendulum is swinging, birds keep singing." His eyes dart around as if looking into the air, "Your grave is waiting." He runs his finger across his neck and says, "Decapitation." Sticking his tongue out.

Puzzlement, confusion, and a loss of words—everyone looks at the man as a bizarre yet terrifying force. His words alone pierce their nerves and shake them, making them question everything from strength in numbers to personal qualities.

Alexander asks profoundly, "Who are you?" his temper rises and he loses composure, "you who kills without hesitation and wears that black cloak. What is it you want!?"

"Now, now." The man says stridently, "My name is Asrath, and all I want is to see chaos unfold."

Michael yells in a booming voice, "Fire!" Bullets fly from the guns of himself and his companion.

Asrath walks forward and says, "Futile."

Essa screams, "WHAT THE HELL IS WRONG WITH YOU!?"

His eyes widen. He licks his lips and says, "You're a tasty one."

Appearing as a white blur, Hex arrives. With his wings stretched out, he slams into Asrath and takes him through an opening in the broken window. They rise into the air and then slam into the ground.

Essa and the others rush to see Hex holding Asrath down with one hand as his other stretches behind him.

Asrath says, "You cannot kill me angel! Not for lack of trying!" And bursts out laughing.

Hex looks at him in fury, "I need not kill you, only restrain your disgusting nature."

The ring on his finger begins to glow and unlocks. It spins, and a white stream of light emits from it. Soon after, a blue spear appears in his hand. He slams it into Asrath's chest. Blue chains burst from it and wrap around him, holding him down, connecting him deep into the earth and restricting his strength.

"This is dirty!" Asrath yells, "I would think an angel would have some pride!"

"There is no sense of pride for me to face off against the likes of you. You only tarnish the light that exists around my being."

"I want to do more than tarnish it. I want to destroy it, twist it and make it mine!" Asrath licks the air and then bursts out into laughter, closing his eyes and pulling his head back. His laughter ceases and he simply smiles.

Watching, Essa tries to think of a way to get down there quickly. She sees a set of ropes that the soldiers left behind when breaking through the windows. She walks towards one of them and tugs on it, looking up to see that it's still anchored in tightly to the wall above. She wraps her hands around it and keeps her legs closed, descending quickly to the ground.

She walks forward and then turns to see the others are following after her. Essa moves towards Hex, who raises his hand forward. She stops.

He says, "You will remain here Asrath, unable to enjoy any more carnage. I will make sure of that." Blue light shines from the chains binding Asrath. They spread across his body further and wrap across his face.

Asrath flings himself around and then calms down. He stares at all of them and lets out a muffled cackle before closing his eyes. He says quietly, "When I get poetic, I always finish." A slumber takes over him.

The underlining threat does not go unnoticed. Hex removes his wings and looks at those around him. Alexander asks, "Are you an angel?"

"Yes."

"I didn't know if you existed. This is a quiet a shock."

"Well don't let it change your opinion on anything."

Michael says, "I just lost a few bets... Well, we should get going."

Alexander turns to Essa and places his hands on her shoulders. Hex looks at him in alarm. Alexander says, "This is sudden, but I must go with Michael. Once I'm in space, I will contact you. We can discuss everything you want to know about your family. I'll always look after you. I promise."

She nods her head and looks towards Hex.

Alexander lets go and follows Michael and the other soldier. They turn to see that Veronica isn't joining them. She heads back towards the building. As minutes pass, Essa is left alone with Hex and Asrath.

She bites her lip and says, "I was rash Hex...I made a mistake. I thought I could do this but I can't. I'm scared. Just now, I...I just stood there and watched as a group of soldiers gave up their lives for a man...I just don't know what is going on. Why do I have a strange book with me? Why did I come across you and Dusk? Why am I different?"

A voice interrupts her, "Hey!" it calls out.

She turns to see Dexter walking with Abigail and Baylee, exhaustion spread across their faces. Essa then sees Cassandra not too far behind them.

Hex looks at Essa adoringly. He says soothingly, "Sometimes people are like stars. They don't know it, but they pull in everything towards them. It's who you are."

She looks into his eyes and begins to cry. "All I really want is for everyone to be okay. I don't want to be responsible for anyone's death. I don't want to just stand in one place."

Hex thinks and then says, "I believe Dusk once said for you to follow him. You can do that. You are able to walk on your two feet and make decisions. You might be scared by the results, but you are walking, Essa. Like a shooting star, you will find your purpose. Even if it isn't on the battlefield." He places a hand on her shoulder and says, "We don't get to choose how we come into this world but we can decide how we live in it, and how we wish too exit."

She hugs him tightly and continues to cry. He places a hand on her head and closes his eyes. The others reach them and wait in silence.

Hex says, "I'm afraid I will have to leave you here Essa. I must find Dusk. His heart is calling for me."

She looks at him, still stricken with wet eyes.

He says, "I've come to notice that there's a lot I need to learn." He wipes away her tears, "Just like you."

His wings return and he spreads them. He looks at Cassandra and says, "Keep her close. You know what to do." He soars into the air and the sunlight hides his presence. Essa stops crying and clenches her teeth, the fire in her heart finding fuel to grow.

CHAPTER TWENTY-SIX
Two Bodies

For a human, birth can be equated as love. Two bodies come together and through such encounter, begin the process of the creation of new life. A newborn will see the eyes of those that bring it into the world. It will begin to learn what compassion and warmth is. It will see those who gave pieces for its creation. It will come to love.

Then, there are those who are not given this opportunity. Born through a different means. Created not by the procedure of love, but by scientific interest. They look not at those who share their DNA, but at a person who's self-interest derails the natural evolution of life.

Sitting in a pile of rubble on the second floor of a building that's lying in ruins, Tern holds Lucil in his arms. They are cast amongst the shadows, where the kiss of the sun can only try to beckon for them to come out.

He looks blankly at the ground before him, thinking of the sound his maker uttered when Tern saw the world for the first time—a gruff noise of satisfaction. He holds Lucil's mangled body, her breathing slow and unsteady.

What was it, he wonders, that brought them to this point in time? It was not freewill, a concept he only knows of through the brief encounters of those running from him. It was not choice. It was simply an order given and the dangling promise for a longer lifespan.

He looks at Lucil and thinks how cruel of a joke it is, to be born with a definitive time clock hanging over one's head, indicating one's death. In a way, dying before the designated time is an action of freewill, but a horrible one.

Lucil looks into his eyes. She places a hand against his face and says, "Don't get lost in your thoughts Tern. It's going to be alright." The blood that trickles from her mouth tells him otherwise, and he holds her closer.

She coughs up blood and moves uncomfortably, letting her head rest against his chest. She listens to his heartbeat, the sound of an unhealthy heart clinging for more time. The sound, she knows, echoes hers.

She finds her mind slipping slightly, and thinks of the first time she saw Tern, a newborn that fell in love with another. Her hand clenches to his clothes, pulling on them tightly. She says, "There are many things I wish I had the time to say to you."

Her delicate nature causes Tern to speak before she can. "I love you."

She smiles, "I love you too."

He runs his hand through her hair and looks into her eyes, "I did from the moment I first saw you. I don't want you to leave me."

Her eyes light up only to fade. Her breathing stops. He looks at her beauty and already misses the clench of her hand, the vibration of her heart. He presses his forehead against hers, his tears land on her skin.

Her voice resonates in his mind, *"Sometimes things are meant to float away. Letting go doesn't mean you failed. It just means you tried. Tern, just let go. Let it go."*

He places her body on the ground and cries. He screams for the world to hear his pain, a world that allowed him to be brought to life, a world not strong enough to love him. And now with his love gone, a loveless child made by a man who is no better than a monster, Tern cries.

His mind experiences something for the first time. It reflects. He enters a place where he sees everything he's experienced. He sees Lucil for the first time. He sees Vince making a joke. He sees Slate looking off at the sky. He sees Echo staring into a mirror.

For five souls, five lives should be lived. But for five clones, only one path exists. Tern visualizes the bastard that greeted them when they woke up, a man who made a promise. To kill and create fear would be enough for them to be given a full life. But why bother now. Tern looks down at Lucil and thinks that Arc, his creator, did not understand the value of love, that the death of it would be the death of a deal.

His mind drifts further. All of the lives that he has taken had also loved. His eyes grow dim and he looks off into the abyss. Everything is cruel.

Lucil speaks to him again. He reflects on the first thing she ever said to him, *"Are you my world?"*

His head hangs low and he sees the pool of blood that's left her body, moving along the wooden planks and dripping off into the broken floor.

Tern says, "I'm so small. But…they took me from you. Left you speechless. Stopped your heart. I'm so small…but I'll make a big impact. I'll show them that we deserved a real shot at life. It's not fair what he did and what we had to do. It's not fair. So I'll fucking show them."

His lifeless eyes gain life. Lucil's spark now lives in his heart. Even though his span to make a move is short he does not care. He understands there's no time to waste. He accepts the fact his story will be short. He knows that even one chance is all he needs.

"I'll show them. Every. Single. One of them."

CHAPTER TWENTY-SEVEN
Echo for Me

Dusk thinks to himself, *when was it that I started to run at life headstrong, without thought, instead of looking to others for advice?* He feels the hand around his throat. He looks past Echo's blank expression.

Dusk questions his weakness, his misjudgment and his fatal mistake in rushing in. He could have asked for help—he should have asked for help. His reflection comes with a reward. Andromeda appears with grace and grabs ahold of Echo, flinging him off of Dusk.

Echo looks at her viciously. He states, "I practically forgot you were here."

She says, "I'm a silent one. Those with too much confidence in themselves tend to overlook my nature." She raises her hands forward, "I will gladly teach you to pay closer attention, just for a moment."

Her silver and blue eyes irritate him. He rushes forward and throws a punch. She pushes the punch away. He continues to attack, and throws a knee. She stops it with her elbow. As this quick encounter progresses, Dusk gets up and wipes the humiliation off of his body. A fire begins to erupt within him. He watches Andromeda stop every single attack from Echo, and thinks of how easily he fell.

Dusk says, "I've had enough of being protected." He pulls out his sword, causing both Echo and Andromeda to turn and look.

Echo says, "What a waste of time."

Andromeda says with a smile, "So that's your decision. Let me do one last thing."

She grabs ahold of Echo and Dusk, and her eyes light up. They're both unable to utter a word—Dusk, filled with confusion—Echo, filled with anger and disgust. She transports them into the top floor of the closest building.

Andromeda lets go of them. Echo spins around and kicks a desk in half. He punches through a wall and reaches out to grab ahold of her. A sword slashes downwards and cuts through the edge of his wrist, leaving him with a deep gash. He pulls back with a yell and glares into Dusk's eyes, seeing a change that looks odd and out of place.

Echo spits out, "What the hell is this? Am I dealing with magic?"

Dusk says soft spoken, "You're too kind." His eyes turn towards Andromeda. He asks, "Why did you move us here?"

She says, "To give you a proper fight. I must leave you here. There's something I need to take care of. Do well. I know you're stronger than you let on." She disappears, destroying the surroundings.

Echo looks back and forth, confused, and yells, "Enough of this! I was right to think there was something odd about you. But this is not what I expected."

"Am I not a worthy opponent?" Dusk says flatly.

"Not even close."

"Then I will change that."

Dusk steps forward and slashes his sword downwards quickly. It meets contact with a sword formed from water. He looks at the weapon closely and sees the ripples move throughout it.

Echo regains his composure and calms down, having finally shown his source of power. The swords remain in the air, pressing against one another.

Dusk looks at Echo and understands that the fight that is about to unfold will be bloody. For the first time, the balance is equal and the footing is fair—something he can control despite the craziness surrounding them.

He taunts Echo, "Magic huh?"

Echo scoffs and says, "This is destiny." He pulls back and slashes forward.

Dusk blocks the attack and they begin to quickly move around, slashing their swords against one another's.

All of the office supplies around them quickly turns to debris, as their sword swings cut through everything. They reach a pillar and spin around it, clashing on the other side.

Dusk moves his blade the way he was taught—years spent forming his body around his sword, to become one with the steel. His years of experience show as he lands the first successful attack between the two of them. He cuts through Echo's side.

Echo's eyes flash in anger. He whips his sword forward and the water on the blade extends. Dusk quickly defends himself the best he can with his blade. The water slams into it and sends him into a pillar. Echo heaves his sword around like a whip. The water cuts through the pillar as Dusk moves out of the way and finds himself running, trying to figure out a way to counter the new fighting style.

He moves his way around the room and jumps over a table. Echo cuts through it and watches Dusk move to his side. Echo returns his sword to normal and meets him head on. They both slash upwards and their swords connect.

Dusk slams his body into Echo and then spins around him, slicing through his back. Echo slams the back of his hand into Dusk's face. They spin around and then slash their swords once more. They leap backwards and then clash, their teeth grinding as they put all of their weight into pushing one another backwards.

Dusk begins to feel his wrists buckle under the weight. He slides his sword and passes Echo, avoiding the water's touch.

He takes a few steps back and asks, "Who are you? Why are you doing this?"

Echo says, "Such a dry question." He attacks with a downward slash. Dusk avoids it.

"There's nothing dry about wanting to know who I am facing. I will want to remember the name of the person who's reminded me of the power I have within myself."

Echo laughs and passes Dusk's guard, slamming his hand into his chest and sending Dusk off his feet and into a table. He says, "I am simply the echo, the echo of humanity."

"What do you mean?"

"What I am is because of you filthy humans. You made me out to be a puppet but I control my own strings."

"Look I don't-"

"Shut up, you won't understand what it's like," Echo clenches his fist, "to be a clone."

Dusk says, "A clone? That's disgusting..."

"Disgusting? Do you not see? I mimic what this world has done to me!" Echo throws his sword at Dusk. It passes above him and cuts through a support beam. Pieces of the ceiling fall down.

Dusk says, "The fact you are a clone and are doing this. I don't care if you're the original or the copy, it's your life and this is how you choose to go about it? Killing for no reason?"

"I HAVE ALL THE REASON IN THE WORLD!"

Another sword forms and he runs into Dusk. Echo raises his other hand forward and forms a second sword. Dusk pushes away and quickly defends himself against a simultaneous strike. He leaps into the air to dodge a low attack, and moves to his right side to avoid another. The water passes through his black jacket, ripping a chunk out of it.

Echo forms his swords into whips and slashes them around. Dusk pushes forward to avoid the lines of water. He enters a trap. The two whips form into one and pull backwards behind him. Dusk ducks in the nick of time, the tips of his hairs being sliced off.

Raising his sword upwards, Dusk slashes down only to meet the resistance of the whip pushing against it. Echo kicks Dusk in the stomach, extends the whip into two and slashes downwards, cutting viciously into Dusks body.

The whip wraps around Dusk's sword and pulls it out of his hand. Echo throws it to the other end of the room and then lets his weapons dissolve into puddles. He raises his fists and hits Dusk directly in the nose.

The punch sends Dusk into a pillar. Before he can push himself off from it, Echo slams another punch into his face. The barrage of hits continues and Dusk begins to feel his sense of balance weaken, as his face grows numb. A heavy hit from the angered Echo causes Dusk to momentarily lose consciousness, the brief second of white light between being awake and out cold.

A familiar voice taunts him, *"What the hell are you doing?"* A smile shows white teeth within the darkness of Dusk's heart. *"Are you just going to let him throw you around like this? Why are you being weak? Why are you ignoring what I can offer? You know you have much more strength than this. More strength than someone's copy."*

Dusk regains consciousness and catches Echo's punch, "Enough…" he says in a hoarse voice. His eyes darken and he slams his fist into Echo's jaw. Echo, with a slight look of bewilderment, forms water around his fists and hurls it forward. Dusk spins around the pillar and avoids the debris of concrete blasting around the room.

Echo chases after him, and Dusk trips. He spins around, lands on his back and raises his own leg to stop Echo's stomp. Their feet collide and Dusk pushes with all of his might to send Echo backwards once more.

Dusk says, "You can't kill me because I'm fighting for something. You don't have a reason do you?"

Echo becomes flustered and says, "I have all I need." He forms a whip and slashes the ground near Dusk. It chases him and then slashes his midsection. The whip wraps around Dusk's wrist. Echo pulls on it and Dusk's feet leave the floor. He goes towards him. A sword forms in Echo's hand. The bloodlust radiates from his eyes, his posture, and his rage.

Seeing this, Dusk feels time slow down. He recalls the conversation between Wish, Hex and himself. He recalls the moment he formed an arrow and fired at the Nightmare, the consequences, and the benefits. He thinks to himself, *I have no choice.*

Yellow light wraps around his left hand. As the blade of water slices downwards towards his neck, he sends his hand into the blade and tears through it. The water evaporates on contact. Echo looks in shock as his weapon leaves his sight and Dusk turns the disadvantage in his favor.

Echo changes the direction of his pull. Dusk goes higher into the air and spins around. As he descends, he cuts through the whip and spin-kicks Echo in the temple.

Tripping, Echo forms water around both of his fists. He throws a punch and collides with Dusk's yellow fist. The water disperses and the impact sprains his hand. He throws his other fist and Dusk moves his head out of the way.

After missing, Echo turns the water around his fist into a short blade that extrudes from it. He slices upwards and misses Dusk's chin by an inch. The water around his other fist reforms and he throws the punch again. Dusk pushes the hand out of the way this time and sends his hand forward with his fingers together sticking outwards like a short knife.

Unable to move out of the way, it pierces through Echo's shoulder. Echo slams his hands into Dusk's head on both sides, screaming. The sound vibrates in Dusk's skull, causing him to bleed from his mouth, ears and eyes.

Reaching out, Dusk wraps his other hand around Echo's throat to cut off the scream. As he does this, the water on the side of his face connects and forms a big bubble, engulfing his head and causing him to intake water. He begins to choke and lose oxygen, bubbles of air leaving his lips.

With no other option but to push forward, he forces his other hand deeper through Echo's shoulder until it pierces all the way through and comes out on the other side. The excruciating pain causes Echo to waver and the water descends, letting Dusk gasp for air.

They both step backwards, struggling to breathe. Echo rubs his throat and looks at his wound. He curses underneath his breath while Dusk heaves, buckled over, keeping his eyes on Echo.

Sweat begins to build on Dusk's brow. His body starts to feel weak. He realizes that since he hasn't killed Echo, the life force he has used now rests within him. He steps forward and stumbles slightly.

With a grin Echo says, "Stubborn bastard, it looks like you are just about ready to collapse. So just do so!"

"And give you the satisfaction?" Dusk stands up straight and lets his power disperse, deciding to rely on his physical strength rather than what's deep within his body.

As they both take a step forward towards one another, the sound of an elevator rising catches their attention. They turn their heads and look over at the far end of the room where the elevator is located. The light indicator above the burgundy coloured doors lights up, showing the floor the elevator is coming from.

Echo asks in a taunt, "Are you expecting company?"

"My closest ally isn't the kind to use conventional ways of transportation."

"Mine either."

They both stare as the elevator reaches their floor. The steel doors open and within it, darkness. They strain their eyes to see who's inside.

A man stands there with an abstract mask on his face that resembles liquid swirling together, a mixture of blood perhaps. A black smile is painted on it, with two eyeholes large enough to reveal a pair of red eyes beneath.

His breathing rattles softly against his mask. He takes a step outside of the elevator and shows his black cloak. His hood raised.

Dusk's face goes pale, the sound to his ears goes faint, and his eyes focus entirely on what the Burden has in his right hand.

He barely makes out Echo's words, "What the hell."

Within the Burden's right hand, fingers wrapped around silver hair, Andromeda's head hangs, her eyes still open, staring upwards. Her jaw is gone. Her neck still oozes both blood and the metallic pieces of her android self.

Echo, his voice shaking, yells, "Get your sword right now! NOW!" Turning, Dusk runs towards the opposite end of the room to retrieve his sword, his mind trying to understand what he just witnessed. Echo's eyes widen and he says, "You're a dangerous one. I'll have to readjust my focus for the time being."

The man tilts his head ever so slightly and says, "That is a wise decision."

His sword appears. The Burden slices through one of Echo's with no effort required.

Echo walks backwards and forms another sword. He swings both of his blades at the Burden while dodging the deadly blade that aims for his vitals.

The Burden spins around and slams Andromeda's lifeless head into Echo's skull, knocking him down onto his left knee. Then the Burden uses the head to uppercut Echo. Falling over a table, Echo gets up quickly and begins to feel rattled, his composure slipping. A lifeless head besting him in battle, the blood staining his clothes and splattering across the room as the Burden swings it around without care.

Jumping onto the table, the Burden kicks Echo in the face and then jumps down, sending his sword forward and cutting the side of Echo's neck. Andromeda's head then comes from the left side and hits him across the face, knocking him off his feet. He stumbles sideways and slams his sword into the Burden's, but is pushed backwards and falls over once more. He turns to see how far Dusk has gone.

Echo stands up and raises both of his swords in front of him to stop the incoming downward slash. It cuts through both of his swords and slams into his shoulder blade. He screams out in pain as the Burden pulls it out.

Stumbling backwards, both of Echo's arms hang at his side, his shoulder blades both torn and wounded deeply. He changes his stance.

The Burden moves forward. Echo throws a sharp kick that passes the Burden's head. He pulls his leg back and blocks the swing of the head with his knee. He leaps into the air and lands a kick from above into the Burden's wrist. He then steps back and throws a kick towards the Burden's head and misses.

With another few steps backwards to keep the distance, the Burden continues to pursue at his own pace. As Echo throws another kick, the Burden steps forward, avoiding the kick and slicing through Echo's waist. He then slams Andromeda's head into the top of Echo's skull repeatedly until he falls to his knees, blood gushing from his mouth.

Echo looks up at the Burden and blinks. The red eyes behind the mask shine as the man says, "You did well...for a clone."

"Fuck you," Echo barks.

The sword rises into the air and comes down. Steel cast in yellow stops the blade. A yell of anger pushes the Burden backwards. Echo sees Dusk move past him and unleash an array of fast and precise attacks towards the Burden.

The blades clash, sparks fly, the two swords slam into one another viciously as their feet move backwards and forwards around the room. The Burden hurls the head forwards and Dusk catches it. It unravels his composure, and the Burden's blade passes through Dusk's cheek.

The head is taken from Dusk's arms and slammed across his face. The Burden sends his foot into Dusk's stomach and it hurls him past Echo.

The Burden says, "You will both end up like this woman—weak prey, weak. Her head will serve as a reminder that neither of you can win this fight. The only difference between her and the two of you is that she was bold enough to embrace death. To give you time to fight. Truly an odd display of comradeship."

Dusk yells, "Enough!" He runs forward and slams his sword downwards. Andromeda's head is sent forward and the blade slams into her skull. The sound vibrates through Dusk's body. He panics. Knowing he must destroy the head in order to regain his power, he slices all the way through.

The Burden says, "Ruthless."

Moving forward, the Burden uses his free hand to slam his palm into Dusk's stomach. The impact hurls Dusk through the air and into the elevator doors on the other side of the room.

Echo turns to see Dusk struggling to get up. His eyes return to the Burden slowly moving towards him.

Echo says, "To hell with this." He stands up and runs towards Dusk, his arms flinging around. He reaches him and slams into him, crashing into the elevator doors with enough force to push through them and fall down the elevator shaft.

Dusk yells, "What are you doing!?"

The last thing he sees is the Burden before the darkness consumes them.

"Saving our lives!"

"I would think that's the exact opposite of what you are doing!"

"Shut up! I know what I'm doing!"

"And what exactly is that!"

"Shut up!" Echo winces in pain as he holds onto Dusk with one arm and moves his other forward, "I'm sorry Tern, but I have no other choice. I'm sorry!" The ring on Echo's finger unleashes a wave that lessens their gravity and so slows their descent.

As they near the bottom the wave increases in pressure to such an extent as to crush the ground below them and blow through the set of doors. They both fall through the opening and the gravity returns to normal.

Dusk asks, "What was that just now?"

"A gift. With a penalty for a friend." Echo responds. He winces in pain, "And before you think we're done fighting, think again. I just need you to help me survive the insanity above us, then I will end you."

"Relying on your enemy to fight another enemy. Huh. That's fine with me. I'll kill both of you."

Echo scoffs. He places his hands to his wounds and closes his eyes. The cuts begin to heal. Dusk watches. Echo opens an eye, "I suppose you want the same treatment."

"You could tell eh? How are you doing that?"

"Water does wonderful things."

After a few moments, Echo finishes healing himself and places his hand to Dusk's face. "If only I could kill you right now."

"Unlikely you would be able to, my sword is already waiting to strike."

Out of the corner of his eyes, Echo sees the blade pointed towards his genitals. He lets out a sigh, "Really now."

Dusk grins, "I got the idea from a friend."

"It's tasteless."

A shadow reveals itself within the elevator shaft. Red eyes pierce through the darkness. They turn. Dusk raises his sword and his face goes stern. His concentration elevates to a new level.

The Burden walks out towards them and attacks Dusk. Their swords collide and sparks ignite. Dusk throws everything he has—elegant moves and sharp angles—while protecting his own skin from the dangerous blade of the Burden. Yet despite all the efforts, he is unable to land a single hit. He goes in for a spin and finds the Burden does the same thing but quicker.

Dusk is pushed backwards. Shock takes over. The move the Burden uses is something that Dusk remembers his brother using when they were younger. The random thought causes him to receive a gash across his face.

Echo yells out, "Be more careful—I'm not your nurse!"

"Damn it, I know!" Dusk yells in retort. He regains his stance and blocks the incoming attacks from the Burden, whose speed and strength overwhelm his own.

Dusk makes a move but fails.

The Burden catches the blade with his bare hand and says, "So weak." He pushes it aside and slams his hand into Dusk's chest, blowing him through the air and out of a set of windows. Dusk tumbles across the ground amongst the shards of glass outside.

The Burden ignores Echo and heads towards Dusk. Taken aback, Echo clenches his fist and looks at Dusk struggling to get up.

Sweating and feeling faint, Dusk struggles to move. Seeing the approaching threat he says, "I've used far too much—this is bad." His sight begins to blur for a moment. He regains his focus, "I can't die here!" he forces himself to get onto his knees and take a stand. He looks around for his sword and sees that it's a few feet away from him.

He lets out a grin and stands loosely in the presence of the Burden. With no strength to move his arms, he puts everything into remaining on his feet.

The Burden looks over at the sword and then at Dusk. He says, "Why are you standing there with such an expression? Prepare yourself and fight me."

"I'm afraid that's impossible."

"Why is that?"

Dusk laughs a little, "I was foolish, that's why."

The Burden says nothing and looks at Dusk for a moment. He then walks forward, raising his sword to strike.

Echo yells, "Do not ignore me!" He bursts from the building and knees the Burden in the mask, flipping over his back and landing between them. The Burden cracks his neck and turns to look at them. A feeling of dread overcomes them but it's coming from elsewhere. They look around for the source while the Burden remains silent.

Surrounding them, spread out amongst the buildings, three figures cloaked in black await them. One stands on a roof, the other on the ground. Another sits on a ledge. If it were a game, checkmate would be called.

The one closest to them speaks. "Well this is a surprise, I was certain I killed you."

Dusk's eyes widen. The hair on the back of his neck rises. He looks at the man and sees the pale skin revealing itself through the shadows of the hood. The smile on his face sets Dusk into a fit of rage as the memories of his death, and the kidnapping of his loved one—her hand reaching out for his as his eyes faded away—flash past his eyes.

Yellow light erupts around his body and causes the ground to shake. Echo looks at him in surprise. The Burdens watch as something new unfolds.

The words that have boiled since that fateful day erupt from his throat. "Where is she!"

"Oh now this will be entertaining." The man replies, "Oh so very entertaining."

Dusk's body grows brighter and his eyes show ferocity that causes Echo to feel extremely uncomfortable—a feeling of fear, a feeling unknown to him.

Dusk says, "I will make you tell me everything."

The Burden crosses his arms and laughs.

Dusk twitches, the yellow light ignites further and bursts all around him, going off into the air. His eyes change, his posture finds complete balance and his emotions leave him. The darkness within him says nothing and simply watches.

CHAPTER TWENTY-EIGHT
Value of Life

Dusk repeats himself, "I will make you tell me everything."

He leaves no room for argument, his tolerance below zero, his anger a full-lit storm.

The laughter continues, vibrating through the sky. Echo looks at the Burden in disgust, wondering how much power he has in order to continue laughing in such a manner.

Almost forgetting about the fourth Burden, Echo turns and looks at the man with the mask, only to see that his sword is sheathed and his posture is relaxed. He leans against a wall.

Spitting out the Burden's name, Dusk says, "Edom, you will tell me all I want to know, and then I will crush your throat so that those words will be your last."

Edom wipes tears of laughter from his face and says, "This is just so annoying. Why the hell are you alive and standing here? This is some poetic justice I suppose. A lover denied happiness, returning to find his bliss. But I have no desire to be the villain in said poem that falters from some weakness. Boy, this is not going to end in your favor. You should have let the despair take over you and pissed off. Your existence is worth nothing."

The other two Burdens remain silent, their faces still hidden. Echo begins to grow angry as well. For whatever reason, he senses a severe distaste towards the man taunting Dusk, unknowing to the past between the two.

Dusk yells, "My existence—my world—is Sarah!" His feet move across the ground quickly. His body posture does not change. The yellow around his body enhances his movement. His steps quickly close the distance while Edom remains still, watching and waiting.

"With no sword, what do you plan to do? Hug me?" Edom taunts.

Dusk's hand moves towards Edom—the same move he used against Echo. It shoots forward at a ferocious rate. Edom catches it between his hands in the nick of time, and his eyes lose joy for a moment, showing concern. Before he can counterattack, Dusk spin-kicks him in the head, snapping his neck.

Edom's body does not move but remains standing. Dusk, emotionless, watches Edom snap his neck back into place as if it were nothing.

Edom says, "If I was someone normal, that would have killed me." He slams his foot into Dusk and sends him backwards. Edom then forms a portal and disappears, reappearing behind Dusk and grabbing ahold of him. He says, "I bet you have always wondered what's on the other end of this portal I can make, haven't you? How about taking a look for yourself!" Edom pulls Dusk into the portal formed from darkness.

Moments later, they appear a few feet in the air. As Dusk falls, Edom disappears and reappears a dozen times, striking Dusk with punches before pulling him into the portal once more. He repeats the process until Dusk catches a kick and propels himself away from Edom.

As he moves closer, Dusk's palm strikes Edom in the chest multiple times, pushing forward with each hit.

Laughing, Edom pulls him in by the wrist and says, "You are still a hundred years too early to be challenging me."

Showing no pain, Edom watches as Dusk forms his hands into a dagger. He dodges the attack, moving his head out of the way, and mimics Dusk, sending his own hand forward. As his hand is about to make contact with Dusk's chest, a white light flashes around them.

Hex proclaims, "You will do nothing to harm him!" as he throws Edom.

The two other Burdens—who have been only watching up until this point—run down the buildings to attack Hex who has abruptly appeared before them.

Echo turns to look at the masked Burden, who still remains silent, watching everything unfold.

Edom yells out, "Bast, Concordia, let's get this delicious meal that's before us!"

The three Burdens attack Hex. He repels them and forms a spear, spinning it around his head and striking one of them across the face. He slams the back of his spear into the other's stomach, and then pierces forward to stab Edom—but misses.

Echo turns once more to look at the Burden behind him. Still seeing no cause for concern, he decides to take the risk and run towards the battleground. He doesn't look back and hopes that the man doesn't strike him down.

Dusk yells out, "My sword, Echo, get me my sword!"

"Damn it!" Echo changes his direction and runs for the blade. He grabs it without stopping and heads towards them.

Echo slips past the Burdens as Hex wraps his hands around two of their cloaks and spins them in the air, throwing them out of the way. Edom takes this opportunity to land a strike in Hex's midsection.

Glaring eyes turn to look at Edom as Hex says, "You will regret that."

He grabs ahold of Edom's face and lifts him up into the air. He slams him head-on into the dirt, leaving his body completely upside down.

Dusk yells, "Throw me my sword!"

"Here!" Echo whips it through the air and Dusk catches a hold of it.

He puts all of his remaining strength into his attack and slashes downwards towards Edom's unprotected body. One of the other two Burdens—Bast—stops the blow with his armguards. His piercing red eyes anger Dusk further.

Dusk screams, "Get out of my way!" He cuts through the armguards and breaks them. Bast pulls away to avoid losing his arms.

With no one in his way, Dusk grabs ahold of Edom's leg and raises his sword into the air. Just then, Edom spins his body around and removes himself. Flipping his body in midair he lands on his feet and slashes Dusk across the face with a small blade.

Dusk returns the blow with a vicious slash down Edom's shoulder. The Burden, bleeding now, stabs forward, aiming for Dusk's heart. As the blade reaches his chest—the same place that killed Dusk the first time—Hex grabs ahold of Edom's cloak and whips him across the ground.

Rushing past Hex, Dusk pursues Edom and slashes upwards. Bast stops the attack with a leg guard, propelling Dusk backwards. Edom then opens up a portal and appears above Dusk in the air, stomping downwards.

Hex moves his spear in the way and stops the attack. Edom slams into it but is unable to break through the guard.

Meanwhile, Concordia, the other Burden, pursues Echo, who in turn is desperately trying to avoid the attacks from her. She lands a blow to his midsection and sends him into Hex who catches him.

The angel then reaches out and grabs ahold of Dusk, "We're leaving."

Dusk yells, "Wait, wait!" He slashes forward, missing all of the Burdens by a long shot. "Damn it let me go!"

As they begin to disappear within the white light—the ability that Hex is able to use because of the ring he wears—Dusk screams bloody murder at Edom with wild eyes. The Burden looks at him with no sense of joy, but pure anger.

Dusk yells, "This is not over! Give her back to me!"

Edom spits back, "I'll make sure to go crush her throat."

They disappear. The scenery changes completely.

Dusk throws himself out of Hex's grip and cries out, "Let me go!"

He throws a punch at the angel's face. Hex does not move, and the impact hits hard.

Taken aback by the fact Hex did not move out of the way, Dusk shakes his hand and looks away in shame. Two free hits now. He clenches his teeth and his fists. Echo moves back, knowing that with different scenery comes a different battle. He looks at both of them as enemies, and is right in doing so. A hand wraps around his throat before he can react—Hex lifts Echo up in the air.

Dusk turns around to see this and yells out, "Hex, don't!"

"Why not, he needs to die."

"Just don't, alright?"

The angel looks at Dusk, bewildered, and says, "But you are not well, you didn't listen to Wish's warning."

Dusk places a hand to his face and feels the sweat. His legs feel light. "It's alright, let's talk with him first. You don't need to go and kill him because I punched you in the face."

"That is not why I want him dead."

Echo looks at both of them, his eyes darting back and forth, wondering if the angel will let him go or break his neck.

Dusk yells, "I said let him go!"

Hex glares at Dusk and says, "Do not order me around. What is your problem?"

"My problem? You just took me away from the very man who killed me! The man who took Sarah from me! That's my problem you inconsiderate prick! Are you brain dead? Can you not feel anything? Fuck you!" Dusk pushes him.

The angel throws Echo down onto the ground and points a finger at him, "If you move, I will not hesitate to slaughter you." He then turns to Dusk and says, "I am aware of your anger, but that was not the proper place for us to fight. You were going to die."

"I had it under control."

"Far from it."

Dusk runs his hands through his hair. Losing his cool, he unravels.

"You don't know that. I wounded him."

The angel lets his spear disappear and says with some compassion, "Dusk, the moment you landed a hit on him, his eyes changed. You had the benefit of the doubt. He was shocked you were alive but figured you were just as weak as before. You proved him but that's all you would have accomplished."

Dusks face goes red and he starts to kick the ground repeatedly.

"Dusk…"

"Just stop it Hex, alright, there's nothing you can say that will make up for the fact you just took away my opportunity to get information out of him. Now I'm back to square one."

"That's not true."

"Are you fucking kidding me, yes it is! Take a look around. You just brought us to a fucking field surrounded by water. I don't see him anywhere, do you?" Dusk mocks Hex by pretending to look around.

"I'm sorry you feel that way. However, she is still alive. Think about what he said."

"What? That he'd crush her…" Dusk stops talking. Placing a hand to his mouth, he bends over and hunches down. "She's alive…" He grabs a handful of dirt and squeezes it.

"For now, control your anger. There's a lot that must be taken care of before we face them once more." Hex turns and looks at Echo, "… For starters…."

Not having moved an inch since Hex left him alone, Echo says, "Look, if you are going to threaten me you're wasting your time. I feel no regret for my actions."

"Yet you fear for your life."

Echo says carefully, "I fear for the ones I hold closest to me."

Dusk looks up, wiping away his frustration. He asks, "Why exactly did you cause havoc to the city? Are you working for the Burdens?"

"Working for them? Did it look like I was? I've never met them before. I did what I did in order to survive—so the five of us could survive. I bet you right now that they've accomplished their goals, that some of your friends have fallen and that Arc is going to let us go as promised."

Dusk asks, "Who's Arc?"

"The one who made us. Our father…if you were to look into his eyes you would see a place of hell. He's that kind of…person. He's used us like instruments until now. He is a bastard and we are his monsters, but we are vindicated because of our limited choices. There is only one way for us and so it is the right one. We find solace within one another, for there is none in this world or the next."

Dusk says, "So, you really were made by someone."

"That is correct." Echo replies. "And we've done this because that was the requirement for our freedom. "

Hex asks, "You had to kill for your freedom? What logic is there in that?"

Echo replies, "It's all about the fear. We had to kill and destroy—ramp up the fear—and then we would be free. We did that perfectly."

Hex begins to glare, "And you couldn't run away or fight back? You simply listened to your order? Why is fear so important?"

"You don't get it do you…he made us. Baring our fangs at him is like trying to fight a god. We couldn't handle it. So, we did what was demanded so we could get our cure. And if you really want to know about fear then just keep watching. The Burdens will do something."

Dusk asks, "What cure?"

Echo's eyes grow distant, a sad calm washes over him. "There's a time limit to our lifespan. It's short and cruel." Beginning to look at them with hatred, he continues, "So excuse me for killing those who've had plenty of time to live, but I want my turn! He has the antidote to grant us that. Blackmail or not, we want to live."

He then pulls down his collar revealing a puncture wound in his neck. "Look at this. This is the wound where the poison began to enter our blood stream. We've been given weeks, maybe months, but that shortens every time we use our inner power. I'm sure you've seen it, the mark that appears on our chests. I refuse to use it. I plan to survive."

Dusk says, "So you killed innocent lives instead of facing Arc himself? Father figure or not, you made the wrong choice."

Echo places a hand to his face and grunts, leaning over as he sits on the ground. "Innocent lives? Innocence is merely ignorance to the way of life. Everyone is subject to the infection of survival. Believe it or not, but our odds were in favor of slaughtering the weak. So we took the job, we got away, and now we just have to kill enough until he is satisfied. And he is no father figure, not even close."

Hex looks at him in disgust, "And what exactly marks the point of satisfaction for this man?"

"That's simple. When the Burdens arrive—which they have." Echo shows a smile. "Now all we have to do is get away. Naturally, I'm in quite a predicament, but the others will do just fine."

Hex reveals the truth to him and says, "Fine you say? I came across two of you before. One was on the verge of death, the other in complete despair."

Echo's face goes pale, "What?"

Hex continues, "That's right, and knowing how cowardly you all are, I feel no sympathy for any of you. It's just as you say after all, the weak and unprepared are easier than facing the harder of two paths. I imagine you are just ants in front of the Burdens and Arc. You don't get it do you. Arc, your creator, does not care about any of you. Not even enough to keep his word."

Echo scoffs, "You don't know that." He begins to think. He points a finger at Dusk, "I recall hearing that you died and now you're alive again. Tell me how you did that."

Dusk says, "It's not that simple."

"How so?" Echo tilts his head slightly, "If one can die and return, why can't another? You're human—so what? I don't care, just tell me."

"I was given an option, to rest in peace or to throw away my sanctuary in order to fight. I chose the latter."

"I see." Echo taps his feet on the ground. "Well then, they will come back."

Hex says, "It doesn't work that way. Dusk is an exception. Your friends, when they die—when you die—you will not even see the light.

That is the fate of a creation not born of natural causes."

Echo falls back on the ground and stares at the sky, "I guess we're fucked no matter what. What a joke...I swear...what a god damn joke." His voice begins to crack and Dusk can see the emotion spill over and overwhelm him.

Dusk says, "Hex, we've said enough."

A moment of silence passes between the three of them as they think and reflect on what has transpired—the truth, the reasons for why people fight and kill. During this time of reflection, large shadows appear over them and cover everything. Looking up, they see ten Federation ships—massive in size, with enough soldiers and military assets to take over a planet.

Echo says, "Well now...wonder if I have to go and blow those up."

"Are they here to help?" Dusk asks.

Hex merely looks up at the sky, wondering why such a massive force is arriving so late.

***

Meanwhile, a small conversation takes place, revealing how humorous yet dangerous the Burdens truly are.

With a hint of sarcasm, Edom asks, "Does Caster plan on leaning against that wall all day?"

To which Concordia replies, "Edom, I'm fairly sure he fell asleep."

Staring at Caster, Edom leans forward, blinks and lets out a loud laugh. He says, "Sleeping at a time like this. My, they must have been boring. Hey Caster, wake up."

His voice travels and causes Caster to open his eyes. He fixes the placement of his mask slightly and looks around.

Caster asks, "Where have they gone?"

"They escaped. They have an angel with them too it seems." Bast replies.

"An angel?"

"Yep, or at least a person with white wings and strong enough to fight us."

Caster stretches, "Ah, I wish I could have seen it."

Edom grins, "You could have if you were awake."

Concordia says, "So what's next, we've got some company above us."

Looking up, Edom's eyes twinkle. "The main course has arrived. I guess I should get going." He opens a dark portal behind him. "After all, it's time I pay our conductor a visit. I'm sure he's just about ready to begin."

CHAPTER TWENTY-NINE
The Colour of Our Hearts

Strong structures of authority block out the sun itself—the ships bear down their presence on the capital city of Eryu like an unwelcome group of bullies. With enough firepower to destroy vast portions of a planet, they head towards a city in need—their fangs already bared.

The organization governs the law throughout space, which protects the peace between planets. One of its fundamental rules is to never interfere with a planet's inner affairs unless directly requested. However, if requested, the Federation itself can lash out. For the laws of preserving a planet are not as concrete as one would hope, so the greed of mankind can seep out, and bullies lash out, and the sky goes black.

This flaw is well known and thus the Federation is feared as much as it is adored. A planet has not requested the aid of the Federation since its creation. And now, Eryu will bear witness to the horrifying truth of how the law can be corrupted when in the hands of those who only seek power.

With the president, Alexander Ixar, safely off the planet, the Federation can now act without worry of a direct backlash, labeling their actions as preserving mankind's existence while wiping out the threat.

The man in charge stands on the main bridge amongst the ten

ships. With his wrists crossed behind his back, he looks out at Eryu confidently. His eyes certain that what lies before him will soon be his.

The destruction of Eryu is evident, with clouds of smoke rising from fires that are spread throughout the city. Even from the sky, piles of bodies can be seen littered throughout the streets below.

A soldier comments on this, "It looks like a complete massacre. How many people got away safely?"

"Half of the civilians were able to safely evacuate. The rest are beneath us. Dead—or soon to be," the man replies with no trace of emotion in his voice.

"Sir?"

"There is no room for compassion. In order for us to wipe away the threat, we must leave no room for error. We must level it all and then rebuild."

Everyone surrounding him—all of the men and woman who bear the crest of the Federation and its dark blue clothing—remains silent. Even if some disagree, to say so loudly would result in their removal from the force.

So the soldier treads carefully. He asks, "How long until we initiate the cleansing?"

To which the heartless man responds, "In twenty minutes this will be over."

Those twenty minutes would mark the time it takes Dusk and the others to gather their strength and figure out the next course of action. Spread apart across a large terrain, all they can do is rely on their combined efforts and hope that the Federation is here to help and not destroy.

In one such location, rest is not plausible; the time to think is not possible, for the battle still wages on. With exhaustion creeping forward, Spike and Kiyo continue to battle Slate. Covered in cuts and bruises, they focus on the adrenaline rushing through their veins, knowing the exhaustion has crept its way into Slate's body as well.

He slams his hands together and brings the two buildings next to him crashing together, the metal fusing and creating a barricade. Spike and Kiyo leap through the openings and press forward, the battle beginning to test their spirits.

As they rise further into the air, they make contact with Slate and engage in a closer combat. Kiyo slams his hands into the top of Slate's head and sends him downwards towards Spike, who slams his second weapon, his wooden long stick into Slate's waist.

The clone moves around the air and lands against a wall, his feet sticking to the metal. His expression grim, he wonders how the others are doing, and how it is that the two before him are putting up such a long and drawn out fight with him.

With the shadows of the Federation's ships looming over, Slate decides to use a move he would otherwise care to avoid—a triumph card.

Well aware of the strange things he's seen during the fight—like the yellow light that shook through them all—he lets himself fall towards the ground. Kiyo and Spike jump after him and leap from building to building, trying to catch up.

Placing his hands together, he lets out a yell that shakes through the whole vicinity. All of the metal around them—even the buildings themselves—warp and join together, forming a dome.

Kiyo and Spike land on the ground and see everything disappear as the last specks of light vanish. They see the devilish look in Slate's eyes and his demeanor of dominance, they the prey, and he the hunter.

Kiyo calls out, "So you can muster up this kind of move, huh? Sort of makes it look like you've been taking it easy with us up until now. Making buildings warp to your will—pretty ballsy."

"I agree, this rubs me the wrong way," Spike chimes in. "Have you been wasting our time? You should have come at us with your full strength from the beginning."

They talk in order to stall time and allow their eyes to adjust.

Slate, who seems to have no issue with it, replies, "I apologize, next time I will not make that mistake, and will crush my opponent with full force. But you see, this is not a move I like to use willingly."

Kiyo asks, "And why is that?"

"It is of no concern to you." Slate says. He raises his hands to his side, the darkness concealing his movements. Two pillars form from the metal in the ground and rise, allowing his hands to rest on them.

His mind begins to wander slightly, wondering how much time is left until Arc rewards them, and if he even will at the specified time. By using his power this way, Slate relies only on the medication.

He snarls and presses his fingers into the metal. Acting as control panels, he avoids touching any of the metal in the dome directly. He controls it with his thoughts, with the consequence of his heart being put under considerable pressure.

The first wave of attacks initiate. Both Kiyo and Spike, still unable to fully see their surroundings, listen to the sound of metal cutting through wind. Kiyo dodges the attack and turns to look in Spike's direction. He sees that it makes contact.

Spike spits out blood and is struck once more. He begins to run forward, only to trip as a piece of moving metal slams into his ankle.

He mumbles beneath his breath, "Stop playing games."

He gets back up and looks around, seeing movement through the darkness despite there being no light. As the metal approaches him, he moves out of the way. It slashes through his clothing but does not hit his skin. The pieces of metal, extruding from both wall and ground, continue to move around in the dark, waiting for the right moment to strike.

As Spike deals with this, Kiyo, able to avoid the attacks, uses his scent, sight and hearing to locate Slate. By focusing in on the sound of Slate's fingertips touching the metal, he pinpoints his location.

He whispers, "Found you."

He dashes forward, avoiding the metal that aims for his body. He slashes through one that suddenly shoots up in front of him. He then finds himself surrounded. Boxed in. Stuck.

He spins around, cutting through all of the metal with his razor sharp nails, yet they continue to rise and block him. He turns to see Spike's condition.

Still in the same place, Spike continues to dodge the metal. Finally, he raises his hand forward and stops a blow with his bare hand. A smile of satisfaction spreads across his face, and even causes Kiyo to wonder if he's human.

A troubled look forms on Slate's face. He twists his hands, causing the metal to eradicate all in its path, with no flow or repetition. The change works and strikes both Kiyo and Spike.

Kiyo coughs up blood, and slashes once more through the metal, this time breaking free. He decides to run, giving no chance for Slate to box him in. As he runs, he recalls the glow that appeared on Slate's chest when he got angry at the beginning of their fight. With an idea now in his mind, he turns once more to see Spike's situation and smiles at his signs of agreement, realization, and a course of action.

Kiyo says, "Alright then—let's change the tide." He lunges forward, faster now, and slides across metal that shoots out. He moves past Spike's body and makes his way around him. He darts through the metal, occasionally using his nails to get a grip on it and shoot himself in a different direction.

He leaps towards the ceiling to buy himself some time. His eyes darting around, he locates Slate once more.

Now to confirm and to ensure an opening of attack, he speaks, "I couldn't help but notice the peculiar scent in your blood. Let me guess, you aren't even human are you? Jealous? Are you acting out like a child because you are different?"

Veins appear on Slate's forehead and he clenches the metal in his palms. Glaring, he replies, "I am far superior to that of a mere human!"

His chest glows and he looks down startled, realizing he fell for the bait.

The long stick that Spike prides himself in, a wooden weapon he keeps on him at all times—appears from the darkness and strikes Slate directly in the centre of his glowing symbol. The impact causes him to fall to a knee, but he does not let go. Yelling, he grabs ahold of the stick.

He says, "You will not make a fool out of me!"

Kiyo drops from the ceiling and grabs ahold of Slate's head. Twisting it, he attempts to break his neck. But Slate quickly forms metal around his skin, causing Kiyo to lose his hold.

Slate slams his elbow into Kiyo and a piece of metal wraps around Kiyo's leg, pulling him up into the air.

"I've had enough out of you." Slate says with a cough, blood now trickling from his mouth.

With his hand still wrapped around the stick, he turns his head to receive a punch in the face. But still he does not let his remaining hand let go of the metal pillar.

Spike looks at it and begins to wonder why Slate refuses to let go. With a daring attempt, he lets go of his weapon and pushes forward with a barrage of punches, slamming each one into Slate's chest, leaving his own guard open.

Slate removes his hand from the pillar. When Spike's expression shows disappointment, Slate says, "What, you thought it held significance? It's a pillar, not your gateway out of here."

Metal wraps around Spike's ankles and takes him to the floor. His head hits the ground hard and his body is dragged. The sound of two gigantic pieces of metal breaking off on either side sends a quivering sound throughout the dome.

Slate says, "It's over now. The two of you have lost."

"Like hell!" Spike yells. He twists his body around and his legs break free from the metal. He stands up, raises his arms out and takes on the impact of two large walls slamming into him. His muscles stretch, his face goes red and his body shakes as he holds off the wall.

Slate looks in awe at the sheer refusal to die and the masterful use of muscles standing before him.

Kiyo yells out, "Spike, hold on!"

"I got it kid!"

"I'm not a kid! Just don't die!"

"I said I got it, kid!", his face flushing, spit leaves his lips as his arms ache. "I won't die like this!"

Cuts begin to appear on his skin, the pressure in his head becoming unbearable. His arms feel the increasing toll as his body struggles not to break.

For the first time since the dome was formed, Slate walks forward, Spike's weapon in his hand. He looks down at the stick and snaps it in half. "My, my, what ever will you do now?"

Seeing his weapon broken, Spike forces his eyes shut. He focuses on the fact that although the stick is broken, his pride is not. Wincing with pain, he asks, "What is it you take pride in? What is it you fight for?"

Walking forward, Slate stops a few feet in front of Spike—close enough to land a final strike. He replies, "My pride is simply within my blood. In the blood of those I fight alongside. Why does it matter to you?"

"I simply wish to know what drives my opponent, so that when I take your life, I will know you died with no regrets."

With a pause, Slate says confidently, "You plan to take my life? I don't see how you can pull that off. You chose to fight me. You chose to desperately try and stop the destruction of this city—but it's all in vain. It's clear who has won. The outcome is in my favor. In a few minutes, I'll be free of all of this."

Kiyo, listening to them talk, remains silent.

"Free of all of this? Don't kid yourself. The scale of damage that you've done will always rest in your heart. Believe me, even if you aren't human, that's a characteristic all living things feel. Regret."

Ignoring his speech, Slate asks, "Are you ready?" as metal forms around his hand.

Spike spits back, "Not just yet. Don't try to rush my death. My muscles can hold off for much longer."

Slate looks at him closely and says, "I don't have time to wait."

Spike hears a crack and looks to his left arm. A piece of bone sticks out of his skin. Blood spills from his mouth and he gulps the rest down. He looks at Slate, "Don't rush my death. Don't run away from the end. Look at me with conviction. A man should never turn his back on what he's done. Look at me with clear eyes!"

Slate raises a hand and presses a finger against Spike's temple. He says, "I could have lived my life differently if I was born naturally. That's not the case for me. We don't always get what we want. You can't blame me if your death seems premature. Things happen." He presses his finger forward. For a moment Slate thinks about his own words, he realizes something sad.

Blood splatters the floor with the sound of bones being crushed.

A hand is jabbed through a chest and eyes dart down, looking to where the wound is screaming out. Slate sees a broken emblem and a sinking feeling runs through his skin. "Why...would you go so far?"

Feeling the pressure of the metal walls crushing against his entire body, Spike says, "I have too much to live for and I've come too far. If I can kill the one who kills me, then no one has to waste their time getting revenge."

Slate's legs grow weak as his power leaves him. With his last bit of strength, he spreads the walls apart, letting Spike fall to the ground. He then lets Kiyo loose from the metal that was binding him.

Struggling to stand, Slate looks up to see the dome weakening and light shining through. His eyes begin to fade and he counts down the seconds until the truth unveils itself. That is, if the man—the devil—would keep his word.

He begins to cry as he feels his heart tighten. The sign of release is not given. The medicine does not spread through his body. He says, "... Everything... It was all for nothing. All of this, pain.... for nothing." He looks at Spike and says, "So live. You needn't worry. My friends won't be able to avenge me...they too are dying."

Spike and Kiyo look at him, unsure of what to say.

"I do regret... I regret my actions. But it's too late." Fighting back pain and tears, he says, "I was never given any other option to live."

As the words exit his mouth, and Spike and Kiyo figure out the meaning behind them, their opponent vanishes before their eyes, along with everything around him.

The ground parts and sends them both falling down. The dome collapses. Steam rises from the air as the metal around them melts from extreme heat.

From the air, the cold-hearted man looks down from his ship, pleased by the direct hit to the metal dome.

A fellow soldier says, "We've struck it sir. It appears we've severely damaged the structure, likely killing whoever was inside."

"Very well." He says with authority, "Fire once more. Make sure that there's nothing left alive in that vicinity. It's been twenty minutes boys and girls. I want to see this city fall to its knees. For we will rebuild it in the colours of our hearts!"

CHAPTER THIRTY
Filling Up the Bucket

Staring off at the sky, Nix stands on a ledge above the city's burning landscape, where both tall pillars of steel contrast the red light given off from the flames below. The Burden—the one responsible for the massacre at Essa's high school—embraces the destruction, the chaos and the darkness.

His eyes weigh heavily on the ten looming ships that block the light, giving everything a gray appearance. It annoys him, for he likes seeing the colour of death, and death is not gray. It is full of each and every colour—wanting, waiting, and wishing to burst free from the clutches of the grim reaper.

The Federation—with its oversized ships, its presence of authority and the hammer of the law—goes against what he likes to indulge in, it ruins the spark to life. So he simply watches for the time being. For the Federation will do what it does best, create fear amongst the weak.

As he waits patiently, a dark portal forms behind him, and Edom steps out from it. As Nix turns to look at him, Edom spins around quickly, raising a dagger towards a third party—another figure wearing a black cloak.

Edom asks, "And who might you be?" His eyes glaring and trying to pierce through the armor that is before him.

Nix replies, "Calm down, you'll see soon enough who it is."

"Precisely." The man's voice rattles in the armor. "Edom, friend, it is I—Keeper."

Letting out a laugh, Edom drops his guard and walks towards the big body of armor standing in front of him. "And what happened to you?" He knocks on the steel body, "Sounds fairly hollow in there."

"Indeed. All that I am is a soul…and steel."

"A soul eh?" Edom tilts his head, "But I can see you also have your red eyes."

The red eyes squint with happiness, "Naturally."

"So what happened, hmm? Why the change?"

"I lost a duel with Bast."

"Bast? He never mentioned anything."

"He assumes I am dead, but Nix had other plans."

Edom turns to look at Nix, "So you had a hand in this?"

Nix, his eyes returning to the sky, says, "Yes. It's only natural seeing as how souls are my source of creativity. I implanted his within that steel armor. Steel, I might add, that is able to withstand bullets, pressure, and the elements themselves. To damage this body would take someone formidable. I didn't see his death being of benefit to us."

Keeper lets out a booming laugh that rocks around inside his body, "After this, I'll settle the score with Bast. Show him the true meaning of a spear versus hand-to-hand combat."

Edom raises an eyebrow, "I'm sure you will. Not like you lost to him once before."

Nix raises his hand and says, "That's enough Edom. Keeper has his pride and so do we. While he might've lost, I think it's safe to say most of us would when Bast gets serious. Being able to blow something up with just the touch of his hand—be thankful he only uses his power when he's in the mood."

Edom places a hand to his chin and looks at Keeper. "I suppose you are a strong bastard after all. Never thought I'd see the day your body of pure muscle would decay."

"Yes." Keeper replies, "It's a shame I lost."

Changing the topic, Edom walks beside Nix. "So, how much longer until you complete what you've set out to do?"

"Once the Federation does what it does best, everything will be ready."

Edom leans forward, turns his head and looks at Nix from below. "And can myself and the others speed this up in any shape or form?"

Nix smiles, "Yes, you certainly can."

Edom returns the smile, "Perfect." He stands up straight and forms a portal, "I'll get things started. Be ready Nix. And Keeper, I hope you can still move well in that damn thing."

He disappears, leaving them.

Keeper says, "He is still the shit disturber."

"Now, now, let him do his thing. This is not the time to be grumpy. We're about to have a splendid show unfold."

Keeper steps forward and stands off to the left behind Nix. "You are right. Well then let's make the men of law know fear, shall we? By the way, what about that girl?"

Nix looks at him from the corner of his eye, "That's a side project, which should be unfolding right about now."

***

Meanwhile, not too far from Nix and Keeper, Kiyo and Spike remove themselves from the debris. The scorching hot metal around them still emits the heat from the Federation's sudden attack.

Spike coughs and says, "That was sudden." With his body worn out—a few broken ribs and torn skin—he wonders how much longer he can continue to move.

Kiyo says, "You're in bad shape Spike."

"I can see that."

Kiyo puts Spike's arm around him.

"No offense, but you're sort of short to be doing this."

"It's this or I drag you behind me."

"Fair enough."

As they make their way from the battlefield, they both take a moment to turn and look back. They think about the final expression on Slate's face, the pain writhing throughout him. His tears.

Spike looks up at the sky and says, "Those bastards had no right to fire. We could have all died."

"I think that was their intention. The fact we are alive is pure luck."

"Luck huh? If it wasn't for the fact we were set free, we would've died."

"So, do we thank Slate?" Kiyo asks.

Spike smiles slightly, "No, we carry his name in our hearts as a man that fought for what he believed in."

"I must say humans are strange." Kiyo's ears twitch and he turns his head. He sniffs the air and his eyes sharpen their focus.

Spike asks, "What is it?"

"I smell Leaf—her scent."

"What, you smell a leaf?"

Kiyo frowns, "No... Leaf. She's a person just like me."

"Did she come from a tree?"

"I swear I am not in the mood. You're lucky you are in this condition."

Spike laughs and stands up straight. He asks, "What condition?"

Kiyo looks him up and down and says, "You still look worn out to me."

"Yes, but," Spike lifts up his shirt, "no broken ribs, just bruises."

"Were you lying then?"

"No, I just heal fast."

"Cool. I could care less. It's good you can walk on your own feet. I'm about to start running."

"Running? Why?"

"Because of a certain tree." Kiyo kicks off and heads down the street.

Spike runs his hand through his hair, sighs, and chases after him, thinking to himself that he finds it interesting that Kiyo doesn't take interest in his own uniqueness.

As they both head towards Leaf's scent, the Burdens make their move. Edom, along with Bast, Concordia and Caster, stand together in a wide-open space directly below the ten Federation ships. With nothing around them but debris and the remains of buildings, they let themselves be a visible target.

The Federation now aware of their presence opens their hangers and unleashes their mobile infantry and their robotic functioning machines—known as R.F.Ms, which are generally piloted by human personnel if not through a remote.

The soldiers and R.F.Ms land and surround the Burdens. With 200 against four, the vast number of troops is only a fraction of what the Federation's ships have in store.

Edom says, "Concordia, Bast, Caster—let's have some fun."

He waves his hand forward and numerous portals open. They all leap into one and the portals disappear. Another portal appears above in the sky. The soldiers and R.F.M pilots look to see a minuscule drop of something dark fall towards the ground.

It lands on the ground and explodes, ripping through all of the soldiers closest to it and destroying a few R.F.Ms. Within the chaos, a portal opens and Bast appears. He slams his hand into a R.F.Ms head and it explodes. He throws down the body and starts slamming his hand into soldiers, sending guts and bodily fluids flying onto their fellow comrades.

As soldiers take aim at Bast, Concordia appears. With a simple blink of her eyes, she sends all of the soldiers in her vicinity into an illusion of torture. They scream and wither in pain.

Two individuals with both of their faces hiding within the shadows of their hoods—nameless to the Federation—viciously slaughter with ease.

As they do so, Caster and Edom make their way towards the ships within the sky.

Caster makes his presence visible and stands in front of a few buildings that have avoided damage up until this point. As he waits, the Federation ships lock onto him. He asks loudly, "Will they refrain from firing upon the innocent?" They fire. "No" he says, "they will not." He runs along the street and everything behind him melts away. As the members of the Federation reload their main cannons, they unleash their secondary fire consisting of heavy machine gun turrets—all to slay one man.

He avoids the bullets as they pierce through buildings, killing those who are in hiding. The bullets raining down on the city cause utter devastation. Further pushing the hope beneath a pile of despair.

The ships fire their main cannons once more. This time aiming behind, in front of and at his exact position in order to clip him.

Caster stops in his tracks and watches as Edom appears and says, "Let's see how they like it."

Edom's portal opens wide enough and absorbs one of the main cannon's beam attacks. He closes the portal, forms another and disappears. He reappears in the sky moments later and opens up another large portal. The beam attack from before comes ripping through and tears through the hull of the ship. It goes through to the other side and slams into another ship. The first ship goes up in flames and begins to explode. The second ship, having taken heavy damage, begins to fall towards the ground.

Sparks, flames and devastation fall towards the city as two ships sink like titans and hit the ground. As they land, they send shockwaves ripping through the city. Fires are put out as new ones form around the ships' remains.

Watching all of this unfold, Gunther's group is unsure of what to do next. They rush through the city in hopes of coming across Dexter and the others.

As Gunther's group searches for them, Essa, along with Dexter, Baylee, Abigail and Cassandra, venture forward at a cautious pace, unsure of what to expect. Uneasy by both the presence of the Burdens and the Federation, the destruction of the two ships causes them to wonder if it's even safe to continue forward.

Essa asks, "Are you able to get ahold of the others?"

Dexter replies, "No, unfortunately not. Hex, Dusk, Kiyo and

Spike don't have a way to communicate with us, and even those who do won't be able to since the interference is impenetrable right now."

"Isn't it times like these when communication is the most crucial?"

"Ya, I suggest you file a complaint to the manufacturer. I'm sure they really care as their city falls to its knees."

The five of them press forward and then, as if luck has taken leave, come across a threatening foe—standing before them almost as if he was waiting.

Keeper waits, his large spear at his side with the tip facing the air.

His voice lets out a slight chuckle within his armor. "Looks like waiting around Nix is paying off. Time to have some fun and let off some steam."

Essa's eyes widen as she says, "Why the hell is such a large set of armor just…waiting for us?"

Cassandra replies, "I think we got some bad luck by going in this direction."

Angry, Dexter says, "We will just have to handle this ourselves. Abigail, Baylee—are the two of you ready?"

Baylee says, "Ready enough to fight."

Abigail replies, "We need to make this quick. It's not safe to linger any longer. We've been separated from the others for far too long. You all saw the look on Gunther's face. I'm sure he's on the verge of a rampage, so we best join him and make sure he's safe."

"What made him so angry when we were on the Trinity? Was it the destruction of the city?" Essa asks cautiously.

They all look at her.

Dexter answers her question by saying, "The symbol that appeared on that young man's chest—the one who was causing the destruction. It's a symbol that Gunther has…had a horrible experience with, and not just him, but also Sapphire and Tail. The three of them will stop at nothing to subdue the person behind it."

Growing impatient, Baylee says, "This isn't the time or place for a talk like this. He's staring at us. Dexter, what are we going to do?"

Dexter nibbles on his lip as he thinks. "Why is he just…waiting there?" He asks.

Baylee persists, "Dexter, seriously, what do we do?"

Keeper beckons for them to move towards him. A soft chuckle rattles around in his empty interior. Although the light is still within the sky, a heavy weight surrounds his presence. The stone buildings around him look evil and full of horrible secrets. His red eyes gleam vicious whispers of what awaits in the seconds to come.

Essa says, "He's a Burden, isn't he…"

Cassandra says softly, "I can't think of a reason how he's not… there's…something incredibly troublesome about him but I can't see what it is."

Dexter looks at her and asks, "What do you mean?"

"I can see souls. I can feel them as well. And right now, I'm getting a similar feeling but he doesn't take on the form of anything I've ever experienced."

Dexter gulps. He looks at Keeper closely. "There is no way out of this. Essa, you need to escape while we buy you some time and join up with you. We don't have enough air gear to get us all away, and this thing, isn't something I want to come find us another day. Cassandra, I want you to go with her. Get her away from this man and keep her safe."

Essa looks at him and, before she can reply, Cassandra places her hand on her wrist and turns to Dexter. "Before we go I'll help."

"How do you plan to do that?"

"Up until now, all I have done is walk around. But fighting is second nature for me. I'll offer you support while Essa and I get away."

"Like I said—how, exactly?"

"By summoning forth a spirit from the other side."

Dexter asks quickly, "Who are you, exactly?"

"That doesn't matter. Look, if the three of you plan to face a Burden on your own, then I have the perfect support for you. A beast of pure adrenaline, blood lust and the desire for carnage." She pulls out her blade, slashes her hand and slams it into the ground, "Come forth! Attila!"

A cloud of smoke appears, sending off steam. The sound of

nostrils snorting can be heard. As the smoke clears, a beast with fur covering the entirety of its body—apart from its stomach—stands on two legs. Its muscles bulging, its face, its horns, and its black skin—it bears a strong resemblance to that of a Minotaur, yet its stature is far larger.

Cassandra says, "I leave her in your hands."

"Her?" Dexter asks.

Cassandra doesn't respond, but hurries off, dragging Essa with her.

Dexter turns to look at Keeper and pulls forth two daggers. He grips them tightly, and the Minotaur stands beside him, its hooves digging into the ground. It snarls and slams its fists together.

He says, "Well then, Attila, let's do this." It roars in approval and they run ahead, Abigail and Baylee following them with their air gear. The two girls latch onto the buildings and run along the rooftops.

Keeper continues to wait.

Dexter reaches Keeper first and leaps into the air with the aid of his air gear. He slams both of his daggers downwards.

Keeper blocks them with his spear.

Dexter flips over his back as the Minotaur reaches them.

Keeper moves his one fist forward and grabs ahold of the Minotaur's punch.

He tries to hold off the beast but it pushes forward and slams into him, taking him through the glass wall behind them and into the building. They land on the floor. The Minotaur stands up and slams its hoof down into Keeper's body. It makes a small dent. He gets back up and slashes his spear forward, cutting the Minotaur's body.

The Minotaur runs forward and slams into Keeper once more, this time pushing him into a wall. It moves back and slams its fists forward, impacting Keeper's body. Keeper grabs the Minotaur by the neck and throws it to the ground. The two beasts, huge in size, fight each other with all their might.

Abigail and Baylee whip forward and slash Keeper across his armor before he can react. Both of their attacks leave the slightest scratches. They look at one another in alarm, seeing that his armor is stronger than their weapons.

He looks up at them and glares. They attack once more. He circles his spear around his body and whips it around. They avoid his attack. Baylee runs along the wall, leaps, grabs ahold of his head and slams her dagger down into the top of his helmet. It punctures it slightly. She pushes down but it doesn't budge.

Dexter yells, "Baylee, get away from him now!" He runs forward, very low to the ground, and slashes his daggers behind Keeper's ankles.

Baylee tries to pull out the blade but fails in doing so. As her heart begins to pound, she looks at her sister and says, "I'm sorry."

Keeper grabs ahold of her and whips her body around like a ragdoll, breaking several bones in her body before impaling her with his spear. He pulls out the blade from the top of his helmet and crushes it. His red eyes enjoy the sight before him as he stands in a puddle of death.

***

As the battle unfolds, Cassandra hurries away with Essa by her side. They cut through the main floor of a building that's still fairly intact. Their feet pound on the black aluminum floor. Essa pulls herself from Cassandra's grip and steps away.

She says shrilly, "Just hold on. Give me a second."

"Essa, there's no time."

"No! Before I go any further with you I want to know why you didn't tell them about your relation with souls? You have a weapon that can extinguish a soul in a successful strike. You have something they don't! Why didn't you stay?!"

"It doesn't work like that Essa…" Cassandra looks around to see if there are any signs of danger. She sighs and steps towards her, "Even if I risked my life to fight someone, something I have no confidence against…even if by some miracle I was able to plunge a Tear of Jessica through that armor, I have no idea what the result would be. He's not a phantasm Essa, and that scares me."

"Then what is he…?"

"I don't know. He could be a man that's at death's door and that's why I got a vibe from him, but that doesn't explain the similarity. If I could guess, someone attached his soul to something in that armor, or possibly the armor itself. If that's the case, any normal weapon should work against him."

"But…if it's the armor…"

"Then they either run, or break him into pieces. Essa, they are professionals. They will figure it out. We need to go. We can't waste any more time."

***

The Minotaur runs at Keeper. The Burden raises his spear to hold off the beast. The Minotaur slams its horns against the spear but is held off. Keeper knees the Minotaur in the face but is then grabbed and thrown into the ground. His black cloak flies off in a tattered mess.

They break the tiles beneath them. Everything they come into contact with turns to debris soon after. Keeper holds onto his spear while the Minotaur pins it down. He uses his free hand to punch the Minotaur in the face repeatedly.

Abigail stares hopelessly and full of shock at her sister's lifeless remains. Dexter screams out for her but she doesn't hear or listen. They need to run—she knows this—but she refrains from moving away. She stares at the battle between Keeper and the Minotaur.

They slam into another wall. Keeper grabs ahold of the Minotaur's horn and pulls on it, freeing his other arm. He slams his spear through the Minotaur's stomach. The beast roars and begins to bleed dark red blood. Keeper feels himself being lifted into the air. The Minotaur slams Keeper into the ground and then throws a vast array of raging punches into Keepers chest, further denting his armor.

Keeper pushes backwards as the Minotaur tries to hold him down, and gets back up onto his feet. Grabbing ahold of the horn again, he pulls the Minotaur down onto a knee and raises his spear.

Just then, Abigail attaches wires around Keeper's legs and pulls. She succeeds in taking him down to his knees, giving the Minotaur the advantage it needs. It slams its horns into Keeper's armor and lifts him into the air. It grabs his arm and leg, and pulls, it roars as it tries to tear him apart.

Keeper yells, "You stupid beast!" He pierces his spear into the Minotaur's chest. The beast drops him. Keeper grabs its neck and begins strangling it.

Abigail rushes forward and aims her daggers at the opening in Keeper's armor. He sees this, lets go of the spear, and slams his hand into her waist, sending her into a wall.

The Minotaur pushes back, knocking Keeper away. It turns around and slams its fist across Keeper's head, putting a severe dent into his jaw piece. Roaring now, the Minotaur presses forward with the spear still in its chest.

***

At that moment, Essa and Cassandra make their way through another building, this one badly damaged.

Essa asks, "That creature you summoned. Could you always do that?"

"No. It's something I was only able to do recently."

"Is it strong?"

"It's the strongest. If Attila fails, then there's nothing I can offer at this time…but she won't. I'm confident though, we've only been partnered together for a short while."

"I'm sorry but this is all just so insane. Dreams, angels, souls, summons… Three months ago I thought the most unique thing this universe had to offer was…"

"It'll be alright Essa. Let's keep going. Attila will keep us safe…" Her eyes glaze over slightly. A feeling of worry sits on her shoulders. She knows she's given up something of high value for Essa, something more valuable than her time.

***

Keeper begins to get excited as the Minotaur attacks in a bloody frenzy. He says, "This is splendid! This is what I need!"

He runs forward, grabs ahold of the spear and pulls it out of the Minotaur. It punches him once more, knocking him down. It raises its hoof and slams down but he avoids it. It slams its fist across a wall, destroying it, but again misses.

Dexter aids Abigail in getting up. "We need to hurry. The Minotaur isn't going to last much longer."

Keeper waits and, as the Minotaur raises its arms to slam down into his body, he slashes his spear and cuts off one of Minotaur's arms. As it roars in pain, he moves past the beast and slams his spear through its back, piercing it into the ground. As it struggles to move, Keeper wraps both of his hands around its neck. It bellows, struggling to break free, blood flowing from its nostrils.

Keeper says, "Rest in peace. I am the more vicious of us dear Minotaur." He twists his arms, snapping the Minotaur's neck and letting its body hit the ground unnaturally.

Keeper reaches for his spear as Dexter and Abigail appear. They slam their daggers into the openings in his armor. As they do so, the same look of confusion appears on their faces.

Keeper turns around and says, "That's right." He pulls the spear out of the Minotaur's body, "There is no flesh or bone for you to cut or pierce into. Your efforts are in vain. To you, I am immortal. You should run."

Dexter yells, "Get away! Now!"

He and Abigail jump back, their weapons snapping within the joints of Keeper's armor. Dexter grabs a flash grenade from his belt and throws it forward. It explodes. As they turn to run, the spear slashes through the light and removes Abigail's head from her shoulders.

Keeper, as if sniffing the air, raises his head. He looks at Dexter and says, "There are things that I miss. While I enjoy killing I can't get that feeling back. I can't smell the blood. I can't feel the goose bumps. This is utter torture, but for now, this fun will do."

Dexter's face turns pale as he watches, helplessly, as Keeper raises his spear into the air. He screams in protest and, with both of his hands, pulls out two grenades.

With wild eyes of fury he screams, "Fuck you!"

As Keeper's spear slashes through one of his arms, he sets off the grenade in his other hand, engulfing both of them in the explosion.

***

Nix, still standing in the same place from before opens his eyes and says in satisfaction, "Now the bucket is full."

CHAPTER THIRTY-ONE
Value of Fear

Nix places his hand into his pocket and pulls out a small cylinder. "Just a little drop should do," he says as he holds onto the cylinder and licks it with his tongue. He turns it over and watches as one drop of black liquid falls to the surface below. Ever so lightly, he presses his finger against the ground and touches the liquid, forming a black ball. He steps on it and it wraps around his feet, securing him in.

This is the moment he has been waiting for, the moment where his efforts come to fruition—a time where everything connects. He rises from the ground and up towards the sky. He reveals his presence. His eyes cast their way towards the Federation ships. He sees a small group of soldiers piloting R.F.Ms heading his way. Nix grins and says, "I love this."

With the cylinder in hand, he continues to rise into the sky. The sun begins to shine on him and he accepts the warmth. He stops and opens the cylinder for a second time. He tilts it slightly. A small drop of black liquid exits its chamber and falls.

As the drop makes its way downwards, Nix chants elegantly, "Creatures of the current. I heard your calling. I saw you fall. I witnessed the disaster. Oh creatures of the current, destruction of my heart. Eat all that is ugly and come forth from the dark. This place is now your home."

The drop of black matters hovers in the sky for a moment. Nix watches it intensely and closes his eyes gleefully as he feels the pressure emitting from it. It shocks the city. Falling, it connects with the drop from the cylinder. This time, the entire city rumbles.

A black line shoots up from the ground and rises through the sky—like a bolt of lightning in rewind—making a loud cracking noise. By now, everyone is looking. Watching. Waiting.

***

Kiyo runs along the rooftops, leaping from building to building. One falls and collides with the one he stands on. It shakes but he keeps his balance. His eyes stare in horror from the feeling the chaos has given him.

He says, "Leaf...please. Where are you?"

Spike runs along the streets before finally stopping to catch his breath. He looks up at the sky and feels a chill run through his body. He thinks back to what Essa said about being someplace else, a place like a dream.

The black line makes a thunder-like sound and a rip emerges. It stretches and opens up, showing nothing but darkness. The darkness then begins to spill out. A claw grabs onto the edge of the rip. A head follows closely behind—teeth bearing, body completely black. A Nightmare looks out at the city below, a dream—a monster—now in reality.

Face growing pale, Kiyo says, "This can't be happening. This... this isn't possible."

Nix looks towards Kiyo and smiles. He thinks briefly about a conversation he had with Edom. *"Your experiment with the dreams of humans is becoming erratic. It's impressive though. Was it your idea to tie humans and theirs dreams together? Was it you, or our leader?"* Edom's words float in his mind.

Nix raises his arms to his side and screams, "Now feast!"

The rips open further and the Nightmares begin to spill out. He looks back at them and marvels over the disgusting things that human's dream of, the malnourished and freakishly conceptual creatures of the dark.

Kiyo feels the skin tighten around his eyes. One feeling, anger, ruptures his balance and filters through his veins faster than blood reaches one's heart. His nails grow sharp. His hair dances in the wind. A black hairless tail rips through his shorts and grows a sharp triangular end that slashes around.

He screams at the world, "I won't allow this! I DID NOT LET NORMA DIE FOR THIS!"

Spike looks up and sees Kiyo leap from the building. He watches the short young man collide with the first Nightmare he comes across. He sees how easily Kiyo rips through it. The Nightmares may have come to the real world, but their hunter was here first.

The Nightmares continue to spill out and quickly fill the sky with treacherous shrills of pain and horror. Their eyes dart around for any source of life and go on a hunt in a rapid frenzy. They spread across the sky and begin to block out the sun.

Kiyo spins around in the sky as he leaps from structure to structure, cutting through every Nightmare in his path. He flips backwards and slashes through one before slamming both of his claws into another. His eyes fixate on Nix, the man that spit on Norma's sacrifice.

***

Far away from the gateway of madness, Dusk watches it unfold. He asks in disbelief, "How is this possible? Hex, I thought a gateway could only be opened by Norma or someone strong like her."

Hex says, "It seems someone figured out another way." He turns to look at Echo and thinks for a moment. He then stares at the increasing number of Nightmares descending upon the city and heading for the Federations ships. He says, "So this is why you were here clone. Does fear have something to do with this?"

Echo says, "Possibly."

Hex says angrily, "Your lives were not worth this. No matter what

you think or how you feel. You chose wrong. This death, this carnage—
it's only going to make things worse."

Dusk asks, "Echo, do you still feel no ounce of regret?"

The clone looks away, giving no answer.

"Dusk, we must act on preventing anymore Nightmares from entering this world." Hex says, "It defies all sense of balance and will
result in only one ending. The destruction of the human race."

"And what exactly are we supposed to do Hex?" Dusk replies
sharply, "Believe me, I don't want those Nightmares to keep spilling
out, but look at how hard it was for us to even get here. Norma gave
up her existence and we even lost sight of Leaf. But someone could
just…open up a damn rift to the other side? Connecting the dream
world and this world? How are we supposed to stop that?"

"There is always a way. All we can do is act to try and stop the flow
from spilling out."

"That kind of logic pisses me off Hex—it just means running into
danger with no plan."

"What would you do for Sarah then?"

Dusk, unsure about what to say, blurts out a rash response full of
anger and confidence, "Run into the depths of hell itself."

Hex, with a shine in his eye, places his hand on Dusk's shoulder,
"Then let us enter that realm of horror together."

Echo speaks up again. "Well now, aren't the two of you just sweet?
I will have no part in this."

Hex turns to look at him and says, "You have no choice. You either
help, or I kill you right here and now. It would benefit Dusk greatly."

Echo scoffs, "I'm sure it would."

"No, you don't understand. You being alive is now a hindrance to
his well-being."

Echo raises an eyebrow and asks, "How so?"

Dusk says, "Hex, it's alright."

Hex looks at Dusk and says, "It's something he ought to know,
in case he ever wishes to fight you on equal grounds again." He turns
to look at Echo for the last time and says, "The moment Dusk struck

you and failed at killing you, he transferred a part of his life into you."

Echo asks, "Now how the hell does that work?"

"By defying all common logic, by existing as a source of his own energy. He saw fit to use it in order to fight you but was naive in doing so."

"This is just...bloody irritating." Echo kicks the ground and rubs his hand through his hair, "Alright, alright already! I don't even get this but," he looks at both of them angrily, "I'll help you, alright? I'll do whatever you two need but then I am out of here, And if either of you try to stop me, I'll kill you. Got it?"

Hex, about to threaten him, is interrupted by Dusk who says, "Sounds like a deal."

Echo steps between them, pointing towards the rip in the sky. He says, "Now, let's start by explaining to me properly what on earth is going on. I don't understand any of this."

Hex lets out a sigh, Dusk wipes his brow and the three of them stare at the hundreds—now approaching the thousands—of Nightmares spilling out.

***

At this time, Kiyo continues to move towards Nix. Spike also rushes through the streets and watches the Nightmares landing, scurrying through the debris to find the remains of those still in hiding.

Stretching his arms out as if to grasp the man himself, Kiyo leaps through the air and heads towards the Burden. Nix, restraining his own desire to smile—not wanting to spoil his intentions—steps off from the dark matter and falls downwards. He grabs ahold of Kiyo and brings him along for the ride.

Using Kiyo as a cushion, they land on a rooftop. The impact cracks the cement and sends fractures running through its foundation.

The Burden stands up and dusts himself off. He looks down at Kiyo in contempt and satisfaction. He says, "It's a pleasure to meet you."

Kiyo looks up at him and coughs up a bit of blood. His body feels unbearably broken but he knows he can still move if he has enough time to heal. He asks in a croak, "Where is she?"

Nix raises an eyebrow and smiles. "So you can sense one another? That's nice to know."

"Tell me…where she is!" Kiyo's nostrils flare and, before he can move, Nix slams his foot into his throat to hold him down.

Nix says, "Now, now, don't get all dramatic. She's in my possession. It's thanks to the two of you that I had renewed faith in my personal goal. My dream was to make this all happen. And wouldn't you know, my dream came true." Nix looks around and admires the Nightmares roaming about. He continues to say, "I made everyone's dream come true."

Kiyo struggles to breathe properly with the weight of a foot bearing down against his airway. He grips the Burden's foot but doesn't have enough in him to extend his claws and strike.

He asks with gasps of air, "What have you done to her?"

Nix says, "The question is what haven't I done to her?" He sees Kiyo's reaction and smiles. He says, "When she first fell from the sky I couldn't believe my luck. So I snatched her up before she knew or could react. Now she's in my special place and, after having studied her and learned things," He pushes down further into Kiyo's throat and says, "I know what makes a dream what is it. I know you can break but also heal incredibly fast. There's more I want to know, so having you in my possession will speed up that process." His eyes return to look at the Nightmares and he says, "I don't feel like observing Nightmares. They have their perks mind you. But," he looks at Kiyo, "they aren't pure."

The sound of incoming R.F.Ms catches Nix's attention. He looks at them and marvels over their bravery but, as soon as they appear, they are destroyed by a group of thirsty Nightmares. They explode and engulf the Nightmares in flames.

A piece of debris is sent through the sky. It strikes Nix in the face. He moves his finger to his cheek and feels the dampness of blood. He looks at his fingers and, as he does so, Kiyo instantly—almost maniacally—lunges like a ferocious beast towards a stronger pray.

His tail slashes upwards and pierces through Nix's hand. Kiyo attacks but a phantasm appears and stops him. He leaps away, able to see the phantasm. Nix clenches his wounded hand and glares at Kiyo.

A pair of hands reaches out and grabs the edge of the rooftop. Spike pulls himself up and huffs, straining his self further. He winks at Kiyo and pulls the rest of himself over. He rolls across the ground and gets up. The two of them stand together—wounds visible—in front of the man who, up until this point, has orchestrated everything.

Kiyo rubs his throat and says, "How nice of you to join us."

Spike says, "I saved your life. I have good aim, don't I?"

Nix says angrily, "A little blood is not worth getting proud over." His eyes ignore them and look towards the main plaza below. "Everything is just beginning. It does not matter how many of you show up. You're in my world now." He rubs some black liquid on his wound from the cylinder and heals his skin.

Kiyo looks carefully at the black cylinder and wonders how much value it holds towards Nix's power over. He remains silent and cautious.

Spike looks down below at the plaza and places a hand on Kiyo's shoulder. "Look, the others are here."

In the plaza Gunther arrives with Tail and Sapphire. They look around before quickly noticing the presence of a nearby threat. On the other end of the plaza, Keeper stands—his armor soaked in red blood dripping down its grooves.

Moments later, Essa arrives with Cassandra. Their hearts drop when they see Keeper. Essa asks, "Cassandra…how did he get here before us…what happened to the others?"

Cassandra thinks about Attila. Her eyes glaze over. "You're right Essa. I should have stayed." Essa looks at her. Cassandra continues, "I should have killed him myself."

They run towards Gunther and join up with him and the others. Gunther asks without thinking, "Essa are you alright?"

Her eyes water and she says, "I'm sorry Gunther."

"What's wrong?"

"I'm weak, just like you said. And now I'm afraid your friends aren't okay."

Gunther looks at her. He feels a weight drop in his stomach. He looks at Cassandra. The way she stands shows her sense of regret. He takes a deep breath and wraps his arms around Essa. He says, "You didn't force them to do anything. Tell me. Who was it that brought you to tears?"

She points towards Keeper. Gunther's eyes slowly move towards the Burden. He sees the blood once more, and knows whom it belongs to. It takes on a new meaning. He sees the dents and scratches in the armor and knows that his friends fought hard in their struggle for survival. A feeling of rage burns in his chest.

Spike screams from above, "You fucks need to pay attention!"

Everyone looks up. A black sphere of gigantic proportions hovers above them in the sky, blocking out the sun. It moves towards them, first slamming into the buildings, oozing past them and then finally descending towards the plaza where it engulfs everyone. They don't know it yet but they are about to be unwilling guests in Nix's sanctuary.

CHAPTER THIRTY-TWO

Those With Wings, Fly

The cries of innocent lives are heard throughout the city as broken families try to find shelter. With no way out, they run aimlessly, some dying from the destruction around them, others by the friendly fire of the Federation.

A large Nightmare wraps around a Federation ship and crushes it, causing it to explode in a massive array of flames and death. Below the Federation ships, the Burdens continue to kill everyone in their presence. Soldiers fall like fragile leaves, their body parts being removed easily and frequently.

Bast and Concordia continue to effectively bring forth a nightmare of their own onto the minds of all those before them while the real Nightmares continue to descend and spread across the city.

In the air, in a spot not yet devoured by the Nightmares, the Trinity hovers. Paige sits at the cockpit with both of her hands firmly gripped on the controls. Her mind urges her to move towards the madness and search for the others.

Rudy says, "We need to do something."

"I know" she says flustered, "but what exactly can we do? We haven't gotten word from them."

He grabs his ponytail and tugs on it, trying to remove himself from thinking. He says, "We both know that they probably can't contact us…we need to do something."

Her face goes red. "I know that alright! I don't want any of them to be there any longer but fuck, what are we supposed to do? I can fly real well—better than anyone—but we don't have the necessary amount of eyes to keep us in the air. With only you watching over this ship, our blind spots will be death of us."

The doors to the bridge open, both Rudy and Paige turn to see Fleur standing at the doorway with her arms crossed.

Paige says, "Who the hell let you out?"

Fleur smiles, "Darling, you just said there's only the two of you. I let myself out." She walks towards them and looks at the chaos in the city. She marvels over it, "So there's something entertaining taking place and I've been cramped up in here. Pity."

Paige says in sheer anger, "What the fuck do you want Fleur? Gunther and the others are out there fighting and you're wasting time by being your usual useless self. Why don't you do something for a change and help us rather than impede our every move."

Fleur laughs and raises her hands as she says, "Impede? Darling I exist to cause a ruckus. But fine. I'll help." She looks at the Nightmares that head towards them. "Something that ugly only makes me feel uncomfortable."

"I'm going to head straight into that hell so we can find Gunther and the others, and get them back on the Trinity. This city—hell, this world—is no longer my concern. And as the pilot of this ship, I'm making it my duty to get us away from here."

Fleur says sarcastically, "How noble."

"So I want you to get off my ship."

Fleur uncertain to her meaning looks at her in alarm.

Paige says, "I know damn well you can stand on the hull of a ship without a problem. Do you think I forgot the last time we tried to capture you? So go out there and put yourself to use."

"By putting those ugly things to rest?"

"Bring them into your territory. Get rid of them."

Fleur smiles again, "I think putting me in harm's way is a laugh but oh well. Let's go save them."

"After we do that, I won't notice your escape."

Rudy looks over at them from the corner of his eye and smiles softly. Fleur looks at Paige and doesn't know what to say.

Paige pushes forward on the controls and yells, "It's time we put our wings to use. Rudy, let's do this!"

***

As the Trinity dives into the heat of battle, Hex soars through the sky and holds onto Dusk and Echo. The clone crosses his arms and looks at the ground below. Ill amused by how he is being treated, he remains silent. Dusk, on the other hand, looks uncomfortable.

He looks up and gazes at the large white wings that, with enough elegance and power, move the three of them towards their goal.

Hex says, "Echo, where do I drop you off?"

Echo glares upwards and says, "You'll do so with my life in mind got it?"

"Oh, it's on my mind."

Echo points towards a set of buildings west of them and says, "Drop me off there and I'll do what I can."

As they reach the location Echo pointed towards, Hex moves close enough to drop him off without needing to stop. Echo lands safely on the roof. He heads towards a door that leads to the inside of the building, not taking a moment to look back at them.

Dusk says, "So, do you think he will keep his word?"

"He will if he wishes to live. If his ally can control gravity, like he says he can, then perhaps with some luck we can close that rift."

"Are you speaking scientifically right now Hex or are you just guessing?"

"I am not a scientist."

"So then you're just guessing?!" Dusk lets out an extremely loud sigh of disgust.

His eyes scan the surface below. He doesn't see any signs of life. He looks to his left and sees the Federation ships in an intense engagement with the Nightmares.

He decides to ask, "Hex. That ring you have. I know it's so you could enter the dream world and eventually get here, but does it have anything to do with how you managed to make us get away from the Burdens so quickly? It seems to do the same thing as what…Andromeda could do…"

"Why did your voice trail off when you mentioned Andromeda?"

"I haven't had the time to mention it…but she's dead."

Hex looks forward and says, "I don't use my ring often because I need to conserve my energy. Once I use it, it takes a long time to regenerate."

"So it's your life support."

"Yes. It removes the constraints on my body and lets me use my full power if I choose to."

"Are you close to running out?"

"No"

"Then why the precaution?"

"So I don't join Andromeda."

The danger begins to move its way into Dusk's pores. He breathes it in. He feels it wrestle with his muscles and urge the voice inside to run but he ignores it as he always has.

Instead of fearing the massive amount of Nightmares they are heading towards, the carnage the Federation is causing rather than helping those in need, the fact that within him another voice is snickering, asking for him to let the darkness take over, Dusk lets Hex bring them closer to where they are destined to go, together, as one.

He asks the angel a personal question. "Hex, if I had gone through that doorway, back when I first met you, what would have happened? Would I be like you? Would I have the strength necessary to fight?" An expression appears on Hex's face, something Dusk hasn't seen before. It looks human, full of emotion. This reaction in the angel's eyes makes Dusk feel vulnerable.

"If you had gone through that door, you would have no part in any of this," Hex replies, "or anything. You would be... nothing." He looks away from Dusk's eyes, surveying their surrounding and continues, "Sarah would never be saved, this band of companions would have never been formed the way that it is now, I would have never associated myself with any of them. You coming with me is perhaps the greatest sacrifice anyone could ask for. Because although you've been granted more time now, you will never rest."

Dusk says, "But people become angels."

"No, humans become nothing. Angels are another...species."

"...Wait, what are you talking about? I thought angels were humans who've gone through the door, and served like...a certain amount of time in the clouds or something."

"...That is as naïve of a presumption as I would expect from a human. But no, Dusk, humans live their life and when it ends, they appear before the gatekeeper known as Truth. He, in turn, leads them through the doorway to where they find peace. I don't know what is on the other side of that door, it could be emptiness, it could be a haven, but one thing is for certain, no human who crosses that doorway ever comes back. Certainly not as an angel."

"But...then what are you really?"

"As I said, I am another species."

Dusk laughs awkwardly and looks off into the distance. He says, "Then there really is nothing true about what they say. You're as mysterious as they come Hex but at least I know now that this is the only road I can take."

"This is no road Dusk" Hex looks at him and says, "this is life."

Dusk looks up at the angel and takes it all in. For the first time, he willingly feels within him that he likes Hex's company and that without him he'd be lost and full of rage and despair. He says, "I wouldn't change my decision even if I could. Following you was the best decision I could have made. We will stop this bullshit fantasy the Burdens are trying to create and you can help me save Sarah. They can't kill me twice."

Hex's eyes look forward into the blackness, they glimmer with radiance and clarity. The thick air that surrounds them temporarily subsides. The angel looks at Dusk and tells him, "No matter how dark the day may become, it fears the light. As it spends all of its strength trying to devour it, one small little flame is enough to hold it at bay. Dusk, you are a source of light for your kind. Humans may differ in opinion but death strikes all. If you exist to stop death from reaching them when death is premature, then you are already more than I. This journey with you has been, worthwhile."

The Trinity appears beside them. Dusk looks over, Hex's words playing in the back of his head over and over. He looks at a woman he's never met. She stands on a ship he's never seen. Fleur looks over at him and grins. She unhooks her cloak and it flies off into the wind. Their eyes both move forward towards the Nightmares and the dome of darkness that dwells amongst them.

Hex says with a small hint of a smile, "But you're still a pain in my side."

CHAPTER THIRTY-THREE

The Eleventh King

For Nix, this is reality. Where both pain and suffering find its home. Where the flick of his mind can send everything spiraling downwards. This place, his sanctuary, is equivalent to a tomb for those who venture into it. It only exists to bring the suffering and pain he has felt, and put it unto others.

Within the darkness, torches are flickering. They give guidance to those who find themselves within Nix's secret little realm. Giving a false sense of security. A small reminder of what they are all about to lose.

This will be your hell. He thinks quietly in his mind.

He watches carefully as his guests stand before him within the wide-open space. Large walls surround them with a long and shallow staircase in front, leading to naught but one man, Nix.

The dimly lit lights of flame cast nothing but a small glimmer into what lies beyond the tall walls that fence them in. Still unsure of where they are, all they can do is let their eyes focus and think carefully about how they wish to dispose of Nix—the Burden who has been the main cause for their grief.

"This place," Nix's voice breaks the silence, "is a special place of mine and you are its first guests. Oh, it hungers and it feels, but that is not all. What it really does is give me sanctuary. I feel the need to tell all of you this because, to kill you without letting you know why you must die, would be feeble and pointless. Every action has a purpose, not just a consequence."

Gunther says boldly, "And what exactly is your purpose for bringing us here?"

"To show you that your actions are pointless. All of you are fighting to survive, yet all there is in life is fake emotions, tedious requirements, laws that restrict absolute freedom. A universe where to break free means to be a criminal. All that is being done now is giving that ugly truth centre stage. All of this carnage and blood is nothing new."

Tail says, "Did you bring us here to preach? No matter how many words you choose to spit out, there is a clear distinction between us. What you are doing is wrong. We're here to stop it."

"No." Nix says, "You are here only because I allow it. Because I feel the need to speak, since none of the others will do so openly. Now, while it may be hard to listen, you're best to do so. A heart that knows the truth dies easy and at peace."

Gunther says, "I do not plan to die."

Nix says, "But you will. I am here. I desire to be. I performed my actions with clear intent. I know what I am doing, I am aware of the pain and suffering of the so-called 'innocent' lives that I have slain. Oh yes I remember that school, all of those pathetic miserable drones who follow so obediently. It was but one of my many enjoyments as of late and I can see that some of you lived through it. So I will speak to you and I will ask, why are you here? Is it because you have full conviction that life is pure and worth protecting or simply because you fear change, death? All you love is merely superficial. I am making a difference. I know the truth."

Spike runs his hands through his hair and groans. "Are you serious right now? We aren't here to listen to your mid-life crisis about the meaning to life. What's pure, what's bad, who gives a shit? We are born with faults and we get through it. We're human and we are full of mistakes but the only person who has control over fixing it is that person himself. Anyone who tries to control everyone else is wrong."

Nix sneers. "Yet you puppets obey the Federation. You follow rules laid out by the High Council. What you're really mad at right now is change. They have had control until now."

Kiyo yells, "What I'm mad at is you taking Leaf! Show me where she is or I will strip you of the ability to speak any further and then you won't have any way of finding the truth before your death."

Nix yells back, "Don't you see the calamity caused by human vices?"

"I AM NOT HUMAN!"

"Very well," Nix says, "I will show you where she is." With a wave of his hand, the sound of a rattling object is heard. Yet the darkness conceals its presence until, slowly, a golden cross bearing Leaf descends into view and hangs behind Nix.

Leaf's head hangs loosely, her body limp and feeble. She breathes slowly, her eyelids barely open. Her life is clearly draining away.

Kiyo, angered beyond belief and startled by her weak state, cries out, "What have you done to her!"

Nix says, "She is feeding this sanctuary of mine. She, a dream, is perfect. However it seems that she's reaching her limits. That's why you I wanted you, Kiyo. I recall her calling out for you, hoping you never end up here. But look at you now, here, and all of her begging futile."

"You've talked enough…your throat is mine."

Essa places her hand on his shoulder to calm him down. She asks Cassandra, "Can you explain any of this?"

"A user of souls can do many things, perhaps infinite but most are generally unfathomable due to the cost and penalty." Cassandra replies, "However, Nix is using other souls for that cost. Dreams in particular. He's stepping further and is bending reality in his favor. This place is his creation, and nothing can get in or get out. If the planet were to explode this place would live, if this place came to an end, the outside would not see a difference…or so I think."

Nix grins slightly and says, "Wise girl. I see you're the one from before. Getting quite good at this passion of ours, aren't you?"

"I'm not like you," she states. "Do not even approach that idea."

"Oh?" he eggs her on, "Different from me hmm. Not by much."

The words cause her to grow angry. Essa and the others, either unsure or unable to focus on it, watch as she steps forward next to Kiyo and whispers something into his ear.

Kiyo nods his head, cracks his knuckles and says aloud, "Spike, let's do something reckless."

Nix opens up both of his arms, his cloak parting and revealing the blood red attire beneath it. He says, "Come then, if you will not listen, then I will gladly slaughter the likes of all of you!" His eyes go wild with excitement, the red within them glowing as he says, "Come on, save this precious girl. Your simple minds are worthless!"

Eight phantasms appear around Nix.

Loudly, Cassandra asks, "Can you see them? If you can't, then do not step forward."

Gunther and Sapphire look at one another, showing signs of concern for neither of them can see what Cassandra is talking about. Tail however, smiles, knowing what he's about to get into, and steps out from between them and says, "There's phantasms around that man. Neither of you can help effectively as of now. But just give me some time and we can do our lovely routine, alright?"

Huffing, Gunther says, "Alright, make it quick and be safe."

Essa, who is also unable to see the phantasms, steps closer to Gunther. He nods his head and Sapphire steps around Essa, making sure to keep her safe from any sudden attacks.

"Stick with us, you'll be alright." Sapphire says.

Essa says to Gunther, "I'm sorry."

"For what?"

"For getting us into this... You're right, I don't have the strength."

He turns to her, places his hand against her forehead. He messes her long red hair up and says, "Listen to me. I don't regret a damn thing. Whatever I do in life is what I do. If it's a mistake then I learn from it. If I lose someone then I never forget them. I make sure that I live each day the best way I possibly can. And you Essa, you're more courageous than I am. You're the most damn courageous little girl I know. Watch this fight with eyes wide open. We're going to make it out of here, all of us."

"But…the others."

He leans in and places his forehead against hers, giving her nowhere to look but his eyes. She sees the sadness in them, deep down, yet surrounding it is hope and love.

He says to her, "Family never forgets. Family never gives in. We're the fire."

"The fire?"

"Yes, the everlasting one."

She sees a flash in her mind of her family. It causes her to blink and shiver. She feels her face flush and wonders if her memories are beginning to return to her. She looks at Gunther carefully, trying to figure out what it is that made her remember. But she's not given the proper time with danger so close.

Tail, Kiyo, Spike and Cassandra step forward. The four of them are able to see the phantasms surrounding Nix with varying degrees of clarity. Cassandra however takes the lead since she has the clearest view.

Spike says, "Before we go into the fray, anyone care to explain how they can see this? Besides Cassandra—you are self-explanatory."

Tail grunts, "Is she?"

She says for herself, "Now's not the time Spike." The four of them widen the space. "Let's put these eyes of ours to use."

Eight phantasms—some large in stature, others skinny and nimble—stand together, each of them wielding a long and wide weapon. As Kiyo and Spike run forward, so do three of the phantasms. The swords are swung and cut through the air, smashing through the ground. Kiyo and Spike avoid the attacks.

Another two phantasms step forward and Tail makes his move. He closes the distance between a phantasm and slams his hand into its chest. Shadows spread from his palm and wrap around the phantasm.

He steps backwards to avoid a punch and a swing of the blade. He runs off to slam his hand into another phantasm. As he does so,

Cassandra directs Spike and Kiyo around the attacks of the phantasms, circling them since she can see more clearly.

With ears perked up, Kiyo uses the sound from the blades to aid him in getting the upper hand. He dodges three sets of swords and slams his hand through one of the phantasms' midsections, ripping out a portion of their armor. He then spins around and hits one of their helmets with enough force to cause it to spin around 180-degrees.

He then leaps in the air, slamming his feet into one of their chests and uses it to propel himself past three that are in his way. He makes a run for the three phantasms that stand in front of Nix, all bearing a more ferocious presence.

Cassandra's eyes dart around as she watches and directs Spike around two phantasms whose eyes focus on him. She says, "Move to the left!" He does so quickly, and then slams his fist into the phantasm's head, smashing the helmet inwards.

Spike then grabs ahold of the phantasm and slams it to the ground. As he raises his fist, Cassandra calls out once more. He ducks just in time to avoid being sliced in half by the large blade from the other phantasm.

Tail appears behind it and slams his hand into it. Shadows wrap around its body. As the seconds pass, he successfully wraps shadows around the bodies of five phantasms. He turns to look at Gunther and winks with his only visible eye.

Sudden heat ignites from Gunther. Essa turns to look at him in alarm as she sees the steam rising from his shoulders. The look on his face showing that of sheer anger and pleasure as he pulls out his sword slightly and with it, flames erupt, spreading across the ground and splitting into five paths. Each flame lands upon a phantasm and set them ablaze.

Cassandra says, "That won't stop them. You need a blade like mine!"

He pulls out his sword completely and runs at the first phantasm. Cassandra sees the shine within the blade and says to herself, "Does he truly…"

His sword rises, and as the phantasm shakes off some of the fire and tries to raise its blade. Gunther slashes through it from top to bottom, splitting the thin and fairly short phantasm in half. It hits the ground with black blood oozing out and shatters.

Spike continues to bash away at the phantasm he threw into the ground. He turns to look at Cassandra and says, "Pass me your blade!" She throws it to him. He catches it and slams it into the phantasm's chest near the heart, finishing off yet another one.

The other three break free from Tail's shadows, yet the flames still reveal their footsteps, letting Gunther continue to participate in the fight.

Nix sees the fate of the two phantasms and doesn't even flinch. His eyes show no sense of concern. He looks down towards Kiyo, who reaches the three phantasms blocking his way. He says, "You are in a rush. I'd advise against that.

Kiyo is within killing distance of Nix, and snarls. The phantasm standing in the middle pulls out two swords and slashes in an x formation. The attack strikes Kiyo, cutting open his shirt and leaving a vicious wound. The other two phantasms pull out long spears. He looks at the three of them and clenches both of his fists.

The two spears shoot forward, slashing him on his ribcage. He steps backwards and raises his arms to protect himself from the two swords. As they swing down, he grabs ahold of the phantasm's wrists. The swords drop. He lets go and receives a cut across his face as one of the swords is caught and used against him.

The combination quickly overwhelms him. Kiyo continues to move backwards as the three phantasms use combinations against him, landing strikes against his body, wounds becoming deeper with time.

However, help arrives as Cassandra grabs her dagger from Spike and rushes forward. She protects Kiyo from one of the spears. It gives him an opening to hand a strike against the phantasm wielding a spear by using his fist.

He grabs the spear and pulls the phantasm in close so he can land a heavy blow on its face. He then pulls it down further and slams his knee repeatedly into the phantasm's head until finally bringing it into the ground and sending his foot down into its head. The damage, although severe, cannot kill it. And so, as Kiyo looks up, he has to jump backwards to avoid the dual sword wielder who presses forward.

The phantasm on the ground stands up and turns its attention to Cassandra. It swings its spear at the same time as the other. Cassandra jumps into the air and spins around horizontally to avoid the two attacks simultaneously. She moves between them.

She rolls across the ground and, as she stands up, one of the spears slams into her side, sending her into the wall. The phantasm then slams its hand into her face and pushes her head in further past the dark brick.

Blood begins to spill from her face as a gruesome wound appears on the back of her skull. She grabs ahold of the wrist and sends her dagger through it. She cuts it off. The phantasm stands back. Spike slams into the phantasm and lifts it into the air with sheer strength. He throws it down. As the other spear wielder attacks Spike, aiming for his neck, Cassandra throws her dagger into its chest.

The rash and risky attack pays off, and causes the phantasm to fall to its knees and shatter. Spike holds the second spear wielder down. Cassandra grabs ahold of her dagger and rushes over. With a great leap and a heave, she slams it down into its face, sending it into the abyss.

Spike asks her, witnessing the blood spilling down her neck, "Are you okay?"

She looks at him and stumbles slightly. "Not entirely." Her eyes roll to the back of her head and she falls forward. Spike catches her and looks at the wound in worry. He looks behind and sees that Gunther and Tail have disposed of the phantasms. He witnesses a subtle fist bump between them as they celebrate victory. The look on his face lets them know that Cassandra needs help so they rush over.

The remaining phantasm wages on against Kiyo as it slashes one of its swords across the wall. Kiyo uses this opportunity to use his claw to rip off the phantasm's arm. As the second sword comes in from the side, Kiyo spins and slams his elbow through the phantasm's chest. He then slams his leg down into its leg, crushing it. He grabs ahold of the second arm and rips it off. Then, with a shrieking roar, he smashes the phantasm into an almost unrecognizable pile of matter.

He walks away from the phantasm and heads towards Nix. The Burden simply claps—unsettling and out of place. Kiyo approaches him with Gunther and Tail. Spike puts Cassandra in Essa's hands and then joins them.

Nix stops clapping and steps forward. He says, "There was once ten kings, oh they all ruled, dividing the lands amongst themselves, enjoying the riches and the glory. But they did so by letting all of the people below them suffer, living in poverty, No safety. No way to look towards a brighter future. Those 'great' ten kings all ruled by only caring about themselves and their selfish desires, seeing the people below them as just dirt."

The others continue to approach him as he carries on, "So one day, a little boy mustered up the courage to fight back and it caused a stir. When riots ensued, the ten kings banded together and had their forces begin massacring their people. You see the kings were all friends. The people were simply pawns. But what they didn't know was that boy was a special boy, a boy with the power to change everything. That boy was the son of the eleventh king. This king did nothing to stop the massacre, hoping to finally be excepted by his peers. He was no different from the others and yet excluded from the table of ten, despite or maybe because of his dominant nature and strength. His real power however became one thing—giving the seed to the womb that brought about this boy."

Kiyo reaches the steps and begins to move up towards Nix, who continues his story, "That boy had a gift. He was able to see the other side—the souls—due to taking the life from his own mother upon birth. With this on his shoulders, and the misery around him, he himself took the lives of each of the kings who wanted their own people dead, saving his father for last. Do you know what that boy said to his father before taking his life? He told his father…" Nix's smile cracks and his face twitches, "That he had no right to be a king, that his armor was being wasted on such a disgrace. For someone like him, who was always an outcast, to throw away his own people for recognition from those who looked at him with no respect. He made the wrong choice, so the boy granted his father his greatest desire and sent him to join the other kings."

The distance now gone, Kiyo rushes ahead and raises his hand forward to grab ahold of Nix, screaming out, "Your throat is mine!"

The Burden says, "That boy is me." His red eyes light up tremendously as an eleventh phantasm appears, surrounding his body with a soul of its own.

CHAPTER THIRTY-FOUR
The Boy

The new form, the tragic bond between father and son, the ghostlike substance wrapped around Nix—it overwhelms Kiyo and grabs ahold of him, pulling him in to the suffocating pressure of death and the feeling of loss.

Unable to break free from the clutches of Nix, who uses the hand of his father, Kiyo is thrown into the air towards Leaf. As his body draws near, he reaches out for her and as his hand grows close to hers, his finger grazing her skin, he is stopped.

He looks at her and then at himself. He sees black rods that protrude out from the walls pierce his body. With multiple wounds, he can only cough up his liquid red regrets at his inability to do more in this situation, and thus, he spends his last moments looking at the most precious thing to him, unable to reach out further and close the distance.

"Let them go!" Essa cries out.

Nix sneers, and the ghost armor of his father—the eleventh king—moves closer to his body, causing them to appear as one. He says, "He may heal fast but this way he will keep bleeding and bleeding and bleeding some more." He walks down the steps towards the others and says, "I brought all of you here to expand my utopia. For as much as I want the rest of humanity to disappear, I'm going to spend eternity as I see fit. As the one true glorious king!"

Essa yells, "You are a selfish bastard! A hypocrite!"

He laughs and digs his nails into his skin, dragging them from the top of his face to the bottom. "Yes I know, but that's okay. I grew up in a worn out world where hardly anyone had enough strength to protect their own selves, let alone the ones they love. But I had the power! I had what it required to survive and so I did. And do you know what I learned? I learned that the weak are no better than the ones that let them rot. I learned that I hate everyone and everything, pure disgusting wretched weight…I learned, that all I need… is me!" He sniffs, "But what's the point of explaining when none of you are capable of listening? You will all die like the rest. I can assure you of that."

Gunther says, "And what? Turn us into your new set of phantasms? Don't think I don't know a thing or two. Your story was fairly obvious. You kill and then force them to be your slaves."

Nix shakes his head and says, "I will have no need when life as you know it comes to an end. What good will it do to have souls wandering around me? Souls I hate and loathe. I'll be a king that simply lives his own ideals. I won't have to listen to the pleading requests of the weak or look at the corrupted men and women I defeated."

Tail asks, "What makes us corrupt?"

"Your very nature."

Essa says, "There are horrible leaders and there are people who have no idea what they are doing but try with good faith. But then there's you—you're the worst. To hate everyone just because times were tough, I can't condone that. You just let them die. You really are a burden."

Those words change the atmosphere in such a way that a calm ripple of water suddenly becomes a whirlpool. Nix barks back, his eyes gleaming red, "Leave them to die? I tried to lead those people to peace and sanctuary! Yet those blithering fools only fought amongst themselves once they realized they didn't have a soldier or king to worry about. Humans are selfish, and when times are rough, they put a smile on and ask for help. I may be a part of the Burdens, but girl, the real burden is people like you. I have every right to be doing this."

Gunther pulls out his sword and says, "Enough. You've said your piece. I'm tired of listening to you." Nix crosses his arms, and his father—the ghost of pale luminosity—raises its large blade to the left.

Gunther glances over at Tail, who appears to be in a deep train of thought. Yet Spike, who in contrast is not thinking at all, decides to make his move with a dash and a mighty punch in its wake.

It slams into Nix's head, yet the father stops the impact from reaching his face. Spike then slams his knee into his stomach but the same thing occurs. He jumps back, seeing that the armor of the ghost is stronger than the phantasms before.

He sees the sword swinging towards him and moves out of the way, but it changes directions and slashes through his leg, then his arm, his chest—until finally, Nix moves in close and unleashes a barrage of quick punches.

The devastation causes Spike to feel faint—the hits as heavy as when he fought against Slate. He tries to focus but he loses sight of the ghost. He mutters, "Bastard." as blood leaves his lips. He reaches out and smears his blood on Nix's father. A fist emerges from the pale light emanating around Nix's stomach, and slams into Spike.

Trying his best to hold on—mad at how quickly he is losing, wondering how much damage he truly took from the previous battles—Spike starts to unload his own assortment of punches. Nix, enjoying the engagement, returns the favor.

The Burden matches the wild look in Spike's eyes and it's clear that, despite all of Spike's hard hits, the ghost absorbs them. Soon after, the sword rises once more. It comes down hard and, with a cry to his companions, the blood soaks through his clothes as they fall away from his skin. His skin leaves his bones. He feels his body go limp, weak like a newborn, defenseless against harm.

He falls backwards and lands hard on the ground but only his confidence feels the hit as it exits along with his blood. A pool forms, and as his eyes begin to dim, tired from the journey and trials, he sees Cassandra struggling to hold on as she hangs in Essa's arms.

A voice speaks to him, *"Grow stronger Spike. Evolve. Make death wait."* His eyelids close and he enters a slumber.

Watching in horror, Essa stares at her fallen companions, at the amount of blood, how it all feels surreal. She sees the vicious wound running along Spike's body, almost separating a portion of his arm from the rest of him. She sees the gash at the back of Cassandra's head. She sees the approach of Tail and Gunther, the expression on their faces revealing nothing but a need to act.

Sapphire says to Essa, "It will be alright. Those two…there's no stopping them now."

Tail grabs ahold of the bandage on his arm and removes it completely. He reveals his completely black arm, as if the skin has rotted and died from lack of life. Gunther pulls out his gun and holds his sword in the other, saying to Tail, "I want to burn this man into the ground."

Tail says, "Don't try to stop me Gunther, his shadow is mine."

"I wouldn't dream of it."

Standing before Nix, the two of them look at him closely and Tail asks one question—the only question on their minds—one that is crucial, one that will decide how much rage they will unleash. Tail asks, "As a boy, you had a desire for change and the courage to fight for it, to fight for your people. Now you want to destroy everyone. Why?"

He gives them their reply and says, "Simple. Even with the change, humans are just humans, and the same issues continue. Idiots who cannot change, there is no purpose to them. They're worthless. They seek after death, they just don't know it."

Pointing his gun forward, Gunther declares, "People…are not… WORTHLESS!" and fires. The bullet makes impact and chips away at the ghost. Nix sees this and takes action. Tail sends his black arm forward. It goes through the ghost and into Nix's chest.

The Burden looks down and sees the darkness digging into his skin. He looks at Tail in shock and feels the first signs of pain riddling through his body. Tail removes his hand.

Flames surround Gunther's sword and press against the ghost that shields Nix. Tail and Gunther quickly run around him, attacking him with shadows and fire, sword and gun, fist and spirit.

The eleventh king begins to show signs of weakness, as it grows weary. Tail sees this. He begins to wrap his shadows around the king. Nix curses and removes his left arm from the protection of his father, grabbing ahold of Tails arm.

The shadows begin to reveal the ghost, the shell of Nix's father, ever more clearly. As well, Nix's view is blocked. Gunther focuses on his flames and stabs the king with a heavy thrust. It pierces through the king and strikes Nix's lower abdomen.

Gunther continues to slash away at the phantasm protecting Nix. The Burden yells in anger. He heals the wound using the black liquid from the small cylinder while his father's sword appears and swings around him, keeping the others away.

Still holding onto Tail, who's been desperately dodging the swing of the sword, Nix looks at him and smiles. He pulls him forward and slams his fist into Tail's face. Gunther doesn't let any opportunity go to waste and attacks the phantasm's sword, slashing through it.

Gunther thrusts his sword forward once more but Nix, along with the aid of his father's hands, catches it. The smile on Nix's face is soon forgotten when flames shoot out from Gunther's sword and send sparks into his eyes. The sword then slashes through his hand. He screams in anger.

Through wrath alone, the phantasm expands dramatically and pushes Gunther and Tail away, knocking them across the floor.

Nix places his hands to his eyes and says, "You fucking pests will regret this." He removes his hands from his face and Gunther smiles at the beautiful art his sparks created on the Burden's face.

Gunther says, "Why don't you just heal and get it over with?"

Nix snarls and reaches for the cylinder.

Gunther yells out, "Now! Tail, Sapphire!" Nix looks up, startled, and sees the three of them rushing at him.

Tail goes down the right side while Gunther runs down the left. Nix slams his hands together and chains rip out from the floor. He says loudly, "I will chain you down and make you my slaves if that's what you want!"

The chains whip around, reaching for them. Gunther cuts through the ones that try to grab ahold of him. He slides his blade across the ground and a path of flames follows him. He then slams his sword into the ground and a wall of fire rises from it, casting its dominance.

Nix looks over at Gunther and raises his hand towards him. The phantasm slams its fist into the wall of fire and bursts through it. The flames don't disperse, and Nix pulls his father's hand back. He turns around and sees Tail. Shadows rise and form another wall that contrasts the flames.

Looking at both the flame and shadow, Nix begins to worry. The two opposing walls quickly merge together and surround him. Unable to do anything, both he and his father's phantasm are engulfed by it and held in a prison. As the heat rises and he feels his father's phantasm reach the end of its use, he hears Gunther yell, "Sapphire, I permit you to use 100 per cent of your power."

She smiles. Her eyes light up. She raises her arm forward and it turns into a cannon. She places her other hand on her elbow to give support. The prison of fire and shadow disperses slightly to give her an opening. Nix sees her and stands there hopelessly. He witnesses the end of his dream.

Sapphire says, "L-Cannon, initiate protocol—ANNIHILATE." A beam of pure red shoots out from her weapon.

Nix sees it strike his father. He sees the phantasm surrounding his body—the embodiment of his past—begin to crack. It breaks and leaves him feeling naked.

A piece of flame licks his skin and engulfs his body. He screams as the fire and shadow tear away at him. Sapphire gasps for air and Essa looks at her with worry. She says to Essa, "Do not fear. It's just taxing to use so much."

Essa looks over and watches Nix's barely visible shadow within the fire that consumes him. She sees his piercing red eyes. Her heartbeat rises when she sees the shadow of something small reach his lips. He drinks it.

Dozens of chains burst from the ground, pulling forth mummified phantasms writhing in pain.

Gunther reacts by sending his fire at the threat. He quickly disperses them which gives Nix the opportunity to escape from the prison. He looks and sees the Burden staring at him with no visible wounds.

The Burden says, "Tell me who you are." His eyes move to the others and he says, "The three of you. I want to know. I want to add you to my collection."

Gunther sweats a little and says, "Well so much for being done with souls."

"Yes, you've changed my mind. Now tell me!"

Tail says, "In my body there is a madness identical to what you've unleashed onto this world."

Sapphire says, "Parts of me are human. The rest simply exists to destroy."

Gunther says, "And I'm just fucking fabulous."

Nix looks utterly bewildered.

Essa feels her legs begin to shake.

Whatever was in the cylinder is now all gone but because of it, despite all of the fighting, Nix looks at them without a single wound. He asks Tail, "How did you infuse yourself with Nightmares?"

"You can ask Arc."

"Arc?! That useless bastard put a Nightmare into you? HOW IS THAT POSSIBLE?"

Essa looks at Tail and then at Gunther. If Tail has a Nightmare inside of him, then that means they knew about the dream world in some shape or form. Gunther's eyes look back at her and he knows she's thought of something.

Nix begins to cough up blood. He looks down and raises his hand. He sees blood drip from his mouth. Then, the sound of a gunshot goes off. He stumbles slightly and looks at Gunther. He sees the smoke rising from the freshly used chamber. Another shot goes off, and then another until five land through his body. He falls to his knees. Flames appear, licking away at his skin, burning away his clothes.

The walls surrounding them begin to crumble as Nix's realm falls to pieces. The ceiling begins to fall. Leaf and Kiyo fall from it and land on the ground. The golden cross breaks along with the black rods.

On the outside of the dome, Keeper watches as it falls apart, pieces landing on buildings and destroying them with their weight. The black substance, unstable, explodes and acts as acid, melting everything it touches.

Yet this corrosive ability quickly subsides as everyone comes falling out of it. Hovering a few feet in the sky, they all land, spread out across the wide-open space of debris and sharp edges.

In the centre of it all, Nix clutches the ground. Keeper sees the state that he is in and stands up straight, watching carefully the fate of the man who gave him a second chance.

He takes a step forward, but Nix yells out, "Do not interfere!" the blood spilling from his mouth, "Don't you dare!" Keeper stops, respecting the Burden's wish, and watches closely as the battle seems to be reaching its finale.

The fire no longer burns away at his body. Nix manages to stand up. He turns and looks around at the others. He sees that the same people are still in the game while the others remain unconscious.

Nix wraps his fingers around one another and says with as much strength as he can, "Feast…" his eyes look up and sure enough, a wide variety of the Nightmares in the sky come rushing down.

Gunther curses, runs forward and says, "Protect them Tail!"

Tail raises his hands upwards and, with all of his strength, he brings all of the shadows in the surrounding area together. They rise and protect Sapphire and the others as nearby Nightmares descend towards them. The shadows rip through the vicious creatures.

Nix doesn't move from where he stands, unable to from lack of strength. Each of the bullet holes in his body draining him of life, his burnt limbs giving no aid. Nix watches as Gunther runs at him, wielding a sword of flame. As the distance closes, Nix feels the approaching death and a memory flashes through his mind.

***

Sitting in a plaza surrounded by people laughing and smiling. The poverty is clear yet the happiness is surpassing it. He looks at all of the people living in the desert, their clothes battered and torn. He watches as they help one another, sharing, caring. He sees the bond between all of them. He sees his younger self, looking at all of them with a warm heart.

The memory changes and he sees himself standing in front of his father, cold eyes bearing down on him. He stares at the man, his long white beard, and the smug look across his face. He sees his father turn around and walk away from him, leaving him alone in the richly furnished room.

One last memory flashes past his eyes, this time the same plaza from before, yet all of the smiling and happy faces replaced with white pale motionless figures. Blood surrounding him, he looks and cries, as everyone is gone. He sees his father standing amongst the bodies. He sees himself run forward, grab a sword sticking out from one of the bodies and rush at his father, raising his sword upwards to attack the man that killed his innocence and love.

***

Nix sees Gunther's sword rise upwards. He sees it come down and slash into his body. He says quietly, "I couldn't change a damn thing."

The blade passes through him.

Gunther pulls backwards and pierces it through Nix's heart. His head falls onto Gunther's shoulder, his body limp. Gunther pushes him off and the Burden falls. His eyes fading, one last thing crosses them, one last image.

As Gunther turns around to face Keeper, Nix sees in the darkness, a man cloaked in black with red eyes reaching out towards him—the man that showed him the way.

His younger self walks towards this man and he hears the words, "What is your wish? What do you desire?"

To which his innocent voice replies, "To be free of those around me."

CHAPTER THIRTY-FIVE
Reflect Maximum

Emotionless. Cold. A body that no longer moves, thinks or speaks. Essa looks at what has become of the man who pushed her towards her spiraling fate. She looks at the blank expression on his face and the faint indication that his eyes found something before his end. Essa sees the death of a Burden and the menace of another. She finds herself in disbelief at what occurs next. What feels instantaneous causes her to feel lost, like some ghost living in an odd shell.

As she tries to digest the overflow of events, yet another man stands before them. A face she has not seen before—the man known as Edom.

He appears from a portal that he creates and, giving no time for introductions or even a quick smile, he grabs ahold of Gunther. With a slight struggle he pulls him into the darkness. Essa sees Keeper enter another portal and, just like that, he's gone. Their fire taken away, leaving all of them to stare in shock.

It comes fast—the shaking, then the pressure on her chest causing her to try and remember what breathing feels like. She looks over, trying to find an answer in the others but their expressions show anything but composure. Even Tail, who is normally the definition of anti-emotion, shows a tinge of concern on his brow. Sapphire too, normally a rock, has a faint look of shock in her eyes. Her nose wrinkles up with concern.

Everything looks, for that brief moment, as a painting perfectly created by an artist trying to muster up a grand reaction and this artist would receive it. Their inner voices make them want to claw their way out of the rigid frame they find themselves within.

What breaks Essa from this painting is something new. A vision. Within this vision, she sees Gunther. His face causes her to let the vision take her in—she doesn't protest. She sees him standing in a room fairly worn out, with marble flooring and a large red carpet in the centre of it all. Chandeliers hang from the ceiling. The wind moves through the room as it pleases.

The vision soon changes and she sees him covered in blood, his brow concentrated as he engages in combat against Keeper. It changes once more and she sees him coughing up blood and spinning around. Then, finally, with one last vision, she sees him falling through the air towards the ground.

With a shiver she breaks from her vision, and as soon as she gasps for air, she's pulled right back in—into this cycle of art. This time she sees Dusk. He lays on the ground in despair.

Tears build on Essa's eyelids.

Sapphire and Tail both notice this, and call out to her but she does not hear them.

The vision continues and she sees Hex, his wings battered and torn as he struggles to remain on his feet, facing a Burden. She sees him pleading.

A voice begins to break into her mind, "Essa!" Sapphire's call reaches her. She blinks and feels herself being shaken. Sapphire asks, "Are you okay? What just happened?"

She shakes her head, unsure as what to say, until Gunther's voice rattles in her brain. *"You're...the most damn courageous little girl I know."*

She touches her face and then looks down at her pouch. She places her hand to her lips and wonders if the book is the cause of her vision. If what she just saw is what will happen. She wonders if she can stop it.

Tail continues to hold up the shield of shadows protecting them from the thirsty Nightmares that cry out for their flesh.

Essa says, "I-I think I just saw Gunther...Dusk and Hex...die."

Sapphire squints and says, "What?"

"I don't know. Just now. I saw it as clear as day."

"How is that possible?"

Essa shakes her head and looks into Sapphire's eyes to erase any feeling of unease. The strong woman before Essa, with her blue hair and eyes, places her hand to Essa's forehead and says, "How Essa? Please explain."

So Essa does just that. And she goes on saying how she believes it's the book but has no factual evidence, because it's impossible. Sapphire and Tail choose to believe her. They are left with the question— what do they do about it and how?

They do their best to figure out a solution in finding the others and keeping them from the fate Essa has foreseen. However, time would not grant them such an opportunity.

***

Gunther stands facing Keeper.

Edom stands at Keeper's side, slightly between them.

The room, large in stature, seems befitting for a showdown between these two who must fight. With nothing in the way, and a lot of room for their footing, Gunther quickly adjusts and the initial shock of being taken away wears off.

Scarlet shadows run along the walls of the room cast off from the chandelier above. The furniture that is present is made with mahogany wood and has gold cushioning. A large red carpet rests across the centre of the marble floor. Each wall has five large sets of windows, none of which are open.

Edom says in disapproval, "Not all that much fear in you is there?"

Keeper lets out a booming laugh and says, "That is precisely what I need, a fearless man to try and face me. Not like those ants before."

A vein emerges on Gunther's brow. "Ants? Did you just refer to my family as ants?"

Edom muses, "Oh my…this one has a short temper. How lovely."

Keeper's eyes gleam with joy as he says, "Yes, yes I did. And what are you going to do about it?"

Gunther places a hand to his sword, grabbing the hilt and leaving his other hand hovering over his gun. "That's fairly obvious, considering the two of you brought me here."

Edom smiles and says, "We did, we did, and do you want to know why?"

"Not particularly. I've heard enough blathering for one day."

"Ah," Keeper says, "Nix does…rather… did like to talk."

Gunther grins with fury, "Yes. Before I cut through him."

Keeper says in reply, "What I did to your family was much worse."

Gunther's expression darkens. Edom says, "And there you have it." He points at Gunther and continues, "Why we—rather, I—brought you here. This hunk of metal can't create lovely portals. He merely swings that wretched spear around."

Keeper replies, "Different tastes, different skills."

"Yes, no matter." Edom continues, "I brought you here since what I saw in the last seconds outside that…dome he made, was you slicing through him. A Burden falling at the hands of…you? So I had this crazy idea. Before letting all of your friends regroup and become hopeful, thus completely undoing the hard efforts of Nix and the Burdens as a collective, why not just take you from them? Pit you against a man that has taken from you."

Edom winks at Keeper and then returns his attention to Gunther, "Let's see how it all plays out. Because while you fight here, as I'm sure you will, mister strong man," his voice egging him on like a child, "I'll be giving all of your friends a nice visit—a fun one too. I just cannot wait," he claps his hands together and jumps up with joy, "to meet them."

Pulling his sword out with care and a natural ease, Gunther rests the blade on his shoulder and smirks. "You are in for a surprise if you think it's going to go easy for you."

Edom's eyes twinkle as he says, "We'll see." He forms a portal behind him and turns one last time to look at Gunther. "It was a pleasure meeting you…for the first and last time."

He enters the portal and it closes behind him, leaving Keeper and Gunther alone in the vast room. They look at one another for a while, until eventually both show that they've seen all they need to see, simply wanting one thing—to kill.

They walk forward, neither of them showing signs of concern or worry. On one face, all that can be seen are a set of red piercing eyes, wielding a weapon responsible for the death of pure hearts. The other set of eyes, accompanied by an actual visible face, show sheer concentration and the desire for revenge. But more importantly, to do so with an utter desire to crush.

If one were to walk in on these two, they would be unable to decipher good from evil. Perhaps that's how it should be. Neither gives time to think about morality or justice. They simply wish to slice flesh.

Yet there is no flesh for Gunther to cut, only metal—sheer metal with few marks on it. The marks that are visible only make him miss his comrades that, without even a proper goodbye, have been taken from him. Gunther wants to watch Keeper burn. Watch him melt.

Was it his fault? He doesn't know, and he doesn't want to think about it. How or why they went out, he doesn't care. He just knows that whatever the circumstances, be it his fault or poor luck, he will use his sword the best way he knows how, and perhaps send a few bullets into Keeper's skull as well.

He feels his body raise the blade as it has done hundreds of times before. Flawlessly, like waking up each morning, the motions come natural. The anger inside his stomach wrenches away at him. If only a pile of vomit were enough to kill a man. He would vomit in rage into that man's egotistic armor.

Gunther does not desire to fall, not now, not with so many things to do. So they exchange blows, landing a strike on one another. He moves in past the swing of the spear and closes the distance. Slicing upward, he watches as his sword sends a variety of sparks off of Keeper's chest. Not getting the result he wants, he spins around, continuing to slice away at the armor, yet mere scratches appear, and annoyance sets in.

A fist strikes him across his face and he loses his footing. Falling to his knee, the spear slashes past his ribcage. He grabs ahold of it and stands back up, piercing his sword forward and successfully digging it into Keeper's armor. Pushing off from one another, Gunther places a hand to his side and feels the warm red gushing liquid of life. So he does what anyone in his position would do, he sets it aflame.

Keeper watches as Gunther shows his true colour—red, lustful and devilish, full of scorn and power. A lick of the flame burns through Gunther's shirt and cauterizes the wound, stopping the flow of life.

The silence between them continues as they move in closer. A small flame spreads across Gunther's blade as he rubs his hand across it. They continue to take a step, over and over, until they both swing their weapons and clash, putting all of their weight into it.

The force of impact causes Gunther's arms to shake and fall away as he receives a disconcerting slice to his lower abdomen once more from Keeper's agile weapon. Gunther quickly burns his skin without thought, however the pain lingers and he wonders how bad it is.

His feet continue to move sideways as he lets Keeper hold the centre of the room. Eyes focusing, despite the wounds, Gunther feels the surge of confidence move throughout him. His body is his vessel. The flames within him are his curse, his gift. Seeing the difference in strength between them physically, he decides to mix things up, turning the room into a familiar and comfortable environment.

Slashing his sword across the red carpet, it ignites and the flames spread quickly, rushing across the room with the force of a tsnumani. Keeper stands in fire moments later, ill amused.

The flames lick away at his armor, scorching his feet and, slowly but surely, turning it black. Seeing this, he moves forward through the flames towards Gunther, slashing away at the fire with his spear, moving the wind with his great strength, spreading the fire to give him the leeway he needs.

He runs, stabbing his spear forward repeatedly. Gunther moves his body around, avoiding the attacks. He dodges the sharp triangular piece of death aiming for his heart.

Using his sword, he stops the blade on his right side and pushes forward. Keeper, unsure as to what Gunther plans to do with but a hand, soon finds out the stupidity in not moving backwards.

With one touch, Gunther's hand melts away a piece of Keeper's chest plate, revealing the emptiness within it. No body, no ounce of flesh to be seen. No bones, no light, just black and hollow.

Gunther stares in disbelief and then anger. He says, "So that's it. That's why they died. You're a man with no body, a coward in a set of armor."

"I am the farthest thing from a coward. Do you know the toll of this fate? It is that of never ending turmoil while my soul slowly decomposes. How I wish I still had a human body which you could burn. That, to me, would be a proper fight. But my body, my life, was stolen from me in an unjust way, as many things are in this world. I will have my glory before my soul fades completely. If my wish is to be granted, then I will die a warrior's death and not like a dog. I am no coward, I am Keeper, I am just." Keeper replies, as he steps outside the boundary of the flames.

"Shut the fuck up. You want a warrior's death? You're fighting without your life on the line. You're taking away the lives of others while you endlessly seek something that will never be. When I kill you, and I will, you will die as the dog that you really are."

The flames from the carpet soon spread to the drapes hanging low to the ground against the windows. They spread up and light the room, causing shadows to scamper towards the depths of any safe corner, bringing forth heat that causes even Keeper to worry.

His response to Gunther is illuminating yet condescending. "The soul is an intangible thing, or so that's what everyone believes. But your body is restricted no matter how much your muscles grow. I do not need to feed, to sleep, to feel warmth. This body of steel is perfection, and while it may seem unfair, this was given at a cost—one I was willing to pay. Your...dogs could not finish me. Do not show anger over the inevitable. If you want to avenge your companions then don't be like them, be a warrior."

Veins reveal themselves on Gunther's forehead. The fire that was subtly showing on his sword now burns brighter, as if gasoline was just set upon it. The same wings of flame that appeared against Vince appear once more. Standing like a raging bird of death, Gunther says, "I'll make sure you pay..." his voice low, rising further, "I'll make sure you regret and think and ponder and regret more and more until you fall to your knees from the unbearable weight of it all. And you will... you will keep regretting. And it will rattle within that empty armor of yours. Filling it up, further and further. Regret, just regret. Nothing else. I will make you regret..." his voice now loud enough for birds outside to hear, "...I will make you regret coming across me and my family!"

He kicks off from the ground and Keeper is unable to defend himself in time. Gunther's sword slashes down and rips through Keeper's armor. He soars through the room, his wings flapping and pushing him through the fire as it latches on, giving him more fuel, more rage.

He attacks once more.

Keeper tries move out of the way yet still receives a blow. This time, Gunther's sword removes two of Keepers fingers on his free hand. They fall like worthless twigs, serving no purpose. Keeper pulls his spear close and watches Gunther rush around and move in once more.

Keeper says, "Honestly, you're just an ant. Just a red ant." A glow emerges from within Keeper, showing that perhaps there is sign of life within his empty shell. Substance. Something that Gunther can cut, tear apart and wound.

The substance—his soul—latches onto the openings and tears in Keeper's armor, and with its faint pink and yellow glow, it heals the openings, repairing the shell.

Gunther can't help but smile wickedly. He lunges forward, his wings of fire rising upwards as he closes in for the kill. He wants to cut, to slice and feel the satisfaction run through his body.

Yet Keeper proves to be more than a pile of armor. He makes Gunther's rash decision to close in result in a regret that quickly spirals out of control.

With a new form of approach, Keeper blocks Gunther's attack by raising his spear into the air, and with both hands on it, he twists it around, slamming it behind Gunther's head. As Gunther turns to try and retaliate, Keeper sends his fist across Gunther's face.

Pushing forward now, giving Gunther little room to maneuver, Keeper becomes the hunter and Gunther the prey. The spear stabs forward and enters Gunther's body, tearing through the nimble flesh and chipping away at the bone deep within.

The spear pulls out and Gunther spins around, trying to stop the loud voice ringing inside his head, warning him of death. He slashes away, cutting at Keeper's armor, but the spear moves through his body once more. Easier now. Like a knife slipping into butter.

Stepping away, the spear pulls out and moves in once more. Gunther cannot help but cry out in pain. His voice leaves him and the spear pulls out and plunges into him once more. His body is now numb. A mess full of large gaping wounds as his sword barely hangs in his hand.

Keeper slams his foot into Gunther's stomach.

His body flings through the air.

He lands, somehow still standing, and pulls out his gun, yelling out a cry of desperation and sheer human emotion—of pain mixed with tears.

Gunther fires, shooting every single bullet in the clip until Keeper's spear rips through the gun, tearing through Gunther's hand and hitting the wall.

Wondering how something has gone so horribly wrong, struggling to even focus on his wounds, Gunther falls backwards and finds he is leaning against the wall. With Keeper moving towards him, he clutches his wounded hand, his sword falling to his side.

His body slides against the wall and he feels the flow of blood— the waterfall of life—leave his body. With a brief moment of focus, he uses his wings of fire to scorch his body, the skin on his stomach now unrecognizable, red and full of blistering agony, yet without the gush of loss.

Struggling, consciousness daring to leave him and fly off into the sunset, memories pouring in, unwelcomed and crushing, an indication that perhaps death truly does bring forth flashes of the past. His flames disappear.

***

"Hey, come on now. Wake up, Gunther. I said wake up!" He opens his eyes and sees, standing in the sunlight, a girl with dazzling blue eyes, short silver hair and a smile that makes his heart warm up more than any flame ever could.

He sees her reach out towards him. He takes hold of her hand, seeing that his own looks so much smaller than what he remembers. She pulls him up and the light becomes brighter. All he can make out is her. Only her. Only Cecilia.

"But…" he says before she places her finger against his lip and smiles.

"It's okay" she says, "You're still alive. You can still fight."

A deafening voice rings loudly, "You will join her, or you can control the gift I've given to you." The familiar and disgusting voice, the one that made everything so complicated.

Gunther looks around and yells, "Arc! You bastard! I will burn you! I will crush and stomp you into pieces!" He screams and doesn't stop until Cecelia hugs him.

He stands there, letting the warmth remind him of everything. He knows there's too much to lose, too much to do, and too much to protect. He can't get hung up on the past.

She backs away and smiles again, "See." She says, "That's the Gunther I know. Strong, composed—the one I could always rely on."

"Cecilia…I…"

"Shh." She says, "I know, and it's okay. I'm proud of you. But even I know you more than you know yourself. We all do. So don't be selfish."

"What...But..."

"Gunther, use that fire. Use it."

"Cecilia..."

"Use it." Her face smiles once more, and her image begins to change, showing another face—Essa's.

He stares in shock and then in sadness, looking at her smiling face. He rubs his eyes, and then images begin to flash through his mind, removing the scene before him and plunging him further into what he can only think of as the end.

He sees Dexter standing together with Abigail and Baylee, conversing amongst themselves. They turn to him and smile.

Dexter says "Hey Pal, why the long face?"

Abigail muses, "It's not cute, not at all."

Baylee nods her head and says, "I have to agree, don't be such a puss."

They wink and smile, wave and gesture their love before the image changes and this time, another voice, the voice he despises, speaks once more.

"Do it. Use the fire or bleed out like the rest."

"Shut up!" he screams at the top of his lungs. "Shut the fuck up!!!!!!"

He cries out in pain, his young self, falling to the floor. He says, "Cecilia... someone... please!"

A shadow spreads across him and he looks up, standing in the brilliant light, the warm and now yellow glow. A boy of his stature walks towards him. That boy is Tail.

With black messy hair and a grim face, he says with the same usual Tail-like presence, "Smarten up man, this isn't you. You are Gunther. You are my friend, and you know how much it takes for me to say shit like this."

Gunther wipes his eyes as he listens.

Tail says, "Whatever happens, you know me, and you know what I'll do." Tail shows a smile and although appearing unnatural for him, it puts hope into Gunther's heart. The boy begins to disappear, and says as he fades, "I'll make sure your flame carries on in the shadows."

Gunther closes his eyes, and the tears spill out, only to land on a hand. The hand rises and presses against his chin and lifts it up. He looks at Sapphire, not young but her normal current self. Her blue eyes look into his as she says, "We're family, we never break. We're far too stubborn. Come on, don't cry."

His eyes light up.

She says, "Everything. I cherish it all. We all do. You know this. After all, this representation of me sounds just like me, doesn't it? So get up, get up once more and be the fire that burns hope into the darkness. We will miss you. We will. And we love you. But please, don't go out like this."

"That's right." One last voice greets him, "Grow some balls."

Sapphire grins and fades away, revealing Fleur standing behind her. Yet Fleur appears different. She isn't in her boyish body, but has messy pink hair flowing long and beautifully rather than short and wild.

She turns and looks at him, giving a huff and then sliding in a compliment, "Look at you—still a hunk."

He looks down and sees that he's no longer in his young body, but his current one, wounds and all.

She says, "You look like quite the mess, hmm. And here I was thinking we'd get to have some fun again—when I get my body back that is—I know you aren't into the whole guy on guy thing." She winks and walks forward. "Course, Paige loves you, so there's that." She pulls on his hair and bites her lip, "But…ha, ya I'll say it," she leans in and butts her head against his, "I'll always love the smart ass kid I had to save."

"I saved myself." He says quietly, regaining his composure.

"Is that so?" she laughs and then suddenly turns sad, "what am I going to do without you?" she asks, playing with his hair. "What am I going to do now that you are gone?"

"I'm not gone."

She smiles slightly, but it doesn't hide the sadness and truth. "Yes, sure, I know you're still alive and kicking."

Her hand slides across his body, touching his wounds. She looks up and into his eyes and says, "You've had it rough. A fate of fire, living on the edge, searching for the truth, you also had something so precious you were able to call it your family. I wasn't a part of that—couldn't be." She places her hand against his face and rubs it gently. "I don't settle down, but…with you…" She leans in and places her lips against his. Pulling back, she says softly, "…I got a glimpse of what a home is. And for that, I'll make sure to…you know."

He nods his head and says "Go on."

She grins, "I'll make sure your heart and soul remain safe. The mere image of…ya, maybe not mere image…you don't have the same looks." She laughs and smiles again, her pink eyes sparkling, "Just wait for me alright? Now wake the hell up. I'm tired of acting cute." She raises her hand and with a slap across his face, his body jolts.

***

He sees Keeper walking towards him. The pain excruciating, Gunther slides his hand over towards his sword and grabs it. He watches as Keeper takes another three steps forward. He slowly gets up, watching carefully to see if Keeper will rush in and end it quickly. But like any true predator, Keeper moves in slowly, enjoying what he believes to be the end to this hunt.

So Gunther raises his sword once more, needing the use of both his hands. He heaves, clearly showing that merely standing is a chore.

Opening his mouth, the only poetic thing he knows leaves his lips, slowly, elegantly, full of purpose and beautiful truth. "I walked out of this skin, revealing my bones. Headed right into the fire, to stop the flames, to atone. Woke up thinking it was nothing but a dream, but the fire that was extinguished was now lit within me." He pauses, breathes and then continues, "For I had become but the bones which fire cannot harm. Within the interchangeable skin of which we all are."

As the sentence ends, he hears the voice of everyone he cares about finish it with him, *"Of which we all are."*

Keepers voice clanks within his steel frame as he says, "Cute."

He grabs his spear from the wall. He raises it and, as he steadies himself to stab forward, Gunther unleashes everything.

He soars forward with no wings—just his body—and his bones feel it, moving throughout his skeleton, giving it purpose, telling the core that they are allowed to move and feel, because where they are going, they need not fear being cold.

His body twists and he avoids the lunge of the spear. He moves in closer, closer, closer. Trying to force Gunther to stop, Keeper's leg becomes the perfect propulsion that Gunther needs. He steps on it and heaves himself into the air. Grabbing ahold of the chandelier, he hangs over Keeper and, in an instant, falls downwards towards him, his sword at the ready.

He lands on Keeper's shoulders and raises his sword, slamming it down into Keeper's head and plunging it into the emptiness.

The sword rattles through the helmet and Keeper flails around, yelling out, "Pointless! This is your final attempt—to disrupt my balance?"

"No." Gunther says while grinding his teeth together, so hard that blood fills between the cracks, "This is why I did it." He twists the sword and a wave of fire ignites within Keeper's body. So much fire—all of it for his family.

Leaping off and falling down, Gunther crawls away as his sword, still stuck inside of Keeper's head, piercing into the centre of his body, melting it and tearing from within, is left behind.

Expecting to be stomped on, kicked or strangled, Gunther turns around, still crawling away from Keeper, staring to see if he will avoid death and witness Keepers' demise.

The Burden does not act as expected. Instead of attacking, he remains still. He admits his defeat.

Keeper asks, his voice echoing in its usual way, "What is your name—your true name?"

Gunther blinks at the question and says eerily, "…You first."

Keeper crosses his arms, "I am Maximilian Keeper." His voice now vibrating even more within his steel body.

Gunther's head nods and he continues to crawl across the ground, his wounds opening up. "Then I'll have you know. My name, my true name," the fire in the room is now engulfing everything, causing the structure inside to start collapsing, "is Gunther. Gunther Starlight."

The words leave his lips with a smile—a smile that remains on his face until the end.

Keeper, hearing the name, says in turn, "Farewell Gunther Starlight." His body, rather than melting, lights up and implodes until reaching maximum density at which point it explodes, sending pieces everywhere.

The blast sends Gunther sliding across the floor, outside of the room through a set of patio doors and across the balcony where he rests against the cold black steel bars. With his eyes darting around, he can see that where he is, is a hundred floors above ground—in the last standing tower in the city.

His head turns and the smile does not remove itself, even when shrapnel plunges itself into his throat and body. He blinks. His head falls downwards; he has no more strength to keep it up straight. The ground at the edge of the balcony begins to crack and break, letting his body slide towards the edge. He sees the colour of red, his eyes gleam with it. The flames approach closely. In their own way they say farewell, and then give him a soft push.

As he falls the cool rush of the air replaces the warmth of the flames. He breathes in a little of the fire to carry with him, to let his heart and his bones know that this is the end. It's okay however, because there's still a star left. A lovely sister he knows will do well.

He falls. He falls. He falls until Gunther Starlight is no more. A light goes dark in the sky.

CHAPTER THIRTY-SIX
White Wings, Black Heart

A ship—so strong, so true—ensures that the falling body, the lifeless body of Gunther, does not become mush on concrete. The Trinity, pulling off a maneuver most pilots would deem mad, flies on its side with its pedestrian door open. That's where Fleur stands, waiting, as her arms open up and she catches Gunther. She notices the faint smile on his face, lifeless and loving.

"Gunther…" she says softly. She holds him tightly and feels the weight of the ship shift. With no intent of ever letting go, she brings his body into the confines of the ship and closes the door behind her.

She collapses while holding him still, and closes her eyes, saying with a shaking voice, "You just had to go up in flames eh? You stupid… damn hero…so stupid." She holds him tighter, clutching his clothes between her fingertips until they turn red. She lets go, placing his head softly on the ground. She then stands up with him and holds his body in her arms, "I won't cry for you." She says, her voice still shaking, "But I promise, I won't disappoint you."

Fleur brings Gunther's body to the bridge, and Rudy, turning first to see who it is, knowing who it'll be, goes pale at the sight before his eyes. Paige, still pushing on the throttle to get them out of danger, doesn't look back. She refuses to. She keeps looking forward, her face wet, dripping, as tears streams down. She eventually calls out, "Is he alive?"

To which Fleur responds, quietly but direct. "No…no he's not."

Paige nods her head repeatedly as if the motion will somehow remove the truth. Her eyes continue to water and her lips tremble. With the tears now accompanied by a sob, she continues to press forward so that they can find the others…alive.

The Trinity soars through, dodging the Nightmares that dare go near it with Rudy piloting the gun system, he tears through any that catch his eye, his anger causing him to yell as he does so, "Fuck!!!!!"

Behind them, the tower—now set aflame—burns brightly. Its light casts smoke and heat that rises above, causing the Nightmares to disperse and let the shine of the light come down, giving great emphasis on the tower itself for all to look and see.

Many faces turn, unaware as to what has befallen the last remaining tall structure. The devastation blends into everything else yet is still different, for the light causes eyes to stare. Even the Federation, with its life on the line, takes a few moments to look at where an unknown, unheralded hero, has fallen for the sake of family.

However, as another Nightmare tears its way through, pulling its long body with sharp black scales into the depths of a Federation ship, paying no heed to the utter chaos unfolding and doing so in glee, the attention of the tower becomes but the backdrop to an unfolding story.

With more than half of its assets gone, almost all of the troops sent to the ground being killed by both Nightmares and Burdens alike, and the R.F.Ms taking equal amount of damage in the sky, the Federation, now with only four ships left, begins considering a retreat.

However, the man leading the Federation ships, cold hearted and still determined, presses forward into the now suicidal standoff. Leading both his ship, and two others.

The crew on the fourth ship questions this, and begins to wonder what good has been done thus far. The man leading said ship, young in both appearance and in heart, has a mind well beyond comprehension.

If the rules binding the Federation were not so convoluted and dense, he would be at a much higher rank than he is. Not following a man who knows not left from right.

So this man, this intelligent man whose name is not important, watches in disbelief at all of the loss of life. And then by chance he, and he alone, sees out of the corner of his eye civilians running in fear down below.

Having had more than enough of the pointless and wasteful efforts, he orders his ship to send down rescue shuttles. No one argues and, within minutes, hundreds of lives are saved—a small smudge against the millions that have perished since their arrival.

To his luck, the other three ships led by the cold-hearted moron do not see or care, and plunge into the depths of the Nightmares, firing their main weapons forward, tearing through them and heading towards the rip in the sky.

Those on the fourth ship watch and after seeing yet another ship get struck by a Nightmare and fall towards the ground, becoming a pile of smoke and ash, the ship departs, signaling its retreat so that the other two ships are aware and can decide their own fate.

The young man does not care. Whatever punishment waits, he will take, for the lives of a hundred mean more than a pointless death.

"Damn it all to hell!" the cold-hearted man yells with sweat on his brow, "this isn't how it's supposed to go! These creatures just won't stop!"

"Sir! The SS Promise is leaving!"

"Cowards! Unable to follow a simple command!"

"Sir!"

"What is it now?!"

"The...SS Dominion just got hit. It's just us..."

"So be it...we will take this ship and get ourselves out of here."

***

As this transpires, Hex and Dusk land softly on a roof not far away from where the rip resides in the sky. Hex, quickly turns to Dusk and says, "Alright, this is as close as I can take you. Do you know what to do? Are you ready?"

Slightly pale, Dusk replies, "You want me to use the arrow, I know. But Hex, what we're going to do is…well suicidal."

"You said you were ready. That you'll do anything for Sarah."

"Well, yes."

"So then what's the problem?"

"The problem is that if I miss, or if it isn't strong enough, or if it all just goes horribly wrong, then, then what…then that's it."

"Do you want to stand here, in doubt, do nothing and certainly die or do you want to take a chance and perhaps live?"

"No, Hex I–"

The angel smiles, "I have faith in you. Just let it all go and it will come back to you. I promise."

The burning tower catches Dusk's attention and he looks over.

"Pay attention." Hex says, grabbing ahold of him.

"Ya…okay let's do this." Dusk pulls himself back into shape, stretching his arms and jumping up slightly to warm up all of his muscles. What they are about to do will be grueling but it is of the upmost importance. There is no one else.

"Now, I'll be using a lot of the power I have stored up. I can do four to five high level moves and, in that time, either your arrow or one of my attempts needs to make a path or strike the rip itself so that it closes."

"It'll have to be you. I don't know how I can possibly close a rip with my arrow."

"Neither do I."

They both look at one another for a moment, and then let out a laugh. A laugh that shows that there is no more reason to cry or run away, or scream in rage. They must simply act. Dusk replies, "Fine, we might as well get this over with."

Hex turns and stretches his wings. He looks up at the rip and the vast number of Nightmares in their way. He feels the wind brushing through his long black hair. He feels the sensation run down his body, kissing his skin.

This is what it feels to be alive, he thinks deeply. *This is what he is fighting for.* He hunches down, bending close to his knees and then, with a great burst, shoots upwards into the air, leaving Dusk behind.

He moves with great speed, his agile body making progress through the hordes of black creatures hurling towards him that are trying to grab ahold of his wings. They fail in doing so and, as Hex finds a suitable position, he stretches both of his arms outwards and with a mighty calling, spears appear all around him, so numerous it causes Dusk to stare in awe.

Hundreds. That is the extent of the spears that Hex creates. All white, all marked with the heavy weight of responsibility and a loud voice of strength. The sight alone makes the Nightmares scream in protest. They dart forward in hopes of bearing down and tearing into Hex's flesh before he attacks. But they aren't fast enough, not nearly. And with one flick of his finger, the spears are sent forward, ripping through the Nightmares, lodging into them and exploding, taking out any that are close by.

The quick massacre impresses Dusk and also wakes him up from his wondrous gaze. He shakes his head and positions himself the same way as he did in the dream world. *Just a dream*, he thinks to himself, *but this time it's real.*

So he focuses, and focuses, and focuses until his mind begins to bend. And as it bends and strains at the limit of breaking, the yellow light appears, stronger than it ever has before, and forms his bow and arrow.

His mind flashes to what came to be the last time he used it, how weak he felt after, the tears of exhaustion and frustration. He thinks about Essa holding him up on his feet and eventually, striking Hex across the face.

He pulls back until his muscles bulge and scream inside him. His concentration causes the images of Essa and Hex to burn into his mind. *Not again*, he thinks to himself, *this time I will make it count.*

His muscles beg for release, for rest. He holds on and waits to see how far Hex can go without needing to shoot the arrow, his life. His existence hangs in the form of a single and possibly final strike.

The angel continues to push forward, now much closer to the rip, its presence so large it makes him wonder how much despair is on the other end of it. He wonders how one man—no, an organization—could fathom up the idea to unleash this and succeed.

Answers he can't find pick away at him as more Nightmares rush towards him. He forms two spears and tears through, spinning around, rising and then falling rapidly to never let them get close enough to grab ahold of him. He does so effectively until, once again, he finds himself in the presence of far too many to handle.

Without the chance to react, before the grip of fear takes hold of his impenetrable heart, a flash of yellow erupts, and then a piercing arrow passes by him.

Hex witnesses, up close, the power of Dusk's existence and life—his desire to press on. The arrow not only kills all that it passes through, by stuns and turns into dust all that it comes close to. The Nightmares scream uncontrollably and scatter like children. *This is what they fear*, Hex thinks to himself, *this is what they cannot handle—life*.

Dusk, now sweating profusely, exhausted and gasping for air, rests on the roof, lying down with his body flat against the tiles and his eyes facing the sky. He looks at Hex and sees the angel form another spear—this one different from the rest, for a red light surrounds it.

The spear is thrown towards the rip, spinning until it makes contact. With the tip of the spear simply touching the edge of the rip without passing through, it sends off a red gleam that covers the hole in the sky.

He turns to see more Nightmares heading towards him—a number he can handle. Deciding to dart upwards, Hex creates a spear and runs it through a Nightmare, slicing it in half. He continues to accelerate upwards, heading towards the white puffy clouds now visible thanks to Dusk's arrow.

As a Nightmare blocks his way, Hex cuts through it, tearing its body into pieces. He breaks through the clouds and turns around, his wings taking in the sunlight. For a brief moment, he looks around and sees the beauty above the clouds, the warm rays of yellow and orange light descending towards him.

His wings stop flapping and he falls through the clouds towards the Nightmares waiting below. *You want a taste of fear?* His mind races, *you will get no such thing from me.*

They reach for him. He sends his spear through one and pulls it out of the dying Nightmare. He then throws it to hit another farther away. He forms a spear to replace it and uses it to kill three more before plunging it into one and leaving it behind to explode.

This continues for a little while, Hex slaying the Nightmares without fear or worry of more entering through the rip. He spins around, cutting through another to catch a glimpse at the last remaining Federation ship. It desperately tries to escape from the reach of the Nightmares.

Wondering if he should help, a large Nightmare gives him an answer. One so large that Hex wonders how it even managed to escape his sight until now. But as it looks at him, it smiles and with one flick of its tail, tears the last remaining Federation ship in half.

With the Federation's presence now gone, Hex watches as the large Nightmare—smaller than the one from the dream world, yet more menacing—heads towards him.

With two large black wings, it flaps through the air. It continues to smile, its teeth bared, its eyes fixated on the majestic whiteness before it. It calls out, "Fooooood." It's voice bellows through the sky, rocking through the city.

"Disgusting," Hex forms another spear with the same red glow from before. He focuses on it and puts enough strength into it until he is satisfied. With a great hurl, it pierces the large Nightmare's frontal lobe, removing its smile completely, and soon after its ability to fly.

It falls downwards, vanishing into nothing. The angel lets out a soft sigh of relief, and then the hairs on his neck rise. A yellow flash and then suddenly an arrow soars past him, striking something outside his vision. He turns to see an arrow knock a Nightmare through the air, the beast still alive.

The angel looks and sees Dusk collapse on the roof. It was an action on par with embracing death. All to protect him—protect him because of the brief moment he didn't pay attention.

Shame trickles onto his skin. He won't let Dusk die in such a way.

Hex turns to look for the Nightmare, but sees only a large group that blocks his visibility. So he turns to Dusk once more and flies towards him, landing on the rooftop.

"Saved your ass there." Dusk coughs up, his skin very pale now.

"You shouldn't have, I would have been okay."

"You aren't a good liar…" Dusk says with a soft voice, "…not even remotely."

Hex smiles weakly. "I'm going to get you away from here, and hunt down that Nightmare. It's going to be taxing on you, but just hold on."

Dusk raises his arms and points behind Hex. "Best hurry up then, because there's a lot heading our way."

Hex turns to look. Sure enough, the Nightmares that had been spreading across the city are now swarming together towards them. His eyes scan the threat and it does not break his will. He lifts Dusk up, runs across the rooftop and, with a push, enters the air.

They fly low between the buildings with a few Nightmares faster than the rest on their heels. They wrap around the remains of a tower on a sharp angle. Some of the Nightmares follow accordingly, others burst through the building in hopes of a short cut.

The Nightmares succeed and enter Hex's line of sight, so he reminds them of who he is. With one hand on Dusk and the other holding a spear, he slices through them and heads towards the sky. With Nightmares everywhere, he has no choice but to raise himself further.

"I can help Hex, especially if you are trying to help me." Dusk says suddenly.

"What do you suggest then?"

"Let me drop, let me use my sword."

"You'll die."

"Not if you catch me."

"So we're going to play a game, are we?"

"Not a game. This is my life we're talking about."

"Very well then."

They both reach the edge of the clouds and the Nightmares surround them. Dusk looks at the soft tranquility above the clouds, knowing the moment he faces the other way he will see hell in all of its glory. Hex lets go.

Dusk falls through the sky, the air whipping against his skin, an unpleasant yet exhilarating feeling. He pulls out his sword and, as the first Nightmare reaches out for him, he stabs his sword through it with the pull of gravity on his body. The cut isn't perfect and so causes him to jerk back, change angles and fall upside down.

Another Nightmare approaches, this time with its mouth wide open. He points his sword forward, and it enters the Nightmare's mouth, tearing through its belly and out on the other side.

Disgust covers his face, but he soon forgets as he changes his body's centre of gravity, down-thrusts his sword through another Nightmare. He witnesses how far he's fallen. Worry begins to build up in his throat, but the angel doesn't let it go much further than that.

Hex grabs ahold of him and quickly hurls him through the sky. Dusk cuts through another Nightmare that approaches and then is caught once more.

"I found the Nightmare that your arrow struck—I'll need your help."

"That's why I'm here Hex."

"I surely can't picture Essa doing this."

Hex's comment makes Dusk chuckle as they head towards a small cluster of Nightmares, the one that matters most being amongst them, looking at them with a snarl.

Reaching the cluster, Hex dives in and hurls Dusk forward. Dusk passes through them fairly easily—most of them caught off guard by the sudden and daring attack. Following him is a set of blazing white spears that kill the majority in his way.

Dusk sees the Nightmare—a wound in its arm where the arrow struck. With one great thrust, he plunges his sword into its chest as he slams into it at a high velocity. The Nightmare's gigantic white-eye looks at him and then rolls around in its head, withering in pain as it cries out.

Dusk tears through the Nightmare's chest, and soon feels his strength slowly returning to him. He's picked up once more and they head towards the ground.

"Thank you Hex."

"For what?"

"For trusting me."

Hex looks at Dusk and doesn't see a pest or an annoyance, but a reliable comrade. He looks up at the rip, at the Nightmares still circling around, wondering if they dare approach. He thinks about the journey, what they've had to accomplish, all of the people they've met, the hardships and trials, the secrets and unlikelihood of surviving.

He wants to say something, something profound that will shape Dusk, something to strengthen his heart. However, a real Burden appears… Not one. Not two, but three.

***

Standing on a large rock, Bast says, "Well what do you know? An angel in the sky."

Concordia taunts, "I wouldn't mind giving it a go."

Caster remains silent. The smile on his mask does enough to unravel Dusk's nerves as they reach the ground.

Hex stands in front of Dusk protectively.

Bast says, "I don't think he has much to say."

"That appears to be the case." Concordia replies. "Maybe he doesn't plan to run away twice in a row."

Bast muses, "Planning to take on three of us?"

Hex forms two spears.

Caster says, "Do not worry." His eyes move towards Dusk, "It will end quickly."

In that moment Dusk looks long and hard at the Burdens. His eyes skim over the detail in Casters mask. It's wooden texture amplifying the horrific rattling of his breath. Standing next to him, Concordia decides to pull down her hood and reveal her long jet-black hair. It catches the suns rays and suffocates it.

Hex says, "I must thank you for revealing yourselves from the shadows. This will be the last time blood is spilt today."

As Bast gets ready to laugh, a spear slams into his gut. He looks down and watches it explode, engulfing him in a dome of white light. The blast, while brutal, doesn't reach Caster and Concordia who are equally spread apart from where Bast is standing.

Dusk pumps a subtle triumphant fist downwards.

The smoke clears and standing before them, displeased, is Bast. The only visible wound being a few faint scratches on his fingers. He clenches his hands, stares with piercing eyes and says, "Caster, don't go giving them the idea to end things quickly. You know how I like to fight."

Caster chuckles beneath his mask but says nothing on the subject. Bast walks forward until he's gotten a good distance away from the other Burdens. He cracks his neck and shrugs his shoulders, ending the quick warm up with a boxers motion, as he air punches and steps back and forth as well as side to side.

Hex forms a second spear and begins to twirl both of them around. He listens to his spears cutting through the wind, the rotation perfect and sound. Bast stretches his arms and twists his body. He lifts up a leg and pulls it closer to his body and then does the other. He then stretches his legs behind his back until finally becoming ready enough to enjoy the approaching battle.

Dusk looks at Caster and Concordia and notices that neither of them are looking his way. All eyes are on Bast and Hex. He can't shake the feeling that something bad is about to happen. That the man Hex is about to face is incredibly dangerous.

"Let's begin, shall we?" Bast proclaims.

"Do not look at me with those eyes."

Bast lets out a laugh. Hex hurls a spear at him. The Burdens raises his hand and as the spear makes contact, it explodes. "I should probably tell you, anything I touch blows up."

Hex grunts and forms another spear. He runs forward and begins a fast array of attacks that require Bast to move out of the way and dodge. As the spear comes swooping around he blocks it and it explodes. As the explosion occurs, Hex stabs his other spear forward. Bast counters that as well. The second explosion tears a chunk out of the ground from its impact and sends dirt into the air.

A quick piercing sound can be heard followed by a white light. Hex forms a spear that isn't solidified. He sends it forward, the power in his wrist causing the air to scream. Bast sees the attack and with a quick reaction, he sends both of his hands downwards to meet the tip of the white spear.

It explodes.

Hex is taken aback. He looks at Bast in alarm. The Burden sneers, "I told you. Everything I touch, everything, explodes."

The angel's expression goes dark. His brow tightens up and in that moment, despite Bast haven shaken the angel up, it is Hex whose inner strength turns the tide of battle. The Burden feels it press into his skin and it aggravates him. It's not the result he was expecting.

Dusk decides to pull out his sword. Caster and Concordia's eyes dart towards him. His legs begin to wobble and his hands shake. Just them looking at him makes him regret having a weapon at all. He thinks about what became of Andromeda and then, he too, calms down. He steadies his breathing and enters a place of focus. The Burdens take notice, and begin to walk forward.

Bast says loudly, "Let me be Caster! I have a certain method."

Concordia replies for him, "We've wasted enough time as is."

Caster makes his way past Bast and closes the distance across the dusty battlefield towards Hex. He swings his sword and attacks. Hex forms two spears and blocks it with one of them, attacking with the other. Caster dodges it and spins around, moving incredibly close to the ground. He slices upwards. Hex stops it with both of his spears crossed together. Caster forward-kicks the spears and pushes Hex off his feet.

Bast appears and reaches out. Hex moves one of the spears in the way. Bast latches onto it and it explodes. Hex swings his remaining spear at Bast and the Burden ducks. The spear catches the tip of his hood and rips it off, revealing his face for the first time beyond the subtle shadows of the hood.

Dusk can clearly see who Bast is beneath the confines of a cloak. The Burden has short but straight black hair. His face is clean-shaven and there are no scars or imperfections. It is the face of someone who rarely gets struck by an opposing attack. The face of someone who can destroy anything that dares dirty his face.

The two Burdens attack Hex simultaneously while Concordia continues to watch. The angel swings a spear around that he forms quickly to push them away. Bast moves from behind, aiming for his wings. Hex uses them to form a strong gust of wind that pushes Bast off his feet. Hex then punches Caster in the face, knocking him forward.

Concordia calls out with a whistle. Hex looks at her and quickly finds himself pulled into a twisted vision. He sees a dozen faces of people he has loved and still loves. He sees them buried in the ground with only their heads sticking out—crying and calling for help. He says quietly, "Don't try to play with my emotions." He disperses the illusion with a wave of his hand. Concordia takes a step back in hesitation, her illusion being thwarted.

As Hex turns his head to continue fighting, Caster closes the distance and strikes him in the shoulder. Caster then runs past Hex and heads towards Dusk. He overwhelms him, taking him by the collar and tosses him across the ground. Hex tries to run forward and protect him but Bast grabs ahold of one of his wings. Without a moment's hesitation, Bast destroys the wing. Feathers rise and the angel's blood spreads across the battlefield.

Hex hurls his arm around. Bast avoids it but the spear that follows lands in the Burden's leg, piercing through the flesh and sticking it into the ground. Hex yells out in pain at the loss of a wing and quickly unleashes a barrage of punches into Bast's face. The Burden begins to wobble. Hex then forms another spear and, as he aims to send it into Bast, the Burden ducks downwards. Concordia greets him once more with a wink and pulls Hex into another illusion.

As he finds himself slipping, things around him changing into his worst fear, thoughts of all those he cares about lying around him dead. His feathers floating around aimlessly, he hurls the spear without focus and successfully cuts through her side, causing her to close her eyes and free Hex.

He rushes forward, slamming his knee into Bast's face. He then rushes past him and towards Concordia. She tries to move away but he overwhelms her and grabs her by the throat. He lifts her up and slams her into the ground. He forms a spear and hears Dusk cry out. He looks and sees Caster slashing away at Dusk, cutting wounds into his body. Hex snarls and aims his spear at the Burden and throws it.

Bast sees this and quickly destroys the spear holding him down. He leaps forward into the air and with the tip of his finger, he reaches the spear in time and destroys it.

Hex grabs a hold of Concordia and throws her through the air and into Bast, knocking them both down. He forms a long spear that requires both hands. He readies himself and then runs forward. As Bast and Concordia make their way onto their feet, the spear reaches them.

Bast reaches out to touch it. Hex twists the spear and it explodes, engulfing both of the Burdens in a white light. He runs through the white light, passing both of them, and hurls another spear towards Caster who turns to see it just in time. He connects his sword with the spear and knocks it away. It explodes soon after, giving Dusk enough time to escape from the Burden.

The placement of the battle however, places Hex in a bad situation. Bast yells out, "Concordia, do something!"

Hex glances backwards. This time he isn't greeted with an illusion, but a powerful force that holds him in place. He can't move a muscle; his heartbeat begins to escalate.

With a beckoning cry, Hex calls out to Dusk for help. The Burdens swoop in from three sides. Bast gets to Hex first and reaches out towards him. A sudden sword cuts down.

Caster and Concordia look at Dusk in surprise. They did not notice his approach and because of that, Bast is now left with one hand.

"You fuck!" Bast yells in pain, he reaches out with his other hand and Dusk cuts off a finger. "You fuck, fuck, fuck, fuck!" Bast yells in agonizing anger. He sends his foot forward and kicks Dusk in the chest, knocking him to the ground.

Concordia sees the situation deteriorate. She pulls out a dagger. The angel sees the approaching blade and touches his ring. A white light shines and forms a white wall, it slams into Concordia and knocks her back. Hex stops an attack from Caster, throwing him over his shoulder. He then turns to Concordia and rushes her. She sends her dagger forward and stabs Hex in the wrist. She then slashes sideways and sends a line across his armor.

He punches her in the face in retaliation and she drops her dagger. She reaches down to grab it and once she retrieves it, she attacks. Hex blocks her advance with his knee guard and grabs her by the hair, whipping her across the ground viciously.

Dusk watches as Hex dominates Concordia. His eyes move over to Bast who walks towards him in anger. "I'll fucking kill you!" He notices that Caster is nowhere to be seen.

He focuses, doing what Hex taught him when they first met and he can't sense anything. The Burden is as much of a ghost as he was moments prior.

Concordia attacks with her dagger once more and Hex grabs her by the wrist. She throws a punch and he stops it. He crushes her hand causing her to cry out in pain. He then breaks the elbow supporting the dagger. He catches it from her and slams it into her eye. As she falls back on the verge of death, he feels a change in the wind.

Bast stops walking towards Dusk. A vein appears on his forehead. "Did…you…" he turns towards Hex and sees Concordia withering on the ground in pain, "just…hurt her?"

Hex says nothing.

"Did you just…HURT CONCORDIA!?" Bast yells in a rage, losing all composure. He runs at Hex, keeping his hand close to his body. Dusk tries to run after him but the Burden is faster than he.

As Hex readies himself for the approaching Burden, a sword passes through his stomach from behind. A look of confusion crosses his face. He looks down at the blade and watches it pull out.

The angel looks at his blood, at his hands, he feels a change in temperature. He feels sweat accumulate on his brow. His sense of sound heightens. *This is bad*, he thinks quietly.

Bast reaches him and slams his hand into Hex's chest, blowing through the amour and putting a small crevasse into his chest. The explosion knocks him backwards, Caster plunges his sword through Hex once more.

Dusk's heart sinks. He feels shock turn into complete and utter anger. A kind he cannot control, a kind he refuses to control. He grips his sword tightly. He grinds his teeth. With a faint glow, his body shines as his life wraps around him, becoming more than a substance to be cast aside. It wants to be seen, felt, and to be feared.

Bast looks over at Dusk. He turns to face him.

Hex cries out, "Face me!"

"You have your hands full." Caster says as he pulls out his sword and pushes the angel forward. He wipes the blood off his blade. "There's no room for kindness."

Hex turns to look at him, holding a hand to the freshest of three wounds. He forms a spear, potentially his last.

Within Dusk, there is no sense of peace. There is nothing to be found or felt. Everything that he is moves across his skin, through his clothes and across his blade. Within him, the darkness remains silent, until it says, *"Make me proud."*

Bast takes a moment to look over at Concordia and see her moving across the ground slowly. He stands between where she is and where Dusk is approaching. She keeps one hand on her face as blood gushes out from where her eye used to be.

"One by one," Dusk says as he walks towards Bast, "that is all it will take." His eyes begin to glow a faint yellow, "To devour my own nightmare."

Bast moves his remaining four fingers around. He keeps his other arm close to his stomach. His blood is soaking into his cloak. His breathing isn't steady, but he has enough in him to kill, to regain composure.

He blinks in surprise as a blade passes through his stomach. Dusk, once more, faded away momentarily. He did not go invisible, but rather, his presence became a faint detail amongst everything else. While Bast pondered over the speed in which he must approach, Dusk had already done so.

Bast sees only cold, empty eyes in front of him.

Dusk says, his voice full of malice, "I, the reaper, wish to see your teeth."

Blood pours out from Bast's mouth and he spits back, "You haven't earned the right to such a luxury." He smiles, his teeth reflecting the colour of his eyes.

CHAPTER THIRTY-SEVEN
Those Who Reap

Bast reaches out for the blade quickly in a daring attempt. Dusk pulls it backwards and out of the Burdens stomach. The tip of the blade is touched and an explosion occurs, knocking Dusk away. He glances at his sword and sees that the tip has broken off, creating two sharper ends. He faces Bast and sees the Burden whip the broken shard of his sword at him. It stabs into his chest.

He pulls it out and throws it back at Bast who knocks it away. Dusk sends his sword upwards and Bast receives the blow head on. A gash moves up his chest towards his right arm. He grabs a hold of Dusks wrist in return.

As the explosion is set off, as it surely will, Dusk creates a yellow light at the area of contact to defend his body. He uses his other hand to slam it beneath Bast's grip, knocking it away. The Burden looks in horror as his remaining hand is taken from him.

Dusk steps forward and stabs his sword through Bast's good leg. The blow brings him to his knees. He grabs the Burden by the back of the neck, "Your teeth. Show me."

The Burden lets out a sad laugh and says, "Whatever my fate, so be it." His head hangs down loosely, submitting to his fate.

Dusk slams his hand into Bast's mouth, taking him by surprise. The Burden's eyes dart in worry. "You think," Dusk says, "after all you have done, that I would end this quickly? I thought I told you, I want to see your teeth!" He yells maniacally and pulls forward. Bast's eyes widen in horror as his jaw is disconnected. He feels his skin peel. He groans in pain as it rips away from his muscles, blood smearing and gushing between bone and the fresh air. His jaw begins to crack and shards break off until it is completely removed from the rest of his skull.

Dusk looks at it. He drops the bloody mess. He watches Bast fall to the ground silently, a gruesome end. He looks over at Concordia. The Burden crawls away. He walks towards her and stands above her. He raises his broken sword.

Hex and Caster look at what's become of Bast. The Burden says, "He's stronger than you are angel. He doesn't mind killing."

Hex looks with worry at his friend who is losing his way. Caster swings his sword and Hex knocks it away with his spear.

Concordia grabs ahold of some dirt and cries. Standing above her is someone just like her, someone who doesn't care about right from wrong.

Dusk with a heavy growl, slams his sword down into her spine with the weight of his entire body. He kneels over her as she twitches. He wipes his face. He pulls out the broken sword and looks over at Hex and Caster. Concordia's remaining eye looks at the ground. She feels the light slip away from her. Fingers wrap around her face. The last thing she sees before death greets her, are the fingers that plunge inside her skull and take her vision away.

Dusk says quietly, "One by one, until only one is left." He squeezes his fist, and the eye within his palm drips through his fingers.

The angel knocks Caster backwards. Dusk rushes forward with the yellow light emitting from his body greatly. Hex sends Caster to the ground and raises his spear. He slams it forward. Caster catches it between his hands and holds it off. Dusk leaps into the air and slams his sword down into Caster's chest before the Burden can escape.

The mask looks up at him. "Don't disappoint me."

Dusk twists the sword. He says nothing. He pulls his sword out from the Burden and remains silent. The angel stares at him. He sees someone completely different from the person he knows.

Dusk says, his voice emotionless, "What? What are you looking at?"

"I'm hoping I'm not looking at the death of someone I know."

"Well you aren't. We won, they've lost." Dusk looks down at Caster, "I don't need to fear these people anymore. They are weak. I can kill them."

"That is not the point." Hex walks forward and pokes Dusk in the chest. "It's not that they lost or even died. It's the fact that you changed. You showed no mercy, no kindness. You simply...acted on a desire."

"I am aware. Hex, my desire was for us to live. I wanted us to live and when I saw that sword pass through you, I worried. I worried so much that I remembered something. I realized that all this time, ever since I died, I've been scared. I've been holding onto that memory and it's been keeping me back from a necessary emotion."

"What emotion?"

"The one that tells me it's me or them. I want Sarah back. Hex, if I don't show mercy I win. If I don't show kindness, I survive. They are the ones who started all of this. They are the Burdens. I'm simply-"

Hex punches Dusk across the face. Dusk feels his sense return to him. He looks at the angel. Hex says, "Don't throw away your kindness. What kind of man do you wish to be when you find Sarah? Wake up Dusk. This isn't you."

Dusk places a hand to his face. He looks at Hex and then at his wounds. He sees that the blood is still oozing out. "Hex...I'm sorry, I -"

"Just don't lose yourself again. That display of cruelty you used towards them was unneeded. In the end...we would have lost if you didn't kill them but I...cannot do that. It goes against my code. Anyone that is human I cannot kill. I can break them...but no matter how close I push, I can't kill."

"But I can."

"Yes, but there are different ways to end a life."

Dusk looks away from the angel's expression and glances at where his wing used to reside. "Are you alright? You're bleeding pretty bad."

The angel pauses. Not ready to let the topic change. Once the pain starts to rock in his skull he says, "I'll be fine. Listen, I need to tell you something."

The ground shakes and interrupts them. Hex and Dusk turn and see something unfathomable. Standing on the other edge of the plain, they see Caster.

Dusk feels his face grow pale. "You're supposed to be dead!" He looks over to where Caster's body laid, and sees that it's gone. His eyes glance towards Bast and Concordia, his heart rests slightly at the sight of their emotionless and gruesome ends.

"Delicious," the darkness inside him says in glee.

Hex says, "We should have known it wouldn't be that easy."

They watch as a portal emerges next to Caster. Edom walks out. He sees the state of Bast and Concordia. He whistles and says soon after, "What's going on here? Is that a dead Concordia?" His eyes widen. "Even Bast is dead."

Caster replies, "That boy." Edom looks over at him and he frowns. "It was him, he killed them both and finished me off as well."

Edom's eyes light up and he sneers. "Now that's interesting. But, you let that happen didn't you? What I want to know is who is he really? I killed him you know. A year ago."

Caster crosses his arms and says, "I suppose we can ask Erick when we return."

"Saying our leader's name out loud? You really are in a different mood. Well, I suppose I'll clean up some of this mess. Bring back the remains of Bast and Concordia. I'm sure Oculus will have a go at that…the damn nut job. Which reminds me…" Edom leans in and whispers to Caster, "…I have to go back and check on Keeper. Nix is dead though. So have fun and remember, don't behave."

Edom waves at Dusk and enters the portal, disappearing. Dusk looks at Caster and feels a surge of fear return to him. His balance fades away and his body loses its yellow glow. He looks at the angel and says, "I'm scared Hex."

"It will be alright. We will stop him as many times as we need. Although…I've put us in a predicament."

"What do you mean?"

"There's one more heading here, because I couldn't kill him."

**

Asrath appears in the sky flying towards them. He hums a soft tune as the wind slides across his face. He spins around and dances past the Nightmares. His eye is on the prize, and it has a white wing.

Hex places a hand to his stomach. He curses under his breath and says, "I can't even heal my wounds. I need everything I have left in my ring. Dusk, do not try to fight that Burden. We must view our success up until now as luck and nothing more. Not all of the Burdens are equal in avoiding death, but causing destruction, they are masterful at."

Dusk looks into the sky and watches Asrath get closer. He sees the Burden lick his lips and descend towards the ground, landing next to Caster. He watches the two of them converse, unable to hear what they are saying. It worries him but he knows there's nothing he can do about it. He clenches his fist and wraps his hand tightly around his sword.

"I don't want to lose this. This taste of metal." Dusk says. Hex looks at him in surprise. He continues, "It's the indication that I'm still here, defying the odds. I'm not going to let them take this feeling from me. They can be the masters of death, but I'm the ruler of my own destiny. I was the moment I followed you. I will be until I am done with what I have to do."

"My…you are growing on me." Hex says in awe.

They stand together, facing the two Burdens. Asrath says aloud in a booming voice, "Angel, did you forget me? Something slip your to do list? Oh, that's right, you didn't kill me, I'm still here, oops!"

Caster says to Asrath, "Remember what I said. Keep the other one alive. Let me handle it."

"Yes, whatever, I'm not interested in someone who killed trash. I want that white light. It's so tasty, calling out for me." His eyes sparkle with joy.

Hex knows there will be no more room for error. He unleashes all of his power with a mighty yell. Dusk watches the ring spin around and send off an incredible pressure of warmth and joy, a thrill for life.

The feeling of being constricted leaves Hex. He feels every fiber in his body and muscles expand, pumping the blood through his veins. Hex feels human. He feels his wounds and he finds a desire to fight relentlessly, for Dusk.

He takes a step forward. His muscles rise to the challenge. He says, "Let me go first. Be safe Dusk." The chains binding Hex's strength no longer in his way, he rushes forward.

The angel collides with Asrath. They push one another and test each others strength. The Burden grabs ahold of Hex's remaining wing and yanks out a few feathers. Hex sends a vicious punch into Asrath's ear.

Hex's eyes grow black at the edges as his hands land rapid and successive strikes. He brings his hands together to contain a force he is about to release. A move so great that it will make his ring unstable. He whispers, "Spear of death."

His eyes go completely black. He slams his body forward with his hands pointing towards the sky. A destructive force emits from him and crushes the ground in his vicinity, pushing the wind away and making everything still.

So still, so translucent, that Dusk doesn't blink. He watches the colourless fight unfold. Why were the angel's eyes black? Why would he have a spear with such a name?

The spear forms. The tip casts a shine from the sunlight as it descends from the heavens a few thousand miles away. Birds chirp as it passes by them, the spear slowly coming into sight. It tears through every single Nightmare in its wake, ridding the sky of their presence for the time being.

Asrath grins and says, "I won't be waiting around to be hit by that."

"You have no choice."

"Pardon?" He tries to move his body but feels restricted. He looks down to see that the chains from before, the ones that he thought were gone for good, were now back, pinning his feet down into the earth.

He looks up and Hex says to him, "I'm an angel. I will do everything I can to make you repent."

Hex runs away and quickly grabs ahold of Dusk. With the use of only one wing, he runs with him rather than flying.

Caster, having not tried to stop this, looks over at the spear in the sky and decides its best to get away as soon as possible.

Asrath doesn't budge. His eyes are locked. With a grin on his face, having been left behind to face his fate, one hand forms a ball of dark energy that has red sparks shooting within it. He then whispers, as the spear makes its way to him, "Obliterate."

The small dark energy expands and as the spear lands, ignites everything around it. Asrath is engulfed in an explosion of white light that reaches the heavens and then descends once more, causing the earth itself to turn white.

Moments of silence pass, until a faint cough emerges from the white dust, Asrath sneers at the oddly coloured blood that sticks to his body. He feels the chains on his feet give way. He turns around, his cloak torn and barely recognizable on his body. He laughs loudly and says, "Am I supposed to repent now?"

Hex lets go of Dusk and steps forward. "Dusk, I think you should run. Find the others. Get away from here."

Dusk, taken aback, asks in frustration, "What the hell do you mean I should run?"

Hex looks at him and his black eyes show that of concern. The angel says, "The Burdens that we've seen are just the tip of the iceberg. There's much more out there. If I die here, then it's up to you to carry on and free your species from this plague."

"Don't talk like you're about to lose. I'm here damn it!"

Hex smiles. "I know you're stubborn but this is getting ridiculous." He looks at Dusk, "Look at my eyes. They are completely black. I'm as true an angel as one can possibly be. But I won't force your hand.

You've done enough."

They turn and see Caster walking past Asrath, picking up speed towards them. Hex forms a spear and whips it forward. Caster dodges it. Hex forms two more and throws them at the Burden. Caster cuts through them and reaches Hex. He slices through his midsection with a speed unlike before. Dusk yells and swings his broken blade. Caster blocks it and then slides his through Dusk.

Hex stares in horror as his friend contorts in pain. Caster pulls out his sword and aims for Hex. The angel overwhelms him and, with a mighty cry, slams his fist into the Burden's chest, sending him out of sight.

He looks down and sees Dusk lying on the ground, gasping. Hex rushes to him. He feels a tremble and notices its coming from his own body, his own skin. Hex begins to feel despair. He looks at Dusk and sees his friend's eyes begin to close. He cries out, "Don't you die on me Dusk! This isn't how it's supposed to be!"

Dusk says quietly, "Shut up, this is nothing." He looks at the angel with a sense of envy and says, "Just make them pay. I can't go running off now, afraid I need to sit for a little while."

Hex stands up tall. He looks at the young man and sees that the wounds from before are healing. A faint yellow light floats around his body. This change is not something Wish mentioned or foretold, this change, is a variable just like Essa's unique book. Hex sees that Dusk is different; he knows everyone he's travelled with up until now is different. He realizes he's the most simplistic thing by comparison. The thought makes him smile inside.

Asrath says loudly, "Listen. I don't have all day. Gods don't wait!"

Hex turns to him, "You're right, Gods don't wait. They are time itself!"

The trembling now confined in Hex's hand, he looks at the maniac who believes his stature to be something more. Yet with so much blood stained on his body, Hex grins, because no god is so weak as to be injured by an angel.

The ground holds the weight of two beings. One, whose darkness holds all colour and weighs his own ideals down into a sickening reality, and another, whose light casts away all colour and lets his heart rise to unlimited heights.

As Hex approaches Asrath, he says, "Let my life be enough to relinquish the evil this man holds and desires to do unto others." A faint white light floats around him for a brief moment as a spear emerges, this time with a golden tip to the blade.

He swings it in front of him and feels the strong connection between himself and it. As his steps close the distance between himself and the darkness, he continues to say, "And if I fail, then ensure that he cannot rise as he desires, and haunt him with such sin. So he knows what cannot be his."

Asrath runs forward with a fist raised, his other palm wide open. He moves his palm to slide the spear across it, yet it still manages to wound his skin in the process. As his blood floats momentarily in the sky, Asrath sends his fist forward, now without the worry of the spear plunging into his body.

It lands upon Hex's face and is the first of many thrown in order to overwhelm Hex with the brutal blows. Hex, only using one arm to fight, brings back his spear that was pushed aside and slices deeply into Asrath's ribcage with his other hand.

Now, with both of his hands on the spear, he thrusts it forward and successfully cuts open the white body, bringing forth the red contents beneath it. In that moment, Asrath takes one hand, and pulls it deeper into his body, using his other to grab ahold of Hex's throat. With a sneer spread across his face, he looks into the angel's eyes as he squeezes tightly.

Asrath says in extreme pain, "Angel or not, you cannot live without air, can you?"

Hex, with his hair covering his face, his head hanging, grabs ahold of Asrath's wrist, and says in the struggle, "You may find out, but not before I learn if it's true."

"What?"

"If the sound of a bone breaking is the same in all beings." Hex crushes Asrath's wrist and, with the spear pierced through his body, raises the Burden into the air and directly upwards.

Light shines on the metal in Hex's spear, causing Asrath's red and white figure to look even more deathly pale as if on the verge of turning to dust like a vampire lost in the sun. The light grows stronger, Asrath points his remaining hand forward and with the tip of his finger, spits out, "Obliterate."

The sphere emerges quickly and sets off, wrapping into a huge explosion with the white light from Hex's weapon. The wind cast from the devastation shoots off in every direction. In the distance, the sound of buildings falling can be heard, showcasing a true wasteland where but a few trees still stand, and the sun has nothing blocking its way.

The spear now broken, Asrath rises from the ground and pulls out the small piece still lodged in his body. He throws it away and steps on it. The wound rests in the centre of his body. He raises his mobile hand and points a finger upwards, stating, "In one of my fingers rests enough power to kill any normal human. But for you, a hand will suff-"

Hex appears before Asrath in a flash. His palm slams into the Burden's face and crushes his nose, sending him spiraling and rocketing across the ground. Before he can move, Hex appears standing above him and slams fist after fist into Asrath's face, burying it deeper into the ground. The adrenaline courses through his veins. Dusk watches closely as light vanquishes evil.

The punches stop and Hex bends down, grabbing ahold of Asrath by the neck and lifting him up. The Burden's legs dangle in the air as he sways slightly. He grimaces and feels the fingers wrap tightly against his throat. Hex says, "What is that word you like to say? Oh yes..." He crushes Asrath's ability to speak.

The Burden places his hand across Hex's face and pushes against it effortlessly until letting it fall, the rest of his body with it. He drops to the ground and looks up at the angel—angry, devastated, and insulted.

In the distance, near a set of rocks, six figures stand together in unison. Six Burdens, six swords, six set of eyes. The blades pull out at the exact same time. Their backs towards the sun, their eyes directed towards the walking light of justice. Hex looks over at them and tries to form a spear. It flickers and then solidifies. Dusk notices the change. He tries to move but his body screams for him to stop.

Hex walks forward and looks at his left shoulder to see the missing wing. He closes his eyes, sighs, and then opens them. He grabs ahold of his broken chest plate and rips it off, letting the remains clunk on the ground. His hand hovers over the hole in his chest. He closes his eyes once more, knowing he doesn't have much left in him.

He points his spear forward. He doesn't bother fixing his hair or wiping away the blood from his face. "I can see you just don't give up. Well come on then! Fight me, he who hides behind the mask!" His eyes open, ready for the next encounter.

Dusk notices the desperation. He sees that amongst the six Burdens, one of them has a torn cloak. He looks and sees the mask, the mask that resides on all six faces.

The six swordsmen rush ahead and quickly reach Hex. One of them attacks the angel's remaining wing. Hex elbows the Burden in the face in response and then slams his foot down into the knee, crushing the leg. Hex moves backwards as another sword shoots out towards him. He knocks it out of the way with his armguard. The impact causes it to break off from his forearm.

The five standing Burdens begin to flicker. They move their swords slowly while their bodies move fast. As Hex tries to ascertain what's going on, he finds himself pushed back, a sword striking from above. He blocks it with his spear. Another sword moves forward. He slides past it. A third comes from his side. He brings his spear down to stop the blow. As he succeeds, the fourth sword comes on an angle. He watches as it reaches his arm, and then takes it away. His arm flings through the air and lands on the ground covered in blood and dirt.

The angel, in clear pain, forms a white light in his fist where the ring still rests, and slams it into one of the Burdens' faces. This motion, this movement, like a failed chess move, results in yet another piece going missing.

The feeling of cool steel rings through the last wing on his back.

Hex swings his arm but misses. He stumbles and struggles to remain conscious. He is losing too much blood, there's no way to stop it. With a large chunk of his chest gone, an arm and both wings no longer his and multiple stab wounds across his body, Hex feels the approaching end.

The angel raises his hand forward and turns his open palm in the direction of the Burdens. They are taken aback, and quickly begin to feel perspiration form on their brows as the angel lets out a howling yell. They see a brilliant light unlike anything other and begin to question why their eyes are closing when something so beautiful rests before them.

Hex breathes heavily. His eyes look at the sky knowing the end is not far away.

Dusk watches helplessly. He crawls towards a broken bench and pulls himself onto one knee. He then stands up and cries out, "Hex! Fight!!!!"

The air around Hex changes as the Burdens regain sight. They see black blood run down his face from his eyes. They see that all of his blood is dark and tainted like spilt ink. The angel screams in rage.

"Not yet!" Hex screams, "Not yet!!!"

All six Burdens ready themselves. They watch as a black spear forms in Hex's hand. A white chain hangs from it and rests across the ground. His white armor barely visible beneath his running wounds.

He moves forward. The Burden who can hardly walk is reached first. Hex swings his spear towards the Burden and watches as the body disappears and leaves behind a cloak hanging on his spear. He glares towards the other five.

He continues to walk forward as they wait. His fist clutches the spear tightly; cracks begin to appear on his ring. Hex runs. He reaches them and withstands five blades at once. His spear knocks them all back as he swipes across the field, cutting against three of them.

The Burdens look at their wounds and then remain still. Caster sheathes his sword. The others disappear. He lets out a soft sigh and says, "No. I won't be a part of this."

"Face me" a heavy and gruff voice emits from Hex's chest.

"This is…not something I wish to be a part of."

Dusk looks at Hex and is unable to hold back his tears. The angel, barely standing, has cracks beginning to show across his skin. His veins start to turn black and rupture. He leans against his spear and says, "There is no escaping me."

"Angel, this has gone far enough-"

"I AM NOT DONE YET!"

The ground breaks between them. Dusk watches the white chains on the spear wrap around Caster. The spear plunges into the Burdens chest and sends him flying forward. His body is yanked in the air and pulled back towards Hex.

As the Burden approaches, he closes his eyes. "This is the end for you." His body disappears along with the cloak. Hex feels the presence of six appear around him. He doesn't listen to Dusks screaming warning. He knows there's no time.

Six blades stab through him. His spear drops to the ground and decays. The angel looks up at the sky with a stained face. *I…better take a long look*, he thinks, Caster moves his hand forward. The Burden stabs the sword deeper into the angel's body. Hex moves closer through the sword and his hand wraps around Casters mask.

His hand lights up and engulfs Caster's head. The swords dig deeper into his body. He throws Caster forward into a wall and walks out of the swords that follow him and slash away at his back. He reaches Caster and as the Burden stands up, he punches him in the mask so forcefully that it breaks open, causing the other Burdens to disappear once more leaving behind falling cloaks that too fade into nothing.

He places his hand against the wall and coughs up blood across Caster's face. The Burden looks at him for a long while. He gently places a hand against the angel's chest and pushes forward, causing Hex to stumble backwards and barely hold up straight.

Caster wipes his face but keeps it hidden from Dusk as he says to Hex, "I don't want you to think you lost to tricks. This wasn't an illusion. I was just stronger than you. I spent my years of youth pleading for a savior from above, somewhere in the stars. When those prayers went unanswered, I took what I had and made it better. You were always fighting me, split into pieces."

Hex says nothing, his consciousness struggles to remain. Caster continues, "Nothing you did to me, nothing, made a difference. But you can do something that matters. You can spend your final moments saying goodbye to someone who will miss you. Maybe then you'll succeed, in finding what you truly seek." Caster fixes his hood and turns away. "Go…before that too is taken from you."

Dusk doesn't wait. He doesn't know what was said but as Caster walks away, he uses all of his strength to move towards the angel who hangs on. Hex looks towards Dusk with a faint smile. Dusk drags his feet, hurrying, reaching out. One hand rests on his stomach, yellow glows softly as it tries to keep the blood from spilling out.

Hold on, Dusk thinks and then says in a plea, "Just hold on Hex!"

Hex's hair blows in the wind, revealing portions of his handsome face. Dusk sees the sadness in the smile and walks faster, his heartbeat beating uncontrollably. Dusk sees that even the ring on Hex's hand grows dim.

***

"What are you planning to do?" A familiar voice beckons Hex.

He looks towards a girl leaning in a field of flowers. She runs her hand through the array of colours and sniffs the air. A wooden cabin rests near them, beyond it, simply beauty as far as the eye can see with hills and valleys, a peaceful place.

"What are you planning to do, when you meet someone just like us?"

"That's not going to happen, there's no one out there who shares our ideals."

He responds as his memory recounts word for word what took place.

"Of course there is," she plucks a flower and stands up. She walks forward, her movement fluid and majestic. She reaches Hex and places it into his hair. "When you find the one who can carry on our ideals, you'll be able to stay here."

"But I-"

"It's not hard." She smiles and rests her hand on his chest, "All you need to do is find someone you'd miss, and would give your life for. A person you can call a friend."

***

Dusk comes to a stop and witnesses standing between them, a Burden who refuses to die. Asrath, breaths heavily. He looks at Hex and then towards Dusk. His eyes show a thirst for vengeance. The Burden opens a black vile and places it to his lips, gulping the contents down greedily for every last drop. Black smoke begins to rise across his wounds, healing them to some degree. He spits in distaste when he realizes not all of the damage is gone.

Dusk looks at his broken sword and sees that a crack runs along the rest of the blade. He sees another piece break off. He drops the remains and takes a deep breath. Asrath looks at Hex and then towards Dusk, he decides his target.

The Burden reaches Dusk and sends his hand into the back of Dusk's skull. He pummels him face-first into the ground, cracking the earth around him. He pulls the young man upwards and looks at his devastated face. He drops him, letting him remain conscious to watch.

He turns around to see that Hex is walking slowly towards them. He moves faster than the angel and wraps his hand around Hex's throat without resistance. "What is this? I turn away and you go and lose your prettiest feature?" He drags him along to Dusk. He places a foot against Dusk's head. "And so will he."

***

"Do you ever question what we are?" Hex asks his closest friend, a girl named Jinx.

"I question who. The 'what' doesn't matter. Why create a line where one isn't needed?"

"Then tell me, why do we reside in such an empty place?"

Jinx looks around at the field of flowers. She sighs softly, understanding Hex's dilemma. "You've been listening to that old mans stories again, haven't you? About those, called humans, who dream of us. We're their saviors against the demons who already walk amongst them, taking the shape of man." She says it sarcastically, though not in total disbelief.

He *looks at her red hair that takes on an orange hue from the light above. She smiles, a large one that no one can replicate. "I'd say those stories are true. But we aren't something special until we prove it. So they've got it all wrong. We aren't them, but we also aren't just a dream. This place is ours, until it changes into something else, and then we will have a new home. That too will change…but, all we have besides this life, are the old mans stories."*

"I hear that there's mention of those who can…go see the humans."

Jinx walks through the field of flowers and lets her fingers touch the petals. "That may be," she pauses, "why?" she turns to look at him happily, "are we going on an adventure?"

"…It's just…the old man being the old man."

"Yes" she raises a finger, "but that's who he is. The old man, does what the old man does. What is it you do Hex?"

"I wish I knew."

She lets out a contagious laugh, "I'll tell you then, who you are."

***

Asrath looks at Hex and says, "Tell me angel, what is more gruesome? Crushing his brain in front of your eyes or obliterating you in front of him?"

Time, distance, and fate—the angel contemplates it all as he stumbles across the ground.

***

"Jinx! What are you doing!?" Hex yells as they stand in front of a castle of legend, one that's formed of marble and steel, constantly shifting into different pieces, one with time and space.

"What needs to be done! We've seen the truth; we know the others helped us get this far for a reason! You need to speak to him and tell him! Tell him to let you through the door!"

"But Jinx, I-I can't just let you do this!"

"This is who I am Hex!"

***

He must do something, anything…everything. He beckons to Asrath with the flick of his finger and says, "You and I both know that I am the one you want. An angel, a being descendant from the heavens—to vanquish me would take you one step closer to being a god. Or you can kill the boy like you state. But know this, you can only kill one of us, because you only have one opportunity."

The Burden takes his foot off of Dusk's head and clenches his fist. "You're right. What good is this boy when so much more hangs onto life in front of me? You best struggle."

Hex feels the desire to scream, but he cannot. All he can do is watch helplessly as a wicked smile spreads across Asrath's face. The Burden raises him higher, his hand now wrapping around the angel's head. A flash of black, and Hex finds himself dreaming, drifting off into space, where the words he had no time to say are finally said.

***

"I have heard your words." A kind voice speaks.

"And? Will you save her?" Hex looks up at the white lights and the giant seat barely visible within it. Streams of faint letters drift in and out of view, like gray strands of a thought being written.

"I cannot."

"But she, she's why I even got here! How we even know about this!"

"And thanks to her, the shift of fate has brought you here, where no other has stood in a very long time. What she and your friends have said is true. Humans, a species worth saving, will die. But I know how you can change that tide."

"I don't care about changing anything! Just bring her back to me." Hex can't withhold his anguish and frustration as the anger causes him to cry.

The voice says words to his heart as a figure begins to emerge from the light, "There's a boy, just like you, who wants to save someone he loves. But because he is human and stubborn, it becomes apparent that he is not willing to accept death yet. Something only humans have a chance at. He can be guided towards the path that saves others Hex. You say you don't care, but that's because of the pain you are feeling. I know the extremity of it, so what I can simply say is, think about what she would want from you. I can't bring her back, but you can achieve what she set out to do. Do this for her, for me, for all of us. Make it so the pendulum of time swings in our favour. Even when all seems dark, keep looking for the light. Make it so the pendulum does not stop. Humans may seem insignificant but we are all connected. If their light goes out, that fate may in turn cause our own demise. For now, what we are is their best chance at life."

"And if I accept?"

"Then a ring you will receive. But you must know, that this young man, he too will be giving up a chance at peace. He would be giving up more than you. If he fails, there is nowhere for him to go. Not even the place I cannot reach."

"That's his concern, his fate....but I'll take him with me. What can I do, how can I make things better for Jinx?"

"First, you must train, then, when he arrives, take him through the world of dreams, where that old man who tells old tales came from. Seek his wife, and once making your way to where humans coexist with many other species, find your lost brethren."

Hex's eyes widen, "Adonis is still alive?"

The figure who still stands in the light, a silhouette giving the idea of how tall its being is, replies, "I believe he goes by the name of Wish now. Hex, will you accept?"

"I..."

"There is one last thing I should tell you."

"What is it?"

"Whether you succeed or not, you too will venture to where I cannot reach."

***

The sound of bones breaking causes Hex to momentarily regain consciousness. He sees Asrath tearing into his body, plunging his hands into places they don't belong. The pain is excruciating, his mind escapes.

***

"I'll tell you then, who you are." Hex watches as Jinx wraps her arms around his neck and leans in towards his lips. She hovers closely with little space between the inevitable touch, "You are," Jinx says happily.

***

Hex moves his arm without Asrath noticing. A light forms. He places it against Asrath's head and the Burden looks at him in alarm. "I am" Hex says, barely audible to hear, the blood streaking between his teeth, "AN ANGEL!"

The white light engulfs Asrath's head, it pulls the Burden off of Hex and upwards into the sky. Asrath claws helplessly at the white orb surrounding his face. It brings him through the clouds and up towards the edge of the atmosphere. He faces the stars and curses, taking in the sight. A black portal forms in front of him, before he leaves Earth's atmosphere completely, it absorbs him and takes him from death's doorstep.

Dusk lies on the ground near Hex and witnesses the angel collapse. His eyes move away from the sky and towards the gruesome and mangled body of his friend. He holds back his fear of throwing up in agonizing realization that the angel has seconds left. He sees Hex's eyes move towards him, and a voice enters his mind.

"This will be the last time you hear my voice Dusk. I'm afraid I can't stay. I don't have time to teach you what I know, or tell you where you should go next. I wish, at this time, you knew what brought us together. How important you are, how fate clings to you like no other. I want you to know that…what you are doing… fighting for love, is exactly what I did. Even when it leaves you, the memories remain, not to be forgotten. You will make choices that will continue to lead you down a path. You will meet people, remember them, because they can be the lights you need in the dark. Focus…but don't focus too much. It's okay to be angry…but don't give in to rage. But most importantly…what matters the most, the most beautiful thing, is having loving faces smiling back at you, while you smile at them."

A soft smile rests on Hex's face, despite the bloody configuration of his body; the ring on his finger loses more light and hangs on for the final bout, struggling, its own life facing oblivion. Tears of clarity fall from the angel's eyes. He heaves. The faces begin to flicker in his mind and warmth unfamiliar to him spreads throughout his heart.

He presses the remains of his lips together, with no energy to let them take in air, his voice continues inside of Dusks mind. *"There will always be despair, the risk of darkness. And it will hurt…I know it all too well...but do not give up, do not set limitations when others say you cannot and should not continue. You must continue...*" his right eye closes, "*you must...*" the warmth in his heart grows as the rest of his body goes cold, "*for that, shows the total dedication for those you carry in your heart.*"

"Hex..." Dusk says with trembling lips. He reaches out towards his friend, his hand struggling to remain up. His tears streak down his face, "Don't leave me." He smiles through the pain, his expression fake and out of place.

Hex's mind flickers. His eyes fade, and in a whisper, he says out loud, "We will find you...Dusk, wherever you end up...we will... find..." the angel drifts away.

"Hex?" The young man goes unanswered. "I'll be the one," his voice cracks, "who finds you." He loses control of his sobbing and hunches over, wishing he could ask more questions, even if the only response was a grin.

***

Where Hex ends up cannot be described. It is a place that cannot be reached by any being. No strength can open it up. There is no light or darkness; it is simply what it is. It is different for everyone and those who find each other, simply do so. It can never be explained, nor can it lead to anything else. It is, what it is. It is a place; it is what you want it to be.

A friendly smile from Jinx greets him. She stands in front of him, and the what, or how, simply makes sense. "Hex, I can tell you who you are." She wraps her arms around his neck and a kiss forms between them. "But first, tell me what it was like without me. And then, tell me how our hero, your friend, is doing." She holds Hex close, "I want to hear all about it, what you've done until now."

CHAPTER THIRTY-EIGHT

Vindication

Shaking, a face covered in tears and stricken by grief, Dusk lingers on the verge of consciousness, knowing something dear has left. Unable to escape from the horror, his mind recounts Hex's monologue and, as it pushes him towards a panic induced fit, he has a blurry vision.

Sarah's voice hits him, *"I love you."*

He withers in distress as the darkness in his heart says, *"So we're just going to lay about are we? Too scared to face it head on?"*

Sarah's voice says, *"I know it hurts."*

The darkness says, *"So weak."*

Sarah says, *"I know."*

Dusk's tears wash the vision away, silencing the voices inside.

*** *

Echo asks, "So are you really going to do it?"

Tern replies, "Yes."

"But Tern, despite all of my…begging, I don't actually want you to. I had no choice. Listen to me; forget these people, this place. It's all right. We can go away and enjoy our remaining time."

"No. I'm tired of rationalizing my own behavior. I'm tired of doing what others tell me to do. Your request came to me as a surprise because it's something I planned to do of my own freewill. I only let you beg because I was still thinking."

"Tern...come on. Let's just get away. We don't owe anyone anything."

"It's not about owing them, it's about causing damage to someone who deserves it. I can do that Echo. I can give a purpose to all of our actions up until now. I can get revenge for our friends."

"It's not a purpose, it's a change in course."

"Same thing Echo, the moment she passed before my eyes, I-"

"I know...alright. I can argue with you all I want but I can see as clear as day what it is you want to do."

"I want to hurt him more than anything, destroy his credibility like he destroyed our chance to live a normal life. He gave birth to us and then killed us."

"Like a god."

"No, he's nothing like a god. He's just a disgusting human."

"So then...what you will do is to hurt one disgusting human but not the rest?"

"Not all humans are disgusting Echo, in fact, most are…"

"…Ya…I know."

***

The shadows still protecting them, Sapphire feels a strain on her heart. She reaches out and places her hand against her chest and, for a moment, an incredible surge of worry spreads throughout her. She looks at Tail, whose eyes say what she fears—that their friend, their puzzle piece to completion for all of these years, is no longer with them.

Essa doesn't see this, doesn't feel this. She finally clues in to the fact that they are both oddly quiet. Essa looks at them, staring, trying to figure it out. *Is it the Nightmares? No, that isn't it. Is it Gunther? Yes, it has to be. That's it—the only possible explanation. But…what about him? Is he okay? When will he be back? When… will he be back?*

Loud roars are heard and the pounding fists increase their attack against the barrier of shadows. Tail begins to struggle. He looks at Sapphire once more, this time telling her with his eyes that they don't have much longer beneath his protection.

She smiles wearily. With Gunther gone, so is the restriction on her body. The loving words that would always contain her are now silent, replaced by the desire to use all her power in his name.

She walks past Essa. Seeing the state of Spike, Kiyo, Cassandra and Leaf, knowing Gunther is gone, Tail being constrained and Essa not ready—she knows it's all up to her. Even the angel from the sky and the boy who cheats death are not with her. Not even the guide she met briefly or the man who guides but does not act.

Something is waiting for them outside of the shadows. She feels it and knows it. She wants to fight them and crush them. She will crush them. She will, for Gunther.

The shadows part and her left arm turns into a machine gun. She runs through the shadow's opening and comes across Edom who stands nearby—a sly grin on his face.

She storms him, effectively passing through his guard. She slams her head into his, causing him to stagger. She then points her machine gun and lets loose. He runs out of the way of the bullets frantically but a few graze his arm and tear through his cloak.

It's a fight like this that shows how empty life can be. A Burden dashing around, fighting for the mere entertainment and knowledge that somewhere someone is having more fun than he is, and Sapphire, fighting with loss and the knowledge that things will never be the same.

The battle continues, until Edom finally slams his hands together and forms a portal that absorbs her bullets. When it appears once more, she moves out of the way.

This time Edom runs towards her, bringing forth the daggers which were concealed underneath his wrists. He grabs onto them and slashes forward. Sapphire lets one pierce into her arm. She throws her own fist and connects with his face. The punch is stronger than what he anticipates and he buckles.

Sapphire doesn't let the opportunity go to waste and grabs him, throws him down and slams his head into the ground ferociously. She repeats this once more before pulling the blade from her arm.

Her arm malfunctions and won't change. With no bullets left, it becomes a hindrance. She whacks him across the head with it as he slips his dagger into her gut.

He throws her off of him and forms a portal. Stepping through it, he appears in front of her and grabs her by the throat. She doesn't buckle, but in turn jabs her hand into his lower abdomen. The strike is strong, and he lets go of her. He backs away coughing. She is unique. This is someone he can't play around with.

Their small battle soon comes to an end. Someone else takes centre stage—a person, who has been used and thrown to the side, one who will make his name known.

***

Eryu, once a bustling metropolis, is now a wasteland with its fallen steel towers and its destroyed landscape. But, there are survivors and they are all looking to the sky. They gaze at something unexpected unfolding before their very eyes. It causes confusion, it causes hope, and it even forms anger in the hearts of a few, one such person being Edom.

He turns and Tail catches his attention. With the barrier of shadows no longer present, there is time to strike, but his eyes return to the boy rising in the air.

***

Moments earlier, Echo and Tern were finishing up their conversation, "Tern…I don't want you to do this."

"It's not about what you want. We all make our own decisions in the end."

"Please…"

"Don't beg. It's not like you Echo, not one bit. I want to see you, in my final moments, as the levelheaded asshole. Can you do that for me?"

Echo smiles, he can't help it. His heart doesn't know what to feel in this kind of predicament. Tern knows this and, with his own heart fumbling with emotions, he smiles back.

His arms raise upwards, both on an angle with one hand missing two fingers. Two fingers for the two friends who used the power he lent them. They knew the penalty, a field of gravity taken directly through Tern's power and when used, the repercussion would show on his body. He's glad they used it, that they relied on him, however in his final moments it serves as a painful reminder that even still, no one is alive besides Echo and he.

The prism on his chest glows, his suit turning brown and black. Echo knows that in less than a minute, the gravity around them will be under the control of one boy.

"It's time, Echo. You need to leave."

He hesitates.

"Echo, you will not survive if you stay here."

"I know."

"Then move!" Tern's voice lets out everything—the anger, the sorrow, the fear, the agitation and edginess—but even more so than all of those combined, he shows his love in those two words.

Both of them stand in a small clearing amongst rubble. Echo takes a few steps back. He takes it in that this will be the last time he ever sees him. So he watches the boy with brown eyes and messy hair rise into the sky, the gravity forming and growing around his body.

Echo turns and runs away, as far and fast as he can without stopping. He isn't going to look back at Tern, at what he does and what the result will be. He's a coward—no—he's already seen the result in his eyes. It's their connection, as brothers born from different DNA, as a group that all shares one heart.

Tern rises in the air and finally reaches a suitable position, with the rip a good distance away. He closes his eyes and breathes in. His act, his decision, one made not for fame, not for glory but to put an end to the madness. To vindicate he and his fallen clones, who were in truth, not evil but merely puppets on a string. It was time to cut the cord.

His eyes open. The remaining rings on his fingers break off, and the gravity around his body grows stronger, expands but becomes for a brief moment, calm. He is a man who cannot be stopped.

He can't help but smile slightly. The gravity picks up and he has complete control. The Burdens are too far to do anything, and with no voices bickering at him, he can witness the beauty unfold. He can pull in everything and make it nothing.

At first it starts off slow, rubble shakes and the few buildings that are barely standing finally fall over. It begins to pick up. Things begin to rise, including deceased bodies. Even blood begins to hover.

The force builds and now more than just loose debris and objects ascend. With the strength of the pull, buildings begin to break more, and huge chunks rise up—eventually pieces of walls and floors—until a few break off entirely and move upwards.

So the debris, the bodies, the blood, odd objects, and even buildings are pulled towards Tern. The gravity continues to strengthen, and it becomes clear it's just starting.

Anyone who's got sense about them grabs something to hold them down. The Nightmares do not calculate what is unfolding and waste their opportunity to escape.

It becomes evident what Tern is setting out to do. His eyes begin to grow fierce as he feels the strain of the gravity on his body. A loud crack punctures his wrist and he sees that his body is beginning to crumble. He keeps going. The Nightmares—all of them, the thousands—move towards him, some of their own freewill to kill, the rest because they have no choice.

He is doing something that no one else can. He does so to give meaning and a true purpose for his existence. He wants to get rid of the door in the sky that leads to humans' dreams, something he envies and will never experience. He, finally, has the strength to control his own life and put an end to this whole ordeal.

Now the gravity, like a black hole, is pulling everything in. It pulls the Nightmares and they scream in wretched agony, trying to lunge at him but stopping as the thin layer protects his body.

He continues to pull them in, the prism on his chest now shining bright. His body tightens and another crack goes off. He doesn't look. He knows what it is.

With the Nightmares being dragged towards him, the sky begins to clear up and the sun bears down on the naked city and its remaining inhabitants.

He says, "This is my will, my vindication." He breathes in deeply and the gravity strengthens further. The Nightmares slam together with everything else, becoming a ball of agony and suffocation.

It's not enough. He continues and then, finally, the rip in the sky begins to stretch and move towards him. This is it. His body lights up and everything is taken, becoming nothing. In a split second it all explodes. Thousands of Nightmares are torn apart. Things that once were become less than dust. The gateway to humans' nightmares is gone. And the boy, the one who never played a major role, never got to live the life he wanted, never got to love and carry on without excruciating pain, leaves this world with a smile on his face.

Echo says while standing far away in the distance, the urge to turn and look having taken over. "Tern, I will always remember the four of you and how at the time when I was greeted by evil, kindness would heal those fears. I know that you think what we've done is wrong...but we did it for us, because no one else would. You went out with a bang, so let me carry on that will of yours. I am the echo after all, and it's what the four of you gave to me that I'll choose to repeat. But how I go about it is up to me now. None of you are here anymore and if I don't find a cure, there won't be any of me left either."

***

With the shadows still wrapped around his legs, Edom holds Sapphire off with one hand while his eyes stare longingly into Tail's. Perhaps the darkness that he controls within himself is longing for the shadows, something that is so close to him, but unseen in the dark. Edom decides brazenly that he will not leave empty handed.

The Trinity comes into view but doesn't unsettle Edom. He merely raises his middle finger and laughs. He throws Sapphire out of his way. The Trinity unleashes its guns at Edom and he runs past it. The ground is destroyed around him, causing a rise of dirt in the air. He appears in front of Tail and reaches out for him, taking hold of him.

Essa sees the expression on Tail's face. She sees him look at her as if saying goodbye forever. He's pulled into a portal and that's it—he's gone. Sapphire's scream echoes loudly. She falls to her knees and slams the ground with her fist.

Things happen quickly. Essa looks around, not really able to take everything in. The Trinity makes landing and Fleur walks out of the ship in a slight daze. Essa sees the blood on her clothing. Paige and Rudy follow behind her. They make their way quickly towards the others. Rudy picks up Cassandra and rushes her to the ship. Paige checks Spike's vital signs and sighs in relief. She looks over to Sapphire for help but sees that she's lost in distress and has a wound of her own. She looks over to Essa and Essa catches a look from tearful eyes. She runs over and helps Paige lift Spike up.

Rudy runs back out of the ship and goes for Kiyo. He grabs him up and looks over at Paige and says, "Where's Tail?"

Essa says, "He was taken…"

Rudy looks away, his expression grim. He brings Kiyo onto the ship. Essa looks at Paige and notices that she's crying. She doesn't know what to say. She sees Fleur pick up Leaf and bring her along. Essa and Paige carry Spike.

Sapphire follows, emotionless.

On the ship, Essa realizes that Fleur isn't locked up. The thought leaves her quickly after—it's irrelevant. She's led down the hall as Paige holds back her tears for the time being.

They turn and enter a room where everyone who is injured is being held. Essa places Spike on one of the beds. She looks over at Kiyo and Leaf briefly, feeling bad for everything they've been through. Her eyes move over to Cassandra and she sees the medic bots working on her.

Essa asks, "Where's Dusk and Hex? Where's Gunther?" She thinks about her vision and begins to shake. Her face goes pale. She looks at

Paige for an answer.

Paige replies, "We saw Dusk and Hex flying through the sky a while ago." She stops there and looks away. "You need to come with me."

Essa follows Paige. She feels the sense of time begin to leave her. Everything looks out of place. Her head begins to heat up and her breathing quickens. Essa feels like she might pass out but she knows it's simply an intense feeling of stress—the kind that brings you someplace else entirely.

They enter a room and there before her, lying on a table with one arm slightly hanging off its side, is Gunther. His chest is covered in burns and spear gashes. She moves a hand to her mouth. She feels her stomach flip. She can't move her legs. Her eyes look up to see Sapphire leaning against a wall, distraught with tears of her own.

A hand presses against Essa's shoulder. Her legs take the notion to walk forward. She reaches the bed where Gunther's body rests. Her throat swells up. She hears Paige crying once more and begins to feel the need to accompany her.

She says quietly, "This isn't fair…I did this to you. I put you through this…and even with a heads-up I couldn't reach you. I couldn't do a thing, and now…you're…" She places a hand to her mouth again, this time bursting into tears. Her hand presses against his and she feels the cold that has taken over his body. She hates it. She wants the warmth to return.

Her eyes move up his still body and rest on his face. She doesn't know why, but she never looked at him longer than she needed to and now, there he lays, his eyes closed, a soft smile still left on his now carefree face.

Sapphire says, "Essa, there's something you need to know." Fleur walks into the room accompanied by Rudy. Paige takes a seat next to Gunther's bed and looks at him longingly. The words that leave Sapphire's mouth confuse Essa, and fill her with despair. She looks at Gunther and can't believe it. "Essa. He's your brother."

The words linger in her mind.

Essa stares at him with trembling lips. She says, "That can't be…" and moves towards him. She finally sees it, like clips of the past re-aligning themselves. Her lack of memory stopped her from picking up on the simple signs of what's been in front of her all along. All of this time, so close, he's been there. A man so stubborn and obnoxious that she failed to look past it and understand his intentions. He was protecting her—his family.

She cries out sorrowful tears, a cry so pure with emotion. The love in her heart spills out. She falls to her knees and places her hands on his stomach. She lets out a symphony of regret; she will never forget this moment.

***

The unknown is like a bucket of fear, a bucket that refills as you wipe up what's already been spilt on you. It fills with the fear of what's to come, the fear of losing loved ones, the fear of failing, the fear of life, the fear of death. The weak can drown under all that fear, but the strong face it, grow from it and persevere. So not everyone breaks. Some go on—stubbornly with no desire to quit. Sometimes after dealing with the reality of the horrors around them, the unknown can be a relief.

The unknown spills on Essa as it does to Dusk who struggles in his own lost mind.

Taunting him, the darkness within no longer sitting in its chair, stands up and applauds with a slow clap and says, "Your eyes are open but you aren't looking, are you? That angel is dead. Now we're just hanging about, aren't we? What are you so damn scared of? I'm not going to hurt you. I need you. Get up. I've had enough of this."

Dusk's eyes focus and he leaves the room of his inner darkness. He finds himself looking up at Caster. The Burden reaches out and grabs Dusk by the collar. He lifts him up and whispers, "Your girlfriend is alive." He lets go of Dusk and walks away, letting a stream of blinding light slam into Dusk's eyes. Before he disappears into the horizon, Caster says, "I hope you listened to Hex."

Dusk moves his hand in the way of the sun. He looks towards Hex, both their bodies next to one another. Dusk turns his attention towards the sky. The darkness in his body edges away. The sun, so bright, causes his vision to become a blur of yellow and white light. He sees hues of orange and red dance around. He moves his hand back up to block the sun. He witnesses a shadow, the unknown, looking at him.

A hand grasps his. He freezes—he can't see. His eyes begin to focus. He sees a face, someone unfamiliar. A smile.

He sees the unknown. Hex's voice rings through his head, still telling him what to do, *"Just open your eyes and look at the world properly."*

His eyes open.

To Be Continued

Christopher Abraham's first love is writing. As a young man living in Châteauguay, Quebec, he honed his craft until moving to Oshawa, Ontario, to continue his education. He loves reading manga, watching anime, gaming and avoiding any meal that consists of pork chops. Along with working as a graphic designer at Toronto's Hockey Hall of Fame, Mr. Abraham is also working on his next novel; Dreams of Youth: Twisted Heart.

For more information, you can reach Christopher Abraham by checking out his website at: www.abrahamauthor.com

Made in the USA
Middletown, DE
30 December 2015